Also by Rosie Goodwin

The Bad Apple
No One's Girl
Dancing Till Midnight
Tilly Trotter's Legacy
Moonlight and Ashes
The Mallen Secret
Forsaken
The Sand Dancer
Yesterday's Shadows
The Boy from Nowhere
A Rose Among Thorns
The Lost Soul
The Ribbon Weaver
A Band of Steel
Whispers
The Misfit
The Empty Cradle
Home Front Girls
A Mother's Shame
The Soldier's Daughter
The Mill Girl
The Maid's Courage
The Lost Girl

The Claire McMullen Series
Our Little Secret
Crying Shame

Rosie Goodwin is the four-million-copy bestselling author of more than forty novels. She is the first author in the world to be allowed to follow three of Catherine Cookson's trilogies with her own sequels. Having worked in the social services sector for many years, then fostered a number of children, she is now a full-time novelist. She is one of the top fifty most borrowed authors from UK libraries and has sold over four million copies across her career. Rosie lives in Nuneaton, the setting for many of her books, with her husband and their beloved dogs.

Rosie GOODWIN
The Rag Princess

ZAFFRE

First published in the UK in 2025 by
ZAFFRE
An imprint of Bonnier Books UK
5th Floor, HYLO, 105 Bunhill Row, London, EC1Y 8LZ

A CIP catalogue record for this book is
available from the British Library.

ISBN: 978-1-80418-307-6

Also available as an ebook and an audiobook

1 3 5 7 9 10 8 6 4 2

Typeset by IDSUK (Data Connection) Ltd
Printed and bound in Great Britain by Clays Ltd, Elcograf S.p.A.

The authorised representative in the EEA is Bonnier
Books UK (Ireland) Limited.
Registered office address: Floor 3, Block 3, Miesian Plaza,
Dublin 2, D02 Y754, Ireland
compliance@bonnierbooks.ie
www.bonnierbooks.co.uk

This one is for all my amazing family, friends and readers who have shown me so much support since my writing career began. You are all stars, many thanks

Prologue

The sky was grey and overcast, and as two pall bearers took the tiny white coffin of Penelope Elizabeth Lilburn to the newly dug grave in Coton churchyard, the clouds opened and the rain poured down as if someone in heaven had turned on a tap. Within minutes the gathered mourners were soaked to the skin, but they continued to pick their way amongst the drunkenly leaning headstones until they reached the child's final resting place.

Dry-eyed, Maggie Lilburn leant heavily on her husband's arm as she watched the coffin being slowly lowered into the small grave, wishing with all her heart that she could have gone with her beloved child. The vicar was slowly intoning the last part of the burial service, but the words seemed to float over her head. For now, she was beyond hearing or feeling anything but an overpowering sense of loss. The tears would come later.

Levi, her husband, however, was unashamedly weeping as he watched the body of his darling girl being lowered into the earth. It was so wrong! Penny had been such a sweet, fun-loving little girl, always laughing and full of mischief. He was finding it hard to believe that he would never hear or see her again, apart from in his dreams.

Penny had been just four years old when the terrible accident occurred. She had been playing with her friends in Abbey Street in their home town of Nuneaton when she had run into the road and straight into the path of two large dray horses delivering barrels of ale to the nearby Kingsholme Inn. There was nothing the driver could have done to prevent what happened. By the time he had managed to halt the two frightened horses, the wheels of the wagon had already run over Penny. After examining her the doctor had informed them that she would have died instantly, for which Levi thanked God. At least he didn't have to think of her suffering.

He glanced towards his three sons who stood solemnly with their heads bowed. Ten-year-old Barney was the oldest of his brood and took after his father, with his dark hair and blue eyes. Then there was eight-year-old Charlie, who also took after his father. Lastly came Harry, aged six, who, with his copper-coloured hair and dark eyes, looked like his mother, just as Penny had. As her face flashed through his mind, a fresh spasm of weeping overtook him and he had to take a deep breath to pull himself together. It wouldn't do to fall apart now – Maggie was depending on him.

At last it was almost over and the vicar solemnly passed around a box of earth so that each of the mourners might throw a handful onto the coffin. When that was done, the man crossed to the family to offer his condolences once more, then with the flaps of his wet cassock slapping against his legs, he strode back to the comfort of the vicarage and a warm fire.

'Come on, hinny,' Levi encouraged as Maggie stared sightlessly down at the mud-spattered coffin. 'Let's get ourselves off to the wake now. There's nothin' more to be done here. We'll go an' get a nice hot cup o' tea inside you.'

He nodded towards the boys, who had silently rounded the grave to stand beside their parents, then they all turned and made for the lychgate, beyond which a carriage was waiting for them. The journey to the Pig and Whistle Inn in Abbey Street, which was just a stone's throw away from where they lived, was made in silence. When they arrived, Levi paid the driver and ushered what was left of his family inside out of the cold and wet.

Quite a few of the mourners were already there; the men with pints of ale in their hands while the women sipped tea or sherry wine and whispered amongst themselves.

'I don't know how Maggie will ever get over this,' one of the women was saying to another with a sad shake of her head. Peggy Walker was the Lilburns' neighbour from one of the courtyards spread all along one side of Abbey Street, and Maggie's best friend, although they were total opposites. While Peggy was plump and easy-going, Maggie was more ambitious and kept her house squeaky clean. 'I can remember the day little Penny were born as if it were yesterday,' Peggy sighed. 'Desperate for a little girl, Maggie were, an' when she clapped eyes on Penny she couldn't stop smilin'. She were a bonny little thing, mind, an' bright as a button an' all. The whole family doted on 'er.'

The woman she was talking to nodded in agreement. 'Ah well, life can be cruel.' Bridie Fellows was the local gossip and was making the most of the free bar Levi had laid on; she was already on her second glass of sherry and was greedily eyeing the plates of sandwiches and hot pies the landlady was placing on a long table to one side of the room. 'Anyway,' she said abruptly as her stomach rumbled in anticipation, 'I'm just goin' to grab a bite to eat. I've had nothin' since last night an' me stomach thinks me throat's cut.'

Meanwhile Levi settled his wife and sons on some chairs close to the fire before hurrying away to fetch them all a drink. He returned shortly with a pint of ale for himself, a large brandy and a cup of hot tea for Maggie and three glasses of lemonade for the boys. Anyone seeing them would have thought they were a very well-to-do family, clad as they were in their smart clothes, but in actual fact Levi ran a thriving rag-and-bone yard next to their tiny two-up, two-down cottage.

Levi had travelled to Nuneaton some years before from Seaton Delavel, a small mining village seven miles outside of South Shields, following the death of his parents. He had come to work on the railways, and soon after he had met Maggie. He had been almost penniless at the time, taking work wherever he could find it once the railway navvies moved on. Eventually he had bought a barrow and walked the streets collecting rags, bones and any scraps of metal he could find, which he would sell on, until eventually he had bought the small yard he now ran very successfully. Shortly after this, he and Maggie had wed and he had thought himself the luckiest man alive. He still did, although he and his wife were as different as chalk from cheese.

Levi had been raised in an overcrowded garret, where he and his six brothers and sisters had slept top to toe on straw mattresses, and they hadn't always known where the next meal was coming from, so he was proud of what he had achieved and thankful that his family didn't have to suffer the hardships he had. Maggie's parents had died when she was young, and she and her siblings had been brought up in the courts by an aunt. Although her aunt did her best, money had been tight, and they, too, had often gone hungry. Sadly, her aunt had died shortly after she and Levi were wed.

Her background had made Maggie determined to pull herself and her family out of poverty and she had worked beside Levi to make their business successful. Once it had started to turn a profit, though, she preferred to mix with the more influential people of the town and had insisted that her children should have the very best clothes Levi could provide. He was happy to oblige, although sometimes he had to gently rein in her spending. Today she was clad in a black bombazine mourning gown and a wide hat covered with a black veil, and the boys were dressed in smart little suits and white shirts with starched collars, as he himself was, although he could hardly wait to get home and get out of it. Levi was never happier than when he was getting his hands dirty and had never been one for dressing up.

'There you go, pet,' he said gently as he placed Maggie's drink before her, but if she heard him, she gave no sign. Instead she sat staring sightlessly straight ahead, just as she had since the day of the terrible accident. People were approaching their table offering condolences and Levi acknowledged each of them with a nod, praying for this dreadful day to be over.

'Can we go soon, Da?' Barney asked. The boys were white-faced and fearful. This had been their first encounter with death and they didn't quite understand it – it was just too hard for them to accept that they would never see their cheeky little sister again.

'Aye, we will, lad.' Levi reached across the table and affectionately ruffled the boy's dark hair. 'Meantime, why don't you take your brothers over there an' get somethin' to eat? I doubt yer ma will be up to cookin' the night.'

Barney obediently ushered Charlie and Harry towards the food table as Levi turned his attention back to his wife. 'Shall I be fetchin' somethin' for you, pet? You've had not a bite between yer lips for days, an' I don't want you makin' yourself ill now. Perhaps a bit o' pork pie or a sandwich?'

Maggie raised a hand to lift her veil back and he was shocked to see the pain and venomous look on her face. 'A bit o' pork pie you say? How can you even *think* of eatin' on such a day? Don't you understand our lovely girl is gone, Levi? We'll not see her again in this life. I just pray she'll be waitin' for us in the next.'

Her words cut like a knife, but his voice was calm as he answered, 'Of course I know that. But I also know we still have the boys to take care of. They need us more than ever now, so we've got to try an' be strong for them.'

'I know that well enough!' she rasped. 'I also know that if you'd bought us that house in Swan Lane that I wanted this might never have happened!'

Levi groaned. 'Oh, not *that* again. Didn't I explain that I couldn't afford it yet? And don't go tryin' to lay the blame for the accident on me, woman. I was workin' when it happened, but where were you? Drinkin' tea from yer dainty china cups an' saucers an' entertainin' yer fancy friends, were you?'

The minute the words had left his lips he wished he could take them back, but it was too late and he cringed as he saw the look of hurt burning in her eyes. 'I'm sorry, hinny. I shouldn't have said that,' he said, running his work-worn hands through his thick mop of hair. 'It was an accident pure an' simple, an' no one were to blame. It was just one o' those terrible things that can happen from time to time. What we have to do now is find a way to come to terms wi' it.'

The boys returned at that moment with their plates piled high with thick ham and cheese sandwiches, pickles and a variety of pies. At least the accident hadn't affected their appetites, Levi thought ruefully.

The afternoon dragged on but when the food table was empty and the bar was almost drunk dry, the last of the mourners left and Levi let out a deep sigh of relief. He went to settle the bill with the landlord before shepherding his family out of the pub and the few yards down the road to the courtyard where they lived.

'Here we are then, me boys,' he said, forcing a note of cheer into his voice as they passed through the yard. Opening the door to their cottage, he ushered them in out of the damp October afternoon. 'How about you go up an' get changed out o' your best suits, eh? An' hang 'em up tidy, mind, else you'll have yer ma skelpin' yer backsides. Then when you come down, we'll all have us a nice hot cup o' tea.'

The cottage was a complete contrast to the rag-and-bone yard outside. Everything was neat and tidy and so clean that Levi often joked he could eat his dinner off the floor. There were two comfortable mohair sofas with gaily coloured cushions scattered over them to either side of the fire, and a good quality mahogany table with six chairs stood in the centre of the room with a matching sideboard against one wall. Thick velvet curtains, which he had collected from a big house on the outskirts of town, framed the windows, and good quality fringed rugs were scattered about the highly polished floorboards. Outside was his domain but Maggie insisted on only the best of what he collected for the inside.

Now she crossed to the side of the dying fire and dropped heavily onto one of the sofas while Levi threw some coals onto the glowing embers before hurrying away to put the kettle on.

'I'll just pop up an' get outta this suit then I'll make us all a nice cuppa, pet.' His words met with no response so with a heavy heart he made his way up the steep narrow staircase to the two small bedrooms. In one he could hear the boys talking as they got out of their best clothes, and as he stepped into his and Maggie's room, the first thing he saw was the small truckle bed that Penny had slept on to the side of theirs. It was neatly made with her favourite teddy bear propped up against the pillows, for all the world as if it was waiting for her to come for bedtime. A lump swelled in his throat as he dropped down onto the side of the bed and buried his face in his hands. It felt as if the whole family had fallen apart and Levi had no idea how he was ever going to put it back together. But one thing was for sure, he was going to have to try to for the sake of the boys.

That evening, after the boys were in bed, the torrent of tears that Maggie had held back suddenly burst from her like a breached dam and all Levi could do was squeeze her hand and speak soothingly to her. He supposed they were better out than in, but as the days and weeks passed with no sign of them ceasing, he wondered if they were ever going to stop.

PART 1

Chapter One

September 1904

It was late afternoon and the light was fading fast as the two boys Levi employed to collect bones for him entered the yard, pushing their small handcart ahead of them.

'We done well today, mister,' the smaller of the two told Levi happily as he swiped his sleeve along the bottom of his runny nose, leaving a shiny trail of snot. 'We went to the slaughter yard an' picked through the bones an' some of 'em will be good enough to make handles.'

Levi crossed to look into the cart and nodded. 'Well done, lads. Yer right. Some o' these will make right good handles fer cutlery for the toffs. The grease from 'em will make some good soap an' all.' The rest of the bones he would sell to a merchant who would grind them down to make glue and fertiliser, so none of them would be wasted.

Fishing in his pocket he took out some coins and paid the boys, who went merrily on their way to buy bread that would ensure their families ate that evening. Levi pushed the barrow to a corner of the yard and threw a tarpaulin over it before crossing to the horse and cart he had just come home in. He too had had a good day, and the cart was loaded with rags and scrap metal, all of which would be sold for a profit. A woman would come in the next morning to sort through the rags to see if any of the clothes were worth salvaging. Those that were would be sold to the rag stall in the marketplace, and those that were beyond reusing would be sorted into whites and coloureds. White rags would fetch tuppence to threepence a pound, depending on their condition and would be sold to paper merchants. Coloureds and wool would fetch tuppence a pound and would be sold on to shoddy factories where they would be ground down to a fibrous mass and mixed with fresh wool before being made into new garments. But as Levi had discovered, it was the scrap metal that would fetch the most, so he spent the majority of his days scouring the streets for what he could find. Old brass, copper and pewter could fetch as much as five pence a pound so were highly valued.

Before unloading the cart, he unharnessed the horse and led him to the stable. Levi had bought old Dobbin some years before, shortly before the birth of his first son, and was more than a little fond of him. He gave him a brisk rub down and a nose bag before leaving him to rest and going back out into the yard where he began the unenviable task of sorting out his day's finds. It was a dirty, smelly job but Levi was used to it, and anything was better than being down the mines – as he had been back in his home town. He had almost finished when the cottage door opened and Maggie appeared. 'Your meal is almost ready. Ten minutes. And make sure you wash before you come in.'

'Right y'are, pet.' Levi hefted the rest of the rags into a shed he had ready for them. They had to be completely dry before they could be sold so he couldn't risk them getting wet. Finally, after swilling his hands and face in the trough of water to one side of the yard, he went into the kitchen.

Maggie was at the stove stirring a large pot from which delicious smells were issuing and the three boys were seated at one end of the table doing their homework.

'Best get that put away for now,' Maggie instructed them. 'And then get the table laid. This is ready.'

'Yes, Ma.' The boys immediately did as they were told. The fun-loving mother they remembered from before Penny died had disappeared over the last almost four years and they had to watch their p's and q's now or suffer a clip about the ear.

Levi hurried off upstairs to change – he didn't dare sit down in his work clothes – returning shortly to take his place at the table with his family just as Maggie ladled out a brimming dish of beef stew and dumplings for each of them.

'This looks delicious, pet,' Levi commented – there was no one could make stew and dumplings like his Maggie – but she didn't react to the compliment, merely carried on picking at her own portion.

Levi watched her from the corner of his eye and frowned. Maggie barely ate enough to keep a sparrow alive and she had lost weight. Since losing Penny she had become a shell of the happy woman she had once been and she rarely smiled anymore. She still took good care of him and their sons, admittedly, but the house was devoid of joy. Even the boys seemed to save their fun for outside the cottage and rarely spoke inside unless spoken to.

They were almost halfway through the meal when Maggie suddenly laid down her spoon and after staring at Levi for a moment she said quietly, 'I dare say I shall be wastin' me breath but there's somethin' I'd like to talk to you about.'

'Oh aye?' He gave her an encouraging smile. 'Talk away then, hinny.'

She shook her head. 'Not until the boys have finished eating.' She rose from the table and carried her almost full dish of food over to the large wooden draining board.

When the boys had eaten their fill, it was Barney who asked, 'Can we go outside to play for a while, Ma?' Of the three of them Barney was the most outspoken.

Maggie nodded. 'Yes, if you wrap up warmly, but only for half an hour, mind. It'll be properly dark soon an' you never know who is about.'

There was a flurry of activity as the children dashed to get their coats on and once the door had closed behind them, Levi retired to the sofa to one side of the fire and lit his pipe before patting the seat at the side of him. 'Come an' tell me what you wanted to talk to me about, pet.'

Maggie dried her hands on a large piece of towelling, and once seated, she folded them primly in her lap. 'Well . . .' She licked her lips. 'I dare say my request will fall on deaf ears as it normally does, but Mrs Clarke called in today for a cup o' tea an' she was sayin' . . .' Mrs Clarke was the local greengrocer's wife and known for her airs and graces.

'Yes?' Levi prompted.

'She was saying that another house has come up for sale in Swan Lane.' She sat back and waited for his reaction. When none was forthcoming, she rushed on, 'Now I know we've had this conversation before but the lads are growing now and there's barely room to swing a cat around in that little bedroom of theirs. It's one of the townhouses that's become available. Three floors it has and four bedrooms, plus another two in the attics. Just think, the lads could have a room each if they'd a mind to.'

Levi puffed on his pipe and stared at her thoughtfully. It had been some time since she had asked to move and he could only take it as a good sign that she was doing so now. Perhaps this would be the start of them getting back to some sort of normality.

'So how much are they askin' for this townhouse?'

Her eyes lit up for the first time in ages. 'I'm not sure but Mrs Clarke gave me the name of the estate agent who's handling the sale. It's here, look. He has a shop in Queen's Road.' She handed him a piece of paper.

He took it from her and stared at it for a minute before saying, 'All right. I'm not promisin' anythin', mind, but I will pop in tomorrow when I'm on me rounds an' make a few enquiries.'

'Oh Levi, thank you!' Suddenly he saw a glimpse of the girl he had fallen in love with, and a flicker of hope flared in his chest. There had been times over the last few years when he had feared that the Maggie he loved was gone forever. If truth be told he could possibly afford to buy a larger place – depending on the price of the property, of course – and if it would bring his wife back to him, he was willing to do it.

Leaning across the sofa, she pecked him tenderly on the cheek before she set to clearing the table as Levi settled down to read the *Evening Tribune*.

Later that evening, when the boys were settled in bed and Maggie sat darning, she said cautiously, 'Actually, there was something else I'd like to speak to you about.'

Glancing up from his seat by the fire, Levi narrowed his eyes. He knew that tone of voice. Was she going to ask for something new for the house that had caught her eye, or perhaps some new clothes for the boys?

'Go on then, spit it out,' he chuckled. 'How much is it goin' to cost me?'

'Oh nothing . . . nothing at all.' A flush had come to her cheeks as she laid her darning aside, and after taking a deep breath she went on, 'It's just that I've been thinking . . . You know that Peggy next door works up at the workhouse, well she was saying that the nursery there is full of little ones waiting to be adopted, so I got to thinking . . . perhaps you and I could consider taking another child?'

Levi's jaw dropped and he stared at her in amazement. '*Us* . . . take in another child? But we have three fine healthy sons already.'

Lowering her eyes, she nodded. 'I know that . . . but I thought we might consider taking a little girl.'

He frowned. 'And what's put this idea into your head? You realise that we could never replace Penny, don't you? So if that's what you were thinkin'—'

'No, no I wasn't thinking that at all,' she said hastily, a catch in her voice. 'I know better than anyone that a dozen little girls could never replace our Penny . . . But I just thought it might help to . . . to ease the pain a little.'

He was instantly sympathetic as he stared at her lowered head. He knew how much she still missed Penny – they all did. During the first year following Penny's death, Maggie had gone to visit her grave every single day come rain or shine. Thankfully the visits had now slowed to three or four times a week, but he knew that she was still grieving.

'I think something like that needs a lot o' thought, hinny,' he said eventually. 'How do you think the lads would feel about introducin' another little girl into the family? And haven't you just said yourself that the cottage is bulgin' at the seams now the lads are growin'?'

'Yes, but that wouldn't be a problem if we moved to Swan Lane, would it? And I'm sure they'd be fine with it. You know how much they all doted on Penny.' Seeing his uncertain expression, she rushed on, 'Won't you at least think about it . . . for me, *please*?'

'Aye, pet, I'll do that.' And for then the subject was closed, although Levi had a funny feeling it wouldn't be the last he would hear of it.

The following day, when the children had gone to school, Peggy popped into Maggie's for a cup of tea. It was her day off from the workhouse and a weekly ritual they had.

'So did yer get chance to speak to Levi about the house an' adoptin' a child from up at the workhouse?' Peggy asked as she dunked a biscuit into her cup of tea. The dainty china cups and saucers that Maggie insisted on always amused her. They only had pot mugs in her cottage.

Maggie nodded as she joined Peggy at the highly polished table. 'I did and he seemed to consider the house, although he didn't seem too taken on the thought of another child.'

Peggy sighed. She and Maggie had gone through school together and had remained close friends, and she knew how much she missed Penny.

'Well, takin' on another little 'un is a lot to ask,' Peggy pointed out. 'Just give him time to get used to the idea afore you broach it again. An' as for the house . . . I dare say you'll not have time fer the likes of us lot if you do move to Swan Lane.'

Maggie frowned at her. 'Don't be so daft, woman. We've been friends forever. You'll still be welcome to come and see us whenever you've a mind to.'

Could they have known it, at that very minute Levi had left the estate agent after picking up the details for the house Maggie had set her heart on as he had promised. He had to admit it looked a fine property, although the asking price was considerably more than he had thought it would be. He could still just about manage it, so long as Maggie understood that money would be tight for a time. There would be lots of rooms to fill and he knew of old that she wouldn't settle for just any old second-hand furniture. Still, if she agreed to be reasonable and bide her time on the furnishings, he would give it some serious consideration. The next step would be to go and view the place if they did decide they wanted to go ahead. It would be nice to see Maggie smiling again and a fresh start in a new house away from all the memories of Penny might be just the tonic she needed. However, he still didn't like the idea of adopting another child. What would be the point? A hundred little girls could never replace the daughter they had loved and lost as far as he was concerned.

Chapter Two

The following Monday morning, Levi took a couple of hours off work to take Maggie to view the house. From the moment they pulled up outside on the horse and cart he could see that she had already made up her mind.

'Oh Levi, it looks so *grand*,' she sighed.

He had to admit she was right. It was a large, three-storey, black-and-white gabled townhouse with huge sash cord windows to either side of the front door. The front garden was surrounded by a low wrought-iron fence, and a path of patterned tiles with a small lawn on either side led to the front door. The estate agent had given them the keys, and as Levi helped Maggie down from the cart, he sensed that she could barely wait to get inside.

Once he had unlocked the door, they entered a spacious hall-way, and Maggie instantly fell in love with the gaily patterned Minton tiles on the floor and the large sweeping staircase that led up from it.

'Why, the hallway alone is bigger than the whole of the down-stairs of our cottage,' Maggie gasped, clasping her hands in glee. The first two doors they came to led into a large lounge with a lovely marble fireplace in the centre of one wall, and a dining room that would have taken a table three times as big as the one they had at present. A third door led into a kitchen that took Maggie's breath away. There was a large range and an inglenook fireplace, and already she could picture a fire glowing and her copper pans gleaming on the beam above it. An enormous Belfast sink sided with a wooden draining board stood beneath a window over-looking the big back garden, which she was thrilled to see had an orchard full of apple and pear trees, and a sizeable vegetable plot. A door from the kitchen led down to a cellar but Maggie decided not to venture down there just yet. Festoons of cobwebs hung from the beams and she had a fear of spiders.

On the other side of the hallway was another room, which, judging by the number of floor-to-ceiling shelves along one wall, had once been used as an office or a library.

'Just imagine,' she sighed. 'The children would be able to sit in here and do their homework of an evening.'

Levi had made no comment as yet. He was more practical and was looking for signs of damp or woodworm, although he had to admit that apart from needing some decorating, he could see no sign of anything worrying.

There was yet another smaller room next to the library, which Maggie declared would make a wonderful snug where they could sit on cold winter evenings. Next, they went to explore the rooms on the first floor, and once again Maggie was taken with them.

'Just look how big they are,' she cried, twirling around with her arms outstretched. 'Even the smallest room is bigger than our largest.'

The top floor, which boasted two smaller rooms, brought yet more excitement. 'These must have been used for the servants' quarters,' Maggie said excitedly.

Levi was worried at this. He just hoped Maggie wouldn't want to employ a maid! But he said nothing. It had been a long time since he had seen her looking so happy and he didn't want to spoil it.

Finally, they went back downstairs to explore the garden, which was a very good size. There was even a stable block to one side of it for Dobbin, which Levi had to admit would be very handy. There was also a rather overgrown lawn beside the orchard where Dobbin could graze, and he could see that with a little time and effort it could be beautiful.

'So . . . what do you think?' Maggie was gazing at him so expectantly that he knew he was lost.

'I think it's a grand house,' he admitted as he slid his arm about her waist.

She stared up at him, her face bright. 'Are you saying we can have it?'

'Well . . .' It would be a stretch financially. 'I'd like to make an offer before we commit ourselves, but yes if I can get it at the right price, I think it would be a grand house for our lads to grow up in.'

Maggie was dancing on the spot in her excitement and he almost had to drag her away after they had done another tour of the place. He could tell that she was already deciding where their furniture would go, which wouldn't be far in a place this size. They'd be lucky to furnish the small snug and the kitchen for a start.

After dropping Maggie back off in Abbey Street, Levi went to begin negotiations with the estate agent. Unfortunately, the gentleman who owned the house lived in the nearby town of Atherstone, so it was going to take some time for the estate agent to contact him to put the offer to him. Levi knew that Maggie would be none too pleased with that, but he was determined to get the house at the best price he could.

While Levi was doing this, Maggie had no sooner let herself into the small cottage, than Peggy tapped on the door and breezed in. 'I'm just on me way to work but I thought I'd pop in an' see how you got on,' Peggy said, although without her friend saying a word, she could see that she was bubbling with excitement.

'Oh, Peggy.' Maggie sighed dramatically. 'It's just the *most splendid* house you've ever seen. Or at least it will be when I've finished with it!'

'Now then, luvvie, slow down,' Peggy said with a grin. 'Don't try an' run afore you can walk. An' more importantly don't go forgettin' your roots. You an' me are both kids from the back streets, an' while there's no shame in hopin' to better yourself, you'd be wise to keep yer feet firmly on the ground. Remember how we used to go to school wi' cardboard cutouts in us shoes, if we were lucky enough to 'ave any, that is. An' how we never knew if there'd be food on the table when we got 'ome?'

Maggie usually hated being reminded of her past but nothing could spoil her happy mood that morning. 'You sound just like Levi,' she teased.

Peggy nodded. 'Happen I do but this will be a big move for you if it comes off an' you'll 'ave to remember, Rome weren't built in a day. But any road, I'm glad the viewin' went well. An' what about the other thing? I mean adoptin' a little 'un from up at the workhouse? Any more said on that yet?'

The smile momentarily left Maggie's face. 'Hmm, well . . . I thought it better not to push that for now. I've planted the seed in Levi's head, but I think I'll wait till we get the house tied up afore I mention it again.'

Peggy nodded. 'I agree, one thing at a time, eh? But I'd best be off now or I'll be late for work an' the miserable bloody old housemistress will 'ave me guts fer garters. Ta-ra a bit.' And with that she left Maggie to her daydreams.

As usual, Barney was the first home from school that day. He had never had a thirst for learning and insisted that schooling was a waste of time. It had already been decided that he would follow his father into the rag-and-bone trade when he finished school and that was about the summit of his ambitions. He was never happier than when he was out and about in the fresh air, kicking a football with his friends or scrumping apples. He was always into one sort of mischief or another, but he had a kind heart and Maggie loved him unconditionally. Of all the boys he was the most like his father in looks and now as he flung his satchel down onto the nearest chair and began to yank at his hated necktie he asked, 'You all right then, Ma?'

'Yes, son, better than all right.' She gave him a beaming smile before rushing on to tell him all about the house she and his father had viewed that morning.

To her surprise, Barney scowled. 'But that's the posh area o' town, ain't it? Why would yer want to live there?'

Maggie shook her head as she poured him a glass of milk, which he swallowed in one go. 'Who wouldn't want to live there?'

'Me fer a start.' Barney swiped the back of his hand across his lips. 'All me mates are 'ere an' all o' them as live in Swan Lane are stuck up. I don't think any of 'em would take very kindly to the likes of us movin' in.'

'And why not?' Maggie was bristling now. 'And what do you mean? The likes of us indeed!'

'Cos me dad's a rag-an-bone man an' they're all posh business folks that go to work in collars an' ties as live there. Just imagine our old Dobbin droppin' a load outside one o' their 'ouses.' He threw his head back and laughed, but his mother was not amused.

'We're just as good as any of them,' Maggie retorted indignantly. 'And it would do you good to remember it, my lad.'

'Aye well, I can't stand 'ere arguin' wi' you.' Barney threw his tie down with his bag and headed for the staircase. 'I've got to meet me mates in ten minutes. We're goin' for a walk around the Blue Lagoon up Bermuda village.'

Maggie looked concerned. 'What, in the dark? An' it's enough to cut you in two out there.'

'Don't worry, I'll be back fer me tea.'

He headed upstairs and Maggie shook her head. Barney was a law unto himself and he was getting worse as he got older.

Charlie and Harry were the next to arrive and they pecked their mother on the cheek. Although very like his brother in looks, Charlie was the scholar of the family and soaked up learning like a sponge. He was rarely to be seen without a book in his hand

and Maggie had high hopes that when he left school, he might be clever enough to go on to university.

Last but not least was little Harry, so like his late sister to look at that every time Maggie saw him her heart seemed to twist in her chest. He had copper-coloured hair that turned to a deep red–gold in the summer and dark eyes, and he also possessed his late sister's sweet nature so Maggie had a huge soft spot for him. He loved nothing more than playing with his tin soldiers and the wooden fort that his father had made for him the year before, and so far he was just a typical little boy who gave no thought to what he wanted to be when he grew up. He was now ten years old and promised to be tall like his father, whereas Charlie was more slightly built like herself.

They were each completely different in temperament and Maggie often wondered how three such different boys could have come from the same womb. She poured cups of milk for them and got on with preparing the dinner. It wasn't long before they heard the sound of Dobbin clopping into the yard. That was one thing about the autumn and winter nights that Maggie liked; Levi always finished earlier because it was hard to work in the dark. Although it would be a good hour yet before he came in, for first he would give Dobbin a good rub down and settle him in his stable, and then he would unload his cart, so she had to wait impatiently to hear what the estate agent had had to say about the offer.

'*Well?*' she asked expectantly the second he set foot through the door.

He smiled wearily as he dragged the flat cap from his head and untied the string that served as a belt about his old overcoat. 'We have to wait to see if the chap who owns the house will accept me offer.' He saw her face fall but there was nothing he could do about it.

'Did the agent think he might?' Her voice was anxious.

'To be honest, pet, no he didn't. He thought the offer might be a bit too far off what the seller wants. But don't get frettin', he's bound to come back wi' a counter-offer.' There seemed no point in lying to her.

'Why didn't you just offer the full asking price and be done with it?' She looked annoyed. 'You know full well how much I love the place!'

Levi drew a deep breath. 'Every pound I can save off the askin' price is a pound you'll 'ave in your purse towards gettin' the place how you want it.'

Slightly pacified, she nodded. 'Yes, there is that I suppose. But what if it sells to someone who offers a higher price?'

'We'll just have to take us chances on that an' if it happens then we'll look elsewhere.'

Something in his tone made her clamp her lips together. Levi looked tired and had clearly had a long day, so for now she dropped the subject.

The next four days seemed to pass interminably slowly but at last Levi came in one evening and told her, 'I called into the estate agent when I was passin' earlier an' it was as I thought: the chap that owns the house rejected our offer.'

'Oh, but—'

He held his hand up to stay her flow of words. 'Hear me out! He came back wi' the price that he would accept, an' I've agreed to it.'

'What? You mean we've got it?' Maggie's whole face was alight and when he nodded, she threw her arms about his neck, and drawing his head down to hers she kissed him soundly on the mouth, even though she usually refused to go near him until he had washed and changed out of his work clothes.

Levi prayed this might be the start of a better relationship between them. Since losing Penny, Maggie had not allowed him to go near her and he had missed the intimate side of their marriage.

'But that's grand news,' she gushed. 'When will we get the keys?'

'Soon as ever I can take the money in' an' the solicitor 'as done the paperwork.' He smiled to see her so happy. 'I reckon a couple o' weeks an' it'll all be done an' dusted.'

Humming happily, she went to finish getting the evening meal ready.

Chapter Three

Towards the end of October, Levi picked up the keys to their new house and when he got home from work late that afternoon and placed them in Maggie's hands, she was ecstatic.

'Oh, we must go round there straight away,' she told him as she jingled the keys at the boys.

'Now, hold fire, hinny.' Levi had had a hard day and it was already dark. 'There wouldn't be much point going now, would there? It's already pitch-black out there and we wouldn't be able to see a thing.'

Maggie's face fell. 'We would if we took an oil lamp with us.'

Levi shook his head. 'No, the boys have school tomorrow and I have work. The weekend will be soon enough for us all to go an' view our new home.' Then seeing her disappointment, he sighed and added, 'Though I dare say you could pop round the morrow if you wanted to.'

Placated, Maggie smiled as she clutched the keys to her chest as if they were made of pure gold. 'I'll do that,' she agreed. 'When can we move in?'

Levi had already given this some thought and, dropping heavily onto a chair and stifling a yawn, he told her, 'I thought the weekend after next. We have to decide what we're goin' to do wi' this place afore we go anywhere. I can't give it up because I need to keep me yard 'ere. I dare say you wouldn't want me taking all me stuff to the new place?'

Maggie shook her head vehemently at the very thought of it. 'Oh goodness me, no, indeed. What would the neighbours think? You must remember they're a different class of people live round there.'

'Aye, an' what you need to remember is that they're only flesh an' blood the same as the rest of us.'

Barney sidled up to him with a frown on his face. 'Do we *really* 'ave to go an' live there, Da? It's dead posh an' the people there will look down on the likes of us.'

'What do you mean – "the likes of us", my lad?' Maggie was incensed. 'I don't mind bettin' our house is as clean, if not cleaner, than a lot o' theirs. An' yer know what they say, *cleanliness is next to Godliness!*'

'All right, all right, you two.' Levi held his hand up. 'I shall start to wish I'd never bought this house if it's goin' to cause trouble.'

Shamefaced, Barney hung his head and darted a venomous look from beneath his lashes at his mother. 'Sorry, Da.'

Hauling himself out of his chair, Levi went off to wash and change.

Much later that evening, after the boys were in bed, Maggie broached the subject of the house again. 'What do you think we should do with the cottage? I understand you need to keep it cos it's attached to your work yard, but it would be daft to leave it standin' empty when it could bring in a bit o' money in rent.'

He nodded in agreement as he puffed on his pipe. 'I'd thought the same, which is why I wondered how you'd feel about me offerin' it to Peggy an' Sid. I know it ain't no bigger than theirs but it's in a lot better condition after the work I've done on it an' I've a feelin' Peggy would jump at the chance.'

'Hmm, you could be right. An' I dare say it would be better to have someone we know here to keep an eye on the yard. Sid could be trusted to do that right enough. Would you like me to ask her in the mornin? She's comin' to have a look at the house with me afore goin' to work.'

Levi smiled. He'd wondered how long it would be before Peggy was round there. 'Aye, go ahead an' ask her.'

Maggie stared at him thoughtfully for a moment. 'And what sort of rent would you be wanting for it?'

Levi shrugged. 'Same as they're payin' now,' he suggested.

Maggie frowned. 'But they don't pay a lot because of the state the place is in.'

'Even so, they're friends an' I don't want to fleece 'em.'

Maggie wasn't pleased with his answer. The way she saw it, the more they charged the more she'd have to spend on the new house, but she didn't push it – for now at any rate. Besides, she was so thrilled with the prospect of moving to her new home that she didn't want anything to spoil it, so she was soon smiling again.

'Have I told you lately what a wonderful man you are, Levi Lilburn?' she giggled as she dropped onto his lap and placed a sloppy kiss on his mouth.

'I don't reckon you 'ave so why don't yer tell me again,' Levi responded. Oh, it was lovely to see his Maggie smiling again and he prayed that this would be the start of happier times for all of them as he cuddled her to him.

The following morning, once she had seen the boys off to school, Maggie was getting ready to go to the new house when the back door opened and her sister Florence walked in. Maggie stifled a groan. She could have done without Flo turning up today of all days, but then she supposed it would be a good chance to boast about the new house, so she raised a smile.

'Morning, Flo, you're lucky to catch me. I was just going to have a look at our new house.'

Flo's hair was the exact same colour as Maggie's but that was where any resemblance between them ended. Maggie was slim and petite, whereas Flo, who had once been fashionably rounded, had run to fat following the births of her seven children who had been born in quick succession. Although they kept in touch occasionally, Maggie and Flo's relationship was strained, for Flo had had her eye on Levi when he had first arrived in Nuneaton. He had taken her out a couple of times and seemed to like her, until he had clapped eyes on Maggie, and then he had dropped Flo like a hot brick. Things had not been the same between the two sisters since.

Their four brothers were scattered far and wide: two had gone to try their luck in Australia and had never been heard of since; another had moved to London; and the oldest brother had died soon after their parents. Their sister, Susan, had also gone to London to seek her fortune, and although she had written to them a couple of times, they hadn't seen her since.

'New house?' Flo raised her eyebrow. 'What's all this then?' She herself lived in a small two-up, two-down terraced house in Fife Street which was bursting at the seams. Jim Myton, her husband, worked in the local bookies and was a drinker, and it was a well-known fact that half his wages went straight across the bar of the Pig and Whistle each Friday night.

Maggie's chest swelled. 'Levi has just bought us one of the big houses in Swan Lane.' She felt a measure of satisfaction at Flo's gobsmacked expression.

'*Swan Lane?* Blimey, has he come into money or summat? What's wrong wi' this place?'

'Nothing at all, but there's nowt wrong with wanting to better yourself.' Maggie gave her a smug grin.

'So what's goin' to happen to this place?'

'We're going to rent it out.'

Flo glanced around enviously. This cottage was like a palace compared to the one she lived in. The trouble was it was no bigger so there wasn't much point in asking if she could have it.

There was a tap at the door and Peggy appeared. 'All fit, girl?' Spotting Flo, she sighed. 'Oh sorry, I didn't mean to interrupt anythin'. I didn't realise you 'ad company.'

'It's only, Flo.' Maggie put on her bonnet. 'You can come to have a look around too, if you like, Flo?'

'No thanks.' Flo shook her head as she rose from the chair. She couldn't think of anything worse than watching her sister show off her fancy new house. 'I only called in cos I 'ad a few things to get off the market an' I were passin'.' She sniffed. 'I'll get off now, ta-ra.'

All the way home, Flo fumed. She had envied Maggie her pretty face and trim figure all her life, even more so since she had stolen Levi right from under her nose. Admittedly he hadn't had much money back then and she had only walked out with him a couple of times, but look at him now! A self-made man about to buy a big posh house in one of the best areas in the town, while she and her brood had to slum it in a tiny terrace where they were jammed in like sardines in a tin. It wasn't fair. But that was Maggie for you; she always seemed to land on her feet. Flo was sure she would have come out with a pocket full of fish if she fell in the local cut!

Had Levi not clapped eyes on Maggie it could have been her moving into that posh house now. It was then that she realised she had quite forgotten the things she had gone to fetch from the market, so with a sigh she turned and trudged back into town. It was either that or there would be nothing to cook for the children's dinner that evening!

As they walked up to the new house, Peggy sighed. 'Eeh, love, it's *beautiful*,' she said generously. Peggy hadn't a jealous bone in her body.

'If you think it's nice from the outside wait till you get in.' Maggie opened the little gate and they went along the path to the front door where she fumbled in her bag for the keys.

Half an hour later they had done a full tour of the house and garden and, like Maggie, Peggy was taken with it.

'It's nice now but I can just picture what it'll be like when you've been in a while. But will you 'ave enough stuff to furnish it? There are so many rooms.'

'Not straight away,' Maggie admitted. 'But it'll come in time.'

'How about I come round an' help yer give it all a good clean afore yer move in?' Peggy offered kindly.

Maggie smiled. 'Thanks, that would be wonderful. I think it's stood empty for some time an' I didn't fancy tacklin' these cobwebs all on me own.'

As they left, Maggie offered Peggy the chance of renting their cottage, and the other woman almost snatched her hand off. Levi had made the place very comfortable and it was so much better than the one they were renting at present.

'Levi says you may have it for the same rent as you're paying now,' Maggie told her. 'On the understanding that Sid will keep his eye on the yard of an evening when Levi's finished his day's rounds. We don't want anyone robbing from us.'

'Sid won't mind that at all,' Peggy assured her, delighted that she too now had a house move to look forward to.

Over the next few days, almost every evening once the children were in bed, Peggy and Maggie set off to clean the house in Swan Lane. They tackled one room at a time, starting at the top and working their way down. Levi sorted the garden on his Sunday off and with the two older boys helping they had soon cleared the overgrown weeds and managed to cut the grass down. Levi had even started to improve the old stable block for Dobbin, much to Maggie's horror. She had hoped he would be left in the stable back at the yard of an evening, but Levi wouldn't hear of it.

'He stays wi' me,' he told her in no uncertain terms.

Maggie frowned at him. It was very rare for Levi to go against her on anything. 'But what will our neighbours think seeing you bringing him back here each evening?'

'I don't give a bloody cuss what the neighbours think, an' you shouldn't either,' he scolded her. 'Just remember it's Dobbin that helped me earn the money to buy this place.'

Maggie pouted. 'I know, but most of the people who live hereabouts have jobs that mean they go to work in shirts and ties. They're doctors, solicitors and people like that.'

'As you quite rightly told Barney, that don't mean they're any better than us,' Levi pointed out. 'An' I hope livin' here won't give you ideas above your station. I'm a workin'-class man as gets me hands dirty an' that ain't goin' to change.'

'No . . . no of course not.' Maggie realised that she'd pushed him far enough for now, although she still cringed at the thought of Dobbin living there with them. He was very old and hardly a racehorse, but what could she do?

At last, every room in the house apart from the attic rooms had been cleaned and they were ready to move in. That was when the next disagreement started.

'I'll move our furniture on the back of the cart after work,' Levi told her one evening as she dished their dinner up.

Maggie looked horrified. 'On that dirty cart!' She paused in the act of ladling sizzling lamb chops onto his plate. 'But can't we hire a smarter wagon to do it?'

'Why would we waste money when I'm perfectly capable o' doing it meself?' Levi questioned.

Maggie cringed, picturing Levi in the old cap and coat that he wore for work.

'You strong lads will give yer old dad a hand, won't you, eh?' Levi smiled at the boys and they nodded, although Barney still didn't like the idea of moving.

'Don't know why we 'ave to go an' live there anyway,' he grumbled as he pushed his meal about the plate.

Maggie forced a smile. 'Don't be so silly. We'll have so much more room there, and don't forget there's a garden where you can play football.'

'Oh yes, an' who will I play with?' he said surlily. 'Harry's too little, Charlie's allus got his head stuck in a book an' all me mates will be back here!'

'We can always invite them round,' Maggie said and, slightly placated, he finished his meal, although he still didn't look too taken with the idea.

The following day while Levi was out doing his rounds Maggie spent the day packing, and by the time he came home that evening she and the boys were ready to go.

Sid came to help Levi lift the heavy stuff onto the cart and at last they were ready for the off.

Peggy and Sid came to see them go. 'I'll be round to see how you're settlin' in in a couple o' days or so when we've got our own stuff in an' sorted here,' she promised as Maggie clambered up onto the seat of the cart and pulled her shawl over her head. The boys were balanced precariously on the furniture in the back and they glanced at the only home they had ever known as Levi urged Dobbin on. Then with a final wave to Peggy and Sid they pulled out of the small courtyard onto Abbey Street and headed for their new home.

Chapter Four

As the cart rattled across the cobblestones towards Swan Lane, the icy November wind bit into them.

'I wouldn't be surprised if we didn't have some snow soon. We'd best get the fire lit the minute we get in,' Levi suggested.

'It's all right. I came round earlier and lit the fire in the drawing room and the kitchen, so it should be warm when we get there,' Maggie assured him. Her eyes frequently swept the streets as she prayed that their new neighbours wouldn't see them arriving in the old cart with all their belongings piled on it. But thankfully, since it was pitch-dark and bitterly cold, there were few people about.

Once they got to the house, Levi urged the horse around to the back, and he and the two older boys began to carry the furniture inside. When it was finally all in place, Maggie couldn't help but feel slightly disappointed. They only had enough to furnish the small lounge and the kitchen downstairs, and while the pieces she had taken such a pride in had looked grand in their tiny cottage, they looked completely out of place and far too small for the larger rooms in Swan Lane.

'We're going to need a much larger sofa,' she told Levi, as he bit into the sandwiches she had made for supper. 'Our others look lost in here.'

'Don't start that already, pet,' he warned. This was just what he had feared. 'I told you when you insisted you wanted the place that it'd take some time for us to furnish all the rooms. There's no money left for anythin' else just yet, so the rooms will just have to stand empty for a time. But come on now, soon as we've eaten this and had a sup o' tea we need to get the beds sorted if we're all to sleep comfy tonight.'

Two hours later, Maggie had hung curtains at the front bedroom window, which was to be hers and Levi's, and the boys were sound asleep in their rooms. She made her way back downstairs to where Levi was sitting by the fire with a cup of cocoa.

'Well, we're in, lass,' Levi sighed as he held his feet out to the fire. For some reason she didn't seem quite as excited as he had expected her to be. 'Are yer happy now?'

'Er . . . yes, it's just that everywhere looks so bare.' She bit down on her lip as she glanced about the room,

Levi frowned. Knowing her as he did, he was concerned that she was going to want to start buying furniture they could ill afford. What with the solicitors' fees and one thing and another, the house had cost a little more than he had estimated, so he had been forced to take out a small mortgage on it. Not that he had told Maggie about that. He didn't want to worry her, but he knew he wouldn't be happy until it was paid off, which meant working even more hours than he already did. Levi didn't like owing money, even to the bank. Only once everything was paid off could Maggie start to spend on new furniture.

After finishing his cocoa, he stifled a yawn and got slowly to his feet. He had been up since the crack of dawn and it was telling on him now.

'Are yer comin' to bed, pet?' he asked with a wink.

Maggie was still gazing about the room deciding where the new furniture could go. Perhaps a lovely long mahogany sideboard along the back wall, and a chaise longue for inside the bay window.

'I'll be up presently,' she said, her mind far away, so with a sigh Levi made his way to bed.

By the time she joined him some time later after damping down the fire and turning off the gas lights, he was already fast asleep, his gentle snores echoing around the room. The small wardrobe and the bed they had brought from the cottage looked lost in such a large room. They would need some more bedroom furniture too, but that would have to wait until she had furnished the downstairs as she wanted it to receive visitors. She was still mentally making a list of everything they would need when she eventually fell asleep curled against Levi's broad back, in a way she hadn't for years.

Over the next few days, as Maggie unpacked the last of their things, she discovered that the bedrooms weren't going to work out quite as she had planned. Charlie and Harry adamantly refused to go into their own rooms, complaining that they were too big and creepy. In the end Levi had no choice but to move Harry's bed into Charlie's room. Barney, on the other hand, was quite happy to have his own space. He was coming up to fourteen and looking forward to finishing school. It was assumed that he would start work with his father, but Maggie had other thoughts on that.

'I was thinkin', we ought to be seeing what the chances are of getting Barney into the grammar school next year so that he can have some further education.'

Barney frowned. They were all seated around the table about to have their evening meal. 'An' why would I want to go on to further education, Ma? I don't need it if I'm goin' to be helpin' me da on his rounds.'

Maggie sniffed. 'There's nothing wrong with trying to better yourself. Oh, and I met the new neighbours today.'

'Oh aye.' Levi had just loaded a fat juicy sausage onto his fork. 'An' what are they like?'

'Well, when I say I met the neighbours, I should have said I met the lady of the house. Her husband owns the mill in Attleborough. They must be very rich if the way she was dressed is anything to go by.'

Levi shrugged. 'Clothes don't maketh the man,' he said quietly, but Maggie was clearly very impressed with the woman.

'Their name is Taylor-Lloyd and can you believe they have a maid, a cook *and* a housekeeper! I've seen a gardener there too.'

'Hmm, just don't get thinkin' we can run to hirin' staff,' he warned.

Maggie pouted. 'She asked me what you do for a living and I told her you were a businessman and you have your own business.'

'Then you were tellin' the truth, weren't you? I *do* own me own business. Did you tell 'er what I do?'

Shamefaced, Maggie shook her head. 'Not exactly.'

'And why was that? Are you ashamed o' me?'

'Of course not, but . . .' Maggie bit her lip. 'It just doesn't sound very posh, does it? If I tell her you're a rag-and-bone man, I mean.'

'There's nowt wrong wi' what I do,' Levi said with a frown. 'I'm sure I work just as 'ard if not 'arder than 'er husband.'

'Yes of course you do.' Maggie could see that she'd upset him, so she hurried on. 'She's invited me round there for morning coffee on Thursday at eleven o'clock. Apparently, some of the ladies who live in the road meet up weekly and take it in turns to have coffee mornin's . . . I mean, morn*ings.*'

'Lucky for them they 'ave the time fer such things,' Levi grunted as he tucked into his dinner and, sensing that he wasn't too happy with her, Maggie sensibly changed the subject.

The following morning, Peggy arrived and when Maggie answered the door to her, she rushed inside out of the cold. 'Brr, it's enough to cut you in two out there,' she said with a shiver as she crossed to the inglenook to warm her hands. 'I pity your poor Levi stuck out in it all day. I can't stay long cos I'm due in at work in the next hour. But 'ow are yer settlin' in?'

'Oh, we're fine, and you?'

Peggy beamed. 'We're snug as bugs in rugs in that little cottage,' she told her happily. 'It's so much better than the one we were rentin' before. The kids love it. But get that kettle on, gel, else I won't 'ave time for a cuppa afore I 'ave to go again.'

Soon after the two women sat at the table with Maggie's precious china cups and saucers steaming in front of them, and Maggie told Peggy about her morning coffee invitation from her new neighbour. 'She talks *ever* so posh,' she told her. 'And she's got live-in staff, can you believe it? Although I can understand why in a house the size of this one. It takes a lot more cleaning than the cottage.'

Peggy raised an eyebrow. 'So, if she's got all them to wait on 'er what does she do all day?'

'From what I can make of it she has a big circle of friends and she does the flower arranging up at St Mary's Church apparently.'

'How the other 'alf live, eh?' Peggy gulped at her tea, keeping one eye on the clock. 'Good luck to 'er, I say, but unfortunately, I've got to get to work. The nursery is chock-a-block wi' babbies at the minute. Poor little buggers. Not all o' the staff are as kind to 'em as I am. One o' the poor little mites 'as got colic an' cries non-stop, an' I got there t'other day to find a rag shoved in its mouth wi' laudanum on it to stop it cryin'. It's a wonder the poor little soul woke up at all. I told the woman who did it that if I came in to find she'd done it to any o' the others again I'd tell the house-mistress – not that I think she'd do owt about it. She's as bad as the rest of 'em. Which leads me to ask . . . 'ave you had any more thoughts on takin' a child in?'

'I have but I thought I'd give us time to settle in before I speak to Levi about it again,' Maggie admitted.

'Is 'e not 'appy 'ere then?'

Maggie sighed. 'I'm not sure. Charlie and Harry seem fine but I think it's taking Barney and Levi a bit longer to get used to the place.'

Peggy laughed. 'Well, it is a big change from where you were livin',' she pointed out. 'Give 'em time to settle. An' what's 'appened to the way you speak an all. Why 'ave you started talkin' all posh?'

Maggie raised her chin and sniffed. 'There's nothing wrong with trying to better yourself,' she said primly. 'And didn't you say it was time you were leaving?' She didn't like the way the conversation was going.

Thankfully, after another glance at the clock, Peggy rose and fetched her shawl from the back of the chair. 'Yer right, pet. I'd best be off. Don't forget where we live, see yer soon, ta-ra fer now.' And with that she was gone, leaving Maggie to her thoughts.

As she wandered around the large house, Maggie paused at the door of the spare bedroom and pictured a little girl in there. She had been so busy over the last few weeks preparing for the move and then settling in that that she hadn't had time to give too much thought to adopting a child, but now the yearning was back. Oh, she knew only too well that no one could ever take Penny's place but surely having another little one to love would ease the heartache a little? She loved each of her sons dearly, but she still missed having a daughter, and now that they were settled, she wondered if she shouldn't pay a visit to the workhouse to see what babies were available. Levi would be none too pleased, but he didn't have to find out, did he? After all, what harm could it do? The move had made her happy for a time but already the novelty was wearing off and the pain and grief of losing Penny were returning with a vengeance. Tears were never far away, although she tried to hide them from the family.

Still, she had her coffee morning to look forward to. Suddenly she wondered what she should wear. If the way Mrs Taylor-Lloyd had been dressed was anything to go by, the rest of the ladies would be dressed in finery and she would stick out like a sore thumb. She had always ensured that the boys were well dressed but the only really decent gown she possessed was the black bombazine she'd got for Penny's funeral. Perhaps she could dress it with a white lace collar and wear that with the string of pearls Levi had surprised her with one Christmas. Feeling better about things she hurried to fetch the dress from the wardrobe.

Chapter Five

It was the day of the coffee morning at Mrs Taylor-Lloyd's and Maggie wanted to make a good impression.

After going to great pains with her appearance, at eleven o'clock on the dot she knocked on the Taylor-Lloyds' door. It was opened by a little maid, who looked no older than nine or ten, wearing a snow-white apron and mob cap trimmed with broderie anglaise. Maggie stepped past her and into the hall. It had much the same layout as her own, but that and the Minton tiles on the floor was where any similarity ended, for this house was extravagantly furnished and decorated. Heavy flocked wallpaper in a rich green, and expensive mirrors and pictures adorned the walls.

'The missus is in the drawin' room,' the little maid told Maggie, and after following her along the hall Maggie was admitted into a room decorated in shades of red and gold that almost took her breath away. Envy coursed through her as she looked around. Two plush velvet sofas, heavily trimmed around the bottom with gold braid, stood either side of a roaring fire, and matching curtains hung at the windows, and an enormous, highly polished mahogany sideboard stood against the back wall, covered in expensive-looking china ornaments. Maggie was so taken with everything that she didn't quite know where to look first.

'Ah, Mrs Lilburn. How nice of you to come. You are the first to arrive. Do come and take a seat.' Mrs Taylor-Lloyd advanced on her in a cloud of heavy French perfume and held out her hand. Suddenly Maggie felt totally out of her depth. 'Eve, the other guests should be arriving shortly so tell Cook to prepare the tea and coffee.'

'Yes, missus.' The little maid bobbed her knee.

The woman frowned at her. 'How many times do I have to tell you, girl,' she snapped irritably. 'It's *ma'am* when you address me, not missus!'

'Sorry . . . ma'am!' Quaking in her shoes, the girl backed out of the room, her cheeks flaming, as the hostess turned her attention back to Maggie.

'I do apologise about the new maid.' Mrs Taylor-Lloyd smiled ingratiatingly. 'I took her from the workhouse and I'm afraid you might say she's still rather rough around the edges. Still, what more can you expect? I dare say I shall have her trained to my standards eventually. Have you managed to employ any staff yet, Mrs Lilburn?'

'I, er. . . no, I haven't.' Thankfully Maggie was saved from having to say more by the sound of the other guests arriving and soon the room was full of beautifully dressed women. They were all decked out in very expensive-looking jewellery, almost as if they were trying to outdo each other, and even in her newly trimmed gown Maggie felt more out of place by the minute.

'How are you settling into your new home?' one woman asked Maggie as she sipped her tea daintily from a delicate bone china cup and saucer.

'Quite well, thank you,' Maggie answered in a small voice.

The woman nodded, 'I believe you have three children?'

Maggie gulped. 'Yes, and I was thinking of going to look at the babies available for adoption in the workhouse. We lost our young daughter you see, and I thought . . .'

'How very noble of you,' the woman cut in condescendingly. 'But are you quite sure you'd be doing the right thing, my dear? What I mean is, you have no idea where or who these children have come from, do you? Your children are boys, are they not?'

'Er. . . yes. Barnaby, Charles and Harold.' It didn't seem right to shorten their names in her present company.

41

Luckily the mention of adopting a child from the workhouse started a debate amongst the women, so Maggie was happy to sit on the sidelines saying nothing. In fact, she was just watching the clock until enough time had passed that she could make an excuse to leave. The morning had been nothing like she had hoped and she certainly wouldn't be in a hurry to come back again anytime soon.

At last, she was able to rise and apologetically tell Mrs Taylor-Lloyd that she had to leave to wait for a delivery, and after saying her goodbyes she scuttled away. As the drawing room door closed behind her, she heard a gale of laughter and one of the women comment, 'Goodness me, *whatever* did you invite *her* for, Eunice? Do you know her husband is a rag-and-bone man and they've come from the courtyards in Abbey Street?'

As Maggie slid through the front door, her cheeks were burning with humiliation. She had looked forward to this visit so much, but she would be in no rush to accept another invitation – if another one came, which she very much doubted.

Maggie's day went from bad to worse when Barney walked in after school with blood spurting from his nose and sporting the promise of a black eye. The sleeve of his coat and the knees of his trousers were torn, and he was valiantly trying to hold back tears.

'Why, whatever's happened?' Horrified, Maggie rushed towards him, but he held his hand out to ward her off.

'Keep away,' he growled. 'This is all *your* fault!'

'*What?*' Maggie frowned. 'How can this be *my* fault!'

'It were *you* as wanted us to come 'ere,' he sobbed. 'We was all 'appy in the cottage. I 'ate it 'ere; the rooms are too big an' it's cold. An' all me mates at school don't wanna know me now. They say I'm a snob an' they pick on me.'

Maggie's chin set. 'Don't worry, I'll nip this in the bud right now,' she promised. 'I shall be at the school to see the headmaster first thing tomorrow. I hate bullies!'

'*No!*' The word shot from his lips like a bullet from a gun. 'That would just make things worse fer me.'

With a heavy heart, Maggie hurried away to fetch a cloth and a bowl of water to clean up Barney's face. She had thought the boys would love living in a larger house and in a better neighbourhood, but it seemed she'd been wrong if the other two felt the same as Barney, who was glaring up at her as she dabbed gently at his nose.

'There,' she said eventually, returning the bloody cloth to the water. 'I think it's stopped bleeding now but you're going to have a right shiner on you tomorrow. Slip up and get changed and I'll see if I can repair your shirt and put the rest of your clothes in to soak.'

Barney slunk off to do as he was told and once upstairs he sank onto the side of his bed and buried his face in his hands. He had never felt so unhappy in his life. Since moving to the new house, he had felt totally unsettled and like a fish out of water. But like the rest of his family, he'd had no say in the matter. As usual his da had done what his ma wanted. And the new house wasn't the only thing he was unhappy about. He would be leaving school soon and his parents had taken it for granted that he would go to work with his da. He sighed. What he really wanted to do, though, was work with the circus that visited the town each year. He had loved the circus ever since his parents had taken him and his brothers to see it a few years before, and whenever it came to town, he would go to help erect the big top or do any other jobs that needed doing. He had got to know many of the circus folk and knew they would take him on. So what was he to do? If he did what he wanted he would hurt his parents, but if he stayed, he would be unhappy. It was a difficult dilemma to find himself in.

Downstairs, as Maggie emptied the water away, the beginnings of a headache started behind her eyes. The day hadn't gone at all as she had planned but hopefully tomorrow would be better. After all, as Peggy had quite rightly pointed out, Barney had barely had time to settle in and he was bound to prefer the house to the small cottage once he had.

'So how did it go today?' Levi asked as they all sat at dinner that evening. Maggie had made a steak pie, one of his favourites, and he was looking forward to it.

'Oh, it was all right,' she answered quietly. 'Pass the potatoes would you, Charles?'

Charlie frowned. 'Since when have yer called me Charles, Ma?'

Barney and Harry grinned, and their mother flushed. 'It's the name I gave you when you were born and I think it's a shame to shorten it. Besides, Charlie is so working class, isn't it? I shall call you all by your given names from now on.'

Levi's laden fork hovered halfway to his mouth. 'But we *are* workin' class, hinny, an' we've allus called our lads Barney, Charlie an' Harry before,' he pointed out.

She nodded. 'I'm quite aware of that, but if we're going to fit into this neighbourhood it won't hurt to make a few changes, will it?'

Levi frowned at her, trying to communicate his displeasure. Ever since Maggie had met Mrs Taylor-Lloyd, he had noticed that she was speaking differently, and now she wanted to change the boys' names!

Aware of his anger, Maggie lowered her eyes and concentrated on her meal, but the atmosphere was tense.

Later that night, as Maggie lay next to Levi, sleep eluded her. The visit to the Taylor-Lloyds had unsettled her and suddenly her own home felt bare and empty. Also, the longing for another baby was burning inside her and again she wondered what harm it would do if she visited the workhouse, just to make enquiries. The more she thought about it the more the idea appealed to her. And after all, if she was going to do it what better time than when Peggy was there?

*

A few days later, once she had seen the boys off to school, Maggie put on one of her warmest gowns and her best bonnet and set off for the Bull Ring, where the workhouse was situated. It was a bitterly cold, foggy morning and the hoar frost crackled beneath her feet as she climbed the hill from the Coton Arches. Her cheeks were glowing from the cold wind and despite the thick woollen gloves, her fingers were numb. But she strode on; she was on a mission now and just prayed that she wouldn't see Levi doing his rounds.

At last, the workhouse appeared out of the fog and she shuddered. It was a dark, depressing place and she could only pity the poor souls that ended up in there. Approaching the large oak entrance door, she took a deep breath, and yanked on the bell that hung to one side. This was it. There could be no going back now.

Chapter Six

The door opened and Maggie found herself staring into the stern face of a middle-aged woman with a hooked nose, clad in black bombazine from head to foot. Her steel-grey hair was pulled into a tight bun on the back of her head and her grey eyes were as cold as the frost underfoot. About her waist was a chatelaine from which a number of keys dangled. She reminded Maggie of a ferret. This, she surmised, must be the housemistress who Peggy had told her about. A woman with no pity and a heart of stone, if what she had heard was true, and after seeing her she had no doubt that it was.

'Yes?' the woman barked.

Forcing herself not to turn tail and run, Maggie straightened her back and took another deep breath. 'I've come to enquire about adopting a child.'

The woman narrowed her eyes. 'Then you'd best come in. What age child are you looking for? Someone to work for you, is it?'

'Er . . . no, I was thinking more of a baby . . . a girl.'

'I see. And are you in a position to afford to take a child?'

Maggie glared at her with defiance. 'Absolutely. My husband has his own thriving business and we own a house on Swan Lane.'

'I see.' The woman nodded her satisfaction. If that was the case and they had a child the woman wanted she could hopefully ask for a generous donation to the workhouse.

She led Maggie along a stark corridor with drab green walls. A child who looked to be no more than seven or eight years old was mopping the tiled floor and at the sight of the housemistress advancing upon her she renewed her efforts. The woman glared at her as she swept past with Maggie close on her heels.

A few feet further along, the woman opened a door and ushered Maggie into a large office. A huge leather-topped desk sat in the centre of the room, behind which sat a portly, middle-aged man with the biggest handlebar moustache that Maggie had ever seen.

'This is Mr Pilkington, the workhouse master,' the housemistress said to Maggie. She went on to explain to him why Maggie was there.

The man stared at Maggie through beady, pale-grey eyes, then nodded as he withdrew a form from a drawer of the desk. 'Do sit down, madam,' he said ingratiatingly. 'I shall have to take your details and then, if you are still happy to proceed, I'm sure Mrs Bentley will show you the children we have available for adoption.'

Ten minutes later, when all the formalities were completed, the housemistress returned and led her to a steep staircase. Maggie was only too happy to escape the workhouse master's scrutiny. There was something about him that she found abhorrent, but now she was feeling decidedly nervous. What would Levi say if he were to return from work to find she had taken a child with-out his consent? But then she reassured herself – it was highly unlikely that she would find the right child on the very first visit. She would probably have to return a number of times before she found exactly the right one.

At the top of the stairs, they passed a row of children, all with hollow eyes, walking in a regimentally straight line behind a hard-faced elderly woman. The children kept their heads down as if they were afraid to raise them and Maggie couldn't help but feel sorry for them.

'They're on their way to lessons,' the housemistress explained. 'We pride ourselves on the fact that our children are all educated and taught to read and write. We have a teacher come in every afternoon for one hour.'

It didn't sound like much of an education to Maggie, but she merely nodded as they moved on. They continued up yet another flight of stairs and as she followed the housemistress into the nursery, it was all Maggie could do to stop herself from crying aloud. Wooden cots were arranged down either side of the room, each contained a baby who was either sleeping or staring dully up at the ceiling. Not one of them was crying. Peggy appeared just then, clad in a white apron and carrying a tray of feeding bottles. Giving no indication that she knew Maggie, she placed the tray on the table and lifted the nearest baby out of his cot. Settling into a chair she began to feed him.

'Mrs Lilburn is looking for a baby girl to adopt, Walker. Perhaps you could show her the ones that are available. I shall be back shortly.'

'Yes, ma'am.' Peggy nodded. She didn't look at Maggie until the housemistress had left the room. 'So, Levi finally agreed to it, did he?' she said, grinning.

Maggie lowered her eyes guiltily. 'Well . . . not exactly, not yet, but I just thought it wouldn't hurt to have a look to see if any of the babies caught my eye.'

'I think I might 'ave just the little one you're lookin' for,' Peggy told her as the child she was feeding finished his bottle and she leant him forward to wind him. 'Let me just change this little one's bindin' an' I'll show yer. She's in the cot by the winder if yer want to 'ave a peep at 'er.'

Maggie walked between the cots, staring into each one until she came to the one Peggy had mentioned. As she gazed down at the tiny infant inside it her heart began to beat faster and tears sprang to her eyes. The baby was swaddled in a dull grey blanket but the head of downy copper-coloured hair peeping out of it immediately transported her back to the day her own daughter had been born. Penny's hair had been the exact same colour.

'She's a little beaut, ain't she?'

Peggy's voice brought Maggie's thoughts back to the present with a start. 'Y-yes, she is,' she stammered as her hands began to shake. 'How long has she been here?'

'She were born 'ere to a young woman who signed herself in. She were at death's door an' could hardly stand when she arrived. She passed away soon after she gave birth, so no one even knows who she were. The little 'un is about two weeks old now.'

'How sad.' Maggie gently stroked the sleeping baby's hair. 'And what is her name?'

Maggie shrugged. 'I don't know as anyone 'as bothered to give 'er one as yet. Yer can pick 'er up if yer like.'

Tentatively Maggie lifted the infant into her arms, and as the tiny girl looked up at her, Maggie's heart was lost. She looked so little and defenceless.

'She's beautiful,' she whispered.

Peggy frowned. 'I'll agree wi' that. But wouldn't you be better to speak to Levi afore you go makin' any hasty decisions?'

Maggie knew that her friend was only speaking common sense but her heart was ruling her head and she didn't want to put the baby down.

'I, er . . . suppose I should,' she admitted reluctantly. 'And per-haps encourage him to come and meet her with me. After all, if he sees her he surely couldn't resist.'

Peggy said nothing but seeing the strength of Maggie's reaction, she was worried. Levi had confided to her how concerned he was about having to take out a small mortgage on the new house. He hated owing money to anyone and Peggy knew him well enough to know that he'd likely work himself into the ground until the debt was paid off. And now here was Maggie thinking to add yet another child to their brood without even asking him how he felt about it.

She was torn. On the one hand, having another baby might help Maggie to come to terms with losing Penny, but on the other, she was worried that it might cause trouble between Maggie and Levi.

At that moment the baby whimpered, and Peggy went to fetch some milk for her, then stood and watched as Maggie sat down to feed her. The child sucked hungrily and when she'd finished, she gave a large burp and promptly fell asleep again.

'See, I haven't lost my touch.' Maggie smiled as she gently rocked the baby. It was obvious that she wasn't planning on leaving anytime soon, so Peggy pottered away to see to the other babies and left her to it.

That evening, Levi came home to a particularly nice dinner, all his favourites, and Maggie with a smile on her face like a Cheshire cat's.

'Is that lamb chops I can smell?' He sniffed the air and grinned as Maggie hurried across the room to help him take off his coat.

'It certainly is and there are roast potatoes, onions and mushrooms to go with it.' She hung his coat on a nail in the back of the kitchen door.

As Levi went to wash his hands, he wondered what she was up to. It wasn't often that he got a greeting like this when he got home – unless Maggie was after something, that was.

'All right, what have you bought?' he asked, raising an eyebrow.

She stared back at him innocently. 'I haven't bought a thing! What makes you think I have?'

He chuckled as he dried his hands. 'I can read you like a book, madam, and I know there's something afoot. So come on – out with it.'

Maggie sighed. She'd been hoping to speak to him privately when the boys were in bed.

'Well . . .' She licked her lips. 'There *is* something, but I'll talk to you about it later.'

Levi frowned but went off to get changed wondering what his wife had up her sleeve.

Much later that evening, Maggie brought him some cocoa, and he looked up from his newspaper. 'Come on then, out with it. You've been like a cat on hot bricks all night.'

'I, er . . . visited the workhouse earlier today,' she began, watching his face closely for a reaction. It didn't look promising. 'And they have the most beautiful baby girl there waiting to be adopted. Oh Levi, if you'd only come with me to meet her, I know you'd take to her. She has a look of Penny about her, the same colour hair and the sweetest little face.'

Levi sighed, running his hands around his face. 'Haven't we had this conversation before, hinny? Penny is gone and there's no bringing her back or ever finding a replacement for her. And we've just taken this place on. We're not really in a financial position to have another child at the minute.'

'But she wouldn't cost much to keep,' she told him. 'I could make most of her clothes and she's not going to cost a lot to feed, is she? I just can't bear to think of her unloved and in that dreadful place.'

Seeing the tears in his wife's eyes, Levi began to weaken, although he really wasn't taken with the idea. 'If she's as lovely as you say, surely someone will take a shine to her? I doubt she'll be there for long. And wouldn't you rather get this place right before we think of taking on any more responsibility? And don't forget, we have Christmas coming up soon. I dare say you'll be wantin' to buy presents for the boys.' Then seeing the tears begin in earnest he shook his head. He always found it hard to say no to Maggie. 'Look, just let me have a few days to think about it, eh? From what I've 'eard you 'ave to give a donation to the workhouse if you take a child from there and I don't have a lot to spare at present.'

Maggie nodded, feeling that at least she had taken a step in the right direction. There was nothing more she could do but wait and see what Levi decided.

Over the next few days, on more than one occasion Maggie tried to talk to Levi about the baby in the workhouse but every time she did, he skilfully changed the subject and she began to get frustrated. It was early December and Christmas was racing towards them, and she had hoped to have the baby settled in with them by then, so eventually she decided there was only one thing to do. She would make the decision herself and suffer the consequences.

'Eeh, are yer sure you're doin' the right thing?' Peggy asked worriedly when Maggie told her what she'd decided the next morning. 'Levi 'as taken a lot on buyin' this place for you, an' it's a lot to ask him to take on another baby as well. They don't come cheap as you an' I know, luvvie.'

'He'll get used to it once he's over the shock,' Maggie said optimistically. 'That baby is so beautiful; how could anyone not love her?'

'Aye, she is,' Peggy agreed, but she looked concerned. 'But you know . . . she ain't Penny. No one could ever replace 'er.'

Maggie's eyes flashed with pain as she rounded on her friend. 'Don't you think I know that?' She took a deep breath. 'But surely having another little one to love will ease the pain a bit? Now come along, there's no time like the present. I know you're due in work soon so I may as well come with you and set the wheels in motion.'

Peggy sighed as she rose from her seat. She knew of old how stubborn Maggie could be when she set her mind to something. 'You know the housemaster will expect a donation, don't yer? Do you 'ave any money spare?'

Could she have known it, Maggie had already raided the housekeeping tin. It would mean they would have to dine on cheaper cuts of meat and smaller meals for the next week until Levi gave her some more money, but she was good at rustling up meals from practically nothing.

'On your own 'ead be it then.' Peggy shook her head. She loved Maggie like a sister and knew how much she missed little Penny, but on this point, she couldn't help but feel she was being rather selfish.

On the way to the workhouse Maggie told her about Barney's fight and of how he was being picked on, and again Peggy was concerned.

'Trouble is, most o' the kids from Swan Lane go to posh private schools an' them that do go to 'is school know where 'e comes from an' probably think that Barney's tryin' to get above 'imself.'

'There's absolutely nothing wrong in trying to better oneself,' Maggie snapped in her posh voice and Peggy wisely fell silent.

Half an hour later they arrived at the workhouse and as the housemistress admitted them Maggie saw the same small girl she had seen on her previous visit mopping the floors as if her life depended on it. She was very slight and scrawny and her long black hair was tied back with string at the nape of her neck. She was wearing a drab grey, shapeless garment that seemed to be the standard uniform for the children who resided there, and wooden clogs on her feet. She glanced up as Maggie and Peggy entered and it was then that she somehow caught the bucket with the mop and it fell onto its side, spilling dirty water all over the floor.

'You *stupid* girl!' the housemistress screeched, advancing on the child like an avenging angel. Lifting her arm she gave her a glancing blow to the side of her head that sent the child sprawling into the dirty water. '*Now* look what you've done. Get it cleaned up at once! You're completely *useless*, and you can be sure there will be no dinner or supper for *you* today. Perhaps that will teach you not to be so clumsy!'

Before Maggie could stop herself, she butted in. 'Excuse me, but it was an accident. I'm sure the child didn't do it on purpose.'

The housemistress sucked in her breath and stood to her full height as she glared at Maggie. 'I would thank you to keep your opinions to yourself.' Her voice was as cold as the air outside and sensing trouble Peggy scuttled away to the nursery. She knew better than to get in the way of Mrs Bentley when she was on the warpath.

'Now, how may I help you?'

'I've come to see about the baby I visited some days ago. My husband and I have decided we would like to go ahead and adopt her.'

'I see.' The woman sniffed. She was aware that Maggie had filled in all the necessary paperwork the last time she had visited, and the housemaster had seemed satisfied with everything.

They both glanced towards the child in the corridor who was choking back tears as she tried desperately to clean up the mess. And it was then that Maggie added, 'I'd also like to take a slightly older girl. One I can train to be my maid. This one would be quite suitable.' She had no idea where the words had come from, but they were said now and couldn't be taken back.

'Are you quite sure?' the housemistress asked. 'As you've seen, the child is very clumsy and not overly bright either. But if you've made up your mind, I'll take you through to the housemaster and he will tell you of the children's history. Or what we know of it.'

In no time at all Maggie was seated in the housemaster's office. Steepling his fingers he stared at her over the top of them. 'So, the housemistress informs me that you have come with the intention of taking not one but two of our children, Mrs Lilburn?'

Maggie nodded. The words she wanted to say were sticking in her throat as she wondered what Levi's reaction would be when he arrived home from work to find they had two more mouths to feed.

'Er . . . yes.'

'Hmm, well the child you saw in the corridor is Annie. She was named after the woman who found her. She was left on our doorstep as a newborn and has been here ever since. We have no idea where she came from or who she belonged to, but we do have the clothes she was wearing when she arrived. They were quite fine, if I remember rightly. I should warn you, though, Annie can be a difficult child and you must be quite sure before you take her on that this is what you want. There can be no returning her if you change your mind.'

When Maggie nodded, he went on, 'The other child, the baby, was born here recently. Her mother passed away shortly after the birth and I don't believe she has even been given a name as yet. You are welcome to take the two of them. It will be a slight financial burden off the workhouse with two less mouths to feed, and I wonder, er . . . if you would care to make a donation towards the good work we do?'

'Of course.'

With trembling fingers Maggie placed the rest of the week's housekeeping money and a few other coins she had found on the table. As the stern-faced housemaster looked down at the paltry amount, she saw disdain on his face and quickly lowered her head.

'I'm sorry it isn't more,' she mumbled, deeply embarrassed. 'We are very comfortable but we're not rich and that's the most I can manage.'

'Hmm, well I suppose something is better than nothing,' he answered as his hand snaked out and he raked the money in towards him. 'And now if you could sign these forms, I shall have the housemistress get the children ready for you.'

The woman appeared as if by magic; she had obviously been eavesdropping. She listened to his request and simpered, 'Of course, Mr Pilkington, I'll see to it right away. Perhaps you would like to wait in the corridor if you've filled in the necessary forms, Mrs Lilburn?'

With a nod towards the housemaster, Maggie followed the woman back out into the corridor and sat down on a hard-backed wooden chair, while the woman approached the child who was still desperately trying to mop up the mess she had made.

'Annie, leave that and come with me to get your things together,' the woman said sharply. 'You're leaving.'

'*Leavin'?*' The child's eyes almost popped out of her head. 'But where am I goin', missus?'

'You'll find out soon enough. Now go and collect your clothes from the dormitory and be back here in five minutes.'

The woman made for the stairs as the child darted away, reappearing shortly after with a small bundle of what looked like rags tucked under her arm. She stood waiting at the bottom of the stairs looking worried and confused until the housemistress returned, clutching the baby, who was wrapped in an old grey blanket, and with a small parcel tucked under her arm.

She dumped the baby unceremoniously into Maggie's lap and handed her the package. 'These are the clothes Annie was wearing when she was left on the steps here. And now I believe our business is concluded. Annie, be sure to behave for your new mistress! Good day.' And she turned and marched off down the hallway with her black bombazine skirts swirling about her legs, giving her the appearance of a large black crow trying to take flight.

'So . . . am I comin' to live wi' you, missus?' the little girl asked.

Maggie rose from the chair and nodded. 'Yes, you are. Do you have a coat to put on? It's very cold outside.'

'I ain't got nuffin 'cept what I'm wearin' an' a change o' clothes in 'ere,' the child answered, looking more confused by the minute.

Maggie sighed, already beginning to wonder if she had been a little hasty. She dreaded to think what Levi was going to say when he got home from work.

Once they were out on the pavement, Maggie gazed down at the baby in her arms, who was staring about with a look of wonder on her face, and bit her lip, trying to hold back the flood of emotion. Already she could picture how she would look when she had dressed her in Penny's old baby clothes – for some reason she had never been able to part with them and now they would be used again.

'Where are we goin', missus?' the child asked in a small voice.

Maggie's eyes turned to the little girl by her side. 'I live in Swan Lane,' she informed her proudly. 'It's not too far, just straight to the end of Greenmoor Road, over the Cock and Bear bridge and we'll be there. Come along, I must have the dinner ready for when my sons get home from school.'

''Ow many sons do you 'ave?'

'Three. Barnaby, Charles and Harold.'

Annie trotted alongside her like an obedient little dog. She had no idea where she was going, but then, she reasoned, anywhere would surely be better than the terrible place she had just left. In the months ahead she would think of that and wonder if she had been right.

Chapter Seven

When they entered the house, the girl stared about her. Although sparsely furnished it was like a palace compared to the cold, drab workhouse, and for the first time in her life, she dared to hope that she might finally find happiness. She had always dreamt of having a family and could hardly believe that dream was finally coming true.

'Is this where you live?' she asked in awe.

Maggie nodded as she centred her attention on the baby. She was beginning to regret her decision to bring the girl already, but she had let her heart rule her head.

'Where will I be sleepin'?'

Maggie unwrapped the drab blanket from the baby. 'You'll be sleeping in one of the attic rooms up in the loft. And I . . . well, I should warn you that I'm going to tell my husband that I've brought you here to help about the house,' Maggie told her. 'He wasn't expecting two of you, you see?'

'Oh!' The girl looked disappointed. Just for a moment she had dared to hope that the lady had brought her here to be a proper member of the family, but it didn't seem like that was going to be the case.

'How old are you, Annie?'

'I reckon I'm eight,' Annie answered.

'Very well, we may as well start as we mean to go on. I had no intention of bringing you here today when I set out, so I'm afraid I haven't had time to prepare a room for you. I haven't got round to cleaning the attic rooms yet. But you'll find all the cleaning things you will need in that cupboard over there. Perhaps you could go and make a start? Go up the second staircase to the top of the house and you can choose which room you prefer out of the two that are up there. You're capable of that, aren't you? Meantime, I need to see to the baby and get the dinner on.'

Annie made her way upstairs and soon found the two rooms Maggie had told her about. The first one she entered was full of clutter, so she opted for the one at the back of the house, which she was happy to see overlooked the garden. She had no doubt it would be lovely up there in the summer but at present it was so cold that her breath hung on the air in lacy plumes in front of her.

There was a metal-framed bed and a chest of drawers on which stood an old pot jug and bowl, but the room had clearly not been used for some time and as she walked across the floorboards to look from the window the dust swirled up and made her cough. With a sigh she went back downstairs for a mop and pail and some cleaning rags, which she took back upstairs and began to clean. By the time she was done her stomach was growling with hunger, but she was used to that – they had never been overly generous with food in the workhouse – and she was covered in dust, but at least she would have somewhere clean to sleep. And it would be the very first time she had ever had a room all to herself, which was a bonus.

When she carried the pail of dirty water and the cleaning things back downstairs, Maggie stared at her in horror. The girl was filthy.

'Oh dear, I shall have to go to the market and get you some clothes off the rag stall tomorrow,' she said, looking worried. 'I can hardly let you walk about like that. You can have a bath tonight and borrow one of my husband's shirts to sleep in. You do have a change of clothes, don't you?'

When Annie showed them to her, Maggie sighed. The second outfit was no better than the first.

She too had been busy, and Annie noticed that the baby was now washed and changed and sleeping peacefully in a drawer that

Maggie would use as a bed until Levi could carry Penny's old cradle down from the other attic room where it had been stored when they moved in. It was another thing Maggie hadn't been able to part with.

'What's 'er name?' Annie asked, crossing to take a peek at the baby who looked angelic in her new clothes.

'She hasn't got one yet,' Maggie told her sadly as she tossed the clothes the baby had been wearing into a rubbish bin by the sink. 'Now, if you've finished your room, you can perhaps make a start on the vegetables for dinner. You do know how to peel vegetables, don't you?'

'Course I do. I worked in the kitchen all the time up at the work'ouse,' Annie said proudly.

'Then you get on while I go and sort some bedding out for you.' Maggie made for the stairs, pausing to say, 'And don't look so worried.'

'Yes, missus.'

True to Annie's word, the potatoes, cabbage and carrots were all standing in pans of water when Maggie reappeared and she nodded her approval.

'Excellent, your bed is all ready for you now. I hope you'll be warm enough up there. Now I must go and fill the coal scuttle from the shed out the back and make the fire up.' It was coming close to the boys arriving home from school and Maggie's stomach was in knots as she wondered what they would think of the new additions to the family.

Just then Peggy appeared, looking concerned. 'So, you've done it?' As her eyes rested on the sleeping baby, she frowned. 'An' I'm told that you also took little Annie.'

'I did,' Maggie answered with a worried glance at the child. 'I felt sorry for her and just did it on impulse.'

Peggy sighed. 'Let's just 'ope you've done right,' she muttered. 'But I wouldn't like to be in your shoes when Levi gets 'ome. To take on one child wi'out him agreeing to it would be bad enough, but two! Anyway, that ain't what I called in for,' she hurried on when she saw Maggie's eyes flash. 'I don't want to tell tales but I thought you ought to know I just saw your Barney up by the Cat Gallow's bridge on me way 'ome. He obviously didn't go to school today. He were skimmin' stones across the cut an' looked right sorry for 'imself. Poor little sod's got a right shiner on 'im, ain't he?'

Maggie bit down on her bottom lip. 'I see, well, thanks for telling me. I'll be having words with him when he gets in, you can be sure of it.'

'Fair enough but don't tell 'im as it were me as told you,' Peggy said. 'From what my lot 'ave said all your lads are havin' it rough at school at the minute. An' goin' back to little Annie . . . just go gently with 'er, eh? The poor little bugger were picked on by that bloody housemistress sommat rotten up at the workhouse. I don't mind tellin' you I felt so sorry for her I'd 'ave taken the child meself before now if we could 'ave afforded to 'ave another one.'

'She'll be perfectly adequately cared for here,' Maggie said primly.

Peggy nodded, although she didn't feel too sure. She was concerned that Maggie had only taken Annie to use her as a maid, in which case the poor little girl wasn't going to be much better off here than she had been at the workhouse. But then she was aware that it was none of her business and her interference might make things worse, so she forced a smile.

'I'm glad to 'ear it. But I'd best be off now. My lot will be 'ome from school soon. Ta-ra.'

Once Peggy had gone Maggie thumped down onto one of the kitchen chairs and rubbed her forehead where a headache was forming behind her eyes. It was turning out to be quite a day one way or another and it was far from over yet.

By four o'clock that afternoon the light was fading fast and Barney was the first to appear. His eyes immediately flew to Annie, who was loading coal onto the fire, and he raised an eyebrow.

'Who's this then?'

'This is Annie,' his mother told him. 'And she'll be staying with us, as will the baby here.'

His eyebrow rose even higher as he threw his satchel onto the table and stared at the baby.

'But why?' He scratched his head, confused. No one had mentioned they were getting new additions to the family.

'Because I said so,' his mother retorted in a voice that brooked no argument. 'Now, what sort of a day have you had?'

Barney avoided her eyes as he helped himself to a glass of milk. 'Oh, same as usual, I suppose.'

'And have you got any homework?'

'Nah, not today.'

'No, I didn't think you would have because you haven't been to school, have you?' she accused.

Barney flushed to the roots of his hair. 'O'-o' course I 'ave! What makes yer think that?'

'Don't you lie to me, my lad!' Maggie was angry now. 'I have it on very good authority that you were messing about by the canal this afternoon!'

'An' what if I was?' he said defensively. 'Look at the state o' me face!' He jabbed a finger towards his swollen black eye. 'What did yer want, for 'em to black the other 'un? I 'ate it here, do yer 'ear me? *Hate it!* Everyone round 'ere are snobs an' we don't fit in, an' it's all your fault. We were all 'appy back in the cottage an' now look at us.' And with that he stormed off upstairs with tears in his eyes.

Maggie's mouth gaped open. She'd known it was taking him a while to settle but she hadn't realised just how strongly he felt about the move. But she didn't have long to think about it because the door opened yet again and Charlie and Harry trailed in looking cold and tired.

They too glanced towards Annie and the baby and Maggie quickly introduced them.

'They're goin' to live wi' us, are they? Like sisters?' Harry asked innocently.

'Well, yes.'

The boys gave Annie shy smiles and she was relieved that at least these two seemed friendlier than Barney.

Over the next hour Maggie became increasingly nervous. By five o'clock it was pitch-black outside and she knew that Levi would be home very soon. She warmed the baby some milk and fed it to her.

The two younger boys were fascinated with her.

'She's really pretty, ain't she, Ma?' Harry said innocently.

'Isn't she,' Maggie corrected. She was still trying to get the boys to stop using slang.

Just as the baby was finishing her feed, they heard the clip-clop of Dobbin's hoofs down the side of the house. Maggie's stomach tightened into a knot as she quickly changed the baby's binding and put her back in the drawer where she lay placidly waving her tiny hands in the air.

Soon the door opened and Levi appeared, his nose glowing red from the cold. 'Hello, boys. Hello, Mag—' He stopped talking abruptly as his eyes settled first on the baby and then on Annie. 'Oh, I didn't know we had company for dinner.'

Maggie gulped and flashed him a nervous smile. 'Well . . . they're not just here for dinner.'

'Oh?' He smiled kindly at Annie, who was standing on a wooden stool washing up the pots in the sink, before looking at Maggie questioningly.

'Children, could you all go to your rooms for a few minutes, please?' Maggie said tentatively. 'I want to speak to your father in private. I'll call you down shortly when dinner is ready to be served.'

The boys mumbled but did as they were told and Annie obediently followed them from the room with her head bent.

'All right, so are you going to tell me what's going on, please?' Levi had had a hard day and had been hoping for a quiet night by the fire. 'Whose children are these?' He crossed to the drawer and stared down at the baby, who was cooing up at him.

'Actually, Levi . . . they're ours now. I went to look at the babies in the workhouse and while I was there, I saw the housemistress mistreating the girl so I, er . . . Well, I fetched her home too. Her name's Annie.'

'You did *what*?' He stared at her in disbelief. He was working desperately hard to pay off the mortgage on the house, and here was Maggie telling him that she'd gone and fetched not one but two more children for him to be responsible for. 'You're telling me that they're here for good?'

She nodded guiltily. 'Yes, but it's not as bad as you think. I'm sure Annie will be a great help about the house. She'll more than earn her keep, and the baby . . . Well, just look at her, doesn't she remind you of Penny? Once I saw her, I couldn't bear to leave her there. She won't cost us much to keep. I kept all of Penny's baby clothes, and even her feeding bottles and her crib so I haven't got to go out and buy anything for her. And I'll go on the rag stall in the market to get some better clothes for Annie tomorrow. The ones she's wearing are little more than rags. Oh, *please* don't be angry with me. You know how much I've missed Penny and I just know this little one is going to bring us so much joy.'

Levi sighed as he saw the tears streaming down his wife's face. He held his hand out to the baby and as her tiny fingers curled around one of his he knew he was lost. He wasn't at all happy with what Maggie had done but how could he send the poor little soul back?

'I suppose we should think of a name for her then,' he said quietly. 'And don't suggest Penelope. There could never be another Penny.'

'I was, er . . . thinking of Eleanor. Eleanor Penelope Lilburn.'

'Hmm, it's a posh name but I suppose we could always shorten it to Ellie,' he said resignedly. 'But what about the other little girl? She can't be more than eight or nine years old. How much help is she going to be? She's only a little dot and looks as if one good puff of wind would blow her away.'

'She's stronger than you think,' Maggie told him.

'In that case, I suppose you'd better go up to the school in Abbey Green in the morning and get her signed in with the boys.'

Maggie scowled. 'Why? I'm sure that can wait until after Christmas. It will give her time to get settled in.'

But on this score Levi was firm. 'Any child in my care will be educated. It's the least we can do for the poor child. I don't want it bandied about that we've only taken her in to work her into the ground.' He had a sneaking suspicion that Maggie had only taken her so that she could boast to Mrs Taylor-Lloyd that she too had a maid, but he kept his thoughts to himself.

'What's her other name anyway? She can't be just Annie, surely?'

'As far as I know, she is. She was abandoned at the workhouse and they named her after the woman that found her on the steps, so she's just Annie.'

'Then in that case she'd better use our surname. She can't be "just Annie" when she goes to school, can she?'

The matter was dropped for then, and Maggie called the children down for their meal. She had set the table for five people and when Levi noticed his wife preparing a tray he asked, 'Who is that for?'

'Why, Annie of course. I thought she could go into the drawing room for her meals while the family eat in here until she feels more comfortable around us.'

65

Levi's jaw set as he strode away and returned with another knife and fork. 'If you've taken it upon yourself to adopt her, she *is* family,' he said quietly but firmly. 'And she will eat in here with us. We'll start as we mean to go on!'

Maggie pursed her lips as Levi made room for another place, but she said nothing. She could sense that her husband wasn't at all happy with the latest developments, so for now she would do as she was told.

Chapter Eight

The next morning Maggie left Annie to look after the baby while she went off to visit the rag stall in the market. Many of the still usable clothes that Levi collected on his rounds ended up there, and she was hoping to buy Annie some clothes that would fit her with minor alterations, as well as some other things that could be cut down and remade into dresses for her.

The night before, when the boys and Levi had retired to bed, Maggie had dragged the tin bath into the kitchen and filled it from the copper before scrubbing Annie from head to toe. She had been shocked to see the bruises all over the girl's small body and how frighteningly thin she was, but she had made no comment. She would soon put a little meat on her bones with some good home cooking.

Annie looked like a different child once she was bathed and dressed in one of Levi's old shirts, and Maggie thought she might actually be quite pretty when she had put some weight on. Her hair was jet black and straight and her skin was like peaches and cream. Her eyes were another striking feature, the colour of bluebells and framed with long, thick dark lashes.

Throughout all this attention, Annie had felt quite bewildered. She liked Charlie and Harry, and the mister seemed kindly too, but she was still undecided about the missus and Barney, who glared at her every time she caught his eye.

Before going to work that morning, the mister had again told Maggie that she was to enrol Annie at the school. At the workhouse she had had only one hour of lessons a day and only then if she was lucky, but she longed to know more and soaked up everything she was taught, so she was excited at the prospect of starting at a proper school. He had also told Annie that from now on she would be known as Annie Lilburn, which she was happy with. She had never had a surname before. And even though everything was still very strange, she loved having her own room, even if it was right at the top of the house and desperately cold.

The other good thing was the food. The meal she had eaten the night before was like nothing she had ever tasted before. Admittedly it had upset her tummy because she wasn't used to rich food and she had had to run outside to the toilet following dinner, but that hadn't put her off. The meal was so tasty it had been worth the discomfort. Breakfast had been the same. Up at the workhouse the porridge was runny and bland, but the stuff the missus had served that morning had been simmering on the range all night and was thick and sweet with honey. She would have liked to ask for a second helping but had been afraid it might make her look greedy. Now Annie was eagerly awaiting the missus's return to see if she had managed to find her any decent clothes. She had never known anything other than the sack-like uniforms the children and adults alike were forced to wear, and she couldn't imagine what it would be like to wear something pretty.

When Maggie walked into the kitchen sometime later, hefting a large bag with her, she was pleased to see that the house was spotless. Annie had tidied up for her while she had been gone.

Maggie had lain awake for most of the night fretting over whether she had done the right thing in fetching the children there. Although Levi had seemingly accepted them, he had been very cool with her and had hardly said a word the night before, but now she thought perhaps things would work out after all. Ellie was quite adorable, and she was sure he couldn't fail to fall in love with her, and Annie could prove to be a very good help indeed.

'How has she been?' Maggie asked Annie as she took the hatpin from her bonnet and dumped the large bag on the table.

'Good as gold, missus. I ain't heard a murmur from her.'

Maggie nodded and proceeded to take some clothes from the bag. 'I think I've found you a couple of dresses that might fit you. I've also bought some larger garments that I shall cut down to make into blouses and skirts for you. Oh, and I got you some boots as well. You can hardly clop around in those unsightly clogs in the winter. Here, try them on.'

Annie was only too happy to oblige. She had never owned a proper pair of shoes or boots in her whole life and she turned her foot this way and that to admire them. Despite the fact they were used, there was still a lot of life left in them and although they were a little large, she could always stuff the toes with paper. Next Maggie held up a dress made in a woollen tartan and Annie beamed with delight.

'Hmm, it's a bit long on you but I can soon take it up,' Maggie told her kindly. 'We'll keep that one for best.' The next dress was much plainer and made from a sturdy light-grey cotton. 'This will be ideal for you to wear around the house.' Even that one was far superior to anything Annie had ever owned before and she beamed again. There were two nightshirts, underwear and some warm woollen tights, as well as a coat that would need slight alterations. 'You can go and put this one on now,' Maggie offered. 'And take some tights and underwear up with you as well. You can hardly walk around in Levi's shirt all day.'

Annie nodded and gathered the things together before licking her lips and asking nervously, 'An' did you 'ave time to ask if there were a place fer me at the school, missus?'

Maggie frowned as she lifted the baby from the crib. 'No, I didn't. The children break up for the Christmas holidays soon so there seemed no point until after that,' she said apologetically. 'Now go and get changed. You'll catch your death of cold walking about like that.'

Annie's face fell but she did as she was told.

When she returned in her new second-hand clothes, the child was almost unrecognisable. Now that her hair had been washed it hung down her back and shone black as coal.

'That's better.' Maggie nodded her approval and smiled. 'You look so different.'

Annie was beginning to think that it wasn't going to be so bad here after all and sat down and watched Maggie fuss over the baby. After a light lunch of bread and cheese, Maggie made a large cottage pie for dinner that evening, while Annie once more volunteered to peel the vegetables.

Soon Charlie and Harry arrived home from school.

'Where's Barney?' Maggie asked and both boys shrugged.

'We ain't seen 'im all day,' Charlie answered as he poured himself a glass of milk from the jug on the cold shelf in the pantry.

'What do you mean, you haven't seen him? Surely you must have spotted him at some stage?'

'No, we ain't . . . sorry, haven't,' Charlie corrected himself as he saw his mother frown.

Suddenly they became aware of a terrible ruckus outside. Maggie rushed to the door and flew down the path towards the front of the house. To her horror she saw Barney sitting astride Mrs Taylor-Lloyd's son pummelling him with his fists as her neighbour screamed in horror.

'Get that *little hooligan* off my boy,' the woman screeched.

With her lips set in a grim line, Maggie rushed forward and, catching Barney by the scruff of his neck, she managed to haul him off the lad. Barney's fists were still flailing about and, in her temper, Maggie shook him.

'Stop this behaviour *right now* and tell me what's going on!'

Barney turned his head to glare up at her and she saw that his nose was bleeding. 'It were 'is fault, *he* started it!' he said without remorse. 'He were callin' me names an' sayin' that the likes of us don't belong round 'ere. He's a bleedin' *toff*!'

'That's quite enough of that bad language, my boy. I shall wash your mouth out with soap if I hear you use it again.' Maggie gave him another shake. By then the other children had come out to join them as well as some passersby, and Maggie was mortally embarrassed.

'I, er . . . I apologise for my son's behaviour, Mrs Taylor-Lloyd,' she muttered. 'But if what Barney is saying is true it seems that your son was antagonising him.'

'Oh, words are an excuse for fists flying, are they?' Mrs Taylor-Lloyd looked as angry as Maggie felt. 'I suggest in future you teach that foul-mouthed little heathen some manners! We're not used to that sort of behaviour around here!'

'My son is *not* a heathen,' Maggie retaliated. Just then, the sound of horse's hoofs approaching reached them, and she felt herself shrivel inside as Levi approached them on his cart dressed in his oldest clothes.

Levi drew the old horse to a halt and strode towards them. 'What's to do here, then?' Bemused, he stared at the bedraggled state of his son.

'That . . . that *bully* just attacked my boy,' Mrs Taylor-Lloyd spat, placing her arm protectively around her son's shoulders and eyeing Levi up and down as if there was a bad smell under her nose.

'Well, missus, boys will be boys,' Levi said patiently, hoping to defuse the situation, but his words only seemed to incite the woman more.

'Not in *this* street. This is a very respectable neighbourhood, or at least it was until you people moved in! Now if you'll excuse me, I must go and see to my boy's injuries. But rest assured, should I need to send for the doctor I shall be forwarding the bill to you! Come along, Reginald!' She grabbed her son's arm and hauled him away, not noticing him smirking at Barney over his shoulder as he went.

'I suggest you all get back inside now!' Levi was clearly furious, and he swung himself back up onto the cart and urged the horse forward towards his stable while Maggie shepherded the children back inside.

It was Annie who felt Maggie's wrath first. 'And who told *you* to come outside. You're not here to gawp. Get back into the kitchen!'

Annie calmly walked away to do as she was told. She was used to being shouted at, although it was the first time Maggie had done so.

'And now you, my lad!' Maggie gave Barney's arm a good shake. 'Missed school again, have you? And don't bother to deny it. The other two didn't catch a glimpse of you all day. I really don't know what's got into you!'

'It's this place,' he muttered, staring resentfully back at her. 'An' that toff next door is a—'

'Never mind about that,' Maggie said hastily as she pressed him none too gently down onto a chair. 'Now sit still while I go and get some water to clean your face up. It looks to me like Reginald gave as good as he got. You're going to have another lovely black eye on you tomorrow, if I'm not very much mistaken.'

By the time Levi entered the room some twenty minutes later, Maggie had cleaned Barney's face up and Annie was busy laying the table while Maggie put the finishing touches to their evening meal.

'I think we'll discuss this later when the children are abed,' Levi told her with a warning glance, and she wisely held her tongue as he hurried away to wash and change.

Everyone was quiet during dinner and as soon as they had eaten, Maggie set Annie to do the washing up while she gave Ellie a bottle. Levi, meanwhile, hid behind his newspaper, but the atmosphere was frosty. So much so that the children were relieved when it was time to go to bed.

'So that was a nice to-do to come home to I must say,' Levi said once they were alone.

Maggie had just started to darn some socks and she glanced over at him. 'Yes, it was, but don't worry, Barney will be punished. He'll not be allowed to set foot outside for a week.'

'Oh yes, and what about if he was tellin' the truth and that lad next door *did* goad him into hittin' him? Are you tellin' me you'd rather believe the word of them than your own son?'

'Even goading shouldn't warrant fisticuffs,' Maggie snapped back, and Levi sighed.

At the sound of raised voices Ellie began to whimper and Maggie went to lift her from her crib.

Levi watched silently for a moment before saying sadly, 'I thought a new house would be the start of happier times for us, Maggie, but now I'm beginning to wonder if we've done the right thing.'

'*Of course* we have,' Maggie snapped as she cuddled Ellie to her. 'We're just having a few teething problems. It's bound to take a while for us all to settle in. This place will be beautiful when we can afford to get it how I want it and we'll all be happy.'

'That's what worries me.' Levi quietly folded his newspaper and rose from the chair. 'All you seem to think about nowadays is what the neighbours think. And as for getting the place 'ow you want it, don't forget we've taken on two more mouths to feed.'

'Oh, don't be *ridiculous*.' Maggie bristled. 'This little one costs hardly a penny to feed and the other one is no trouble. She's a great help about the house.'

'Hmm, and that's another thing that worries me.' He ran his hand through his thick thatch of hair, something he always did when he was concerned. '*The other one* 'as a name. It's Annie, and she's just as deserving of love an' kindness as that one there in your arms. She's still only a child.'

'*Now* who is being silly?' Maggie tossed her head, setting her copper-coloured curls dancing on her shoulders. 'You haven't seen me be cruel to her, have you?'

'No,' he admitted. 'But I haven't seen you be particularly loving to her either. If it wasn't for me, I doubt you'd have even let her sit at the table with us to eat.'

'Oh, now you're just being over-sensitive!'

Levi shrugged. He could sense that this was fast developing into a row. 'Well, I'm going up and you can just think on what I've said. Are you comin'?'

'No, I have Ellie to see to. You carry on and I'll be up in a minute.'

Levi left her to it. He knew there would be no point in remaining when Maggie was in this frame of mind.

Chapter Nine

Maggie had just entered the kitchen early the next morning when she was startled by a loud hammering on the back door. It was still pitch-black outside, so after laying Ellie in her crib, she lit the oil lamp and tentatively went to see who it was.

'Who's there?' Her voice must have betrayed her unease but the voice that answered was gentle.

'It's me, Maggie, Sid. Can yer let me in?'

Maggie unlocked the door just as Levi appeared behind her in time to see Peggy's husband enter the room looking concerned.

He nodded towards Maggie and quickly snatched his flat cap off before addressing Levi. 'I'm afraid I've got bad news, mate. I checked the yard same as I allus do each evenin' afore I turn in, an' everythin' were fine. But when I got up a while ago, I saw the gate had been prised open an' I'm sorry to say whoever it was broke in 'as stolen all the brass an' the lead you've been gettin' ready for a weigh-in.'

'Aw no!' Levi looked shocked. Only the day before he had checked the brass and lead piles with satisfaction. There had been enough there to easily pay for Christmas and a bit left over but now it looked like it was all gone.

'I'm so sorry, pal.' Sid shuffled from foot to foot looking uncomfortable.

Levi shook his head. 'It's not your fault,' he told him. 'I can't expect you to stay awake all night listenin' for thieves. It ain't the first time this 'as happened and whoever this was clearly knew there was a lot of money's worth there, the lousy sods!'

'Do yer think we should call the peelers?' Sid asked.

'Nah, they won't do anythin' over a bit o' metal. I reckon we'll just 'ave to write it off. It's me own fault really. I should 'ave got it weighed in but I've been so busy I never got around to it. Anyway, thanks for lettin' me know, Sid. Do yer want a cuppa afore you go.'

Sid shook his head. 'I won't, if yer don't mind. I don't wanna be late for work. Luckily Peggy ain't got to work today so I've told her to keep an eye on things an' then I'll fit a stronger padlock on the gate when I gets back this evenin'.'

Once Sid had gone Levi plumped down on the nearest chair looking devastated. 'I were relyin' on that weigh-in to get gifts for the kids for Christmas,' he said despondently. 'But I suppose we'll just 'ave to pull us reins in a bit now.'

Maggie frowned and was about to answer when Charlie and Harry appeared, knuckling the sleep from their eyes and yawning, closely followed by Annie who looked guilty.

'Sorry, missus, I overlay.' She had made it her job to get up first in the morning and coax the fire back into life but today she had failed.

Maggie ignored her, and glanced towards the boys. 'And where's Barney?' They had seen nothing of him since he had shot away up the stairs following the fight the night before.

'Don't know, Ma.' Charlie shrugged. 'I just went to 'is bedroom to tell 'im to get a shufty on but 'e weren't there.'

'What do you mean, he wasn't there? Where is he?'

Charlie shrugged again, and Maggie looked at Levi who held up his hands. 'Sorry, but you're goin' to 'ave to sort this yourself. I've got to go an' earn us some money, 'specially now the metal's gone missin'.'

'But you haven't even had a drink,' she objected.

'Don't want one.' And with that he left without so much as a goodbye.

Maggie bit her lip. The day before had ended badly and this one didn't look set to be a good day either.

'Right, get yourselves to the table while I get the porridge,' Maggie barked sharply. Her head was all over the place. Where could Barney have gone at this time of the morning? He never usually went off without telling her, but she needed to make sure the others got to school on time, so there was nothing she could do right now. Ellie started to whimper at that moment and Maggie sighed. 'Annie, could you get that porridge served up to the boys, I need to give Eleanor a bottle.'

'Yes, missus.' They could all sense that Maggie was in a bad mood and Annie didn't want to do anything to make things worse, so she shot off to do as she was told.

An hour later the boys had left for school and Ellie was settled back in her crib, but there was still no sign of Barney.

Snatching her shawl from the back of the door, Maggie told Annie, 'Keep your eye on Eleanor, would you? I'm popping round to Peggy's to see if they've seen Barney.'

Annie nodded. But once she was alone, she sighed. Because she hadn't started school yet she had volunteered to do lots of jobs about the place and she'd worked almost as hard here as she had in the workhouse, although at least here she did have her own room and plenty of food, so she supposed things could have been worse. Even so, she did feel sad when she thought of the home she had always dreamt of. But then straightening her back she looked at the pile of dirty pots on the table. All her life she had believed that one day her real mother would come to the workhouse to take her home and they would live happily ever after, but there was no chance of that happening now and there was no sense in upsetting the missus, so she set to with a will.

When Maggie turned into the court in Abbey Street her eyes were immediately drawn to the empty spaces where Levi's brass and lead had been piled. His rag-and-bone business brought in the main of their income but the money he made on the metals paid for their luxuries, and she knew how upset he was. She had only got halfway across the yard when the door to the cottage was flung open and Peggy appeared brandishing a rolling pin.

'Oh . . . it's you.' She sighed. 'I thought it were someone come back to try an' steal sommat else an' I were ready fer 'em. I'm so sorry about what's happened, Maggie. An' so is Sid. We feel as if it's our fault but we never dreamt anybody would manage to break the padlock on the gate. They must 'ave used bolt croppers.'

'Aw well, it's done now. But it isn't that I've come to see you about. I was wondering if you'd seen anything of our Barney. There was some trouble between him and the neighbour's son last night and afterwards he went to his room and stayed there. But then when we got up this morning he was gone and we don't know where he is.'

'Oh dear.' Peggy turned and walked back into the kitchen with Maggie close on her heels. 'Our Ricky did confide that Barney weren't 'appy but we ain't seen 'im around 'ere. I did 'ear, though, that the circus an' the fair were camped up in Riversley Park again fer a couple o' nights on their way to their winter quarters. Didn't he keep disappearin' off to see 'em earlier in the year when they were there?'

'Yes, he did.' Maggie strummed her fingers on the table. The circus and the fair had always held a fascination for Barney ever since she and Levi had taken the children when they were smaller. 'The trouble is I can't go to check if he's there because I've left Annie looking after Eleanor.'

'That's easily solved. I'll come back wi' you an' I'll watch the baby while you go an' look for Barney,' Peggy volunteered.

'Would you?'

'I just said so, didn't I? Just wait while I get me shawl.'

They were just approaching Swan Lane when Peggy said hesitantly, 'It don't look like your new 'ouse is turnin' out to be the happy place you 'oped, does it?'

Maggie was instantly on the defensive. 'And just what is that supposed to mean?'

Peggy chose her words carefully. 'Well, fer a start off Levi didn't seem any too pleased that you took the two kids from the work'ouse wi'out talkin' to him about it. And your lads don't seem none too 'appy either. Our Ricky were sayin' the other kids at school are givin' 'em a hard time. Takin' the mickey like.'

'It's just taking them time to get used to the change,' Maggie said crossly.

'Oh yes, an' 'ow are you gettin' along wi' the neighbours? Weren't you goin' for mornin' coffee a few weeks ago? An' was it their son who Barney had the trouble wi' last night?'

Maggie's cheeks burned as she thought back to her coffee morning with Mrs Taylor-Lloyd and what the other women had said about her as she left. It had been humiliating, but her pride wouldn't allow her to confide that to Peggy.

Instead, she merely said, 'The coffee morning was very pleasant, and yes, it was Mrs Taylor-Lloyd's son who had a bit of an altercation with Barney, but it was only a spat, I'm sure.'

'Hmm, if you say so!' Peggy clearly didn't believe a word she was saying and the rest of the walk passed in silence.

When they entered the house, Annie's little face lit up when she saw Peggy and she rushed over for a hug. Peggy was the only one who had ever shown her an ounce of affection during her life in the workhouse, and Annie idolised her and wished that it had been her who had taken her home to live with her.

As she snuggled into the kindly woman's ample bosom, Maggie glared at her. 'Have you washed up?' she asked, looking towards the sink.

'Yes, missus, an' I've made a start on moppin' the floor, look.'

'Oh, come on, 'ave a 'eart, Mags,' Peggy chided gently. 'She's only a little slip of a thing. I'd 'ave thought you'd 'ave her at school be now wi' the rest o' the kids, instead o' keepin' her 'ere workin'.'

'I fully intend to, but it isn't worth it until after Christmas, and I didn't ask her to mop the floor,' Maggie answered defensively as she checked on Ellie, who was still sleeping peacefully with her tiny thumb jammed into her rosebud mouth. 'Anyway, if you're sure you don't mind keeping an eye on the baby I'd better go out and see if I can track Barney down. He can't have gone far.'

'Yes, you get off.' Peggy was already settling herself in the chair by the fire and meant to make the most of a short break.

Within minutes Maggie was toiling through the town, which was no mean feat when the ground was as slippery as an ice rink with frost. Her breath hung on the air and soon her hands and feet were so cold they were painful. They'd had a similar situation to this the year before. Barney seemed to be fascinated with the circus folk and their way of life and more than once Levi had been forced to go and find him when they were camped in the Pingle Fields and haul him home. By the time Maggie reached the edge of Riversley Park, she was breathless and had to pause for a moment. Then she moved on towards the Pingles, as it was commonly known, and eventually the circus trailers came into sight.

Rabbits and muntjacs startled her as they ran across the rough path ahead of her, but she ploughed on. She had a rough idea where Barney might be and had no intention of turning back now after coming so far. She heard a sound and paused to listen. It sounded like children laughing so she turned in their direction and soon came across a number of the fair children skimming stones across the frozen surface of a stream.

'*Barney!*' She saw him amongst them almost immediately and now the fear she had felt that he might be lost was replaced with anger.

Barney paused in the act of throwing a stone as he turned startled eyes towards his mother and colour flooded into his cheeks.

'What? What do yer want?' He was painfully conscious of his circus friends sniggering.

'Why aren't you at school?' his mother snapped. 'And why did you just go off like that? I've been worried sick.'

'Why? I'm big enough to look after meself.' He glared at her as she advanced on him.

'You just get yourself back home with me right now, my lad,' she ordered in an ominously quiet voice. 'I shall let your father deal with you this evening. But in the meantime, you can get your uniform on and get yourself off to school.'

'I ain't goin' back there,' he replied mutinously.

His mother caught his arm. 'Oh yes you are, even if I have to drag you kicking and screaming.'

'All right, all right. Gerroff me.' He shook her hand from his arm, and turned to stride away through the trees with his head down and his hands jammed into his trouser pockets.

Maggie set off after him and when they reached the road she sighed. 'All this silly behaviour has to stop, Barney,' she said in a gentler tone, but he merely scowled at her, so the rest of the journey was made in silence.

When they arrived back at the house they found Peggy feeding Ellie, and as Maggie rushed over to check that all was well with the child, Barney's temper erupted.

'It's no wonder I don't wanna be 'ere,' he said bitterly as he headed for the door leading into the hall. 'That baby's only been 'ere fer five minutes an' already you ain't got time fer the rest of us!'

'That's not true,' Maggie denied, but her words were lost as Barney slammed the door resoundingly behind him.

'Oh dear, I think it's time I was makin' meself scarce.' Peggy lifted her shawl and after a nod at Annie she quietly left as Maggie sank into the chair and cradled Ellie to her.

Chapter Ten

A few days before Christmas, Levi came home one evening with a Christmas tree on the back of the cart. Annie's eyes almost popped out of her head. They had never had a Christmas tree in the workhouse and she thought it was beautiful.

'We put baubles an' tinsel on it,' Charlie informed her. 'You can 'elp us after dinner this evenin' if yer like.' She and Charlie were getting on like a house on fire.

'No, she can't, she'll have no idea how to do it,' Maggie said sharply. She was seated at the side of the fire giving Ellie a bottle.

Levi frowned. 'Well, she'll never know how to do it unless someone shows her, will she, hinny?' he said persuasively.

Maggie glared at him. Already she was beginning to regret fetching Annie home, especially as Levi seemed so taken with her.

Levi scowled as he headed outside to get a bucket of earth to set the tree in. He didn't know what was happening to Maggie lately but whatever it was he didn't much like it. He knew she'd been bitterly disappointed that she hadn't received any more invitations to the neighbourhood coffee mornings since the first one at Mrs Taylor-Lloyd's, but personally, he thought she was better off keeping herself to herself. From what he'd seen of the neighbourhood ladies they were all terribly stuck up. The only time Maggie ever seemed to be happy recently was when she was attending to Ellie, and although he was pleased that she loved the child, he couldn't help feeling that she was becoming rather obsessive with her, to the point that the rest of the family was being neglected.

As for Annie – strangely enough it was her that Levi had taken to. She was such a hard-working, pleasant child that it would have been hard not to. She never complained; just took every-thing in her stride, despite the fact that Maggie was quite strict with her. If truth be told, he felt that Maggie was being a little hard on her. She was only a child after all – not that he dared to voice his opinion. Maggie had already distanced herself from him again and he knew that were he to say anything it could only make matters worse.

When he returned with the bucket, he placed the tree in it and stood it to one side of the fireplace.

'Does that suit you there?'

Maggie sniffed as she winded the baby. 'I suppose so. Mrs Taylor-Lloyd has one twice that size in her bay window in the front lounge but seeing as I've hardly any furniture in there, I suppose it will have to do in here.'

Without another word, Levi went to get washed and changed.

Soon after, as they were all seated quietly at the table, Levi tried to jolly things up a little when he suggested, 'Why don't we *all* have a go at decorating the tree this evenin', eh?'

Charlie and Harry nodded enthusiastically but Annie kept her eyes lowered and Barney just sat there scowling as he picked at his food. Because of his escapade with the circus folk, he wasn't allowed out until after Christmas and he was bored sick.

'I tell you what,' his father said, smiling at him. 'I know your mam has kept you in from playin' out wi' your mates, but what about if you came to work wi' me fer a few days on the cart? I could do wi' the help an' it would give you somethin' to do.'

Barney's ears instantly pricked up. Anything was better than being stuck in with his mam all day watching her fawn all over the new baby.

Maggie didn't look any too pleased. 'But I told him he wasn't to go out of the door until after Christmas!'

'Aye, I know you did, pet,' Levi placated her. 'But it ain't as if he's goin' out wi' his mates, is it? An' I ain't lyin' when I say he'd be a good help. My job can be pleasant in the summer but it ain't much fun in the winter stuck out in the cold on the cart all day. He could be me little runner. Goin' to knock on the doors an' such an' save me old legs.'

Maggie sniffed, clearly not happy with the idea but then she supposed anything was better than having to watch Barney's miserable face all day.

'Very well,' she agreed. 'But only until after Christmas, mind. Hopefully those dreadful fairground people will be gone by then and Barney can get back to school.'

The evening was spent pleasantly decorating the tree and the next morning, on Christmas Eve, as agreed, Barney was up bright and early to accompany his father on his rounds. Levi had been forced to work extra hard following the theft of the metal from the old yard and he had managed to earn enough to get the children a few small gifts each for Christmas, and so he was in a good mood.

'We'll finish shortly after lunch today,' Levi promised Barney as he guided old Dobbin down the drive and out onto Swan Lane. The sky was grey and leaden and Levi was expecting snow. They had just turned onto the lane when Mrs Taylor-Lloyd appeared with her two sons. Reggie and Barney glared at each other as Mrs Taylor-Lloyd sniffed her disapproval.

'I do hope you won't be allowing that . . . that . . . *dirty* old horse to soil our road again,' she said caustically.

Levi stared at her calmly. 'You're the first I've heard complain, ma'am. Most o' the people I pass are only too 'appy to clear up after Dobbin. That soiling, as you put it, happens to be very good fer roses. And Dobbin may be old but I assure you 'e is far from dirty, I make sure of that.'

He clicked his tongue and Dobbin moved on leaving Mrs Taylor-Lloyd fuming. As far as she was concerned the Lilburns were lowering the tone of the street. Unfortunately, there was little she could do about it, apart from hope that they would soon get the message that they weren't welcome and move on.

'Come along, Reginald.' Grabbing her son's arm she yanked him along beside her with Monty, the younger of the two, following on behind as they set off for the town.

Inside the house, Maggie was feeding the baby while Annie mopped the enormous kitchen floor. Charlie and Harry were sitting at the table drawing pictures with coloured chalks. Even though Annie was still expected to help around the house, she couldn't help but feel a little excited. This would be her first Christmas outside of the workhouse and ever since Levi had hinted that she might receive a small gift on Christmas morning, she had been in a happy frame of mind. Admittedly, the guardians up at the workhouse had always ensured that each child received an orange, but a real gift was something she could scarcely envisage.

When she slid between the cold sheets in her attic bedroom that night, instead of falling asleep almost instantly as she normally did, she tossed and turned anticipating the day ahead, until eventually sleep claimed her.

Annie woke the next morning to an eerie grey light from the skylight window in her room and, hopping out of bed, she breathed on the lace-like frosted pattern on the glass and scrubbed at it with the sleeve of her nightgown until she could peer out. She gasped with delight, for spread in front of her was a snow-white wonderland. It had snowed heavily throughout the night and now everything looked crisp and bright. With a murmur of pleasure, she broke the thin layer of ice in her bowl and washed before tugging her clothes on, then she shot downstairs. She lit the oil lamp and set the fire blazing before putting the kettle on to boil just as Maggie appeared, still in her dressing robe with her hair in a long plait across her shoulder and baby Ellie cradled in her arms.

'Have you put her milk on to warm?' Maggie greeted her.

Annie nodded. 'Yes, missus, an' the water for the tea.' And then she added boldly, 'Merry Christmas, missus.'

Maggie opened her mouth to say something but then thought better of it and snapped it shut. It was Christmas Day after all, and Annie was only a child. A very excited one if her face was anything to go by. For the first time Maggie noticed how pretty she was becoming. She had gained some weight and lost the gaunt look that she'd had when she first arrived, and her coal-black hair was gleaming in the light from the fire. Her deep-blue eyes were sparkling and Maggie noticed dimples in the cheeks of her heart-shaped face when she smiled.

'You look happy today,' Maggie said kindly.

Annie nodded. 'I am, missus. I think it's me birthday as well as Christmas Day. The housemother up at the workhouse told me that I were found on the steps there nine years ago today.'

'Really?' Maggie was shocked as she wondered how any mother could abandon a child like that, especially on Christmas Day. Suddenly she remembered the small parcel the housemother had given to her at the workhouse.

'That parcel the housemistress gave you; where is it?'

Annie was busily pouring the warm milk into Ellie's bottle, which was just as well because she was becoming fractious.

'It's up in me room, missus.' Annie handed the bottle to Maggie, who sat down to feed the baby.

'Perhaps we should have a look at it. I believe she said it contains the clothes you were wearing when you were left at the workhouse. It might give us some clue as to where you came from.'

Annie nodded, but at that moment Levi and the three boys appeared, all with smiles on their faces as they eyed the presents beneath the tree.

'Can we open 'em now, Ma?' Barney asked excitedly.

Maggie smiled and shook her head. 'No, you know the routine – or you should do by now. It's breakfast first and then you can open your presents. Oh, and I think we should all attend the service at St Mary's this morning once I've got the dinner on. Now that we live so close it would look disrespectful to the neighbours if we didn't.'

'Aw, *must* we?' Barney didn't look at all happy with the idea but on this Levi backed his wife.

'Your ma is right, son – it's a mark o' respect an' it'll only be for an hour. Come on, let's get this breakfast eaten so you can all open yer presents.'

The boys needed no second bidding and soon they were all seated around the table with smiles on their faces. It was the happiest they had all looked since moving there and Levi offered up a silent prayer that this might be the turning point.

The boys ate their breakfast in record time and then Levi lifted the presents one at a time to look at the names written on them. 'Ah, looks like this one is for you, Harry.' He smiled as he handed the little boy his gift and went on to the next one. 'And this one is for you, Barney, but I want you to use it sensibly or I shall confiscate it, do you 'ear me?'

'Yes, Da.'

'There's one here for you, Charlie. Oh, and look, there's one here for you an' all, princess. We hope you like it.'

Annie's eyes almost popped out of her head. She had never in her life been referred to as a princess before, let alone had a real present to open.

'Come on then, let's see what you've all got.'

Harry was the first to tear the paper from his gift and he whooped with joy as he stared at the apple, orange and the set of tin soldiers it contained. For Charlie there was his apple and orange and a book – *Peter Pan in Kensington Gardens*, by J. M Barrie, and he instantly opened it and began to read, oblivious to all the excitement surrounding him.

Barney then tore the paper from his gift and after putting aside the fruit he stared at his gift in awe. It was a shiny new penknife that folded away when not in use.

'I just want to say I shall be watching you with that to make sure it's only used sensibly,' Levi warned him sternly. 'I thought it would come in useful when yer go fishing wi' your friends, but should I ever find out that you've been usin' it as a weapon I shall confiscate it immediately.'

Barney nodded, his eyes shining. This was far smarter than some of the ones his friends had and he could hardly wait to show it off. 'I will, Da,' he promised.

All eyes turned to Annie who was standing back looking a little overawed.

'Come on then, hinny, let's see what's in your parcel,' Levi said gently.

With shaking hands Annie carefully began to unwrap the parcel, smiling as an apple and an orange rolled out onto the rug. Then she gasped as she stared down at the most beautiful rag doll she had ever seen. She had a cloth body and long black hair tied back with a ribbon. She even had a little dress with bloomers beneath it and two blue embroidered eyes much the same colour as Annie's own.

'One of the ladies on my rounds was makin' them so I got her to do it for you.' Levi explained. 'I thought you should have somethin' a bit special. Oh, an' Maggie informs me that it's your birthday an' all so happy birthday, Annie. Do you like her?'

Annie was too taken aback to speak and could only nod. She had never owned anything so lovely in her life and she knew she would treasure it always.

For Ellie there were two carefully knitted matinee jackets that Maggie had painstakingly made for her. And finally Maggie and

Levi opened their gifts. There was scented soap for Maggie and she had knitted Levi a thick woollen scarf with matching mittens, which he said would be perfect for keeping the cold at bay on dark winter mornings.

It had been decided the night before that Annie would stay behind to keep an eye on the baby while the rest of them went to church, so after breakfast they set off in their Sunday best, leaving Annie in charge of Ellie and the goose that was cooking.

As they entered the beautiful old church Maggie smiled at Mrs Taylor-Lloyd and some of the women she recognised from the coffee morning, but they all turned their heads and whispered to each other. Maggie felt the colour rise up her neck and into her cheeks as she ushered her family into a pew.

Maggie had seemed to be in a happier frame of mind that morning, but Annie noticed that she didn't seem quite so happy when they arrived home, although the rest of the family were in a cheerful mood. The Christmas dinner was like nothing Annie had ever tasted. As well as the goose, which was cooked to perfection, there was home-made sage and onion stuffing, creamy mashed potatoes, crispy roast potatoes, turnips, brussels sprouts and cabbage, and gravy. This was followed by a large Christmas pudding, which Maggie had had soaking in brandy for weeks, and thick creamy custard. By the time they had finished eating, Annie was sure she would never have room for food again.

Without being asked, she stood up to clear the dirty pots.

'I'll help,' Charlie volunteered, and he was as good as his word. Harry was far too busy playing with his soldiers and Barney was whittling away at a piece of wood with his new penknife while Maggie and Levi put their feet up beside the fire for a while.

Later in the afternoon they sang Christmas carols, much to baby Ellie's delight, played Snap, and then Maggie began to prepare the tea. Annie was certain she wouldn't be able to eat a thing but when she saw the delicious blancmanges and the quivering jelly she couldn't resist.

All in all, it was the happiest day she had ever spent and when she finally went to bed to cuddle her rag doll, who she had named Cissie, there was a broad smile on her face.

The next day, Levi went to the yard to collect a sledge he had made for the boys the year before, and Harry, Charlie and Annie took turns in dragging each other around on it – Barney had declared he was far too old for that sort of thing now. Next, they made a snowman and by the time they went back into the warm kitchen they were smiling and had red noses and rosy cheeks. Once again Maggie had prepared a lovely meal and they tucked in, wishing the holiday could go on forever.

Chapter Eleven

January, 1905

On the first day of term following the Christmas holidays, Annie started at the little school on Abbey Green. Maggie still wasn't at all happy with this as, during the short time Annie had been with them, she had become invaluable and had slowly taken on more and more of the household chores. But Levi had insisted and nothing Maggie said would make him change his mind, so now it was down to Maggie again, at least until Annie got home from school.

On that first morning, Maggie was making her round of the bedrooms tidying the beds and as she paused at the foot of the attic stairs, she thought again of the package Annie had brought with her from the workhouse. She had forgotten all about it in the lead-up to Christmas but now she was consumed with curiosity, so she climbed the stairs to the small room beneath the eaves. Annie had left the room meticulously tidy – she knew she'd be in trouble if she didn't – so Maggie made her way to the small chest of drawers that held everything Annie possessed.

As Maggie peeped in each one, the rag doll that was sitting against the pillow on the bed seemed to watch her reproachfully. Maggie spotted the package and quietly drew it out of the drawer and placed it on the bed. It was a brown paper package tied with string and had Annie's name written on it. After untying the string, Maggie slowly turned back the brown paper and frowned at the contents. There was a tiny, hand-made nightgown, trimmed with what appeared to be guipure lace, and a little knitted matinee jacket with matching bootees and bonnet. Although these items were well made, there was nothing remarkable about them. But it was the shawl that took Maggie's breath away. She had never seen one so beautiful. It was heavily fringed and made of pure silk, so fine that it slipped through her fingers. It was clearly an adult's shawl and was brightly coloured, with an exquisite pattern of light blue flowers intricately woven through it. It was the sort of shawl that would stand out from the crowd, and she was confused. Whoever had owned this and these baby clothes had plainly put a lot of thought into them, so why then would they have abandoned Annie? It just didn't make any sense.

'Maggie . . . are yer up there, gel?'

Peggy's voice cut through her thoughts and she quickly rewrapped the clothes and placed them back in the drawer before going downstairs.

On entering the kitchen, she was surprised to find not just Peggy but Flo too. Her sister had only visited once since they had moved in.

'Hello, Florence. I wasn't expecting you,' Maggie greeted her as Peggy filled the kettle at the sink.

'Well, seein' as yer never bother to come an' see me I thought I'd better make the effort.' Flo sniffed as she glanced around enviously. 'An' is it true what I've 'eard? That you've taken a couple o' kids from the workhouse to live wi' yer?'

'Well . . . yes it is. But, er . . . one of them is my maid.'

'*Maid?*' Peggy scowled disapprovingly. 'How can yer say that? The little mite is only just ten years old.'

'She's quite old enough to train up,' Maggie responded defensively. She had started to regret taking Annie from the workhouse, so she had decided she would tell people she intended to train her as a maid, although this hadn't necessarily been her original intention.

Flo meanwhile was staring down at Ellie in her crib. 'Hmm, an' I can see why yer took this one,' she said. 'She's got the look of our Penny about 'er, ain't she?'

'I, er . . . suppose she has.'

'So where is the little maid?' Flo glanced around.

'She started school with the boys this morning.'

'School? Since when did maids go to school?'

'It was what Levi and I wanted.'

'Huh! More like it were what Levi insisted on,' Peggy said disapprovingly – she was never one to pull any punches. 'An' quite right he were too. After bein' shut up in that bloody place since she were born, she deserves a life.'

'And she has one now.' Maggie was beginning to feel ganged up on and hastily changed the subject. 'Anyway, now you're both here I dare say you'd like a cup of tea.'

'It wouldn't go amiss.' Flo moved away from the baby and plonked herself on the sofa by the fire as Maggie prepared the cups and made the tea. 'An' I also 'ear that you're havin' a few problems wi' your Barney.'

'Not really.' Maggie was on the defensive again now. 'But how are your lot?'

Flo shrugged. 'Same as ever. They're right little buggers, I don't mind tellin' yer, 'specially our Walter. So, when yer gettin' some new furniture then? This place still looks a bit sparse.'

'Oh, we thought we'd wait till the spring.' Maggie was too proud to tell her that they still couldn't afford any.

Flo nodded as Maggie handed her a bone china cup and saucer. Ellie stirred and Maggie hurried to make her a bottle as Flo watched on with a frown. 'Ain't that one of our Penny's nightgowns she's wearin'?' When Maggie nodded, she shook her head. 'Yer can't bring 'er back yer know.'

'I'm not trying to,' Maggie said irritably, but oh, how she wished that she could. Over the last couple of days she had begun to realise that perhaps she had made a mistake with both girls. Despite her best efforts, and her original infatuation, the novelty of having a baby again was beginning to wear off and she found that she wasn't bonding with Ellie as she had hoped. In fact, she had begun to feel increasingly dissatisfied about everything in her new life. She had thought that moving to her dream home would be the answer to all her prayers but now when she looked about all she saw were empty rooms that they couldn't afford to furnish, and it felt unfair.

'In actual fact, I come to tell yer that I've 'eard from our Susan. Fer some reason she's comin' back to visit an' she wanted to know if she could stay wi' me. I wrote back an' told 'er there ain't room to swing a cat around in our 'ouse an' I gave her your new address. No doubt you'll be hearin' from her in 'er own good time.'

Maggie's heart sank. She and Susan had never got on particularly well when they were younger, but she supposed she could put her up for a few days if she was only coming to visit. And at least it would be nice to show the new house off, even if it wasn't as she wanted it to be just yet.

Thankfully the conversation moved on to safer topics and soon, much to Maggie's relief, Flo left.

'I should be makin' tracks too,' Peggy said shortly after, and soon Maggie was alone with Ellie again. She chewed her lip as she thought on what Flo had said about her sister. Maggie couldn't imagine that Levi would be too pleased if Susan were to turn up on the doorstep. He'd always thought she was a flighty piece, and he still hadn't completely forgiven Maggie for taking Annie and Ellie without asking him, although he did seem to have taken to Annie now.

With a sigh Maggie pushed it from her mind. There was every chance that she wouldn't hear from Susan. She could change her mind with the wind and might well decide to stay in London with her fancy man so there was no point in worrying about it unless she had to.

When Annie, Charlie and Harry appeared after school that afternoon, Annie's face was beaming.

'Miss Mackintosh, me teacher, reckons I'm really bright,' she told Maggie. 'An' she says she reckons I'll catch up wi' the others in no time if I attend regularly.'

'Did she now?' Maggie answered straight-faced, and Annie instantly became solemn, as if all the joy had been suddenly sucked out of her. 'That's all well and good but it doesn't alter the fact that I've a list of jobs as long as my arm waiting to be done, so I suggest you go upstairs and get out of those decent clothes and come down and give me a hand. I haven't even had time to start preparing the dinner yet with having Eleanor to look after and no one to help me.'

'Yes, missus.' Annie quietly left the room and made her way upstairs. For just a few hours that day she had been allowed to be like any other child, but now Maggie was acting as if she shouldn't have gone to school. Perhaps she had started to look at her as no more than an unpaid maid. Still, she considered herself to be slightly better off than she had been in the workhouse and there was always school tomorrow to look forward to. The thought put a spring in her step and she hurried on her way.

'How did your first day at school go, princess?' Levi asked Annie over dinner.

Maggie scowled at him. She hated him calling Annie princess.

With her eyes sparkling Annie smiled. 'It went ever so well.'

'It did,' Charlie backed her up. 'She's been put into Miss Mackintosh's class wi' me an' she said that Annie is as bright as a button.'

'Well done,' Levi praised warmly.

Maggie's frown deepened. It was no good, she was going to have to have a few words with him about how he treated the girl. Anyone hearing him might have thought she was one of their own.

'And did she give you any homework to do?' Levi asked.

Annie nodded. 'Yes, some sums.'

'Hmm, in that case you must have a go at them after dinner, hinny. As it happens I ain't too bad at sums so I might be able to 'elp you if you get stuck.'

'There'll be washing up to do after dinner, Levi,' Maggie snapped, unable to contain herself.

He looked at her calmly. 'I'm quite aware of that but I'm sure it can keep for half an hour while Annie gets her homework done wi' the boys. You wouldn't want Miss Mackintosh to find out that you'd kept her from doin' it, surely?'

Angry colour flooded into Maggie's cheeks and rising from the table she went to fetch the jam roly-poly pudding from the oven.

The rest of the week passed in a blur for Annie. She loved going to school and had even made friends with a couple of girls her age. It was this that caused the next disagreement between Maggie and Levi on Friday night when Annie said innocently over dinner, 'It's Emma Morgan's birthday tomorrow an' she wondered if you'd allow me to go to her birthday party?'

'I'm afraid that's quite out of the question,' Maggie snapped. 'There's more than enough work here for you to do at the weekends.'

'Aw, come on now, Mags,' Levi said cajolingly. 'I bet the kid's never been to a birthday party afore.'

'And there's no reason why she should now.' Maggie's eyes flashed as she glared at him. 'In case you've forgotten, a big house like this doesn't run itself. I need some help about the place. She's hardly one of the family!'

A muscle twitched in Levi's cheek, a sure sign that he was annoyed. 'As far as I'm concerned, she *is*,' he retaliated. 'All the children under my roof should be treated the same, no matter how they got here. I won't 'ave fish made o' one an' fowl of another so get it into your head, woman. You were the one that chose to bring 'em 'ere, so now make your mind up to treat 'em equal.' Then turning his attention to Annie, he asked gently, 'What time is this party an' where is it, hinny?'

'I-it's at three o'clock an' Emma lives in Bracebridge Street.'

'Right, so you can walk 'er round there so she's on time,' Levi told Barney, who screwed his face up in disgust. 'I'd do it meself but I'll still be at work so mind yer get 'er there or you'll 'ave me to answer to when I get in.'

'Yes, Da,' Barney sighed resignedly.

For then the subject was dropped, although Maggie was determined to have her say about it when the children were all in bed.

'I don't like it when you speak to me as you did earlier in front of the children, Levi,' she scolded when they were finally alone.

Lowering the paper, he stared at her. 'Then perhaps it's time you made a little more effort wi' Annie.' His voice was calm but she could see he was annoyed. 'Since the day she arrived you've shown the poor kid no affection, an' it's only gettin' worse. You're beginnin' to treat the child like a skivvy an' I won't have it. Bear in mind I was quite 'appy wi' our family how it was. It were *you* as chose to bring the two girls here. But now they are 'ere I want to see 'em both bein' treated fairly, do yer 'ear me?'

'I hear you.' Clearly miffed, Maggie laid down her darning. 'If you don't mind, I can feel a headache coming on so I think I'll have an early night.'

Levi grinned at her with a suggestive twinkle in his eye. 'Now that sounds like a good idea. How about I come up and join you?'

She put her nose in the air. 'As I said, I have a headache coming on, so I suggest you stay down here and read your newspaper. Oh, and don't disturb me when you do come up, please.'

She turned and flounced out of the room leaving Levi to stare sadly into the dancing flames of the fire. He had thought coming to this house would be the making of Maggie. That it would help her to put what had happened to Penny behind her and give her something else to focus on, but that didn't seem to have happened. She was becoming so unlike the woman he'd married that sometimes he barely recognised her. She had changed drastically from the little lass who had been happy to work beside him to build them a home and be content with what she had. Now all he heard were constant gripes and demands. It was as if nothing he did was good enough. But the worst of it was that he didn't know how to change things, especially as he had less time now that he had a mortgage to pay as well as two extra mouths to feed. With a sigh he leant back in the chair as a lonely night stretched ahead of him.

Chapter Twelve

March 1905

'Did you see Barney at school today?' Maggie questioned Annie as she arrived home from school one afternoon. The weather had finally changed and spring was in the air.

Annie flushed, avoiding Maggie's eyes. She hated having to tittle-tattle, so instead she scuttled away to get changed. Once school was over, she was expected to work in the house and the sooner she got the jobs done the quicker she could get on with her homework.

It was Harry who answered his mother's question when he piped up, 'None of us 'ave seen him, Ma. He left us at the top o' the road this mornin' an' he ain't been in school all day.'

Maggie scowled. It wasn't the first time that term he'd bunked off from school and she dreaded to think what his father would say when he found out.

Only the week before Charlie had come back from school with a message from the headmaster asking if Maggie could pay him a visit. She had set off the following morning thinking that he probably wanted to talk about Annie. After all, she could hardly be expected to fit in after spending her life in the workhouse.

On arriving at the school, she had been shown into Mr Deacon's office and he had greeted her cordially. 'Good day, Mrs Lilburn. I apologise for having to ask you in.'

She had smiled back at him. 'That's quite all right, sir. Is it something to do with Annie?'

'Oh goodness me, no.' Mr Deacon had beamed at her. 'Annie is doing remarkably well, all things considered. In fact, were she a

99

boy I would be recommending that she might be grammar school material. Every one of her teachers has nothing but praise for her. I just wish all my students were as enthusiastic to learn as she is . . . Which brings me to the point of today's meeting.' He coughed and looked mildly embarrassed before going on, 'I'm afraid we are having rather a lot of problems with Barney. There have been quite a few fights in the playground with different boys and it appears that Barney has incited them all. And then there is the matter of his attendance. Were you aware that he hasn't been in school for one full week since the Christmas holidays? He's so close to leaving now that it seems a shame.'

Maggie had been mortified. 'Er, no . . . I wasn't aware,' she had mumbled. 'And I'm so sorry, Mr Deacon. I shall be telling his father what you've told me this evening and you can rest assured that it will be addressed.'

'Good, good.' The headmaster had stood up from behind his desk indicating that the meeting was over as Maggie stumbled to her feet. 'Because as I'm sure you can appreciate, I cannot allow this disruptive behaviour to go on. It sets a very bad example to the other students and if Barney doesn't settle down soon, I shall have no option but to expel him, which would be most regrettable with only a few months before he leaves.'

Maggie's hopes of Barney going on to further education had died in that moment, and as she made her way home, she fumed. She had found the whole meeting thoroughly humiliating, especially as the headmaster had sung Annie's praises.

Levi, however, didn't seem half as concerned about it when she had told him that evening. 'Well, he's never been much of a scholar 'as he? An' it ain't the end o' the world. He'll be more like me probably, 'andy wi' his hands, so I shouldn't worry too much about it, hinny.'

Now she nodded at Harry. 'All right, go and get changed all of you then you can play out in the garden until your dinner is ready.'

Once the children had disappeared, she lifted Ellie from the crib and started to feed her. She was almost five months old now and Maggie was just starting to wean her on pobs and runny porridge. She was a sunny-natured little soul who rarely cried unless she was hungry or thirsty, but Maggie's initial obsession with her was waning badly. Ellie had failed to replace her departed daughter in her affections and she was gradually sinking back into the awful depression that had taken hold of her following Penny's untimely death. Sometimes all she felt was guilt when she looked at the child. After all, how would Penny feel if she knew her mother was caring for another little girl?

Things were going from bad to worse with her and Levi, too, as he always took Annie's side and felt that Maggie was too harsh on the child. To make matters worse, the house hadn't turned out to be the Utopia she had expected either, and she was painfully aware that the neighbours looked down on them because of what Levi did for a living. She would walk around the large empty rooms when Levi was at work, frustrated that she couldn't furnish them. Oh, it was all right for Levi to say that everything would come in time, but he wasn't the one who had to rattle around in the place all day.

As soon as the baby was fed and her binding changed, she returned her to the crib and had just started preparing the vegetables for the evening meal while Annie got the coal in, when there was a tap on the back door. Maggie went to answer it and the moment the door opened she was met with the scent of expensive French perfume.

She gasped. It was her sister Susan, but she was nothing like she remembered her from the last time she had seen her. This woman might have stepped from the pages of a magazine. She was dressed in a smart burgundy velvet travelling gown trimmed with black braid, with a long skirt and a fitted peplum jacket, and about her shoulders was a stole that looked to be made of real fur. On her head was the most beautiful hat Maggie had ever seen, trimmed with peacock feathers that danced with her every movement, and her shining hair was dressed in a chic French pleat.

'S-Susan!'

The woman laughed as she stepped past her, peeled off her expensive leather gloves and glanced around. 'Well, hardly the most rapturous welcome,' she commented drily as Maggie continued to gawp at her. 'And actually, I prefer to be called Susanne now.'

'Oh, er . . . sorry. It's just such a surprise to see you.' Maggie hastily dried her hands on her apron. 'I wasn't expecting you. Florence did say that she'd heard from you and that she'd sent you my new address, but I thought you'd write to let me know if you were coming.'

'I wasn't aware that one had to make appointments to visit family,' Susan responded.

Maggie was shocked to hear that she didn't even sound the same anymore. The local dialect had gone from her speech and she sounded more like Mrs Taylor-Lloyd now.

'Of course, if it's a problem I can quite easily book into the hotel in town. I have the funds, I assure you, and I haven't come to sponge off you if that's what you're worried about.'

'No, no of course it isn't,' Maggie said hastily as Annie entered the room hefting the heavy coal bucket.

'Ah, and this must be Annie. Flo told me all about you in her letter.' She flashed a smile at the child. 'But didn't you take two children from the workhouse, Maggie?'

'Yes . . . Eleanor is over there.'

Susan crossed to the crib and briefly glanced down at the sleeping baby. 'Hmm, she's a pretty little thing.' Susan had never been very maternal and she went to the mirror to take the pin from her hat and pat her hair into place.

'Would you like a cup of tea?' Maggie suddenly remembered her manners and hurried to fill the kettle from the pump on the sink. 'How long will you be staying?'

Susan laughed. 'Regards to the first question – yes, I would, please. And goodness, I only just got here and you're trying to get rid of me already.'

'No, of course I'm not. But the thing is I only have one empty room and that's up in the attic next to Annie's. I'm afraid it isn't what you're clearly accustomed to nowadays.'

Again, a tinkling laugh. 'Oh, I'm sure it will be quite acceptable.'

'In that case I'd best get Annie to make it ready for you. Annie, get the cleaning things and the mop and bucket and go and get that room cleaned. Then when you've finished be sure to make the bed up.'

'Yes, missus.' Annie dropped the heavy bucket onto the hearth and scuttled away to do as she was told.

Susan watched her go thoughtfully. 'I reckon you're going to have a beauty on your hands with that one when she gets a little older,' she commented.

Maggie bristled. 'I suppose she'll pass,' she said reluctantly. 'That's if I keep her. I only brought her here as a maid, really, but Levi treats her like one of the family. He even insists that she goes to school.'

'And why shouldn't she?'

The boys bounded in from the garden then and stood staring at their visitor uncertainly. They had all been very young when Susan went off to London to seek her fortune and they clearly didn't remember her. She and Maggie had always been very different. Even as a child Susan had craved excitement, so it had been no surprise to anyone when she ran away to London as a teenager.

'This is your Aunt Susan,' Maggie informed the boys. 'She's come to stay for a while.'

Susan looked as surprised as they did as she stared at them. They'd shot up since the last time she'd seen them. 'Shouldn't there be three of them?'

Maggie flushed. 'Yes, Barney isn't home yet. This is Charles and Harold.'

'Didn't they used to be Charlie and Harry?'

'We did,' Harry told her with a grin. 'But now we live in a posh 'ouse, Ma allus calls us by our full names.'

'Oh, I see.' Susan chuckled. Maggie had always been a bit above herself and it appeared that nothing had changed. 'Anyway, which of you strong lads is going to carry my cases upstairs and show me where I'll be sleeping?'

They both rushed forward, eager to help, and when they had finally puffed their way to the top of the stairs, they found Annie busily mopping the floorboards in the spare room.

Susan stared around; it wasn't what she was used to but she supposed it would do. She wasn't intending to stay for long and the thought of what she had come for brought a frown to her face.

Two hours later, as Susan sat on a sofa at the side of the fireplace, they heard Dobbin clip-clop up the side of the house, and some twenty minutes later Levi appeared, looking tired.

As soon as he saw Susan, he hurried forward with his hand out-stretched. 'Why, Susan – just look at you. You're all grown up and doing well for yourself by the look of things.'

The jewels on her fingers and wrist flashed in the firelight and she smiled. 'Oh, I can't complain, and it seems you are doing well too.'

He inclined his head. 'We're gettin' there, lass. Though I 'ave to say there's still a lot to do 'ere. We need some more furniture for a start off, but it'll come in time.'

'Huh, it needs to,' Maggie said ungraciously as she slammed a pan of boiled potatoes onto the draining board. Levi hadn't even acknowledged her once he set eyes on Susan, and she felt a pang of jealousy. Susan was very pretty now and he seemed quite taken with her.

'So, what brings you back to this neck o' the woods?'

Susan batted her long eyelashes at him. 'Oh, you know . . . I just thought it was time I paid my family a visit. But don't worry – I shan't be staying long.'

'You can stay as long as yer like, hinny. But tell me, what are you doin' in London these days?'

'This and that,' she said sketchily. 'I work in hotels mostly.'

'Oh yes, doin' what?'

Barney barged in then and the conversation stopped as all eyes turned to him.

'Late again, my lad. I'll have words with you later,' Maggie warned as she carried a large steak and ale pie to the table. She didn't want to start an argument in front of Susan, but she had no need to ask where he had been. She'd heard that the circus was back in town, so no doubt he would have been with them all day.

Over the next couple of days Susan was fairly quiet but then one evening, as darkness was painting the sky, she put on her hat and coat.

Maggie stared at her. 'Where are you off to at this time of night? It's getting dark.'

'Oh, don't worry about me. I'm a big girl now and can more than look after myself. I just want to pop out and catch up with a few friends and get a breath of fresh air. Don't wait up for me.'

'This is an odd sort o' time to go out, ain't it?' Levi commented as the back door closed behind her.

Maggie shrugged as she glanced up from the little matinee jacket she was knitting for Ellie. 'Like she said, she's a grown woman now, as I'm sure you've noticed,' she said sarcastically, causing Levi to blush as he lifted his clay pipe from the rack and packed it with tobacco.

Meanwhile, Susan was hurrying along the road and once she came to Abbey Green she turned left and started to make her way up Tuttle Hill. At the top of the hill she turned sharply left to follow an unmarked lane that led down to the Coventry canal. She could only hope that the person she had come to see was still living in the tiny cottage further on, otherwise she didn't know what she was going to do.

As she drew closer to it, feeling her way along the hedgerow, she was rewarded by the glow of an oil lamp through the drawn curtains. She just prayed that the woman she remembered was still there. Looking up and down the lane to make sure no one was about, she knocked on the door, her heart in her mouth.

Chapter Thirteen

After a moment she heard shuffling footsteps coming towards her and a voice called, 'Who's that knockin' on me door at this bloody time o' night? Ain't you got a bed to go to?'

'Granny Keen, is that you? I- I need your help,' Susan said in a small voice.

The bolts were dragged back and the door opened a crack. A wizened old face peered out at her. 'In trouble are yer, gel?'

When Susan nodded, the old woman held the door wider and ushered her inside. As Susan looked around her heart sank. A large dog lay snoring on a worn rug in front of the fire while two cats were fast asleep in one of the wing-back chairs to one side of the fireplace. An identical chair stood at the other side of the fire, but they were both so worn and shabby that it was hard to distinguish what colour they might once have been. The floor was packed earth and looked as if it hadn't been swept for months and just for a moment Susan panicked and wondered if she was doing the right thing. She had known many girls visit the old woman for the same reason she was there now, but she had never thought she would have to. Perhaps she would be better off going back to London and finding someone who might help her there.

'So 'ow far along are yer?' the old woman asked bluntly.

Susan gulped. 'A-about ten weeks, I should think.'

'Hmm, an' the bloke's left yer 'igh an' dry, 'as he?'

'Something like that.' Susan didn't want to go into detail. She just wanted to get this over with.

'Hmm, well yer early enough along that we shouldn't meet wi' too many problems, but it'll cost yer.' The old woman eyed her sternly. 'An' should anythin' go wrong, my name ain't to be mentioned. Is that quite clear?'

Susan nodded numbly.

'Right, well the price is two guineas. Money up front afore I lift a finger,' she warned.

Susan nodded and laid some money down on a dirty table. The woman hastily snatched it up and dropped it into her apron pocket before pottering away. She returned a few minutes later with a bowl of soapy water and an evil-looking tube.

'Get undressed from the waist down an' lie on the table,' she ordered. 'Seein' as you ain't too far along we're gonna flush it away, all bein' well. If this ain't worked in the next couple o' days, come back an' we'll 'ave to resort to a knittin' needle.'

Burning with humiliation and fear, Susan did as she was told.

'Right, now bring yer knees up and let your legs drop open.' The old woman plunged the tube into the water, then rammed it inside her. Susan winced with pain and started to shake. But worse was still to come, and she gasped as she felt the greasy water being pumped into her body. It seemed to go on and on until she was sure that her stomach would burst, but at last the old woman stood straight and swiped the sweat from her grimy forehead.

'There yer go. That should do it. Now just lie there fer a few minutes an' let it do its job.'

Susan was crying by that time, but she did as she was told. Her stomach was already growling ominously as if she hadn't eaten for a month, and she felt sick, but she didn't say a word.

After what felt like hours, but was in fact only a few minutes, the old woman nodded at her. 'Right, yer can get dressed an' be on yer way now.'

Susan rolled off the table clutching her stomach, and somehow managed to struggle into her clothes again.

'Wh-what will happen now?' she asked in a quavering voice.

'Give it a few hours an' the pains should start. Just make sure as yer close to the privy,' the old woman answered unfeelingly. 'You'll know right enough when it's over. If it don't 'appen wi'in two days as I said, yer to come back an' we'll try the other method. An' just remember, girl, yer were never 'ere.'

Susan nodded and walked unsteadily towards the door. Her face was as pale as lint and she only just made it out onto the lane before she leant forward and was violently sick into the bushes.

Somehow, she made it back to Swan Lane and when she entered the kitchen she found Maggie in her nightrobe making a mug of cocoa. She took one glance at Susan's face and frowned.

'Good grief, what's happened? You look ghastly!'

'I, er . . . think my monthly course is due,' Susan told her as she headed to the door leading to the hallway. 'It always knocks me about. You don't mind if I go up, do you?'

'No, of course not, but wouldn't you like a last drink first?'

Susan shook her head and left the room, then stared at the staircase in dismay. The way she felt it might have been a mountain, but somehow, she managed to climb the stairs. Once in her room she collapsed onto the bed and started to cry. When she'd found out she was having a baby, she had thought Theo would be pleased and happy to make an honest woman of her, but it had been quite the opposite. Her memory drifted back to when she had first met him and she found herself smiling through her tears.

She had been working in a little backstreet café at the time, earning barely enough to pay for the squalid little room she was renting when Theo had walked in one day, and for her it had been love at first sight. He was tall, dark and handsome, and dressed like a toff in his smart suit and silk top hat, so when he smiled at her, Susan had felt as if all her birthdays and Christmases had come at once.

After that he came into the café every day for a couple of weeks, and finally he asked her out to dine, and she could hardly believe her luck. Everything had moved fast from then on and before she knew it, he had installed her in a smart little apartment and bought her a whole new wardrobe of fancy clothes. She had waited patiently for him to ask her to marry him, but then he had revealed his true intentions and for a while she had been heartbroken. She, it seemed, was just one of many girls Theo controlled as a pimp. Even so, he told her that she was his *special* girl, and so she had begun to earn her living as a whore.

Theo arranged her clients and took the money she earned, but he gave her a more than generous allowance so she couldn't complain. Most of the married men he found for her preferred to visit her at her small apartment, while the single ones were happy to book into a hotel. And she soon discovered that many of them could be very generous indeed! She was showered with gifts of clothing, jewellery and expensive perfume and eventually she began to enjoy the lifestyle, although her heart still belonged to Theo.

But then the worst had happened, and she had found that she was carrying a child. Theo had given her an ultimatum, 'Get rid of it or I don't wish to see you again. Why, there's no saying who the father of this brat is! And a pregnant whore is no good to me!'

Susan knew that she should have walked away right then, but she found that she couldn't. He was the love of her life and she was putty in his hands, hence the unexpected visit to her sister, praying that old Granny Keen was still alive and able to help her. And her prayers had been answered. Once this was over, she could go back to the life she had become accustomed to, but deep down she couldn't help but feel a little guilty about the tiny life that she had helped to extinguish that night. As Theo had quite rightly pointed out, though, she had no idea who the father might be, and she had never been very maternal, but even so . . .

With a determined shake of her head, she pushed these thoughts aside. She had to concentrate on getting through the next few hours, or possibly days, and then she would put the whole sorry interlude behind her.

During the night she started to bleed heavily and as dawn painted the sky, she was tossing and turning with griping stomach pains. More than once during the dark hours she had been forced to vomit into the chamber pot, for she felt too ill and weak to manage it to the outside privy. She was aware that the room stank of sweat and vomit but there was nothing she could do so she just tried to be as quiet as she could.

Eventually she heard the door across the landing open and close and guessed that it would be Annie going down to get the fires lit. It seemed that she did most of the work around the house, from what Susan had seen. The poor kid was just an unpaid skivvy. Already Susan's mind was racing ahead a few years. What a little beauty Annie was going to be when she got a little older. She could just imagine how delighted Theo would be with her if she could only tempt the girl to go to London with her. She knew that many of his clients preferred the young ones – the younger the better for some of them – and she would be well rewarded for finding Annie. But not yet. Perhaps in five years or so.

'*Argh!*' As another pain cramped her stomach, she gasped and curled herself into a ball and for the time being all else was forgotten.

It seemed to be hours later when a tap came at her door and Maggie popped her head inside. She wrinkled her nose at the sour smell.

'Good grief. It reeks in here. Are you all right, Susan?'

'Y-yes. It's just me monthly course. I've got the cramps.'

With a frown Maggie crossed the room and felt her forehead. 'Why, you're burning up. Are you sure that's all it is?'

'Of course it is,' Susan snapped more sharply than she'd intended to.

'Perhaps I should send Annie for the doctor?'

111

'No! Don't do that . . .' Susan forced a weak smile. 'Another day or so and I'll be right as rain. You just go about your business and forget I'm here.'

'Well, at least let me go and empty this chamber pot and get it washed out for you, then I'll send Annie up with a cup of tea. Is there anything else I can get you?'

Susan shook her head as Maggie lifted the pot and quietly left.

It was mid-afternoon when the pain became unbearable and Susan knew that she was going to have to get outside to the privy. Somehow, she made it down the stairs on shaky legs that seemed to have developed a life of their own and, keeping her head down, she hurried through the kitchen. The walk to the privy seemed to take forever but at last she was safely inside and not a minute too soon, for as she sat down on the hard wooden seat, she felt the urge to push and then something exploded out of her.

It was over, the baby was gone and relief washed through her.

'You're looking a bit perkier today,' Maggie commented when Susan came downstairs a couple of mornings later.

'I am. In fact I think I might manage a bit of toast if there's any going.'

It was Annie who hooked some bread onto a toasting fork and held it out to the fire, then she spread it with butter and handed it to Susan.

Susan watched Annie closely. Yes, if she wasn't very much mistaken this girl would be very beautiful when she was a little older.

Maggie had gone upstairs to strip the blood-stained bedclothes from Susan's bed and with a smile Susan asked innocently, 'So have you settled here, dear?'

'Yes, thank you.'

Susan could hear from the way Annie spoke that the child's heart wasn't in her answer, and she didn't wonder at it, considering the way Maggie treated her.

'I was thinking when you get a little older that you might like to come and have a little holiday with me in London?'

'London!' Annie's eyes sparkled at the thought. She'd seen pictures of London in books at school and couldn't imagine ever going there. It seemed like the other side of the world to her.

Ellie started to grizzle at that moment and Annie hurried over to lift her from her crib. The missus didn't seem to be quite so devoted to her lately and often left her to cry.

The back door opened then and Peggy appeared, looking in surprise at the visitor.

'Well, stone the crows . . . is that you all growed up, Susan?'

Susan smiled. 'Yes. I thought I'd pop back for a few days and pay a visit to the family.'

Peggy narrowed her eyes. Susan was ghastly pale and didn't look at all well.

'I've just had my monthly course and it always knocks me about,' Susan explained as she noticed the way Peggy was looking at her.

'Does it now.' Peggy had thought it was Susan she had seen going up Tuttle Hill a couple of nights before, but had dismissed the idea – Susan had been gone for so long now. But here she was, and she couldn't think of a reason why she'd have been heading that way, unless . . .

'Oh hello, Peggy.' Maggie came into the kitchen with her arms full of dirty bedding and smiled at her friend. 'Put the kettle on, Annie, and make yourself useful. We'll have a fresh brew once I've got these to soak in the laundry room.'

Both Peggy and Susan noticed the way the girl jumped forward to lay Ellie back in her crib and do as she was told, and they both felt a little sorry for her.

An hour later, when the tea was drunk, Peggy left to go to her job at the workhouse, but her brain was still working overtime, particularly after seeing the stained bedding Maggie had fetched down from Susan's bed. Was it a monthly course that had caused the young woman to look so drained or had she paid a visit to Granny Keen to rid herself of a little problem? After all was said and done, though, it was none of her business. Even if her suspicions were right, Susan wasn't the first girl to find herself in that predicament and she wouldn't be the last. Drawing her shawl more closely about herself, she hurried on.

Chapter Fourteen

It was the following morning when Maggie's problems began. She'd had a restless night, not aided by the fact that Ellie had been fretful, and so when she trudged downstairs, she was not in the best of moods. Annie was already up, the fire was blazing in the hearth, and the kettle was singing on the hob.

'Cup o' tea, missus?'

'Yes, and put plenty of sugar in it.'

Maggie had changed recently and Annie no longer expected a please or a thank you for anything, so she hurried away to do as she was told just as Levi appeared, knuckling the sleep from his eyes and yawning.

'Mornin, Maggie, mornin', princess.'

Maggie scowled. Every time Levi called Annie princess, it grated on her nerves.

'Is there a cuppa goin' spare?' he asked. Levi was always in a good mood in the morning, unlike his wife.

'Just seein' to it now, mister.'

'Good lass.' There was another scowl from Maggie but he chose to ignore it and settled down at the side of her. 'So, what 'ave you got planned for today, pet?' he enquired with a smile.

'Same as always.' She sipped her tea. 'Washing, cleaning, cooking, ironing. What else do I ever do?' she answered peevishly.

Levi could have said that he thought Annie did most of the housework when she wasn't at school but he couldn't face an argument this early in the morning, so he wisely kept his thoughts to himself. 'And what about Susan? How much longer is she plannin' on stayin'?'

'How should I know? And anyway, is it a problem?'

'No, o' course it ain't.' He quickly drained his cup and rose. Maggie seemed to have one of her moods on her that morning so the sooner he could get himself off to work the better.

'Aren't you staying for breakfast?' she enquired when she saw him pulling his heavy boots on.

He shook his head. 'Ner, I'll pop back around about lunchtime an' grab a bite to keep me goin' till dinner tonight.'

Maggie looked horrified. 'Well, if you do, just see that you take Dobbin and the cart round the back where no one can see them.'

'Aye, I'll do that.' He sighed and with a wink at Annie he left.

The boys were the next to come down and Annie cooked them some bacon and fried bread while Maggie went to fetch Ellie for her breakfast. They were almost finished when Susan joined them, and Maggie was relieved to see that she looked slightly better.

'I think I might head back to London today,' Susan informed her sister as she pinned her hair up in front of the mirror above the mantelpiece.

'Already? But you've only been here for a few days.'

'I know, but now I know where you live, I can always come and see you again very soon, can't I?'

Susan refused any breakfast and after two cups of tea she went upstairs to pack her bags.

'Would yer like me to 'elp you carry yer bags to the train station?' Annie offered later that morning when Susan was ready to leave.

It brought a glare from Maggie. There was plenty for the girl to do at home, but she could hardly say anything in front of her sister.

'That would be grand.' Susan flashed her a smile and Annie hurried away to get her shoes on.

'Right, I'm all set.' Susan slipped into her jacket and pinned her hat on at a jaunty angle. She still looked pale but much better than she had. She just wanted to get home now and see Theo. Deep down, although she knew she was only one of a string of women he controlled, she hung on to the hope that one day he would realise that she was the one he wanted to be with. 'Thanks for having me.'

Maggie inclined her head graciously. 'You're very welcome. Just don't leave it so long next time, eh?'

Annie arrived back, her face alight at the thought of getting a little time out of the house. Thankfully, because it was a Saturday, she was able to. Had it been a weekday she would have been at school.

They left together, with Annie carrying the heaviest bag. Although small she was surprisingly strong and she smiled as she trotted along Swan Lane and through Abbey Green with Susan, who she thought looked as pretty as a picture. She had never met anyone as glamorous as her before and was quite taken with her. She just wished she could have stayed longer.

'Do you see yourself staying here?' Susan asked innocently, peeping at the girl from the corner of her eye. 'When you're all grown up, I mean. Have you decided what you'd like to do yet?'

'I haven't really thought about it,' Annie admitted as she stared at the spring flowers that were sprouting through the grass on Abbey Green. 'I think per'aps I might like to be a nurse.'

'Hmm, well if ever you change your mind, you could always come and stay with me in London when you leave school. I'm sure we could find a much more exciting job for you.'

'Really?' Annie stared at her adoringly. 'Doin' what?'

'Oh, there's all sorts of things. But best not mention I've said that to Maggie just yet. She might think I'm trying to tempt you away.' She took a piece of paper from her jacket pocket and handed it to Annie. 'That's my address, put it away somewhere safe and, as I said, not a word to Maggie, eh?'

'Right you are.' Annie thrust the piece of paper into her pocket.

'Do you ever get any time off?' Susan asked.

Annie nodded. 'Yes, if I get all me jobs done then I'm allowed to go out for a while wi' Charlie an' Monty. Monty lives next door an' he's nice. His brother Reggie ain't though.' She scowled. 'He's a bully.'

It was then that Nuneaton Railway Station came into view and the conversation came to an end.

'Have you ever been on a train?' Susan asked as they went to wait on the platform.

Annie shook her head. Until Maggie had taken her from the workhouse, the furthest she had ever been was to Coton Church for services, so this was like a whole new world.

Susan went off to buy her ticket then while Annie waited by the bags and soon after the train belched into the station in a cloud of steam and smoke that rose into the air.

'Goodbye, pet.' Susan bent to kiss the girl's soft cheek. 'For now, at least. And don't forget, if you ever decide you want to come and stay with me, you have my address, so just write and let me know and I'll send you a ticket and meet you at Euston Station.'

She lifted her bags aboard the train and Annie watched enviously as she made her way into an empty carriage and took a seat at the window.

A lump came to Annie's throat as the train drew away, and she waved so hard she felt as if her hand might drop off. She waved until it was out of sight, deciding then and there that one day she would have beautiful clothes just like Susan's.

Back at the house, Maggie was feeling sad too as she walked from one empty room to the next. Levi was still working all the hours God sent to pay off the mortgage, so there would be no chance of any new furniture for the foreseeable future, and added to that only the day before Mrs Taylor-Lloyd and some of the other neighbours had passed her in the street with their noses in the air.

The boys had gone out to play immediately after breakfast and Ellie was fast asleep in her cot in the bedroom Maggie shared with Levi. She tiptoed in so as not to disturb her to collect some dirty washing, and as she glanced towards the cot her heart did a somersault. There was a small shape standing at the side of it, staring down at the sleeping baby and on hearing her enter, it turned towards her with a look of reproach on its face. It was Penny. *But how could that be?* Maggie's tortured heart cried silently. Penny had been gone for a long time now. And yet when she blinked and looked again, she was still there.

'Oh, my angel,' Maggie whispered in a strangled voice. 'I've missed you so much.' She took a step towards the child with her arms outstretched but even as she took the first step the image started to fade and within seconds it had gone. 'No, Penny, come back,' Maggie screamed, waking the baby, who started crying lustily.

'Oh, *shut up*, Eleanor,' Maggie snapped. Why had Penny looked so sad as she stared at the baby? Could it be that she felt her mother had replaced her? Stumbling from the room, Maggie leant heavily against the wall with her hand pressed to her heart as she tried to steady its erratic beat. Then, ignoring the baby's cries, she fled down the stairs and collapsed into the chair in the kitchen, sobbing as if her heart would break.

How could she ever have thought that another baby could take the place of her beloved girl? She knew now that nothing and no one could ever do that. And why had Penny looked at her so reproachfully? Could it be that she felt hurt? If that was the case, then Eleanor would have to go. Nothing must prevent Penny from coming back to her again.

Maggie was still sitting there when Annie returned. The girl stared at her, perplexed. Usually, the moment Maggie set eyes on her she gave her a job to do, but today she was just sitting there hugging herself and crying. And why was Ellie sobbing all alone upstairs?

'Er . . . missus, the baby is cryin'.' Annie stood uncertainly waiting for some reaction, but it was as if Maggie was locked in a world of her own and hadn't heard her, so she set off up the stairs.

Ellie had cried herself into a frenzy and was thrashing her tiny fists in the air. As Annie gently lifted her from the crib the child gave a hiccup of indignation and sagged against her shoulder as

Annie carefully carried her downstairs. Maggie was still in the same position so after laying Ellie down, where she instantly started to wail again, Annie hurried away to warm some milk for her.

Minutes later the baby was hungrily sucking at her bottle, but it was as if Maggie didn't even realise she was in the room. When Ellie had finished, Annie changed her sodden binder and rocked the baby in her arms until at last her eyelids fluttered and she dropped into an exhausted sleep.

Annie was at a loss what to do then. There was clearly something wrong with the missus but who could she get to help? Peggy was the only one who sprang to mind, but what if she ran all the way round there and she was away at the workhouse? After a few minutes she decided there was no other option, so she gently lay the baby back in her crib and once she was sure she was properly asleep, she raced from the room and started to sprint up the road. Thankfully, when she turned into the courtyard at Abbey Street, she saw Peggy with her mouth full of wooden pegs hanging clothes on the washing line.

'Why, pet, whatever's the matter?' the kindly woman asked as she spat the pegs out. 'You're all of a dither.'

'I-it's the missus.' Annie leant over and rubbed the stitch in her side. 'She's actin' all peculiar like, an' I don't know what to do.'

Peggy looked concerned. 'What do you mean – peculiar?'

Annie flung herself into her arms. 'She's just sittin' rockin' in the chair an' she don't seem to know what's goin' on around her.' As Annie quickly explained how she had walked Susan to the station and found Maggie like that on her return, Peggy looked worried. Ever since Penny's death she had been expecting something like this. The poor love had been living on her nerves trying to cope with her grief, but it sounded as if it had caught up with her now.

'You wait there a minute, pet.' She patted Annie's shoulder comfortingly. 'I'll just go an' put me shoes on an' take me pinny off, then I'll come round an' see 'er with you, eh?'

Annie sighed with relief and soon after they set off hand in hand. On entering the house on Swan Lane, they found Maggie exactly as Annie had left her. Bending down in front of her, Peggy asked gently, 'Are you all right, love?'

Maggie looked straight through her as if she wasn't there.

Straightening up Peggy asked Annie, 'Make a pot o' tea, would yer, love? It appears she's had some sort of a shock, though goodness knows what it could be. A cup o' hot sweet tea might be just what the doctor ordered. I could do wi' one meself an' all.'

When it was ready, Peggy pressed the cup and saucer into Maggie's hands, but she was shaking so hard that the tea immediately slopped into the saucer and soaked into Maggie's skirt.

'Hmm, I don't like the look o' this at all.' Peggy chewed on her lip as she stared at her friend, then, making a decision, she rose and told Annie, 'Do you know where Doctor Brain lives, pet?'

Annie nodded. 'I had to fetch him when Harry fell over a while back and cut 'is knee.'

'Right, run round there an' if he ain't in, leave a message wi' his wife to ask 'im to call as soon as he can, there's a good girl.'

Annie set off obediently, wishing with all her heart that it had been Peggy who had taken her from the workhouse. She was kind was Peggy. But then Annie supposed beggars couldn't be choosers and she did love Levi and the boys.

Thankfully, the doctor was just climbing into his pony and trap as she approached his house and when she told him what was happening, he nodded solemnly.

'Hmm, you're lucky you caught me, young lady.' His smile was kindly. 'I was just about to start my rounds, but I dare say I can always make Mrs Lilburn my first visit. Hop up here with me.'

Annie had never ridden on a trap before and despite the concern over what was happening to Maggie she couldn't stop smiling all the way back to the house.

Once there the doctor advised Annie to stay outside while he had a word with Peggy and examined Maggie, so she happily slipped into the garden to admire the spring flowers. Primroses were peeping from beneath the hedge and daffodils, with their bright yellow trumpets pointing towards the sun, stood erect in clumps of gold. After being used to the confines of the concrete yard at the workhouse this was still like heaven to Annie, and she never grew tired of being outside in the sunshine.

'How do, Annie.'

Glancing up Annie saw Reggie leering at her over the garden wall. He had never laid a hand on her, yet for some reason she always felt uncomfortable in his presence.

When she merely nodded and looked away, he sneered, 'What's up with you then? You should answer when your betters speak to you.'

Annie turned around and made for a spot in the garden where she couldn't be seen rather than cause a row. Why couldn't Reggie be more like his brother Monty, who had become a good friend?

She seemed to wait there for a long time but eventually Peggy called her from the back door and she went inside. The doctor was just leaving and he nodded at her as he slipped away after promising to call back and speak to Levi later that evening.

Maggie was still sitting in the chair. She had stopped rocking back and forth but was staring sightlessly ahead as if she was the only person in the room.

'What's wrong wi' the missus, Peggy?' Annie's eyes looked huge in her small pale face.

Peggy was holding Ellie on her hip and she stroked Annie's hair. 'It's all right sweet'eart. She's just 'ad a bit of a funny turn, but she'll be all right. Meantime I 'ave to get back to my brood. Do yer think yer can manage the baby till I can get back later on?'

'Oh yes.' Annie nodded confidently. She was used to seeing to Ellie, especially as Maggie hadn't been paying her so much attention lately. She was used to doing most of the chores about the house – and cooking too, if truth be told.

'I'll be back just as soon as I can be,' Peggy promised as she passed the baby to Annie. 'Hopefully in time to get yer all some dinner on the go.'

'I can do that.' Annie kissed the baby's soft curls and seeing that she was getting tired now that she had a full belly and a clean binder again, she gently laid her in her crib.

Peggy left soon after, but despite her words Annie could see that she was worried. When the boys came in at lunchtime Annie made them all some bread and cheese, but Maggie hadn't moved and when Annie offered her some, she seemed not to hear her.

'Why is Ma sittin' there like that?' Harry asked, nervously eyeing his mother. Normally when they came in for something to eat or drink, she would make them all wash their hands and faces but today she hadn't even glanced at them.

'She ain't too well. Peggy 'ad me fetch Dr Brain to 'er earlier on so don't go upsettin' her.' Annie pottered away to make the baby some pobs and once their bellies were filled the boys went back out to play.

Peggy came back later that afternoon and was impressed to find everything tidy, the baby fed and the vegetables for the evening meal gently simmering on the hob along with a large pan of potatoes.

'I'm doin' sausage an' mash fer dinner,' Annie informed her.

Peggy stroked the girl's coal-black hair. She really was a little treasure. 'How's she been?' Peggy nodded towards Maggie.

Annie shrugged. 'All right, but she ain't said a word. I made 'er two cups o' tea but she didn't touch 'em. She did get up once, though, to go out to the privy, but other than that she ain't moved.'

When the meal was almost ready, Peggy was relieved to hear Dobbin trotting towards his stable, and smiling at Annie she asked, 'Go an' find the lads an' tell 'em to come in fer their meal, would yer, love? I just want to 'ave a quick word wi' the mister.'

After Peggy had told Levi what had happened and of the doctor's visit, he crossed to his wife and, kneeling in front of her, he gently took her hand. 'So, what's wrong, hinny?'

For a while he thought she hadn't heard him, but eventually she turned her eyes towards him and told him dully, 'It's Eleanor . . . Penny doesn't like her.'

Levi felt as if a knife had been thrust into his heart, but he remained calm as he told her softly, 'Now you know that can't be right, pet. Penny ain't with us anymore. Don't you remember?'

Colour mounted into her cheeks and she glared at him. 'But she *is* here! I saw her . . . and she doesn't want us to have Eleanor. She'll have to go back to the workhouse.'

Levi was shocked. 'But we can't do that to the poor little mite. It was you that wanted her. How can you change your mind so quickly?'

She snatched her hand from his and her eyes flashed as she leant towards him. 'It doesn't matter, she has to go, I tell you! I won't have my Penny upset! Do you hear me?'

Peggy crossed to Levi and placed her hand comfortingly on his shoulder. 'Dr Brain is poppin' in to explain her condition to you later this evenin',' she whispered, drawing him away. 'But he seems to think she's had some sort of a mental breakdown.'

Levi sighed and shook his head. 'I've been expectin' this for a long time,' he said miserably. 'But what will I do now?'

'Well, for a start off I can take Ellie home wi' me for a while. That'll take some o' the load off yer.'

'But how will you manage? You 'ave enough o' your own brood to look after an' what'll you do wi' her when you go to work?'

'Oh, don't you get frettin' about that.' She smiled at him sympathetically. The poor chap looked as if he had the weight of the world on his shoulders. 'There's allus women in the courts who'll be happy to babysit for a few bob.'

Seeing no other option, Levi nodded his agreement.

Chapter Fifteen

September 1905

Although it was early in the morning, the day was already uncomfortably hot as Annie packed the boys off to school. Over the last few months, she had become head cook and bottle washer and she had been forced to miss far more school than she liked to. But what other option was there? Rather than get any better, Maggie was worse, if anything, and some days she chattered away to her deceased daughter as if she was sitting right next to her.

Peggy and Levi had both been wonderful, helping Annie as much as they could, but they both had jobs to go to, so the majority of running the house fell to Annie. Luckily, her teacher had been understanding about the situation, and often popped in with homework for her to do – not that Annie had much time to do any. Charlie and Harry helped as much as they could when they were at home, fetching the coal in and doing any jobs that Annie hadn't managed during the day, but Barney, who had now left school, was away from home for most of the time. Annie knew Levi was gravely concerned about him, but she didn't concern herself with what Barney was up to. He came and went as he pleased without his mother there to keep him on track.

Annie was closest to Charlie, and he could do no wrong in her eyes. They had become good friends, possibly because Charlie would sit with her every spare minute she had, to help her with her homework. He had even helped her with French lessons, and they fascinated her. He was as much of a bookworm as she was and the shared interest in learning meant they had a lot in common.

Now, though, with the house quiet, Annie looked around and sighed. It was Monday, which meant it was bed-changing day, a job she dreaded. Maggie was sitting as usual rocking to and fro in the chair at the side of the empty grate, so Annie set off up the stairs and began to strip the sheets from the beds. She was just carrying them downstairs when she heard Peggy talking to Maggie in the kitchen, or at least she heard Peggy talking. Maggie was trapped in her own world as usual and was oblivious to everyone around her.

''Ello, pet. How you managing?' Peggy glanced at the pile of soiled laundry in Annie's arms. The way she saw it, it was a crying shame that a little lass like her should have such responsibilities on her shoulders. She should have been going to school with the boys and playing out with friends instead of being stuck indoors with an invalid all the time.

'I'm fine.' Annie returned Peggy's smile and looked at Ellie, who was balanced on Peggy's hip. The baby was coming on a treat and seemed to be thriving.

'And how's she been?' Peggy cocked her head towards Maggie.

Annie dropped the washing by the door ready to take to the outside laundry room and shrugged. 'She just sits there chattin' to someone we can't see fer most o' the day. She don't even notice the mister when he comes in from work anymore. I know he's really worried about her.'

'Hmm, so am I.' Peggy chewed on her lip for a moment. 'When is Dr Brain comin' out to see 'er again?'

'Tomorrow, I think. Levi said he's goin' to be 'ere to listen to what the doctor 'as to say. But I'll make you a cup o' tea, shall I? The missus will be ready fer one now anyway.'

Soon after they sat together at the table sipping the tea as Ellie sat on the hearth rug playing with a saucepan and a wooden spoon.

Suddenly, Maggie became distressed. 'I'm sorry, Penny, sweetheart,' she wailed as she held her arms out, and the hairs on the back of Peggy's neck stood to attention. 'Don't worry *she* isn't my baby! *You're* my baby, you know that . . .'

'This is gettin' ridiculous,' Peggy said grimly. 'I reckon the poor soul is seriously mentally ill.'

Annie nodded in agreement. 'That's what the mister says an' why he's asked the doctor to come back tomorrer. Last time he came I heard the doctor say that if she didn't start to improve soon 'e'd 'ave to send her to somewhere called Hatt . . .?'

'Not Hatter's Hall?' Peggy was horrified, and yet what alternative was there? Instead of getting better, if anything Maggie was getting worse by the day.

'Yes, I think that's what they called it. Is it a sort of hospital?'

Peggy gulped as she thought of the dark forbidding place. 'Yes, it's sort of a special place for people like Maggie.' How could she tell the child that it was a mental asylum?

'And will they be able to make 'er better?'

Peggy nodded and forced a smile, praying that it wouldn't come to that. 'I should think so, pet. But don't you get worryin' about it. You're doin' a grand job o' holdin' the fort 'ere. I don't know what Levi would 'ave done wi'out yer, an' that's the truth.'

Soon after Peggy took Ellie and set off to tackle her own housework while Annie began the tedious job of washing the sheets and getting them pegged out onto the line where they flapped gently in the breeze.

The following day Levi returned at lunchtime to meet the doctor. He looked worried and grave-faced and Annie felt sorry for him. Maggie hadn't even acknowledged him when he came in, but he was getting used to that now. She was sitting in her usual chair wearing creased clothes that she had worn for days, and her hair was limp and tied into the nape of her neck with a piece of string. She had lost so much weight that her clothes hung from her frame and her face was gaunt, her eyes haunted.

She no longer resembled the pretty, ambitious woman he had fallen in love with, and Levi had no idea how he could help her. A couple of days before he had filled the bath in front of the fire and tried to tempt her into it so that he could wash and change her, but she had fought him like a wildcat and eventually he had given up. He dreaded to think what the doctor would think when he saw her. She looked so unkempt and almost wild.

'Any change, hinny?' he asked Annie hopefully, and when she shook her head he sighed. 'Ah well, we'll see what the doctor has to say when he arrives, eh?'

The doctor arrived shortly after and Annie was told to go out and get a bit of sunshine in the garden while Dr Brain examined Maggie, who didn't even seem to be aware that he was there.

Annie stood admiring the late roses. Through a gap in the hedge, she could see Mrs Taylor-Lloyd's husband smoking a pipe. She didn't think much of it until their young maid appeared. Annie had become friendly with Eve and they often chatted over the garden wall as they were both hanging the washing out. Today Eve was carrying an ash can and didn't notice Annie but when she caught sight of Mr Taylor-Lloyd the colour drained from her face and she quickly turned about as if she was hoping to avoid him. It was too late, he had spotted her and Annie heard him say, 'Ah, Eve. Come over here, m'dear.'

Reluctantly, Eve placed the ash can down and approached him, and what happened next shocked Annie to her core, for suddenly Mr Taylor-Lloyd grabbed Eve and began to run his hands down her back.

Annie blushed to the roots of her hair as she stumbled over the hillocky grass heading for the orchard to escape the scene. Young as she was, she was quite aware that that sort of thing shouldn't be happening, but then she supposed it was no business of hers. Unfortunately, Mr Taylor-Lloyd glanced up at that moment and, spotting Annie, his eyes flashed with anger and he pushed Eve aside as he made towards the hedge that separated the gardens.

'*Girl!* Annie, isn't it? Come here.'

At his command, Annie stopped dead in her tracks and reluctantly turned towards him. Out of the corner of her eye, she saw Eve scuttle away, leaving just the two of them outside.

His face was wreathed in a smarmy smile as he fumbled in the pocket of his smart suit jacket. 'I was just, er . . . giving the maid a list of jobs to do.'

Annie didn't believe a word of it and she stared back at him, her face pale.

'But perhaps it wouldn't be wise to mention you saw us together, eh?' Taking something from his pocket he handed it over the hedge. Annie automatically took it and gasped as she opened her palm to reveal a shiny half a crown. She had never had so much money in the whole of her life, but it made her feel uncomfortable.

'Our little secret, eh?' He tapped the side of his nose.

Not knowing what else to do, Annie nodded.

'No good ever came of idle tittle-tattle,' Mr Taylor Lloyd went on threateningly. Then he turned and strode away.

Annie gulped and licked her lips, then scooted away to the other side of the garden where she sat down on the grass and waited for the mister to call her back inside.

It seemed to be an awful long time before he did, and when she entered the kitchen, she could see that he was upset. The doctor had left and looking towards Annie, Levi asked in a choked voice, 'Could you pack a bag for the missus, please, hinny? Dr Brain thinks it might be best if she went into hospital for a little while, so she'll need some of her things to take with her. Clothes and such like. He's gone to arrange for a carriage to fetch her a bit later.'

Annie nodded solemnly. 'Aye, I can do that, mister.' He looked so sad that her young heart went out to him. She turned and made her way to the bedroom the mister and missus shared and after finding a carpet bag she began to pack underwear and a change of clothes into it.

It was almost two hours later when the carriage arrived and two men in white coats entered the house.

'Mrs Lilburn?'

Levi nodded towards Maggie, and as the men approached her, she looked up and her eyes filled with fear.

'Come along.' One of the men gently reached towards her. 'We're going to take you somewhere where you can have a nice little rest for a while, m'dear.'

'I-I don't want to go,' Maggie mumbled as she wrapped her arms protectively about herself. 'I have to stay here to be with Penny.' She slapped out at his hands and edged herself further back in the chair.

'Now come on, missus, we don't want to have to drag you.' As the man firmly took her elbow Maggie began to struggle.

Levi quickly stepped in to say soothingly, 'It's all right, my pet. You can take Penelope with you.' It was all he could think of to say, but it seemed to do the trick because looking at the seat beside her Maggie told the unseen presence, 'Come along, sweetheart. We're going on a little holiday.'

Annie felt a shiver of fear run up her spine as Maggie smiled sweetly and nodded. Then as meek as a lamb she rose and walked beside the men to the door.

Tears were streaming unashamedly down Levi's cheeks as he promised, 'Don't worry, hinny. I'll come and visit you regularly until you're well enough to come home.'

Maggie paused to stare at him vacantly for a moment then looked down to the side of her. 'Come along, darling,' she whispered, and minutes later the carriage rattled away.

Levi dropped onto a chair and buried his face in his hands.

'D-don't be upset, mister,' Annie said, feeling at a loss as to how she might help him. 'We'll manage just fine an' the missus will be better again in no time.'

'I just hope you're right, princess.' Levi's voice was wooden. 'I just hope you're right!'

Chapter Sixteen

As the carriage rattled towards Hatter's Hall, Maggie glanced to the side of her and became agitated. 'Where's Penny gone?' she asked the attendant. 'She was here with me when we got into the carriage.'

The man shook his head. He was used to dealing with lunatics.

'But she was right here next to me!' Maggie began to cry as the man tried to calm her. 'She *was* here I tell you!'

He sighed as he pressed her back onto the seat, glad that they didn't have too far to go. From what he could see, this poor woman had totally lost her marbles. As the carriage rattled up Tuttle Hill and down Chapel End, she became more and more upset and he breathed a sigh of relief when his colleague shouted from the driving seat, 'Almost there now, Fred!'

Maggie was struggling to reach the tightly secured back door of the closed carriage and Fred was trying his best to restrain her, but she fought him with a strength that surprised him for such a frail-looking woman. At last, the carriage pulled up outside the enormous oak doors of the asylum and Fred shouted, 'Go an' get some assistance, Jim!'

Minutes later the doors to the carriage flew open and a huge woman and a man in white coats reached in and grasped Maggie's arms.

'Come along quietly now,' the woman said sternly. 'It will be all the better for you if you do.'

Maggie took an instant dislike to her. She looked more like an all-in wrestler than a woman to Maggie's mind and she had no intention of going anywhere with her. The woman was at least six foot tall and as ugly as sin, with thinning grey hair tied up in a bun on the back of her head, and a bulbous nose that looked as if it had done a dozen rounds with a boxer.

Maggie managed to pull her arm free of the woman's grasp. 'Get off me and take me home *at once!*' she commanded in her sternest voice.

The woman simply grinned as she nodded to the man at her side. 'Slip back in and get a straitjacket,' she ordered. 'Looks like we're going to have our hands full with this one. Never mind, once we get her inside a nice cold bath will calm her down.'

Maggie stared into her cold snakelike eyes and her stomach turned over. The man soon returned with a strange garment that they forced her into. It had very long sleeves that tied at the back and rendered her unable to move her arms, so she had no choice but to stumble along at the side of them.

Once inside the enormous hallway, the smell of boiled cabbage, stale urine and disinfectant assaulted her. She shuddered with fear. What was this place and why had they brought her here? They hauled her up a large staircase that ran from the centre of the hall to a galleried landing, and the further up they went the louder the noise of people wailing became. Who were these poor people and what were they doing to them? On and on they dragged her through so many locked doors that she lost count of them until at last they threw open a door into a small cell-like room.

'Right, in you go and if you're quiet we'll come and take that straitjacket off in a while. I'm Nurse Stone and you'd be well advised to do as I say!' The woman gave her a hard push in the back and Maggie fell forward onto the hard stone floor, grazing her chin and biting her lip. Somehow, she managed to roll over and struggle to her knees before crawling to the small bed at the side of the room. It was the only thing in there apart from a bucket in one corner. There was one small window high in the wall that let in a little light and the drab green walls were scratched with names that spoke of the despair the people who had been incarcerated there had suffered.

'*Levi!*' she screamed as she somehow managed to throw herself onto the bed. 'Levi, *help me*, please!' But the only answers were the heartbreaking groans of the people in the neighbouring cells. On and on she screamed until her voice was hoarse and her throat was sore. Suddenly the door was flung open again and the same ugly woman, who she would come to fear in time, entered with two male nurses clad in uniforms the same drab green as the walls.

'Tut tut, all this fuss,' Nurse Stone said as the two men bore down on Maggie. 'We're going to take you and give you a nice little bath. That usually makes people feel better.' She smiled spitefully. The men proceeded to take Maggie's straitjacket off and once she was free she began to fight them like a wild cat.

'I demand you take me home *immediately*!' she screamed.

The woman laughed as she jerked her head towards the door. '*Ooh*, do yer now! Right, boys. Bathroom, if you please!'

Once they reached the room, Maggie was subjected to yet more humiliation as they stripped off her clothes. Several tin baths stood along one wall and she noted that one was full. All too soon she was as naked as the day she was born and she lowered her chin to her chest with humiliation as the two men dragged her towards the bath. Then before she realised what they were going to do, they lifted her as if she weighed no more than a feather and unceremoniously dropped her into it.

The cold water took Maggie's breath away as she sank beneath the surface before struggling back up, choking and spluttering.

'Right, let's have her nice an' clean,' the woman barked.

The men were on her in an instant, rubbing harsh carbolic soap into her hair and onto her body. The indignity seemed to go on forever until at last, the nurse instructed, 'All right, that should be enough for now. Get her out!'

The men grasped her arms and deposited her none too gently onto the cold tiles where she lay shivering as she tried to get her breath back. Next, she was hauled to her feet and a shapeless shift was flung towards her. 'Get that on and come along quietly unless you want more of the same,' the woman ordered.

Maggie was so exhausted after her ordeal that she could do nothing but obey and soon she found herself back in her cell where she sank onto the bed, trembling, her dripping hair forming little puddles on the floor. She was fearful and resentful now. Why had Levi sent her to such a dreadful place? Did he not love her anymore? And then suddenly a thought occurred to her – could this place be Hatter's Hall? The thought made her gasp with dismay, for she had heard so many dreadful stories about the place and the poor people who were incarcerated there. It was whispered that once you were committed here you never came out, and if this was true, she knew she wasn't going to be able to bear it. Somehow, she was going to have to get home to Levi, the children and Penny. The poor child would be looking for her, she was sure of it. Another thing she was sure of was that if she wasn't allowed home very soon, she would take her own life. Rather that than stay in this hellhole, and at least she'd be with her darling daughter again!

Lowering her head she wept bitter tears but there was no one to comfort her.

Back at the house the mood was sombre. Levi had not returned to work and Annie could see how distressed he was.

'We're goin' to have to work out how to get you some help around here, hinny,' he said as she pressed a mug of tea into his shaking hands. 'I can't expect you to do everythin' about the place single-handed. You're only a slip of a lass.'

Annie could have pointed out that she'd been virtually doing it all herself for weeks now, but instead she told him, 'It's all right, mister, I'll cope, an' Charlie an' Harry will 'elp me.'

'I notice you don't mention Barney,' he said bitterly. The lad seemed to be completely out of control now and Levi was at a loss as to how to deal with him. He was hardly ever at home and showed no interest in anything. Levi was aware that the circus was once more staying at the Pingles Field, which probably explained why they'd seen hardly anything of the lad recently. Barney seemed at his happiest when he was at the camp helping them to care for the animals and mucking around with the lads, but as Levi had tried to point out to him, what future was there for him with the circus?

He himself was working from dawn to dusk every day trying to build up his business so that one day it could be passed to Barney as the oldest son. Until recently Barney had seemed to like the idea, but now he showed no interest in anything but going his own way and doing as he pleased, and Levi was beginning to despair of him.

It was late that evening before Barney showed his face. Everyone had been in bed for some time apart from Levi, who had waited up for him.

As Barney entered the kitchen he looked about for his mother.

'If it's your ma yer lookin' for, yer wastin' yer time,' his father growled. 'She were admitted to Hatter's Hall earlier today.'

'Hatter's Hall . . . the *lunatic* asylum!' Barney was shocked.

'Aye, that's the place, an' I've no doubt it's partly your behaviour lately that's put her there,' Levi accused him bitterly.

Barney scowled. 'Don't you go tryin' to lay the blame fer her at my door,' he retaliated. 'Everyone knows she ain't been right in the 'ead since our Penny died. Why, she's done nowt for the last few weeks but sit rockin' in the chair talkin' to 'er as if she were still 'ere. How long will she be in for?'

Levi sighed and ran his hand through his hair, suddenly bone weary. 'Your guess is as good as mine, lad,' he answered quietly. 'I dare say it all depends on 'ow she responds to the treatment.'

'An' will we be allowed to go an' see 'er?'

'I will on Sunday afternoons, but they told me they don't encourage the children o' the patients to go. It's too upsettin' fer 'em apparently an' sets 'em back. But what you can do, at least till she's 'ome again, is pull yer weight about the place. I've got to work an' we can't leave everythin' to young Annie.'

Barney sniffed, feeling rather guilty. He supposed he had been going a bit off the rails lately.

'An' where yer been till this time o' the night anyway?' Barney hung his head and Levi sighed. 'Let me guess, over at the circus camp?'

Barney nodded. 'Aye, I was, I was helpin' 'em get the horses bathed an' doin' a few jobs fer 'em. Yer should just see the horses, Da. They're beautiful.'

'Happen if you're that taken wi' horses yer could spare a bit o' time to bathe our Dobbin,' his father replied sarcastically.

At that Barney's mouth set in a grim line and he stormed towards the stair door, slamming it behind him.

Levi shook his head sadly. He had thought when he finally gave Maggie her dream home in Swan Lane that it would be the start of better times for all of them, but in actual fact, it felt as if it had been just one disaster after another since the day they had moved in. Still, they were there now and hopefully once Maggie was recovered, they could start again. Crossing to the table he lifted the oil lamp and made his way upstairs and let himself into the bedroom he had shared with Maggie, and lying down on the bed, he cried himself to sleep.

Barney, meanwhile, was pacing his room, his thoughts troubled. He knew he'd behaved badly recently and hoped that this hadn't contributed to his mother's admittance to the asylum, because despite his behaviour he did love his parents. The trouble was, they seemed to have his future mapped out for him and he knew that working with his dad wasn't what he wanted. He wanted to be on the road with the circus, visiting different towns and working with the animals each day. He felt another twinge of guilt.

He was aware he should be doing more to help about the place. He'd noticed how Annie seemed to have taken the main load of the work on. He'd been quite unwelcoming to her when she first arrived, but over the last month he'd seen first-hand how hard she worked to keep the house running, and he hoped she'd forgive him. With a sigh he stripped his clothes off and threw them into a pile on the floor before clambering into bed where he tossed and turned, wondering what he should do.

On Sunday afternoon Levi stood outside the huge doors of Hatter's Hall in his Sunday best, waiting to visit Maggie. The starched white shirt collar he was wearing felt as if it was choking him and he was apprehensive about how he might find his wife. In his hand was a bunch of roses that Annie had picked from the garden for him, and he tapped his foot impatiently until the doors were opened by the matron and the visitors were allowed in. Once inside, they were pointed towards the day room, a large room at the back of the house. Tables with hard-backed chairs stood around them were dotted about the room and large windows gave a nice view of the enormous lawn, which was surrounded by a tall brick wall.

Those of the patients who were expecting visitors were already seated at the tables and Levi's eyes swept the room for a sight of Maggie. Seeing her by one of the windows, his heart sank into his boots. If possible, she looked even worse than she had on the day she had been admitted. Her lovely copper hair was tied at her neck with a piece of string, and she was clad in a very unbecoming, shapeless shift dress.

'Maggie . . .' She looked up at him as he approached and he gasped as he saw the look of raw anger in her eyes.

'What are *you* doing here?' she rasped. 'I thought you'd had me put away so that you could forget about me.'

'Aw, Maggie, pet.' He dropped into the chair next to her and tried to take her hand, but she snatched it away. 'I could *never* forget you. You should know that. I love you an' it wasn't me who wanted this. It was Dr Brain who said they could help yer here.'

'Help me with *what*?'

'Well . . . help you with your grievin' fer Penny.'

'Just because you don't grieve for her doesn't mean that I shouldn't,' she snapped.

Levi felt like crying. 'Now you know full well that ain't true,' he protested. 'I loved that little 'un as much as you did, but we have other children too. We have to try an' go on fer them.' He gently laid the roses in front of her but she swept them onto the floor, sending petals flying in all directions.

'You can have no idea what it's like in here. It's *hell*, so you can keep your bloody flowers,' she screamed. 'And don't come here again. I don't wanna see your face. Do you hear me?'

At that moment two male nurses approached and before Levi could say another word, they grabbed Maggie by the elbows and began to drag her away.

'It might be as well if you left now, sir,' one of them told Levi as they hauled a kicking and screaming Maggie between the tables. 'Try coming again next week. Happen she'll be a bit more settled by then.'

'Next *week*?' Levi was devastated. Somehow, he had hoped that her stay might last for days rather than weeks.

People at adjoining tables were watching with interest and Levi's cheeks burned with embarrassment as he picked his way through them. Once out in the enormous hallway he could only watch helplessly as the two men forced Maggie, who was still screaming at them, up the stairs, before turning towards the doors with a heavy heart.

Chapter Seventeen

October 1905

Life in Swan Lane had settled into a new routine since Maggie had left. Ellie was doing well with Peggy and Annie was managing to keep the house running, with the help of the two younger boys, who, although they were still coming to terms with their mother being away, pitched in whenever they could. Barney, however, was still a law unto himself, coming and going as he pleased, but for now Levi was turning a blind eye to his behaviour. He had other far more pressing things on his mind.

Although Annie would never admit it to anyone, she actually found things easier without the missus being there snapping out orders. At least now, once she had seen the mister off to work and Harry off to school, she could tackle the chores her own way, and slowly she was getting into a routine. As for Charlie, he was now attending the local grammar school for further education, which he seemed to enjoy.

Peggy had given her a few lessons on ironing the clothes and although Annie had a few small scars to show for her efforts, she was getting better at it. Her cooking was improving too, but she still felt sad each evening when she saw the mister sitting alone by the fire with his head in his hands. She could see how much he missed his wife and hoped for his sake that Maggie wouldn't be gone for too much longer.

Now they were into October and the leaves on the trees were changing from green to rusts and golds, and there was a distinct nip in the air. Levi had visited Maggie every Sunday since she had been admitted to the asylum, and each time he had come home disheartened after seeing no improvement in her. If anything, he'd confided, she seemed worse, but the doctor had assured him that it was often the case that patients got worse before they started to get better, so he hadn't given up hope.

Ever since the day Annie had witnessed Mr Taylor-Lloyd and the maid in the garden she had made sure that no one was about next door through the gap in the hedge before venturing into the garden, and the half a crown he had given her to buy her silence was tucked firmly beneath her mattress. She had tried to speak to Eve once about what she had witnessed but the girl had closed up like a clam, so Annie wisely asked no more. At the tender age of ten she still wasn't sure quite what it was that she had witnessed, but something told her that it was wrong, so she kept what she had seen a closely guarded secret. There had been times when she had wanted to confide in Peggy, who had shown her nothing but kindness, but she never did.

She still secretly wished it had been Peggy who had taken her from the workhouse, which made her feel guilty. She'd feel guiltier still whenever she saw the mister. He was kind, was the mister, and she would have done anything for him. But it was still Charlie she was closest to. He would spend a few hours each evening helping her with her homework and he always carried the coal in and did any of the heavier jobs that needed doing with not a word of complaint.

On this blustery October morning, Annie loaded the sheets she had just passed through the mangle into the large wicker wash basket and carried it out to the line, peeping through the hedge dividing the houses just to make sure there was no sign of the mister from next door. There wasn't but Eve was there pinching a breath of fresh air and when she saw Annie scuttle past, she walked to the hedge and smiled at her.

'How's your missus doin' now?' she asked in a friendly fashion. 'Word 'as it she still ain't well an' she's in Hatter's Hall.'

Annie dropped the heavy basket and hooked some wooden clothes pegs from the large pocket of her apron. 'Not so good at present, accordin' to the mister,' she admitted. 'But we 'ope she'll start to pick up soon.'

The girl nodded. 'Let's hope she does. We could per'aps go fer a walk on me Sunday afternoon off, if you've time?'

'I'd like that. Monty and Charlie might like to come too,' Annie agreed. They often went off together for a few hours if they were all free.

'Right y'are.' Eve straightened her broderie-anglaise-trimmed mob cap on her halo of dark curls. 'Well, I'd best get in, as yer know the missus is a tartar,' she said in a low voice with a grin. 'But I'll see yer again soon, hopefully. Ta-ra fer now.'

'Ta-ra.' Annie watched her go before turning back to the job in hand. Eve was nice. She was the only female friend her age that Annie had now, as she had lost touch with the ones she had made at school.

'Any sign of Barney?' the mister asked when he arrived home early that evening. The nights were drawing in and he couldn't work such long hours.

When Annie shook her head, he sighed. That lad of his would be the death of him. 'Ah well, I dare say he'll be back when he wants his belly filled. So, what have we got for dinner tonight, princess?'

'I've made a steak an' kidney pie – Peggy showed me 'ow,' Annie told him, feeling slightly nervous. 'I dare say it won't be as good as the ones the missus makes but I 'ope it'll be okay.'

'I'm sure it will be.' He smiled at her and hurried off to get changed. Maggie had always insisted on it before he sat down to eat and some habits were hard to break.

Minutes later Charlie and Harry came in and helped Annie set the table before they all sat down to eat.

'Florence came round earlier to ask after the missus,' Annie told Levi as she spooned vegetables onto his plate. Charlie and Harry had grown some of them in the garden and were very proud of them.

'Oh aye, an' I bet she didn't offer to lift a finger to 'elp out,' he answered drily.

'No, she didn't, but she did ask if we'd thought to let Susan know what 'ad 'appened.'

Levi paused with his fork halfway to his mouth. He hadn't given it a thought, although he supposed he should have done.

'I could do it if yer like?' Annie volunteered, keen for an excuse to get in touch with her. 'She left me her address afore she went back to London. It'd be no trouble.'

'In that case yes, yer go ahead. You'll find some envelopes an' writin' paper in Maggie's bureau an' I'll give yer the money for the stamps.'

Barney still hadn't arrived by the time they'd finished eating, though his food was keeping warm over a pan of hot water. But if he didn't arrive soon, it would be ruined.

When she said as much to Levi, he replied drily, 'Serves him right if it is. He'll 'ave to make do wi' some bread an' cheese. Happen it'll teach 'im to be 'ome at mealtimes.'

Up at the asylum the patients were being herded like cattle down to the communal dining room, and Nurse Stone was surprised that Maggie went without a murmur. Normally she had to be dragged from her cell but this evening she followed the nurse as meekly as a lamb. Maggie had finally realised that she was doing herself no favours by kicking up a fuss, and so she had decided to use another tactic and do exactly as she was told.

Once in the dining hall she joined the queue of patients as they waited to have their plates filled, and for the first time, she raised no complaint at the slop they were served. She even managed to force the meal down, aware that Nurse Stone was keeping an eye on her.

The nurse was seated next to Dr Makepeace at the staff table and leaning towards him she muttered, 'I don't know what Lilburn is up to but suddenly it's like she's a completely different woman from the one that was brought in.'

Dr Makepeace was not an unkind man, and he smiled. 'Then let us hope that the poor woman has turned a corner, Nurse. Grief is a terrible thing and maybe she has found a way to come to terms with the loss of her child and is ready to move forwards. We shall have to keep a close eye on her for the rest of the week and hopefully we'll have some good news for her husband on Sunday.'

The nurse frowned. She wasn't so sure, but she agreed with the doctor on one point: they would have to keep a *very* close eye on her for the rest of the week.

The other missing member of the Lilburn household, Barney, was at that moment sitting before a fire outside one of the fairground trailers with a group of boys in the Pingles. He had spent the afternoon taking the horses down to the stream and helping the lads to bathe them. It was a job that he loved. Barney was now a strapping lad and recently he had started to notice girls – or at least one girl in particular. Her name was Mercy and she was the younger sister of Noah, his best friend. On most of his previous visits to the fair, Mercy had been nothing more than a nuisance, who loved trailing along with the boys and making a pest of herself. But now she had turned fifteen and this year when Barney had made his first visit to the camp, he had been shocked at the change in her.

Her long hair was dark and shiny, and her eyes were a lovely blue-grey colour. She wore large gold hoops in her ears and he could only sigh at the creaminess of her skin and the womanly curves that were beginning to develop beneath her colourful clothes. Everything about her was perfect to him and it was plain to see that when grown-up she was going to be a great beauty.

Of course, like all the circus girls, she was closely guarded and never allowed to be alone with a boy or a man, but that didn't stop Barney's eyes following her wherever she went. She was the most beautiful girl he had ever seen, and he would have walked over hot coals for her if asked. Especially when she gave him a shy smile.

Mercy was the daughter of Luca, the circus owner, and his wife Charity, who for some reason lived in separate trailers and were rarely seen speaking to one another. Barney had questioned Noah about this once but Noah's curt reply that 'it was their business' ensured that he never poked his nose in again.

For Barney, Mercy was now as much of an attraction at the circus as the horses, and he was upset that they were planning to move on later that week. It could be months before they returned and Barney dreaded the time stretching miserably ahead of him. Things were not good at home without his mother there and his father seemed to do nothing but nag him nowadays. Deep down Barney supposed he deserved it, but then he was young. Why should he have to spend his time stuck at home when he could be out in the fresh air with his friends enjoying himself? They'd be gone soon enough so for now he intended to spend every spare minute he could with them.

'Penny for 'em, boyo?'

Barney started as Noah's question jolted him back to the present. Flushing, he began to pick at a loose thread in his trousers, avoiding Noah's eyes. 'Oh, er . . . sorry, I was just thinkin' how much I'm gonna miss you all when you leave.'

'Ah.' Noah frowned and, leaning towards him, he lowered his voice. 'And perhaps my sister most of all, eh?' He shook his head and the gold hoop he wore in his ear glinted in the late afternoon sun slanting through the trees. 'We have accepted you into our company even though you are not one of us, but you must remember it would not be a good idea to form an attachment to Mercy, or any of our girls. When they are of age and our families consider it the right time, they will all be married to men of our own kind and of our parents' choosing.'

Barney flushed. 'Don't know what you're on about. I come 'ere to see you an' the horses.'

'Good.'

'Any road, it's time I were headin' off home. I dare say I'll get a flea in me ear fer bein' missin' all day again.' Barney was so embarrassed he could scarcely wait to get away. He was mortified that his friend had noticed his attraction to Mercy and vowed that he wouldn't even look at her in future. Although that would be easier said than done. There was something magnetic about her. Perhaps it would be good when they left. At least he could try to get over his silly crush.

Just as Barney had feared, a grim-faced Levi was waiting when he got home. He'd hoped to sneak in and hurry up to his room but it was obvious that wasn't going to happen.

'I dare say I've no need to ask where you've been, eh? Off down the Pingles wi' yer circus friends, were yer?'

Barney shrugged, as Annie hurried over to the range to fetch him his dinner. Sadly, it was dried up and looked very unappetising.

'Sorry, I did try an' keep it warm. I could get yer some bread an' cheese instead if yer like,' she apologised.

Levi frowned. 'You'll do no such thing, hinny, sit yerself back down. You've done more than your fair share of work fer today. If he can't be bothered to come home in time fer the meals you've cooked, he can damn well make somethin' fer himself or go hungry.'

'I ain't hungry anyway,' Barney snapped.

Annie sank back into her seat and nervously bit her lip. She hated it when Barney and the mister argued, she just hoped this didn't develop into another full-scale row.

She needn't have worried, though, for without giving her a glance Barney stormed off to his room, and his father didn't stop him.

'I, er . . . think I'll go on up an' all now, less you want anythin'?' she told Levi in a small voice.

He smiled at her. 'No, you go on up an' get a good night's sleep. I'll lock up down here.'

Annie scuttled away, glad to escape.

Chapter Eighteen

'Hello, pet, I thought I'd just pop round to see if there were anythin' I could be doin' for yer,' Flo said as she entered the kitchen a few evenings later, shortly after Levi had got in from work.

'Well, that's very kind o' yer, Flo, but at this time o' day young Annie 'ere has pretty much seen to everythin'.'

Flo had clearly made a big effort with her appearance, and she batted her eyelashes at him. It had occurred to her that with Maggie shut away in the asylum this could be her chance to win Levi back. 'In that case we can enjoy a bottle o' this together.' She produced two bottles of brown ale from her bag and Annie hurried away to get them a glass each.

'I, er . . .' Levi was clearly feeling uncomfortable but Flo wasn't about to take no for an answer.

'Now come on, man. Everyone needs a bit o' pleasure in their life an' you certainly ain't had much o' that married to our Maggie, have yer? Especially not recently. She allus were high-strung mind, wi' ideas above her station. Now me . . .' She spread her hands to encompass the kitchen. 'Had *I* been taken to a house like this I'd 'ave thought I'd died an' gone to 'eaven.'

'Maggie is ill,' Levi said defensively.

Flo looked contrite. 'O' course she is, pet. But all the same, she's got everythin' goin' for 'er, ain't she? It's you as I feel sorry for. A man needs a woman aside him. But never mind that fer now. Have this drink an' relax a bit, eh?'

147

With a sigh, Levi accepted the drink but he didn't feel comfortable. Flo had always made it more than obvious, even before Maggie took ill, that she was still his for the taking, but he had never regretted his choice of sisters. Maggie had her faults, admittedly, but until they lost Penny she had been a wonderful wife and mother and he still loved her.

Looking towards Annie and Charlie, Flo said, 'Ain't it time you two young 'un's were abed now? I dare say Harry's already gone up, ain't he?'

Obediently, the two children rose and after saying their goodnights retired to their rooms.

The nights were cold now and as Annie entered the sparsely furnished bedroom her breath hung in the air and she shivered as she hurriedly changed into her nightclothes. Before she got in between the cold sheets she pulled the small parcel containing the things she had been wearing on the night she was abandoned from beneath her bed and carefully unwrapped it.

The silk shawl shivered through her fingers, and she bit her lip. Since Maggie had pointed out how beautiful the shawl was, she had taken to examining it frequently, her imagination running wild. The mister often addressed her as 'princess' and she wondered what sort of family she might have come from and why they would have abandoned her.

When she was younger, she had dreamt that her mother would come to the workhouse to claim her one day, but that hope had gradually faded over the years as she had watched other children be chosen for adoption while she was always left behind. Admittedly, the missus had freed her eventually, but it had hardly turned into the happy-ever-after life she had wished for. If anything, she had simply swapped one life of drudgery for another. Still, the mister made up for that. He was the nearest thing to a father she had ever had, and then there was Charlie. She loved Charlie. Oh, she really did. He was so kind.

With a sigh she put the things away and hopped into bed and, after blowing out the candle that guttered in the draught from the skylight window, she was soon fast asleep.

It was early in November as Annie was clearing the dirty pots following the evening meal that there came a knock on the door. Hurrying to answer it, she found Dr Brain standing on the doorstep.

He smiled at her. 'Good evening, Annie. Is Mr Lilburn in?'

'Yes, sir. He's in the kitchen – come on through.'

The doctor entered the hall with a blast of icy air and followed Annie back to the kitchen where he found Levi quietly smoking his pipe and reading his newspaper on the sofa to the side of the fire.

'Ah, Levi, I'm glad you're in,' Dr Brain said, removing his hat.

Levi paled. 'Evenin', Doctor . . . is . . . is something wrong wi' Maggie?'

'Quite the opposite, dear chap.' The doctor smiled at him. 'In fact, I've just come back from Hatter's Hall where the matron informed me that they are so pleased with Maggie's progress that they're hoping she'll be well enough to come home in time for Christmas.'

'Why, that's grand news.' Smiling broadly, Levi stood and shook the doctor's hand. 'So, what should I do now?'

'Nothing at all, my dear chap. Just go and visit Maggie as usual on Sunday and if all is still well, I've no doubt the matron will be having a talk to you.'

That proved to be exactly the case when Levi arrived at Hatter's Hall the following Sunday to find the matron waiting for him in the hallway.

'Ah, Mr Lilburn, a word in my office if you please!'

Levi left the room a short time later with a wide smile on his face after hearing what the matron had to say. He could hardly wait to tell Maggie the good news. He had been visiting her as regularly as clockwork every Sunday since she had entered Hatter's Hall and it felt as though she had been there forever instead of weeks.

He was delighted to know that Maggie would soon be home for several reasons. The first, of course, was because he missed her. The second was because he knew that a little of the weight of running the house would be lifted from Annie's shoulders. Thirdly, Flo was becoming rather a nuisance, turning up most evenings and demanding his attention, so hopefully that would stop once Maggie was home.

He found his wife sitting by the window in her usual position and this time when he greeted her with a kiss on the cheek, although she didn't respond, she didn't flinch away.

'I've got grand news for you, pet.' He quickly told her what the matron had said.

She nodded. 'Good, and is there a date set yet?'

'No, but hopefully if you continue to make good progress it will be in the next couple o' weeks.'

She nodded again, secretly smiling to herself. How easy it had been to trick them all simply by doing as she was told. Soon she would be able to go home to her precious girl and the boys. But she'd be more careful this time and never let any of them know that Penelope was still with her.

Maggie was released from the asylum two weeks later. It had been arranged that Dr Brain would bring her home in his carriage and on the day she was due, Levi took the afternoon off work so he could be there to welcome her.

Washed and changed, Levi paced up and down by the large bay window waiting for a sight of the carriage, and when it drew up outside at last, he ran out to greet Maggie, being careful not to slip on the icy pavements.

'Aw, pet! Welcome home. This place ain't been the same wi'out you, an' that's a fact.' He swung her down from the carriage, shocked to find that she was as light as a feather, and hurried her inside.

Dr Brain followed with her bag and as they entered the kitchen Maggie heard the kettle singing on the hob and saw a large sponge cake oozing with jam and cream standing on the table – Annie had made it for her especially. She glanced around, and there was little Penelope, patiently waiting for her in the corner. Of course, Maggie was careful not to draw attention to the fact – she had learnt her lesson on that score. From now on she would only speak to her when she was on her own.

'It's good to 'ave you back, missus,' Annie said tentatively.

Maggie inclined her head to her, although she didn't say anything.

'I'm makin' some tea, an' I made you a cake an' all,' Annie went on. 'It probably won't be as good as the ones you make but Peggy's been givin' me cookery lessons an' the mister reckons I'm gettin' better at it.'

'Thank you.'

When the tea was ready, Annie placed a large slice of cake and Maggie's favourite bone china cup and saucer down on the small table at the side of her.

Meanwhile, Levi moved away to have a word with the doctor. 'See as she takes her time getting back into the swing of things over the next few days,' Dr Brain advised kindly.

Levi nodded. 'Aye, I will. An' thanks, Doctor, fer everythin'.'

'You're welcome. I just hope things will return to some sort of normality for you.' He left, then, hoping that he wouldn't be called back for some long time.

The two youngest boys were ecstatic when they came home later that afternoon, although the same couldn't be said for Barney. He'd been down in the dumps for days, ever since the circus had moved on, and even his mother's homecoming couldn't cheer him up. It didn't help that his mates had been teasing him, saying that he had a head case for a mother. He eyed her worriedly, hoping they weren't right.

For the first time in weeks, they all sat down to dinner – cooked by Annie – as a family, and they were almost finished when Flo put in an appearance.

'All right?' She nodded towards Maggie, looking none too pleased to see her. She'd hoped she was going to be away for a lot longer – not that Levi had made any move towards her despite her best efforts.

'Yes, I'm all right . . . and you?' Maggie answered.

Flo shrugged. 'Same as always. Levi told me yer were comin' home today so I thought I'd best pop round.'

'Actually, I'm feeling a little tired. I think I might go and have a lie-down.' It felt strange to be back at home and Maggie just wanted to be left alone so she could talk to her darling Penelope.

'Come on then, pet.' Levi was at her side instantly, helping her to her feet as if she was an invalid, and for a moment, she felt like screaming at him to leave her alone, but she managed to remain calm.

'It's fine. You stay and see to the children. Goodnight, Flo.'

After she'd gone, Flo frowned. 'I'd say they've let her out a bit early,' she said nastily. 'She still don't seem herself to me!'

'I'm sure they wouldn't let her come home unless they were certain she's on the mend,' Levi answered irritably.

Instantly Flo was contrite. 'Aw well, yer know where I am if yer need anythin'.'

Levi sighed. All these offers of help, yet she never seemed to come round until all the jobs had been done.

Disgruntled Flo left and she had just reached the pavement when she almost bumped into Mrs Taylor-Lloyd, who was just coming back from decorating the altar in the church with greenery.

'Have you just come from the Lilburns'?' the woman asked, her curiosity getting the better of her. Normally she wouldn't lower herself to speak to such a blowsy-looking woman, but she'd spotted her coming in and out for some weeks now. 'Only I heard that Mrs Lilburn was coming back from . . . er . . . the asylum today. Is that right?'

'Aye, that's right,' Flo answered, still in a huff. 'Though if you ask me, it's a bit premature.'

'*Really?*' Mrs Taylor-Lloyd loved nothing more than a good gossip. 'And why is that, may I ask?'

'Nutty as a fruit cake, she is,' Flo responded spitefully. 'An' I should know. I'm 'er sister. Allus had ideas above her station, she 'as, but she's gone to pot since she lost 'er little girl.'

'I see.' Mrs Taylor-Lloyd was in her element. She would certainly have something to share with the ladies at her coffee morning the next day. The woman inclined her head at Flo and went on her way with a spring in her step.

Chapter Nineteen

December 1905

As Maggie boarded the carriage bound for Coventry, she smiled. It was almost three weeks since she had been discharged from the asylum and the time had passed without incident. To all outward appearances, she was doing well. Only she knew the turmoil bubbling inside her. She and Levi were now once again sleeping in the same bed, although she had made sure that sleeping was all they did. If Levi felt spurned when she rejected his advances, he had made no complaint, presumably thinking that she just needed some time to settle back in. But Maggie knew differently. She would never forgive him for allowing her to be committed to Hatter's Hall and now she meant to make him pay for it.

As yet, no mention had been made of Ellie returning home, but Maggie knew that it was only a matter of time before it came up. The child was thriving with Peggy and Maggie was happy for her to stay there. She was not prepared to risk upsetting Penelope again by bringing her back to the house. Thankfully, Levi had been too afraid to mention Eleanor, but when he did suggest her coming home he wasn't going to like her answer.

Only the night before, when she had asked if he would mind her going shopping in Coventry, he had been thrilled, thinking that she meant to go for Christmas presents, which was a good sign, surely. He had willingly given her his bank book and his permission to withdraw as much as she would need from the bank, and she had certainly done that. The teller in the bank had raised an eyebrow when she'd told him how much money she wished to withdraw, but it was none of his business, and so he'd counted out the money.

Now Maggie intended to spend every penny of that money. She smiled as she thought of Levi's face when he realised what she had done, but it would be too late by then, and it would serve him right. She doubted he would raise too much of a rumpus – he was still too afraid of upsetting her and sending her on a downward spiral again. And after all, she reasoned, he had promised her a beautiful home, hadn't he? Well, now she intended to have one.

She was heading for a very upper-class furniture store on the outskirts of Coventry where people with money tended to buy their furnishings. As well as brand-new furniture the shop also sold excellent second-hand pieces that had been taken in part exchange for new, and it was there Maggie was aiming to visit now. She was sick of walking around empty rooms and being confined to the kitchen, and she intended to have the house looking fit for a king by Christmas.

It was mid-afternoon by the time she returned home and found Annie preparing the evening meal. The girl greeted her with a smile before looking slightly surprised when she saw she had no shopping bags with her. 'Were there nowt that caught yer eye, missus?'

Maggie smiled as she removed her gloves and warmed her hands in front of the fire.

'Oh, there were quite a few things that caught my eye,' she smirked. 'And they're all being delivered tomorrow.'

Annie thought this strange. It was usually only the toffs like Mrs Taylor-Lloyd next door who had things delivered but she didn't dare to question it.

'How did your shopping trip go, hinny?' Levi asked as they all sat down to their meal that evening.

Maggie kept her eyes on her plate. 'Quite well as it happens.'

'Good, good, I hope yer treated yerself to somethin' nice. Yer deserve it.'

'Oh, I did,' she assured him.

'Then per'aps yer can show me what you've bought after dinner?' he suggested.

She shook her head. 'Can I show you tomorrow? I have a slight headache coming on, so I think I'll go and lie down after dinner.'

'Aye, you do that, pet. We don't want yer bein' ill again. Especially not just afore Christmas.'

The next morning a letter arrived for Annie with a London postmark, and she tore it open eagerly.

'Who is writing to you?' Maggie questioned with a lift of her eyebrow.

Annie smiled. 'It's from Susanne.'

'Susanne?' Maggie frowned. But when she realised who Annie meant, she snapped, '*Susanne* indeed! She's always been Susan to us. What does she want?'

'She's just writin' to see 'ow you are,' Annie told her as her eyes scanned the page. 'I can read it to you if yer like.'

And so, sitting down at the table she began.

Dear Annie,

Do forgive this message for being rather short, I'm so very busy at present that I barely know if I'm coming or going! Thank you for writing to inform me that Maggie is home again. I'm so relieved and I'm sure she must be too. What perfect timing, just ahead of Christmas. I was hoping to come and see you all over the holidays but I'm afraid that work dictates that I won't be able to. I hope you all have a lovely time. Hopefully I'll find time for a flying visit with you in the new year. Do please give Maggie and the rest of the family my love and don't forget if ever you fancy a little break in London, you are always welcome to come and stay with me. Tell Maggie I would of course meet you off the train – London is no place for a young girl on her own – and I would be happy to send you the money for your ticket. Do keep me informed of Maggie's progress,

   With much love to you and the family,

   Susanne xx

Maggie wrinkled her nose. It was a poor lookout if her sister couldn't even spare the time to visit her family at Christmas. But then Susan had always been a law unto herself.

Maggie spent the rest of the morning peering from the front bay window and pacing up and down, no doubt waiting for her delivery, Annie thought. She was like a cat on hot bricks.

Suddenly a shout went up. 'They're here.'

Annie sidled into the hallway to see what was going on as Maggie flung open the front door, letting in an icy blast of air. The young girl's mouth dropped open as she spotted a large wagon loaded with what looked like very good quality furniture standing outside. Three men began to unload it and as they carried a huge highly polished mahogany table into the house, Maggie instructed them, 'In the dining room, if you please.' She ushered them into the room to the left of the front door. 'In the centre . . . yes, just there.'

When the table had been positioned to her satisfaction the men went to fetch the eight ladder-back chairs that went with it. Next came a matching sideboard that almost stretched the length of one wall. And still they weren't finished, for next came a very luxurious-looking heavily tasselled velvet three-piece suite in a soft shade of pale green.

'That's for the drawing room on the other side of the hall,' Maggie instructed the men. A long, low polished table that was to stand in front of the settee came next, and then they brought in a very ornate glass-fronted china cabinet. And finally, two enormous bags were brought in and placed in the hallway.

'That's the lot then, ma'am.' The older of the gentleman touched his cap to her. 'Will there be anything else we can be helping you with?'

'No, that will do nicely for now,' Maggie told him with a girlish giggle as she handed him a handsome tip and, after closing the door on them, she went back into the drawing room and did a little jig of pure pleasure. Annie had never seen her look so happy.

But as beautiful as the furniture was, Annie couldn't help but wonder what the mister was going to say when he saw it. She was no expert, but even she could see that this was all very high-quality furniture, the like of which she'd never set eyes on before.

Maggie, meanwhile, had turned her attention to the two huge bags from which she took enormous velvet curtains with matching swags and tails. There was a green set for the drawing room and a rich burgundy set trimmed with gold tassels for the dining room.

'I think these are going to be just perfect for those two front rooms.' Maggie sighed with pleasure as she stroked the soft fabric. 'You can come and help me and between us we should be able to get them up for when Levi comes home to surprise him.'

Annie hurried away to fetch the step ladders and soon she and Maggie were busy hanging the new drapes. It was no easy task, for they were extremely heavy, but as Maggie had said, they were a good fit for both windows and looked very luxurious. They were just finishing when Charlie and Harry came home. Barney was helping his father out on his rounds again now – it wasn't what he wanted to do, but he supposed anything was better than sitting about all day.

The boys' eyes stretched wide with surprise when they glanced around the newly furnished rooms.

'Crikey, 'ave we come into some money?' Charlie asked.

Maggie scowled at him. 'Go and get washed and changed,' she barked, then turning to Annie she ordered, 'And you get a fire lit in both these rooms. We'll eat in the formal dining room this evening like civilised human beings.'

Annie went off to fetch the coal. Personally, she liked living in the kitchen. It was warm and cosy, whereas these two rooms with their high ceilings and large proportions tended to be cold in the winter. Still, if that was what Maggie wanted, she would do as she was told.

When the children had left, Maggie stood back and smiled as she ticked off in her mind what they needed to finish the rooms off. Definitely some china pieces for the cabinet, and some big rugs for the highly polished floorboards. But first she would have to wait and see what reaction she'd get from Levi when he found out how much she had spent. In fairness, she had spent even more than she had intended, but how could she have resisted such bargains?

Soon after, Levi and Barney arrived home. Barney went straight inside to get changed, and after giving Dobbin a good rub down, throwing a warm blanket over him and feeding him, Levi entered the kitchen, surprised to see that only Annie was there putting the final touches to their evening meal.

'Where is everyone, hinny?'

'They're in the, er . . . the dinin' room.'

'The dinin' room? What are they doin' in there?'

When Annie didn't answer he strode past her and along the hallway and when he pushed open the door his mouth fell open.

'*Good grief!*' His eyes slowly swept the room as Maggie rose from the table to greet him. 'Where did all this bloody lot come from?'

'Don't swear in front of the children,' she scolded him. 'What do you think? It looks splendid, doesn't it? And come and see the drawing room. You won't recognise it.' Taking his hand, she drew him across the hallway.

On seeing the second room he was momentarily struck dumb. 'B-but I thought we'd agreed we wouldn't get spending money on furniture till I'd paid the mortgage off,' he managed eventually.

Since they had moved in, he had worked every hour he could to do just that and he had almost saved enough. But one glance at all the new stuff was enough to make his stomach turn over. From what he could see it was all high quality and would have come at a rare old price.

'Oh, don't be upset,' Maggie wheedled, taking his hand and giving it a squeeze. 'It didn't cost nearly as much as you might think. It's all second-hand and I . . .' She forced a few tears to her eyes and dabbed ineffectualy at her cheek with a tiny white handkerchief. 'I was feeling so low after all that's happened that I thought it would give me a lift.'

'How much?' he asked.

With a sigh she took the bank book from her pocket and reluctantly handed it to him.

As he looked hard at the amount left in the account his heart sank. Maggie had spent almost every pound he had earned since they had moved in, and there would be no chance of paying the mortgage off any time soon. And yet, he didn't have the heart to tell her off. As she had said, she'd had a rough time of it lately, so should he really be angry with her if these furnishings had given her a lift? There was just about enough money left to see them over Christmas with a few treats for the children, and then he would have to start saving again, although he would be sure not to give Maggie access to the bank account in future.

'So do you like it?'

She stared at him so hopefully that all he could do was nod.

PART 2

Chapter Twenty

Seven years later, Christmas Day 1912

'Merry Christmas and a very happy birthday, Annie,' Levi greeted Annie and the boys as they entered the kitchen early on Christmas morning. Maggie was still in bed, but Levi had come down early to light the fires so it would be warm for them when they got up.

'Sweet seventeen eh?' Levi chuckled as he handed Annie a small parcel wrapped in bright paper. 'That's from all of us,' he told her.

Annie blushed with pleasure, and opened the parcel carefully to reveal a small velvet box. When she sprang the lid she gasped as she looked down upon a slim gold chain from which was suspended a small locket.

'Oh, but it's lovely.' She had never owned a piece of jewellery and could hardly believe this was really for her. 'B-but it's too much.'

'Rubbish,' Levi snorted. 'You deserve it and a whole lot more besides for all you do for us. Come here and I'll fasten it for you.'

Once it was fastened around her neck, Annie crossed to the mirror and smiled broadly as she stared at the delicate locket. 'Thank you . . . thank you so much. I'll treasure it.'

Delighted she was so pleased with the gift, Levi poured them all a cup of tea.

The last few years hadn't been easy for the family. After Maggie had returned from the asylum and settled back in, she and Levi had had some very heated debates about Ellie. Eventually Levi had been forced to agree to Peggy and Sid keeping her, for Maggie had flatly refused to have her back in the house and had told him she'd rather she went to the workhouse. Peggy had blanched at the very thought.

On top of that, two years previously, Levi had got up for work one morning and found Barney's bed empty, and they'd not seen hide nor hair of him since. Levi had known he was no happier working the rounds with him than he had been at school, and he didn't have to wonder long about where he had gone, for that same day he heard that the circus had left town. He had no doubt that Barney had chosen to go with them and for a time he'd considered trying to track them down to bring him back home. But then common sense had kicked in. Even if he did find him, Barney would probably only run away again and he was a young man now and entitled to make his own choices, so against Maggie's wishes he had let him go. Eventually Barney had written to tell them that he was safe and well doing a job he enjoyed so they shouldn't worry about him. Maggie hadn't forgiven Levi for this. She still felt he should have brought Barney home.

Sometimes Levi barely recognised Maggie. Over the last seven years she had hardened to the point that she only ever seemed to be truly happy when she was spending money on fancy gowns to wear to church or on things for the house.

Through all this Annie had been a rock, keeping the house running and being at Maggie's beck and call with never a word of complaint. But now on this special day he was determined all that must change. Annie had been little more than an unpaid servant, but she was of an age to find a job outside the house. He was going to have a fight on his hands when he suggested it to Maggie, but on this point, he was prepared to stand up to her. Not today though. As well as being Annie's birthday it was Christmas Day, and he didn't want to do anything to spoil it.

Soon the family were seated about the table with steaming mugs of tea in front of them while Harry toasted bread on the fire. This was usually Annie's job but they were all determined that she should have a day off. As Levi peeped at her over the rim of his mug it struck him just how much she, too, had changed. Her hair now hung down her back as sleek and black as a raven's wing and her eyes were a brilliant blue, with long dark lashes that curled on her silky cream cheeks when she closed her eyes. She wasn't conventionally beautiful, though. The trend women favoured was to be curvy with curly hair, and although she was no longer skinny, Annie's figure was still slim and she was perhaps just a little too tall to be fashionable. But she was a striking girl who drew looks wherever she went.

More than a few of the local young men had shown an interest in her, including Mrs Taylor-Lloyd's son Reginald, who stalked her every time she set foot out of the house – but Annie wasn't interested. The only man she had eyes for was Charlie. They spent every spare moment they could together discussing books they had read or clips from the newspapers, but as yet there had been no romance between them.

After leaving the grammar school Charlie had gone on to college to train to be an accountant the year before, much to his mother's delight. He was the only one of her brood who had been interested in learning – apart from Annie, who Maggie still didn't consider to be a true member of the family. And anyway, the way she saw it education was wasted on girls. They would marry and have children – that was their purpose in life, surely – so why waste time and money on educating them?

They had almost finished their tea when the hall door opened and Maggie appeared, still clad in her dressing gown with her long coppery hair hanging in a plait across her shoulder.

'Merry Christmas,' she said, stifling a yawn. Then looking towards Annie she added, 'And happy birthday, Annie. I see Levi has given you the present he chose for you.'

'Yes, missus, thank you. It's beautiful.' Annie fingered the dainty locket happily as Maggie sniffed. She had considered it a rather extravagant present and had told Levi so when he showed it to her, but he had refused to take it back to the jeweller's to change it for something a little less expensive, insisting that Annie deserved the best. But Levi was always the same when it came to anything to do with Annie. He treated her as he would have treated a daughter and made no secret of the fact that he loved her as much as the boys. She was his little princess, and it rankled with Maggie.

Levi upset her further when he said, 'I've told Annie that she's not to lift a finger today. We can see to the Christmas dinner between us. She's already prepared everything, so how hard can it be?'

'It will have to be a late dinner in that case,' Maggie answered peevishly. 'Unless you want to see to it yourself. I'm going to the Christmas service at the church.'

'I don't mind cooking, really,' Annie piped up.

Levi held his hand up. 'No, you won't, hinny. I've told you this is your day and it's going to be one of rest.'

'Aye, we can chip in an' help,' Charlie and Harry said in unison. 'Though you might need to tell us how long everythin' takes to cook.'

Annie grinned. 'Of course.'

After two cups of tea the family exchanged their gifts and Maggie went to get changed for church. Annie was made to sit and watch while Levi and the boys popped the goose she had prepared the night before into the oven.

Throughout the morning, under Annie's supervision, everything was cooked to perfection and when they finally sat down to eat, the meal passed pleasantly.

'I think I might go outside for a while and get a bit of fresh air,' Annie said after dinner, feeling like a spare part while she watched the men coping with the washing up.

'What? Yer must be mad,' Levi told her glancing towards the window. 'It's enough to cut yer in two out there. I wouldn't be surprised if we didn't 'ave snow afore the day's out.'

Annie grinned as she put on her coat. 'I'll be fine,' she assured him and slipped out into the garden. Everywhere was coated in frost and looked magical as she wandered around admiring the red berries on the holly trees and the robin redbreast who was diligently pecking at the lawn in the hope of finding worms. She could hardly wait for the spring. The year before she had planted dozens of daffodil bulbs and snowdrops and she was looking forward to seeing the flowers come up.

Gradually, she became aware of a noise from over the hedge. It sounded like someone crying, so approaching the gap she cautiously peeped through and saw Eve. She looked broken-hearted and Annie was dismayed to see her so upset.

'Psst . . . Eve come here.' She frantically waved through the gap in the hedge and after a quick look over her shoulder, Eve approached.

'What's wrong?'

'Huh! It'd be easier to tell yer what's right.' Eve looked thoroughly miserable but after taking a deep shuddering breath she whispered. 'Oh, Annie, I'm in *such* trouble, I don't know what I'm gonna do.'

Annie frowned. 'What sort of trouble?'

Eve hesitated before telling her in a shaky voice, 'The worst sort . . . yer know?' She pointed to her stomach and when Annie continued to stare at her blankly, she sighed. 'You're such an innocent. I've missed two courses. *Now* do yer get me meanin'.'

As it dawned on Annie what Eve was saying, she gasped and put her hand over her mouth. 'Oh no! You mean . . . you think you're goin' to have a baby?'

'That's about the long an' short of it. An' when them bleedin' lot in there find out I'll be chucked out on me arse wi' nowhere to go.'

Like Annie, Eve had been taken from the workhouse so had no family to fall back on. They often spoke of what it would have been like to have been brought up by their birth mothers.

'It'll be back to the work'ouse fer me,' Eve went on, as more tears bubbled from her eyes.

'But won't the baby's father stand by you?' Annie asked softly. Eve had never mentioned having a boyfriend, so she was feeling slightly confused.

'The baby's father? Why it's the master's, ain't it? An' can you really see 'im leavin' the missus fer the likes o' me?' she snorted.

'B-but why did you let him . . .' Annie's voice trailed away at the look on Eve's face.

'*Why?* Well, I could 'ardly tell 'im to bugger off, could I? He's the gaffer an' if I'd turned 'im down he'd have found a reason to get rid o' me long before now. I've 'eard rumours that I ain't the first maid he's got in the family way, but 'is sort allus get away wi' it, don't they? Fer two pins I'd do a runner. Owt's better than endin' up back in the work'ouse, ain't it? But then I ain't showin' as yet, so I dare say I could stay 'ere fer a bit longer till the weather warms up.'

Annie nodded. 'Yes, do that, and we'll try and sort something out between us.'

'Like what?'

'Ah, here you are. I'd get back inside if I was you, girl. The kitchen is full of dirty dinner pots and Cook is ready to rip your head off if you don't get back in there soon.'

Both sets of startled eyes turned to see Reginald strolling across the frozen grass towards them, puffing away on a large cigar and blowing blue smoke into the frosty air.

'Er . . . right y'are, sir.' Eve cast one last despairing look at Annie before scuttling away like a cat with its tail on fire.

Poor, poor thing, Annie thought as she watched her go. What a terrible position to be in. And worse still, she didn't have a single clue what she could do to help.

'Having a nice Christmas Day are you, Annie?' Reginald asked smarmily.

Turning her attention away from Eve and back to him, Annie shuddered. Why was it that men of his class thought they could treat women as they pleased? Giving a curt nod she turned to leave, but his hand snaked out and he caught her arm through the gap in the hedge.

'Oh, don't go rushing off yet. I was going to ask you if you fancied going to the picture house one evening?'

She shook his hand away and glared at him. 'Thanks, but I'm rather busy at the minute.' And with that she strode away.

Reginald watched her walk away with a frown on his face. She was a feisty little devil there was no doubt about it, and yet the more she rejected his advances the more he wanted her. He supposed it was because most girls fell at his feet the moment he batted his eyelashes at them, but that certainly wasn't the case with young Annie. She should be grateful that someone like him was showing an interest in her. Still, he'd bring her to heel eventually, he was sure of it.

Dropping the cigar onto the frozen earth he ground it out with the heel of his boot and made back for the house.

Chapter Twenty-One

That night Annie barely slept as she thought of poor Eve's dilemma. But try as she might, she couldn't think of a way to help her. Boxing Day passed peacefully with the family all at home, apart from Barney, but as usual Maggie chose to spend most of the day in her room. Annie would often hear her talking away to someone when she passed her bedroom door, and she had a funny feeling she was speaking to her dead daughter, although she never mentioned it to the boys or Levi. As far as they knew, that disturbing episode in Maggie's life was over, but Annie knew differently.

The following day, as Annie was tackling the breakfast pots after Levi had returned to work, the back door opened and Susan breezed in sporting a large black eye that a boxer would have been proud of.

'Good grief, what happened to you?' The words were out before Annie could stop them.

The young woman self-consciously pulled the brim of her hat a little lower. 'Well, that's a nice greeting, I must say!'

Annie blushed guiltily. 'Sorry, Susan . . . I mean Miss Susanne. We weren't expecting you, but it's lovely to see you.'

Susan glanced around the room. 'Where is everyone?'

'The missus is still in bed, the boys have gone out for a walk and the mister started back to work today. I can nip up and fetch the missus for you if you like.'

'No, no, I think I'll just have a cup of tea first, if you don't mind. I've been travelling since very early this morning and I'm rather tired now.'

'Of course.' Annie filled the kettle at the sink.

Susan watched her thoughtfully. They had kept in touch by post, but it had been almost a year since she had seen Annie and just as she had expected, the girl had turned into a beauty. She took off her hat, coat and gloves and sank down onto the sofa at the side of the fire, feeling exhausted.

'Did you have an accident?' Annie asked innocently when she carried a cup of tea over to her.

Taking the cup, Susan nodded. 'Er . . . yes, I did actually. I slipped on the ice outside my flat a couple of days ago and banged my face on a wall.'

Even to Annie this didn't ring true but she didn't say anything.

'So, how has Maggie been?'

'Oh, not so bad,' Annie said cagily.

Susan nodded. 'She's still talking to Penny then?'

'I'm not sure, but I do hear her talking to someone.'

'Hmm!' Susan took a sip of tea. 'And how are you?' It was such a waste for Annie to be skivvying. With her looks she could have been anything, given the right introductions, which, could Annie have known it, was one of the reasons she was there.

'Oh, I'm fine. Would you like something to eat?' Annie asked.

'No, if you don't mind, I'll go up and have a lie-down after I've drunk this.'

'I'll run up and put some fresh sheets on the spare bed,' Annie volunteered. 'When the missus gets up it'll be a lovely surprise for 'er to know that you're 'ere.'

As soon as the girl had hurried away Susan's hand rose to tentatively touch her black eye and a lump formed in her throat. It wasn't the first time Theo had hurt her over the last couple of years, but this attack had been particularly brutal, and yet still she couldn't find it in herself to leave him. She tried to convince herself that eventually he would make an honest woman of her and they would move away from London to a little cottage in the country with roses round the door. They would start their family then: two girls for her

171

and two boys for him. But it still seemed a very long way off. Biting back the tears, she went to the mirror and patted her hair into place before going upstairs to see if her room was ready.

She had fled from Theo's attack the night before after throwing a few gowns and essentials into a bag, and she had spent the night on a hard wooden bench in Euston Station before catching the mail train to the Midlands early that morning. Now she just needed to sleep. Surely everything would look so much better when she was rested. She could only hope so.

'So how long are you here for?' Maggie asked Susan later that day, and Annie wondered if perhaps she wasn't quite as pleased to see her sister as she had thought she would be.

'I thought I might stay for at least a week this time. If you don't mind having me, that is?'

'Of course we don't,' Maggie replied.

Annie didn't think she sounded sincere, although she herself was delighted with the idea. She had never met anyone as glamorous as Susan before and loved listening to her telling them about her trips to the theatres and music halls. She seemed to lead such an exciting life, and Annie couldn't help but envy her.

The next morning, when Annie took her up a cup of tea in bed, Susan pulled herself up onto her elbows and pointed to a beautiful gown laid over the back of a chair.

'Try that on,' she ordered.

Annie's mouth fell open. '*Me?*' she squeaked, stroking the luxurious fabric. It was made of a very fine corduroy in a rich plum colour trimmed with black braid. Annie had never seen anything so lovely in her life. Even the expensive gowns Maggie favoured couldn't compare to this one.

'Yes of course you,' Susan encouraged. 'I packed it by mistake, to be honest. It's a little tight on me now but I think it might fit you. Go on, try it on.'

Feeling a little embarrassed Annie took off her plain blouse and drab skirt, and slipped the dress over her head before fumbling clumsily with the row of tiny black buttons that ran from the waist right up to the high neckline.

'It's perfect on you,' Susan declared when Annie turned to face her, her cheeks glowing. 'Go and have a look at yourself in the mirror on the landing.'

Annie didn't need asking twice and lifting the skirt she tripped away. Staring into the mirror, she twirled, barely recognising herself. Susan came to stand beside her with a broad smile on her face.

'You're a very beautiful young woman,' Susan told her. 'So, what do you intend to do with your life?'

Annie frowned. 'Do? Well . . . I dare say I'll stay here for as long as I'm needed, seein' to the family.'

'And what a waste that would be,' Susan admonished her. 'Why, with your looks you could be anything you wanted to be. In London there are countless opportunities for girls like you.'

'Really?' Strangely enough, Annie had never really given much thought to her future, but suddenly she felt excited. 'Such as what?'

'Anything, really. Although with your looks you could be on stage. An actress, a dancer or a singer perhaps?'

Annie sighed and shook her head. 'It all sounds well an' good but I don't think that would be fer the likes o' me. It's like this gown, it's just beautiful but where would I ever go to wear it?'

'There are lots of places you could wear it if you lived in London,' Susan said cajolingly. 'And lots more jobs you could do if you don't want to be in the public eye. Levi tells me you're quite bright?'

'I ain't too bad,' Annie said cautiously. 'An' I would like to be a nurse more than anythin', though that takes a lot o' training. I did think I might get a job in an office or sommat like that though.'

'There you are then. Though I think we'd have to work on the way you speak a bit, get rid of that local dialect. Anyway, just give it some thought. I'm sure Levi wouldn't want you to stay here and miss opportunities.' She didn't say the same about Maggie, because she'd seen how hard Annie worked and knew her sister wouldn't want to do all her own household chores again.

A thought occurred to Annie, and glancing up and down the landing to make sure no one was about, she asked cautiously, 'Could I ask you something? In private like?'

'Of course. Come back into my room.'

Soon they were seated side by side on Susan's bed. 'Go on then, spit it out. I can see there's something bothering you and I don't bite.'

'You said there's opportunities for girls like me in London an' I was wonderin' . . . Well, a friend o' mine 'as got 'erself into trouble an' she needs to get away from 'ere but she ain't got nowhere to go.'

'I see.' Susan guessed immediately what sort of trouble Annie was referring to. 'And how old is this friend?'

'About a year or so older than me,' Annie told her.

'And is she a pretty girl?'

Annie frowned as she thought about it. 'I dare say she is.'

'Hmm, perhaps I ought to meet her. I'm not making any promises, mind.'

Annie nodded eagerly. 'Oh yes, I could arrange that easy enough.'

'Then let's see what we can do for her, and in the meantime, you think about coming with me too. I would put it right with Levi. Now, are you going to accept this gown?'

Annie twirled, then bent and placed a kiss on Susan's cheek. 'All right and thank you. Even if I never get to wear it at least I can look at it.'

Susan's hand rose to touch the place Annie had kissed and she felt a sudden surge of protectiveness towards her. Perhaps Annie wasn't cut out for the sort of life she had lined up for her after all. She was so sweet and innocent.

Annie, meanwhile, was taking the gown off before getting back into her working clothes. 'I'd best get on. I've a list o' jobs waitin' to be done as long as yer arm, an' the missus will be after me if I don't get on wi' 'em.'

With the gown folded across her arm she left the room and Susan suddenly felt like crying. She could remember when she had been innocent like Annie, but it all seemed a very long time ago now. With a sigh she lifted her hairbrush and began to pin her long fair hair into the chic chignon on the back of her head that she favoured.

It was two days before Annie was able to fleetingly introduce Susan to Eve. She had arranged to meet her at the end of Swan Lane on the pretence of going for a walk.

'Why would yer want to go out in this weather?' Levi questioned from his place at the side of the fire when they started to get into their outdoor clothes. 'It's freezin' out there, take my word fer it. I've been out in it all day.'

'Oh, we shan't be long,' Susan said breezily as she wrapped a scarf about her neck. 'I just feel like I need a bit of fresh air.'

'Must be mad,' Levi muttered with a wry grin. 'You're likely to catch yer death o' cold.'

They set off, picking their way carefully along the pavement and soon they saw Eve waiting forlornly for them in a pool of yellow light cast by the streetlamp.

'Hello dear, you must be Eve.' Susan held her hand out. 'Annie tells me you're in a bit of bother.'

'Huh! That'd be puttin' it mildly,' Eve said miserably.

Susan was studying her carefully. She was certainly an attractive girl, or at least she could be with the right clothes and a little make-up. If Eve was agreeable, she was sure Theo would welcome her into his little band of girls once her problem was out of the way.

Susan dipped her hand into her coat pocket and drew out some change. She handed it to Annie saying, 'Pop down to the corner shop, would you, pet? I fancy some pear drops. I'll stay here and have a chat to Eve.'

Annie left them to it and once she was some distance away, Susan said, 'I may be able to help you but there would be conditions. Here's what I'm proposing – you could live with me and act as my maid until after the baby is born and then we'll get it adopted or fostered out. And then . . .'

As she went on with the rest of her proposal, Eve's face paled. Susan was telling her that she would be an escort for gentlemen, which in her language meant being a whore with a pimp who would take the majority of her earnings. But then, wasn't that what she had been for Mr Taylor-Lloyd for as far back as she could remember? And she hadn't been paid at all for that. And what was the alternative? If she turned Susan's offer down, she had no doubt she would be turfed out onto the streets once the baby started to show, even if she told the missus that the child was her husband's. She had no doubt the woman would never believe her and then the only place she would find shelter would be in the workhouse.

Seeing her hesitation, Susan went on cajolingly, 'Theo would see that you had a lovely flat to live in and beautiful gowns to wear. He would never expect any of his girls to entertain wealthy gentlemen in rags. And, of course, the men would be more than generous and no doubt shower you with expensive gifts. I quite understand if you need some time to think about it, but my only request is that you don't tell Annie or any of my family what I really do for a living. I don't think they would understand. Will you do that for me?'

'O' course, an' thanks fer the offer, missus.'

They both noticed Annie coming towards them and, making a hasty decision, Eve told her, 'An' yes please. I'd like to take yer up on yer offer.'

'Excellent. We'll tell Annie that you're going to maid for me till the baby's born and that I'm going to get you a job in London when it's over. She needn't know what the job is. I shall be going back to London early in the new year. Can you be ready to travel with me?'

'You just tell me when.' Now that she was getting over the shock of Susan's proposal, Eve was beginning to feel quite excited about the idea. 'I shan't be tellin' the family I'm goin' either. I don't feel I owe 'em owt.'

Annie came abreast of them and they started to walk back towards the house.

'I've agreed to let Eve stay with me in London until the baby is born. She can be my maid,' Susan told Annie. 'Obviously she doesn't want to keep the child, but it will be no problem getting it adopted in London, and then if she likes living there, I shall find her a job.'

Annie's face lit up. 'Why, that's great news.' She smiled at Eve. She'd been really worried about her but it sounded like her luck was about to change.

'So why don't you come back with us too and have a little holiday?' Susan suggested.

Annie frowned. 'Oh, I don't know about that! I don't reckon the missus could spare me.'

Susan giggled girlishly. 'You just leave my sister to me.'

A little worm of excitement wriggled in Annie's belly. *Her* go to London? It sounded like a different world. But if only she could! She would get to see all the famous landmarks that she had only ever seen and read about in books. Buckingham Palace, the Tower of London, the River Thames to name but a few. Still, she told herself, she mustn't get carried away. There was every chance the missus would refuse to let her go, but at least Eve would be all right, which was the most important thing.

Chapter Twenty-Two

The following evening after dinner, Susan put her suggestion that Annie should return to London with her for a short holiday to Maggie. It was met with exactly the response Annie had expected.

'*Holiday?* London? Whatever for?' Maggie was clearly very unhappy with the idea.

'What do you mean what for?' Susan retaliated hotly. 'From what I've seen of all the work she does, the girl deserves a break, and I thought you'd be happy for her to have one.'

'All the work she does,' Maggie scoffed. 'Why, she has it far easier here than she did in the workhouse. If it wasn't for me, she'd no doubt still be languishing there!'

Susan had hoped that if she could make Maggie feel slightly guilty about all the work Annie did, she might agree to it, but it seemed her plan was failing dismally.

It was then that Levi stepped in. 'Now hold on a minute, Mags,' he protested. 'You can't deny the girl has been a godsend to us all. How do you think me an' the lads would 'ave managed when you were ill without 'er? To be honest I was plannin' to 'ave a word with you any time now about her future.'

'What do you mean?' Maggie was incensed. It wasn't often that Levi stood up to her. He was too afraid of her getting ill again, but it seemed that if it was about his little princess, he was prepared to stand his ground.

'The lass is seventeen,' he pointed out. 'Most girls of her age are already walkin' out with young men an' goin' to dances an' the picture 'ouse, an' what have you, but she barely sets foot out o' the door. I reckon it's time she started to build a future fer 'erself. She needs to find a job, sommat she enjoys doin', an' have a bit of a social life. You did at her age, didn't you?'

'Well . . . I . . .' Maggie tossed her head, at a loss as to how to answer.

'I think a little break in London would do 'er a power o' good. Broaden 'er horizons a bit, so to speak. Susan, er . . . I mean Susanne would look after 'er,' Levi went on, sensing an advantage.

'But she doesn't have the sort of clothes she would need to wear in London,' Maggie pointed out quickly, desperate for an excuse to stop this happening. 'And we certainly can't afford to rig her out just for a short holiday; chances are she'd never wear the clothes again.'

Levi found this statement mildly amusing. Maggie certainly didn't mind paying out for her own expensive gowns or things for the house.

'That won't be a problem,' Susan assured her with an angelic smile. 'I'm afraid I've put a little weight on and I have an armoire full of clothes at home that Annie is welcome to. I've already given her one gown, as it happens.'

Maggie's shoulders slumped. It seemed that this holiday was going to go ahead whether she liked it or not. Which meant that she would have to be head cook and bottle washer and she didn't like the idea at all.

'So that's settled,' Levi said when there were no further objections forthcoming. 'When Susanne goes back, Annie can go with her and have a break.'

Maggie's face was set in grim lines, but she didn't argue further.

Annie had kept quiet throughout the argument, never dreaming that Maggie would agree. And though she could see Maggie was furious, she was too excited to care!

Later that evening Annie managed to catch Eve outside when the young maid took some rubbish to the bin. 'Stand by, Levi has agreed for me to come to London with you and Susanne when she goes back. Are you sure you still want to go?' she hissed.

'Not 'alf!' Eve glanced back towards the house. 'Far as I'm concerned, the sooner I get out o' this bleedin' place the better. I owe that lot bugger all, an' I ain't got no intentions o' tellin' 'em I'm goin' either.'

'All right, nearer the time I'll tell Susanne to get three train tickets. Just be ready. Try to get your things packed.'

Eve snorted with derision. 'Huh! That won't take long. You just gi' me the word when you're ready.'

'*Eve!*'

Both girls looked towards the door of the Taylor-Lloyds' kitchen to see a red-faced cook glaring at them.

'Get yerself in 'ere this minute,' she barked. 'You ain't paid to stand about gossipin'.'

'I ain't usually paid at all,' Eve muttered beneath her breath, as she turned and went back in.

The next day, while Levi was at work, Maggie had two visitors. The first was Flo, who had come to see Susan.

'Is that a black eye I can see?' Flo narrowed her eyes and peered at Susan closely.

Susan had tried to hide it with make-up but although it was fading it was still visible. 'Yes, I had a fall,' she answered challengingly, taking in her sister's blowsy appearance. She really had let herself go.

'Hmm, I'll believe yer, though thousands wouldn't.' Flo took a seat opposite Maggie and asked, 'An' how are you feelin'?'

'Fine. Why shouldn't I be?'

'All right, all right, leave me bloody 'ead on.' Flo sniffed. Turning to Annie, she said, 'So what about a cup o' tea then? An' a slice o' that cake on the table wouldn't go down amiss.'

'I would have thought you'd be avoiding sweet stuff. You've put on an awful lot of weight,' Susan observed.

Flo seemed to puff up to twice her size. '*Cheeky mare!*' she snapped. 'Just cos you go round like a painted lady decked out like a Christmas tree!'

'I make no apology for making the best of myself,' Susan answered serenely.

Seeing that this was in danger of blowing up into a full-scale row, Annie quickly poured some tea and carried it over to Flo, before going to cut a large slice of the cake for her. It had only just come out of the oven and she'd been hoping to save it for the lads when they got home.

'Ta, ducks.' Slightly mollified, Flo tucked in as if she hadn't eaten for a week.

'I hear that Peggy's Sid ain't too grand,' Flo told them when she had gobbled a second slice.

Maggie frowned. 'Oh really? I wondered why she hadn't been round for a while. What's wrong with him?'

'He's 'ad that flu thing that's goin' round an' it's settled on 'is chest, apparently. He ain't been to work for a few days now, accordin' to what I 'eard.'

'Oh dear.' Sid was a good worker and would never take time off unless he had to. 'I'll have to try and pop round over the next few days and see how he is.'

The conversation turned to other things but none of them were sorry when Flo finally heaved herself out of the chair, dropping crumbs all over the floor before leaving.

'She doesn't get any easier, does she?' Susan grinned.

Maggie shook her head. 'No, she doesn't.'

Because they usually had their main meal in the evening, Annie made them all a light lunch of bread, cheese and pickles and they had just finished when the back door opened and Barney strolled in.

'*Barney!*' Maggie leapt out of her seat and flew across the room to her son, hugging him tightly and causing him to flush a dull brick red. 'Where have you been? We've been worried sick about you.'

'Yer know where I've been, Ma. I don't wanna be a rag-an'-bone man like me dad. I earn me livin' bare-knuckle fightin' now, an' I live wi' the circus folk.'

Maggie held him at arm's length and could hardly believe the change in him. It was a long while since she had last set eyes on him and in that time, he had changed from a gangly youth into a very handsome, muscly young man. His hair was now past his collar with a tendency to wave and he towered above her. He wore a gaily coloured kerchief about his neck and a gold hoop glistened in one of his ears.

'Oh Barney,' she choked. 'Isn't that rather dangerous?'

He laughed. 'Not fer me. I'm more than able to look after meself.' He looked towards Susan and nodded, ''Ello, Auntie Susan.'

'Susanne,' she corrected him with a smile.

Next, he looked at Annie and his mouth dropped open in surprise. She had changed drastically in the last two years and didn't resemble the young girl he remembered. With her beautiful black hair tied into her neck with a blue ribbon the exact colour of her eyes, she had turned into a beauty just as his father had always predicted. Even so, he had never had eyes for any girl but Mercy and he couldn't see that changing.

'Are you ready to come back home now?' Maggie asked hopefully, drawing his attention back to her. 'You don't have to go into the family business if you don't want to. I'm sure we could find you some other job to do.'

'Sorry, Ma, but I like the way o' life I 'ave now.' He shook his head apologetically. 'I wasn't even sure if I should come an' see you. I didn't know what sort of a welcome I'd get after I cleared off the way I did.'

'You will *always* have a welcome here,' she told him, gripping tightly to his hands. She didn't want to let him go in case he disappeared again. 'But how long are you here for? A week? A month? Longer?'

'I'm afraid this is only a flyin' visit. I've got a fight on in Sibson wi' a pugilist from Leicester this evenin', so I've not got long. I just thought I'd come an' check how you all were.'

'But you *will* come and see us again before you leave, won't you?' she implored him. 'Your father will want to see you.'

'Aye, all right, I'll do that,' he promised.

He sat down beside her then and told them about all the places he had visited with the circus, and what he'd been doing since he left them. They all listened, enthralled. He clearly loved working with the animals and even enjoyed his fights, and in fairness, Maggie had to admit that his way of life didn't seem to be doing him any harm. He looked as fit as a fiddle and certainly seemed content enough.

It was shortly after that Charlie and Harry arrived home and they too were impressed with the change they saw in their big brother. The boys made a huge fuss of each other and Barney asked, 'An' 'ow is little Ellie doin'?' He'd always felt a little guilty because he'd been slightly jealous of her when she had first come to live with them.

'Oh, she's thriving with Peggy,' Charlie told him. He still hadn't quite forgiven his mother for refusing to have her home when she'd returned from the asylum. 'Though she isn't so little now. She's a tyrant and I heard today that Sid isn't doing so good.'

'We heard that too. I must go round and find out what's going on.' Maggie shook her head.

All too soon it was time for Barney to leave and when he rose, Maggie reached for him. 'Must you really go?'

He nodded. 'I'm afraid so, but don't worry, I'll be back to see yer all again afore we move on.'

As he made for the door, he looked towards Annie. 'And how are you? I must say I 'ardly recognised yer. Yer seem to have grown up all of a sudden.'

'So have you,' she countered with a grin.

Maggie watched him go with tears in her eyes.

'He's happy,' Susan assured her as she saw the tears glistening on her sister's lashes. She patted her arm. 'That's all you can ask for your kids, surely?'

Maggie nodded. 'I know but I can't help but think I've lost him as well as Penelope.'

'Rubbish. He said he'd be back to see you, didn't he? All young people fly the nest when they're ready. It will be Charlie and Harry's turn next, so you'd better be prepared for it. Now come on, get your shoes and coat on and we'll pop round to the courtyards and see what's wrong with Sid, eh? There's no point in sitting here and getting all maudlin, is there!'

Chapter Twenty-Three

It felt strange to be returning to her old home – Peggy usually visited her on Swan Lane – and as Susan and Maggie crossed the courtyard to the tiny cottage, Maggie lifted her skirts and wrinkled her nose.

'I hadn't realised just how cramped we were, living here,' she commented.

Susan frowned. Maggie really was a dreadful snob.

On entering the cottage, they were greeted by Ellie. She was eight years old now, attending the local school, and the apple of Peggy and Sid's eyes, which reflected in her bright little personality. Her curly hair, which no amount of brushing seemed to tame, was tied back in a pretty red ribbon and she smiled a greeting.

'Mammy is upstairs wi' Daddy. He ain't very well,' she told the visitors regretfully.

'Then why don't you and I wait here while Maggie goes upstairs to see how he is?' Susan said tactfully. 'Is this your dolly here? Why don't you tell me what her name is.'

Ellie got Clara, her rag doll, and took her across to Susan while Maggie crossed to the narrow steep staircase in the corner of the small room. At the top of the stairs, she tapped on the door to the room that used to be her and Levi's bedroom.

It was opened by a tired-looking Peggy. 'Oh, it's you, pet.' She held her finger to her lips. 'Come on in but be quiet, he's just dropped off. He were awake all night coughin' 'is lungs up, bless 'im.'

Maggie glanced towards Sid and she was shocked to see how ill he looked. His eyes seemed to have sunk into his face and he was as pale as putty. His every breath was laboured and she could hear his lungs rasping.

'Poor love,' Maggie whispered. 'Why didn't you tell me how ill he was? And why didn't Levi tell me, come to that? He must have known. He drops his loads off here every day.'

'I asked him not to,' Peggy answered as she swiped her hand across her brow. 'There's nothing you can do and I was hoping he'd be on the mend by now. But to be honest, he seems worse. The doctor called in again this mornin' an' the fear is that it could turn to pneumonia if he don't start to improve soon. But come on, we'll go downstairs an' have a cuppa an' let him rest while he can.'

They made their way back downstairs and Peggy put the kettle on while Maggie sat down, carefully arranging her skirts about her as she glanced around the room, wondering how she had ever managed to live here.

'Is there anything we can do for you?' Susan asked kindly. She'd noticed that Maggie hadn't offered, but then Maggie was used to young Annie waiting on her. To her mind it would do her sister the power of good to realise just how much work Annie did once she took her off to London.

'No, pet, we're managin', but thank you fer offerin'.' Peggy gave a weary smile as she measured some tea leaves into the big brown pot standing on the table. Poor Sid hadn't worked for almost two weeks now and money was tight, but Peggy's pride would never allow her to tell them that. Luckily, her two youngest boys were working now. Ricky, her oldest, had left home some time ago to go to sea. Wilf worked on the railways, and Tom, her youngest, had recently started working down the pit, and they had been happy to tip most of their wages up while their father had been ill, otherwise Peggy didn't know how she would have managed.

Ellie had retreated to the hearthrug where she was happily chattering away to Clara, but Maggie barely gave her a second glance.

'Our Tom is doin' well down the pit,' Peggy told them proudly when the tea had mashed and she was pouring it into mugs.

'Hmm, it's just a shame that you'll still have this one reliant on you,' Maggie said unfeelingly as she glanced towards Ellie, quite forgetting that it had been she who had fetched the child from the workhouse.

'Oh, she's no trouble at all.' Peggy smiled lovingly at the little girl. 'She's the daughter I allus wanted an' I don't regret havin' her for a single moment.' She handed them their drinks. 'Sorry I ain't got no sugar. I seem to 'ave run out an' I ain't 'ad time to get to the shop yet.'

'She's a lovely child,' Susan commented and Peggy's chest puffed with pride.

'So, when are yer goin' back to London, pet?' Peggy asked after a time.

'Next week, and I'm taking Annie with me for a little holiday.'

'Really?' Peggy was shocked that Maggie had allowed this. 'How long for?'

'As long as she wants to stay.'

Maggie sniffed her disapproval. 'I can't say as I'm keen on the idea,' she said peevishly. 'But Levi seems to think it will do her good. Says it will broaden her horizons and perhaps give her some idea what she wants to do in the future.' She shook her head as she took a sip of tea from the stoneware mug and wrinkled her nose. Tea always tasted so much better when it was served in a china cup and saucer, but then Peggy had never been one for wanting the finer things in life. 'Personally, I would have thought it was obvious what she'll do,' she went on. 'She'll meet some young man, settle down and have a family. Isn't that what all young women do?'

'Not quite all,' Susan reminded her with a wink at Peggy. 'I'm not married, am I?'

'More fool you,' Maggie said shortly. 'I'm sure you would have had offers.'

Peggy quickly steered the conversation in another direction, but shortly after, the sound of Sid having a terrible coughing fit floated down the stairs. Rising, she told her visitors apologetically, 'I'm so sorry, but I shall 'ave to go up to 'im, poor love.'

'You carry on,' Susan told her with a warm smile. 'And if you need anything, be sure to send one of the lads round to get us.'

She and Maggie took their leave and as they walked along Abbey Street Maggie shook her head as she saw the children playing in the road. This was where her beloved Penny had met her end.

'I'd forgotten just how rough it was around here,' she commented.

Susan could have said, *Yes you have, and now you've forgotten your roots*, but she clamped her mouth shut. Anything she said could only lead to another row and she was trying to spend her last few days with the family in peace.

Before Annie knew it, it was New Year, and on Sunday evening she packed a carpet bag in preparation for setting off for London very early the next morning. She and Susan had told Eve of the arrangements and she had promised to be waiting for them at the end of the road.

'You just be careful now, and don't get venturing out wi'out Susanne,' Levi told Annie gravely when she went downstairs that evening to say her goodbyes, knowing that the house would still be sleeping when they left early the next morning. 'London is a big place for a young girl to get lost in.'

'She'll be fine,' Susan assured him with a gentle smile.

Levi dipped a hand into his pocket and gave Annie some coins. He would have liked to give her more but it was the best he could do at that time. They had a very expensive Aubusson rug due to arrive that week that Maggie had ordered, and it would have to be paid for.

'Just in case yer need anything,' he told her as she opened her mouth to object. She could see Maggie wasn't happy about him giving the money to her.

'I'm sure Susan will see to her needs,' Maggie said waspishly.

'I certainly will, but it'll be nice for her not to have to ask me for every penny if she sees something she likes,' Susan told her.

'An' when you come back, we'll talk about what yer want to do,' Levi went on fondly. 'You're old enough to have a job, if yer'd like.'

'Huh!' Maggie tossed her head in disgust. 'Since when do women have jobs?'

'Lots of women work now. Times are changing,' Susan pointed out. 'I work and Peggy works, so why not Annie?'

Maggie clamped her lips together. It felt as if they were all ganging up on her so she might as well hold her tongue.

Even Monty next door had managed to catch Annie when she ventured outside to put some scraps into the pig bin so that he could say goodbye too.

'I won't be gone forever, you know,' she told him with a smile.

'I'm pleased to hear it. But please take care, won't you? London is a big place.' It was plain to see that he was more than a little fond of her.

'So I'm told.'

Annie had smiled as she made her way indoors. Monty was nice, nothing at all like his brother Reggie or his horrible stuck-up mother!

It was only when Annie had gone to her room that evening that the first little seeds of doubt began. She would miss Levi and Charlie very much, Monty too, but then as she had told him, it wasn't as if she was going away forever, was it?

Smiling again she clambered into the icy cold bed and despite being sure that she wouldn't sleep a wink, she was asleep in seconds.

Chapter Twenty-Four

'That's it then; we're all ready for the off,' Susan told Annie cheerfully the next morning as she secured her hat with a large hat pin. It was still pitch-black and bitterly cold outside and the rest of the house was silent save for the ticking of the clock on the mantelpiece.

Annie was dressed in the gown Susan had given her and felt like a princess. It was such a shame that she'd been forced to put her old coat on over it and wear her old worn-down boots, but then she was grateful for the gown.

As they set off into the darkness and started up the road, their feet crunching on the frosty pavements, Annie's stomach was in knots. What if Eve hadn't managed to slip away? What would become of her? But then they saw her standing under the glow of the gas lamp on the corner, and Annie heaved a sigh of relief. Hopefully this would be the start of a better life for her.

'Eeh! I ain't slept a wink an' I were gettin' worried yer weren't goin' to come,' Eve greeted them. 'Mrs Taylor-Lloyd will 'ave a dicky fit when she gets up an' finds the fires ain't lit, the table ain't laid fer breakfast, an' I've done a flit!'

'Serves her right, the way she treats you,' Susan responded. 'Don't give her another thought. She's had more than her money's worth out of you over the years and you owe her nothing! Now come along, girls, don't dawdle. We have a train to catch.'

Soon they were on the platform of Nuneaton Railway Station watching the train chugging towards them. It pulled into the station in a hiss of steam and smoke, reminding Annie of a great fire-breathing dragon, and once again her nerves kicked in. Eve wasn't much better. Neither of the girls had ever travelled on a train before and were shocked at just how big it was close up.

'Come on, we should have a carriage to ourselves this early in the morning.' Susan ushered them aboard and sure enough they found an empty carriage and lifted their luggage onto the overhead luggage racks before taking their seats.

'Don't look so worried, girls,' Susan chuckled. 'It's as safe as houses, I promise you.'

Just then, the station master blew his whistle and once again the train chugged into life. It was too dark to see anything beyond the windows, so the girls sat back and tried to relax. As it gradually grew lighter, they stared from the windows at the passing fields and began to feel a little better. Susan had fallen into a doze, so they spoke in whispers so as not to disturb her.

'Are you excited?' Annie asked. This was much more of a life-changing event for Eve than it was for her after all. Annie was only going for a holiday whereas Eve had no intention of ever coming back.

'Yes, I am,' Eve admitted. 'Although I feel bad about givin' the baby away when it comes. The poor little sod didn't ask to be born, did it? But then, after the way it came about, I don't think I could ever 'ave any feelin's fer it. I'd see the master's face every time I looked at it, an' Susanne 'as promised it'll go to a good 'ome, so it's fer the best all round, ain't it? Once that's over, I can get on wi' me life. I must admit I'll miss Master Monty though. He were the only one o' that family that ever 'ad a kind word for me.'

'Yes, he is nice,' Annie agreed.

'Handsome an all, an' I reckon he's got a soft spot fer you.'

'For me?' Annie looked shocked. 'No, I don't think so. Can you imagine what his mother would say if he were to show an interest in someone like you or me?'

'Ah well, we're all entitled to us own opinions an' I'm tellin' yer that young chap is sweet on yer an' yer could do a lot worse.'

When Annie frowned Eve decided enough had been said on the subject and they lapsed into silence enjoying the views from the window.

After some time the fields beyond the windows gave way to more built-up areas and the girls realised they must be nearing London. Susan had slept the entire way but when she woke and glanced around, she smiled.

'Ah, we'll be coming into Euston shortly. Lift the luggage down, girls.'

As soon as they arrived at the station, they stepped down onto the platform and both Eve and Annie were shocked. They had never seen so many people all in one place before and suddenly it felt as if they were a million miles away from the little market town they had grown up in.

'Now, a word of warning.' Susan looked at them both seriously. 'Hang on tightly to your bags; this place is alive with thieves and pickpockets. Once we get outside, I'll hail us a cab.'

In truth neither of the girls had anything worth stealing but they clung on to their bags just the same as they followed Susan. It was even busier when they emerged from the station onto Euston Road and they looked about in amazement. There were horses and carts of all shapes and sizes, the new-fangled motor cars that Mr Taylor-Lloyd was always talking about, and people of all nationalities milling about.

'We haven't got far to go now, girls,' Susan assured them as she saw the dazed look on their faces. She could remember the capital having much the same effect on her when she had first arrived.

Stepping to the edge of the pavement she raised her hand and a hansom cab pulled up. Ushering the girls inside, she gave her address to the driver.

'I live in a flat in Russell Square,' Susan told them as they set off, and soon they merged onto the busy roads. Both girls leant forward and stared at the hustle and bustle from the windows. They passed elderly ladies standing on street corners selling little bunches of lucky heather and tiny bags of birdseed from trays hung about their necks for the many pigeons that were flying about. There were barrows of jellied eels that looked disgusting, and homeless people listlessly begging for money or food from anyone that passed.

After a time, the cab pulled into a square lined with huge houses with a large fenced-in lawn in the centre of it.

'This is it,' Susan trilled happily. 'We're home.'

They alighted the cab and once Susan had paid the driver and added a generous tip, she led them towards a Georgian townhouse that seemed to stretch up into the sky. It looked very grand, and as they climbed the marble steps that led up to the door, it was opened by a young man in a smart uniform.

'Good day, Miss Belle,' he greeted Susan with a welcoming smile.

Annie was slightly confused. She was sure that she'd heard Levi mention that the missus's and Susan's maiden name had been Willis.

'Is there any mail for me, David?'

He crossed to some small wooden pigeonholes in one wall, took out some letters and passed them to Susan.

'Thank you.' She bundled them into her bag and beckoned the girls to follow her along the ground floor hallway, pausing to unlock a door.

'Each of the floors in this building has its own self-contained flat,' she told the girls. 'And this one is mine.'

They found themselves in yet another hallway, slightly larger than the one in the main foyer, with several doors leading off it. Susan marched on and threw open the one at the end, and they stepped into a lounge that quite literally took their breath away. It was lavishly, and obviously very expensively, furnished with a thick-pile carpet in a soft cream colour, that stretched from wall to wall. A set of French doors led out to a charming small garden, and comfortable velvet settees and chairs were strategically placed about an ornate marble fireplace in which a fire was burning brightly.

Heavy velvet curtains hung at the windows and small, highly polished tables covered in what appeared to be very expensive trinkets and plants were dotted about.

'So, who lit the fire if yer've been away?' Annie enquired curiously.

Susan laughed. 'Oh, that would be Milly, my daily. She always lights the fire if one is needed whether I'm here or not.' As she spoke, she removed her coat and threw it across the back of a chair. As if the mention of her had conjured her up, a young woman in a cotton mob cap and a voluminous white apron appeared from another doorway leading off from the lounge.

'Welcome back, Miss Susanne.' The girl bobbed her knee at Susan, glancing at Eve and Annie.

'Ah, there you are, Milly.' Susan smiled at her as the girl hurried forward to retrieve the discarded coat. 'I've brought some friends to stay for a while. They'll be sharing the twin bedroom. Would you see that it's made ready for them? And then perhaps you could make us all a cup of tea and a late lunch. We're rather hungry after all the travelling.'

'O' course, miss.'

As the girl disappeared, Susan turned to her visitors. 'I hope you won't mind sharing a room? I do have three bedrooms, but I like to keep one free for . . . unexpected visitors.'

'I certainly don't mind sharin',' Eve told her, dropping the heavy carpet bag. This was feeling more like an adventure every second and she was very glad she had come.

'I don't mind either,' Annie assured her, crossing to the French doors to peep out at the garden. There was a thin coating of snow on the grass and not much to see, but she guessed it must be pleasant in the spring.

Turning back to Susan, she asked, 'I heard the doorman call you Miss Belle. But I thought I'd heard the missus say your name was Willis?'

194

Susan chuckled. 'You're quite right, but Susan Willis is so ordinary, isn't it? Here I prefer to go by the name of Susanne Belle because I think it has a more glamorous ring to it, don't you?'

Milly soon appeared again. 'I've put a light lunch in the dinin' room, miss. Anyfin' else yer want, just give me a shout.'

Susan smiled at the two girls. 'As you've probably noticed by her accent, Milly is a Londoner through and through, born within the sound of Bow Bells and proud of it.'

She led them through to another room, this one not quite as large as the lounge but just as beautifully furnished. A delicately inlaid rosewood table stood at the centre of it, surrounded by six chairs, and against the wall was a matching sideboard with a steaming tureen standing on it.

'Mmm, Milly's delicious stilton and broccoli soup,' Susan said happily. 'Do help yourselves, girls, and there's a basket of rolls on the table.'

Annie and Eve didn't need telling twice. Just as Susan had said, the soup was absolutely delicious and the girls tucked in, delighted to be waited on for a change. There was tray of fresh-baked scones with jam and cream to follow and by the time they were finished, they felt bloated.

'Right, I'll get Milly to show you to your room now.' Susan smiled at them. 'Do let me know if there's anything you need.'

After the dormitory in the workhouse and the cold, draughty attic room in Swan Lane, Annie's eyes popped out at the sight of such a beautiful bedroom. Against one wall, two beds stood either side of a cream baroque table; on the other side of the room was a matching armoire and a dressing table with triple gilt mirrors. A tiny spindle-legged settee and a marble-topped washstand took up the other wall, and thick damask curtains hung at the window, which overlooked the garden. Pretty paintings and gilt mirrors adorned the walls.

'Stone the bloody crows!' Eve gasped. 'I've never seen anywhere so posh in me whole life! I thought Mrs Taylor-Lloyd's 'ouse would take some beatin' but this does it hands down. We've even got us own little fireplace wi' a fire burnin' in it, look.'

'It is lovely.' Annie was feeling a little out of her depth and could only stare around, almost afraid to touch anything.

The same couldn't be said for Eve who bounded over to the bed, leapt on it and bounced up and down, shouting gleefully, 'Bloody Nora, I reckon this is a feather mattress. Try yours, Annie.'

In a rather more ladylike fashion, Annie went to perch on the edge of the other bed and smiled. 'It is lovely and soft,' she agreed. 'And the pillows are soft too. I think we're going to be very comfortable in here.'

There was a tap on the door and Milly stuck her head around it. 'Anyfin' else I can get for yer, ladies?' She was quite looking forward to having two girls close to her own age to stay. ''Ave yer got plenty o' blankets an' wharravyer?'

'I'm sure we do,' Annie assured her as the girl stepped into the room. 'How long have you worked for Susan?'

'Miss Susanne, yer mean,' Milly corrected her with a cheeky grin. 'Ooh, about a year or so now, I reckon, but I don't live in. Me an' me family live not so far away so I go 'ome of an evenin'.'

'And do you like workin' ere?' Annie asked.

'Nor 'alf! She's all right is Miss Susanne. But 'ow long are you two 'ere for? I only ask cos o' gettin' the shoppin' in.'

'Well, I'm just havin' a little holiday,' Annie explained. 'But Eve here will be stayin' longer, all bein' well.'

'Brilliant, well I get Sundays off so if eiver o' yous ever want a bit of a tour o' London, just give me a shout, eh?'

'I think I'm going to like it 'ere.' Eve sighed contentedly when Milly had gone, and she dropped back onto the pillows. If only she wasn't carrying an unwanted child, everything would have been just perfect. But the child was very much there, so first she would have to get over that hurdle before her fairy-tale could begin.

Chapter Twenty-Five

They spent that evening quietly at home with Susan, but when they rose the next morning, they found her warmly dressed and ready for the outdoors. They could hear Milly clattering about in the kitchen, and Susan told them, 'Milly is preparing some breakfast for you. You don't mind entertaining yourselves for a few hours, do you? There's someone I have to see.'

'Course not.' Eve, still clad in her nightclothes with her hair tied in a long plait across her shoulder, stifled a yawn. She had slept like a log and had been reluctant to get out of bed.

'In that case I shall be off.' Susan patted her hat and pulled on her gloves. 'Bye for now, girls. Have a pleasant morning.'

The two girls made their way into the dining room and soon Milly appeared with two platefuls of steaming bacon, eggs and sausage. At sight of it, Eve turned a dreadful shade of green and clapping her hand across her mouth made a mad dash for the toilet.

'Oh! Is she, er . . .' Milly didn't like to ask outright but she'd seen her mother pregnant enough times to know the signs.

Annie merely lowered her eyes and didn't answer, not feeling it was her place. If Eve wanted her to know, she'd no doubt tell her herself.

Eve appeared back shortly after and smiled apologetically at Milly. 'Thanks, but I don't think I'll bother wi' breakfast today.'

'Then 'ow about I make yer a nice cup o' rosy-lee wiv some ginger in it? Me ma swears by it when she's pregnant . . . But it's good fer all sorts o' upset stomachs,' she added quickly, not wishing to offend.

'Thanks.' Eve sank onto one of the chairs looking pale and wan.

'I think she's guessed, but I didn't tell her, I swear,' Annie told her.

Eve shrugged. 'Don't worry about it. It ain't as if I'm goin' to be able to 'ide it fer much longer, is it?' She grinned sadly. 'I wonder what's happenin' back at 'ome? They'll 'ave realised I've gone now. The missus will go mad!'

'Serves her right for the way she treated you,' Annie responded, helping herself to a thick rasher of sizzling bacon.

Could they have known it, at that precise moment, Mrs Taylor-Lloyd was hammering on Maggie's front door with a face like a dark thundercloud. Because Annie wasn't there, Maggie hurried to answer it and when she found her neighbour on the step, she blinked with surprise. She had never come to her door before in all the time she had lived there, but it was soon apparent that Mrs Taylor-Lloyd wasn't on a social call.

'Where is she?' The furious woman demanded through gritted teeth.

'Er . . . where is who?' Maggie looked confused.

'Oh, don't come the innocent with me!' Mrs Taylor-Lloyd spat. 'I'm talking about Eve, my maid.'

Maggie shook her head. 'I'm sorry, but I have no idea what you're talking about. How should I know where your maid is?'

'She's gone . . . run away, and don't you find it strange that it happened on exactly the same day that your maid and your sister went to London? Did they plan it between them?'

'I assure you, I really don't know anything. Neither Annie nor Susan said anything to me about Eve going with them. As far as I am aware they've gone alone, just the two of them.'

'I should have known I wouldn't get the truth from the likes of you,' Mrs Taylor-Lloyd screeched in a most unladylike manner. 'It was a sad day for our neighbourhood when you guttersnipes moved in!'

'Now just hold on a minute—' Maggie was getting rattled, but before she could say anymore, the woman turned and stomped away.

'They'll be sorry, just you wait and see, because when the slut decides to come back, she'll find herself out on the streets,' she shouted over her shoulder.

Later that morning, Susan reappeared accompanied by a tall, dark-haired man.

'This is Mr Theodore Fitzroy, a good friend of mine,' Susan introduced him.

'I'm delighted to meet you,' Theodore said, eyeing both girls up and down.

Much to Annie's embarrassment, he bowed gallantly and kissed the backs of their hands.

'This is Eve and this is Annie,' Susan told him.

Eve stared at him, completely enchanted. The same couldn't be said for Annie, however. Admittedly he was extremely good-looking but there was something about him that she didn't take to, although she couldn't figure out what it was.

'I hope we shall become friends too, and do call me Theo.' He flashed the girls a charming smile that made Eve go weak at the knees.

'We've only called in for Theo to meet you,' Susan informed them. 'We have an appointment, so do try to entertain yourselves. I should be back for lunch and then hopefully there'll be time to take you to see a few of the famous London landmarks. Are you ready, Theo?'

'Of course, my dear.' He offered her his arm and once they had said their goodbyes to the girls they left.

It was only when they were back outside in Russell Square that Susan asked him, 'So, what did you think of them?'

'Hmm, very rough diamonds but both have potential. Particularly the dark-haired girl, Annie. They'll need some polish to get rid of their rough edges and completely new wardrobes, but I dare say I can leave that to you?'

She felt a pang of guilt as she nodded. She hated it when Theo asked her to recruit girls for him, but she was so under his spell she found it hard to refuse. 'Absolutely. But don't forget it will be some time before we will be able to set Eve to work. Meantime, I'll employ her as a maid to help Milly and work on her elocution. And Annie . . . well, I just hope that if I give her a good enough time she might decide to move here in a few months. At the moment, to all intents and purposes, she's just having a holiday.'

'Then make sure you impress her. I have a feeling she would be much in demand with our clients. Speaking of which, we ought to get on. I have someone I'd like you to meet. You'll be escorting him this evening.'

Susan's heart sank. She had hoped she and Theo could spend a little quality time together before she returned to work, but she was in no position to argue. After all, he had forgiven her for running away. She tried not to think of the reason she had fled, but even so her hand rose to touch the faded bruise around her eye, now skilfully concealed with make-up. She pushed it from her mind. He loved her! Of course he did, she told herself, once again ignoring the little warning voice that said he was only using her for his own ends. Each client she entertained for him brought them a little closer to having a future together. She had to believe that, for the thought of a future without him in it filled her with dread.

Back at the flat, Eve was almost swooning as she thought of Theo's handsome face. 'Weren't 'e just the *best-lookin'* bloke you ever saw?'

Annie shrugged. 'I suppose he were all right, but he weren't my type. He were a bit smarmy, if you ask me. Come on, let's give Milly a hand wi' these dirty pots, eh? It'll help pass the time till Susan gets back.'

As promised, Susan arrived back shortly before lunchtime and they dined together on juicy lamb chops, winter cabbage and crispy roast potatoes that Milly had cooked to perfection. Eve was feeling much better and more than did the meal justice.

'Cor, that were lovely,' she declared, patting her full stomach. 'So, when are we goin' sightseein'?'

'Just as soon as you're ready,' Susan told her and shortly after they set off in a happy mood.

Back in Nuneaton, the mood in the Taylor-Lloyds' house was anything but happy as Mrs Taylor-Lloyd sat at the dining table having lunch with her sons.

'I can't believe that ungrateful little bitch has run away,' the woman complained. 'And after I was good enough to take her from the workhouse as well!'

'I wonder if she's gone to London with Mrs Lilburn's sister and that maid of theirs,' Reggie said slyly.

'I've already been round there to enquire,' his mother told him primly. 'But of course she lied through her teeth and denied all knowledge of it. I shouldn't have expected any more from the likes of her. Her sort are incapable of telling the truth.'

'That's a bit harsh, isn't it, Mother?' Monty looked concerned. 'It won't look very good on you if word gets out, will it? I mean people will wonder why she had cause to leave, surely?'

His mother paused. 'Hmm, I suppose you do have a point,' she admitted reluctantly as her pride reared its ugly head.

Monty smiled at her. 'I'm sure word will reach us soon as to Eve's whereabouts, and until then I'd say nothing if I were you.'

'I dare say you're right,' she admitted reluctantly. 'I've no doubt she'll be back with her tail between her legs when she realises which side her bread is buttered. Meantime I shall have to decide if I want to give her another chance.'

Monty stifled a smile. His mother really was a terrible snob and he just hoped that Eve was all right wherever she was.

Eve was having the time of her life. She loved everything about London. It seemed so busy and full of life after Nuneaton. Plus, she had become good friends with Milly, who had offered to take both Eve and Annie home to meet her family on the next Sunday, which was her day off.

The same couldn't be said for Annie, however, who after a few days began to miss Levi, Charlie and Monty.

'I think I might stay fer about another week an' then get Susanne to get me a ticket home,' she confided in Eve one night after Susan had taken them to a music hall. Eve had loved every second, but Annie had found it rather noisy.

'What?' Eve was appalled. 'But *why*? We're havin' a good time, ain't we? Sorry, aren't we?' she corrected herself. Susan had begun to give her elocution lessons but she wasn't doing too well with them as yet.

'Oh yes.' Annie looked slightly shamefaced. 'Susan has been lovely to us, but I just feel a bit like a fish out o' water here. Everythin' is so hustle an' bustle an' I reckon I prefer a quieter way o' life.'

'Then yer must be daft,' Eve scoffed. 'How can yer prefer to spend yer days skivvyin' fer Lady Lilburn to bein' waited on' and took out an' spoilt?'

'Ah, but I won't be doin' that when I get home, will I? Levi told me that now I'm seventeen I can get meself a job if I choose to.'

'Doin' what?'

Annie shrugged. 'I'm not sure. I could get a job in a shop, or better still an office, but I'd have to do a course to make sure me writin' and arithmetic were up to that. Anyway, don't forget that when I go back, you'll be officially helpin' Milly till after you've had the baby. That was your agreement, weren't it?'

'Well ... yes.' Eve flushed. She still hadn't told Annie what Susan had in store for her once the baby was born, nor did she intend to.

'So, let's just enjoy the next week, eh? And then I'll decide when I want to go home.'

Chapter Twenty-Six

Early the following Monday morning, as Levi was getting ready to leave for work, someone rapped on the back door. Hurrying to open it he found Tom, Peggy's youngest son, standing on the step.

'Hello, lad. Come on in outta the cold. What brings you out so early in the mornin'?' He ushered him inside.

'Sorry to bother yer, Mr Lilburn, but me mam says can yer come straight away? Me dad's had a real bad turn.'

Levi frowned as he pulled on his coat. Things must be dire for Peggy to send for him, so without even waiting to get old Dobbin and the cart sorted, he said, 'Come on, lad. We can be there in ten minutes if we get a shufty on.'

They set off at a run along Swan Lane and minutes later crossed the yard to Levi's old home.

'Me mam's upstairs wi' me dad,' Tom informed him.

Grim-faced Levi nodded. 'Good lad, just wait there, would yer? I might need yer to run fer the doctor.' Then he took the stairs two at a time to the bedroom.

Tapping on the door, he opened it and the sight that met his eyes caused his breath to catch in his throat.

Sid was propped up on pillows in the bed, with Peggy crying broken-heartedly as she lay across his chest, and at a glance Levi knew that it wouldn't be the doctor they were needing, it would be the undertaker. Sid had passed away.

'H-he developed pneumonia, an' 'e couldn't breathe . . .'

'Aw, lass.' Dragging his cap from his head, Levi twisted it in his hands as tears filled his eyes. He'd been a good bloke had Sid, one of the best. 'I'm so sorry. Come away downstairs now an' let me make yer a nice cup o' tea, eh?'

As if in a trance, Peggy allowed Levi to take her elbow and gently lead her down the stairs where he helped her to a chair before hurrying away to put the kettle on to boil.

'Mam, is me dad . . .' Tom asked in a wobbly voice.

Peggy nodded and held her arms out to him and he rushed into her embrace with tears streaming down his cheeks.

'I'm so sorry.' Levi knew his words were inadequate, but what more could he say? Nothing would relieve their pain. 'Have a hot drink, son, then perhaps yer could run round to the undertaker an' ask him to call. The doctor will need to come an' all to sign the death certificate.'

Tom nodded and extracted himself from his mother's arms. 'Afore I go, I need to tell yer that the yard was broken into again last night. I'm sorry, Mr Lilburn. Me dad asked me to keep me ears open, seein' as he weren't well enough to, but I must 'ave dropped off to sleep. I'm afraid they've taken a fair amount o' the copper you'd collected.'

Levi waved his concerns aside. 'Don't you get worryin' about that just now, lad. Copper can allus be replaced, yer dad can't, God bless him.' He thrust a steaming mug into the young man's hand and another into Peggy's but she just sat staring down into it.

Soon after little Ellie came downstairs clutching her rag doll and when she saw the tears on Peggy's pale cheeks, she ran to her and threw her arms about her waist, sensing that something was seriously amiss.

'I'm gonna get back home while you break the news to the rest o' the family. I'll fetch Maggie back to keep yer company, pet,' Levi told Peggy kindly. 'Yer shouldn't be on yer own today.'

He left with a heavy heart. He had known Peggy and Sid for as long as he'd known Maggie and had always thought what a happy couple they were. In fact, looking back he could never remember them having so much as a cross word.

Maggie had just come downstairs when he got back home and she looked surprised to see him. 'Oh . . . I thought you'd left for work!'

'I was just about to when I had a visit from Peggy's Tom . . .' He told her what had happened, and she sighed. Poor Peggy, she would be devastated. 'So, I was thinking you could perhaps go round there and keep your eye on her today?' he ended hopefully. 'I really don't think she should be left on her own.'

'Hmm, I suppose I should.' Maggie wasn't too happy with the idea. She had a fitting at the dressmaker in town today for the latest gown she had ordered, but she supposed she would have to put that off for now. 'But how will she manage to pay the rent on the cottage with Sid gone?'

Levi was shocked at such an insensitive question, and he stared at her as if he could hardly believe what she had just said. Poor Peggy had just lost the love of her life and here was Maggie only worried about how she would get their rent.

'I really don't think that's something we should even be *thinking* about at a time like this,' he said harshly.

Realising she'd been rather tactless, she nodded. 'No, of course you're right . . . I, er . . . was just worried about how she'll manage. Just give me a moment to get dressed and I'll come back round there with you.'

Sid was laid to rest the following week in Coton churchyard. It was a cold, rainy day and as the mourners stood at the side of Sid's grave the rain mingled with the tears on their cheeks. Maggie had laid on a small spread back at their house in Swan Lane for any mourners that chose to attend, but Levi had a nasty suspicion that it was more to show off her lovely home than to help Peggy. Maggie had already shown her displeasure when Levi had offered to buy Sid's coffin and pay for the funeral. He knew Peggy could ill afford it, and it was the least he could do, but Maggie didn't agree and had wasted no time in telling him so. However, on this Levi had stood firm and there was nothing Maggie could do about it.

Soon after the interment was over, the mourners from the court-yards in Abbey Street began to arrive at the house in Swan Lane, and Maggie greeted them as if she was royalty.

'Do come in and go through to the dining room,' she told them imperiously. 'There will be tea and coffee coming shortly. Mean-while, do help yourselves to sherry or a short.'

Levi cringed at their expressions as they looked around the lux-urious rooms.

'By, Levi, lad, you've done well fer yerself, ain't yer?' old Lil Cotton from the next courtyard to Peggy said in awe. 'It's like a bloody palace in 'ere!'

'Thank you, Mrs Cotton,' Maggie said with a simpering smile. 'Now, do help yourself to a sandwich, there's ham, egg and cress or salmon, if you prefer.'

Throughout the next hour Peggy sat staring into space as if she had been turned to stone and Levi felt for her, although Maggie didn't seem to notice. She was too busy showing off in front of her old neighbours.

'Come on, Pegs,' Levi urged, carrying a plate of pork pie over to her. 'Try a bit o' this, pet. You've not eaten a thing.'

'Thanks, but I ain't hungry.' Peggy raised a weary smile. She didn't know what she would have done without Levi over the past week. He had organised everything, as well as popping in at least twice a day to check how she and the family were. 'Actually, I need to 'ave a quick word wi' you when everyone's gone,' she went on, lowering her voice. 'It's about the rent. Don't get wor-ryin' about it. We've worked it out that wi' what I earn up at the work'ouse an' wi' the lads pitchin' in wi' some o' their wages we'll be able to manage.'

Levi bristled with indignation. 'I wasn't worrying about it,' he told her sternly. 'And you shouldn't either. Your rent 'as been the last thing on me mind this week, believe me.'

By that time most of the food and drink had disappeared, the mourners began to disperse, each muttering their condolences to Peggy as they left.

'I should be goin' now an' all,' Peggy muttered as she rose stiffly from her seat. 'But I'll give Maggie a hand wi' all this clearin' up first. She put on a lovely spread fer Sid an' I'm very grateful.'

'You'll do no such thing. You just get yourself home and into the warm and put your feet up.'

'But Annie ain't 'ere to help,' Peggy pointed out.

Levi smiled as he leant towards her. 'Well, it won't 'urt 'er to get 'er snow-white 'ands dirty fer a change, will it?' he whispered.

Peggy smiled; really smiled for the first time since Sid had passed away, then she gently slapped him on the arm and made her way to the kitchen with her sons close behind her. She had left Ellie with a neighbour because she believed she was too young to attend a funeral, and after how inclement the weather had been she was glad she had.

'Thanks fer everythin', Maggie, yer did my Sid proud,' she told her old friend.

Maggie nodded. 'You're most welcome.'

It was only when Peggy had gone that Maggie's smile slipped and she stared around in dismay. There were dirty pots and glasses on every available surface, and the floors throughout the down-stairs were covered in muddy footprints and crumbs.

'Damn Annie for clearing off on a holiday when I most need her,' she muttered as she tied an apron around her waist to cover the beautiful black silk mourning gown she had bought especially for the occasion. It had cost almost as much as the funeral.

As Levi fetched a tray and started to help, he smiled to himself, but he didn't say anything. He knew better than to make Maggie's mood worse.

'How much longer do you think the young madam will be away?' Maggie queried irritably as she filled the sink with hot soapy water. It was going to take hours to get the house back to rights.

'I dare say she'll be back soon enough.' Levi lifted a tea towel ready to help with drying the pots and a silence settled between them.

As he worked, his thoughts turned to the robbery at his yard. He was gravely concerned, although he couldn't tell Maggie. With Sid gone he had lost not only a good friend but the night watchman. Recently, the yard had been targeted far too often, despite Sid's diligence. It was something he would have to give serious thought to.

Chapter Twenty-Seven

On Sunday, as promised, Milly took Eve and Annie to visit her family. They took a cab from Susan's house to the East End, and then Milly led them through a labyrinth of twisting alleys.

'This is it, Pear Street where I live with me ma,' she told them eventually. The girls stared around them at the narrow street with rows of shops along one side and tall terraced houses that opened directly onto the street on the other. Grubby-looking children were playing on the cobblestones, and the place was alive with people coming and going.

''Ere we are then.' Milly stopped in front of one of the houses opposite a tobacconist's shop 'Now, don't get expectin' too much. Me mam ain't as posh as Miss Susanne, but she does 'er best, bless 'er.'

The outside of the house was sooty and grimy, but the lace curtains hanging at the windows were surprisingly white and the stone doorstep was spotless. Milly turned the handle on the door, beckoning the visitors to follow her into a small front parlour, which although scantly furnished was also spotlessly clean.

Three small children instantly hurled themselves at her. ''Ave yer bought us any sweeties, our Milly?' one of the children piped up.

Milly chuckled as she ruffled his dark blonde curls. 'No, I ain't 'ad time to call into the shop yet, but 'ere yer go, 'ere's sixpence. Go down to the shop an' get yerselves some gobstoppers, eh?'

Taking the money, the little boy and his siblings sped out of the front door and Milly led her visitors into the next room, which was a kitchen-cum-sitting room. A cheerful fire burned in the grate and a plump woman with a kindly face sat in a chair at the side of it feeding an infant from a glass bottle with a rubber teat.

'Ah, Milly, me love.' She turned her head to receive Milly's kiss on her cheek before beaming at the two young women. 'An' you two must be Eve an' Annie. Milly told me all about yer last week. She's quite enjoyin' havin' yer stay wi' Miss Susanne.'

'Hello, Mrs Froggett. Thanks fer invitin' us,' Eve said as she looked to another chair where a young man was sitting. Her eyes widened in surprise as she recognised him.

'Oh, but aren't you David, the doorman at Susanne's flat?'

He grinned. 'I am that. Didn't our Milly tell you I was her brother. An' it's Davey while I'm at 'ome.'

His mother rose from her seat and dropped the baby and the bottle into his lap. 'Here, finish feedin' him for me while I make me visitors a cup o' char. Come on, luvvies, come an' sit yerselves down. Will yer be stayin' fer dinner? It ain't no trouble.'

'Oh, no thank you, Mrs Froggett, we're havin' dinner with Susanne at 'er apartment,' Annie told her as she and Eve settled onto a horsehair sofa at the other side of the fireplace.

'But will yer find yer back awright wi'out our Milly?' the woman asked with concern. 'The alleyways round 'ere are like a maze! I wouldn't want you to be gettin' lost!'

Annie smiled as she jingled some coins in her pocket. 'It's all right, Mrs Froggett. Susanne gave me some money so that we could get a cab back.'

'Well, not afore you've had a drink an' some cake, I hope,' she said, putting the kettle on the hob.

Once the tea was ready, she placed a pot and a large sandwich cake oozing jam and cream on the table, and the children clustered around waiting for her to cut them a slice.

They spent a pleasant hour with Milly and her family but eventually Annie glanced at the clock. 'I think we ought to be going now. But it's been lovely to meet you all,' she told Mrs Froggett.

'It's been lovely to meet you an' all. Make sure as yer come again. Next time you'll per'aps get to meet me old man. He's down at the Dog an' Duck at the minute enjoyin' 'is weekly pint.'

'I'll walk yer back to the main road an' get a cab for you,' Davey offered as he rose from his seat and went to collect his coat.

As they walked through the alleyways, Annie couldn't help but notice that Davey and Eve were getting along like a house on fire. Once they were back on the main road, he hailed them a cab and saw them safely inside it, before setting off back home.

'Did I detect a little spark between you two?' Annie teased as the cab rattled across the cobblestones.

Eve blushed. 'I think Davey is the nicest chap I ever met,' she admitted. 'An' he's good-lookin' an' all. But there can't ever be owt between us, can there?' She stabbed a finger at her belly. 'Once this starts to show he'll run a mile. No, my life is mapped out fer me now. Once this is born, Susanne will get it fostered or adopted an' then I'll work for her.'

'Exactly what sort of work will you be doin'?' Annie asked. It had never occurred to her to ask before.

Eve quickly looked out of the window. 'We ain't exactly decided yet but I dare say she'll get me fitted up wi' some sort o' job,' she lied. How could she tell Annie the truth? Since leaving the workhouse to live with the Taylor-Lloyds, Annie was the only friend she had ever had and she couldn't bear to think she might look down on her.

When they arrived back at the flat, Theo was just leaving. He smiled at them, his eyes lingering on Annie. How he wished that it was her who would be working for him soon. Eve was a pretty enough girl, admittedly, and he had no doubt she would be popular with his clients, but Annie was stunning. Still, hopefully if Susanne played her cards right, she would encourage her to join them eventually.

'Had a good morning, have you, girls?' he asked affably.

'Yes thanks. Milly took us to meet 'er family an' they were lovely,' Eve replied. Meeting the Froggetts had brought home to her just how much she and Annie had missed in their lives. They obviously weren't rich financially but the love they felt for each other was plain to see and she envied them their closeness. Once she had dared to hope that she would find a loving home with the Taylor-Lloyds, but she had soon discovered they only wanted her as a skivvy. It had been pretty much the same for Annie, although Levi and Charlie had always been kind to her. Deep down she was concerned about the life she would shortly be committing herself to. But what choice did she have? There could never be a happy-ever-after ending for her now.

'I'm pleased to hear it,' Theo replied. 'I thought perhaps it might be nice if we all went out to an eating house one evening before Annie returns home – that's unless I can persuade her to stay, that is?'

Annie shook her head. 'That would be very kind of you, but as regards stayin' I can't do that. I'll be needed back in Nuneaton.'

As time passed, she was growing increasingly concerned about how Maggie would be coping. The rest of the family thought she was over her grief, but she knew better.

'Ah well, if ever you decide that London living is more to your taste there will always be a home for you here, isn't that right, Susanne?' Theo flashed her a smarmy smile.

'Of course.'

Susan, Annie noted, was dressed in a low-cut floaty peignoir trimmed with feathers that left little to the imagination and she felt herself blushing. She must have had a lie-in after her evening out the night before, she decided.

Milly had prepared a lunch before she'd left that morning, so after eating, they went sightseeing again. But although she enjoyed it, Annie was yearning for her hometown. Added to that she found herself missing Charlie dreadfully; they had always been close, but since being away, she had started to wonder whether her feelings might be developing into something different.

213

She mentioned her desire to go home that evening as Susan was getting ready to go out again.

'What? So soon?' Susan said regretfully. 'I was hoping I would be able to persuade you to stay a while longer.'

Annie shook her head. 'That's really kind of you but I'm ready to go back now. I thought I might go midweek?'

'If that's what you want.' Susan sighed. Theo wasn't going to be pleased with Annie's decision but there wasn't much she could do about it apart from hope she would decide to come back. She would be in Theo's bad books again if Annie didn't.

Eve was sad to hear the news too, and once Susan had left for the evening she asked, 'Can't yer stay fer just a *bit* longer? I'll miss yer when yer go.'

'I'll miss you too.' Annie gave her a quick hug. 'But I don't reckon I'm cut out fer livin' in the smoke.'

The girls decided they would make the most of the few days they had left together, and the following morning they went on a shopping spree with Susan in Bond Street. As well as ordering herself two new gowns, Susan treated both girls to a new blouse and skirt each before taking them to lunch.

'We can wear 'em tonight when Theo takes us all out to dinner,' Eve said excitedly.

Theo arrived promptly at seven o'clock and ushered them into a waiting cab, which took them to a grand-looking hotel. Following Theo and Susan inside, both girls stared around open-mouthed. It was like entering another world. Potted palms stood about on marble plinths and a grand staircase led up to what they imagined must be the hotel bedrooms. The walls were covered in gilt mirrors, and sparkling crystal chandeliers hung from the ceilings, throwing rainbows of colours across the walls.

'Ah, Mr Fitzroy.' The maître d', who looked almost as smart as the guests, hurried forward to greet them. 'How nice it is to see you again, sir. Do follow me, your table is all ready for you.'

Impressed, Eve and Annie glanced at each other. Theo was clearly well known there if that greeting was anything to go by.

The man led them into the restaurant, which was full of the most wonderful smells. The tables were covered in crisp white linen cloths, each laid with silver cutlery, crystal wine glasses, a candelabra and a bowl of hot-house flowers. The scent of wax mingled with the cooking smells and the expensive perfumes the lady diners wore.

'Here we are, sir.' The maître d clicked his fingers and a waiter in a black coat and white shirt appeared at his side and handed them each a menu. Another appeared with a wine bucket in which stood a bottle of champagne. 'Please accept this to drink while you study the menu, sir, with compliments of the house.' The maître d inclined his head.

'That's very kind of you.' Theo looked completely at home and Annie realised that this must be his normal way of life rather than a treat as it was for her and Eve.

The waiter popped the cork and poured them each a glass and Annie grinned as she sipped at hers and the bubbles went up her nose.

'Have you ever had champagne before, my dear?' Theo enquired.

Annie blushed. 'No, sir. I can't say as I 'ave . . . but it's very nice.'

He grinned. 'Good, but a word of warning: sip it slowly. It's a lot more potent than it tastes and I'd hate it to make you ill.'

They studied the menu but it was all double Dutch to Eve, because it was written in French, although Annie could read most of it thanks to the French lessons from Charlie. To make it easier, Theo kindly ordered for them.

They began with a melon starter, which was quite delicious, and then Susan, who was always watching her figure, chose to have a Dover sole while Theo had a fillet steak, and Annie and Eve had the chicken breast covered in a delicious Dijon cream sauce. After the main course they chose a dessert from the trolley and by the time they had finished Annie felt as if she might burst.

'I ain't never tasted owt like that in me life,' Eve sighed as she rubbed her full stomach contentedly.

Susan giggled. She really would have to start giving her some more elocution lessons – and soon, if the disapproving stares they were getting from the neighbouring tables were anything to go by.

Annie and Eve then went back to the flat in a cab, while Susan and Theo went on somewhere else, promising to see them later.

'Cor, 'ow the other 'alf live, eh?' Eve grinned as she leant back against the squabs. 'Did yer see the price o' that food we just ate? Why, just the main course were more than I earn in a month an' Theo paid it as if it were nuthin'!'

Annie nodded. She had thought the same thing but after living in the workhouse where the inmates were always hungry, she wasn't sure if she could condone it.

'It must be nice to be that rich,' Eve mused as they pulled up outside the townhouse.

Davey was waiting for them in the foyer and Annie couldn't help but notice how both his and Eve's eyes lit up at the sight of each other.

'You carry on. I'll catch yer up in a minute,' Eve said with her eyes still fixed on Davey.

They were clearly attracted to each other but as Eve had pointed out, what could come of it considering the position she was in? It was a crying shame to Annie's way of thinking.

Chapter Twenty-Eight

'Are yer quite sure I can't persuade yer to stay a bit longer?' Eve said tearfully as Annie prepared to leave for Euston Station the following Wednesday morning.

Annie shook her head as she packed the last of her things into her carpet bag. She seemed to be going home with a lot more than she had arrived with thanks to Susan's generosity.

'No, but don't worry, we'll be seeing each other again and I'm sure Susan will take good care of you.'

'I know she will, but now you're goin' my 'oliday will be over an' all, an' I'll 'ave to start helpin' Milly about the place. That were the deal, after all. I'd work fer Susan till the baby comes.'

Annie had said her goodbyes to Susan the night before as she had told her that she wouldn't be returning that evening. There were lots of nights when she hadn't come home and Annie wondered if she was spending them with Theo – not that she dared to ask. It was none of her business, after all. Susan was a grown woman and could come and go as she pleased.

'So do yer want me to go out an' hail you a cab?' Eve offered.

Annie shook her head. 'No, I can find my way to Euston in no time. It's only a hop, skip and a jump away.'

'Then I'll come with yer, shall I, an' see yer onto the train?'

Again, Annie shook her head. 'No, you stay here in the warm. It's stopped raining but it's still cold out there. No point in both of us going.'

Milly, who had been washing the breakfast pots in the kitchen, joined them and she too looked sad that Annie was leaving.

'I hope you come back an' see us again soon,' she said with a catch in her voice as she gave her a hug. 'An' don't get worryin' about Eve. She'll be fine 'ere wi' us, we'll see to that.'

'Right, that's it then. I'm ready,' Annie said brightly as she pulled on her gloves. 'Goodbye for now, both. Take care o' yerselves.'

They both saw her to the door and waved until she disappeared round the bend. Davey was in the hallway standing by the door in his porter's uniform. It was his job to to make sure that no unsavoury characters entered the building and to carry any of the tenants' things to their flats for them if requested, and he took his job very seriously.

'Ready fer the off, are yer?' He gave her a cheeky smile. 'I hope we see yer again. Have a safe journey, Annie.'

'Thank you, and goodbye, Davey.' And with that she set off across Russell Square on the first part of her journey home.

It was late afternoon by the time the train pulled into Nuneaton Railway Station and Annie set off for Swan Lane. It was already dark and bitterly cold, and she was longing for a cup of tea.

The first person she saw when she entered the kitchen was Maggie huddled by the fire talking to someone, but when Annie looked around she saw that she was alone, and a little finger of fear crept up her spine.

'Hello, missus, I'm back.'

Maggie's head swung towards her as Annie surveyed the room. The draining board was piled high with dirty pots and the fire was almost out.

'Where is everyone?'

Maggie sniffed. 'Levi is round at Peggy's as usual. He has to spend longer round there now sorting the yard out because Sid died while you've been away having fun.'

'Oh no.' Annie's eyes filled with tears. 'Poor Peggy. What happened to him?'

'Pneumonia,' Maggie responded shortly. 'And Charlie's gone off to Coventry again. I can't think what the draw is over there. Every Sunday and Wednesday he goes now. And Harry's off out with his mates somewhere.'

'I see.' Annie unpinned her bonnet and laid it on the table. If the rest of the house was in as bad a state as the kitchen, it would take days to bring it back to rights, but at the moment she was more concerned about Peggy. She had adored Sid and Annie could only imagine how heartbroken she must be. She wondered how she would manage without him. Even so, Annie was also aware that there was no meal prepared, so after taking off her coat she threw some coal onto the dying fire and went to check the pantry. It was sadly depleted, although she did find a string of sausages and some potatoes.

'I'll do some sausage and mash for dinner, shall I?' she asked Maggie.

The woman shrugged. 'Please yourself.'

As she peeled the potatoes, Annie wondered how long it had been since Levi and the boys had come home to a cooked meal. Once they were cooking, she popped the sausages into the oven and attacked the washing up. There were an awful lot of dirty pots and she was just coming to the end of them when Levi appeared. His face looked gaunt and tired, but it brightened at the sight of Annie and, crossing the room, he pecked her on the cheek.

'Welcome 'ome, princess. Eeh, it's good to 'ave yer back. Did yer 'ave a good time wi' Susan? An' 'as Maggie told yer what happened to Sid?'

'Yes, I had a good time, thank you; and yes, Maggie did tell me about Sid. I can't believe it. He was such a lovely man. Poor Peggy, she must be devastated.'

'She is.' He shook his head and lowering his voice he said apologetically, Sorry you've 'ad to come 'ome to such a mess. Maggie ain't been 'erself fer the last few days. We 'ad Sid's wake 'ere an' she seemed fine up till then, but after it were over, she sort o' shut down again. I'm just hopin' she ain't goin' back to the way she were before.'

'Hmm.' Annie shared his concern. She glanced at Maggie who was sitting quietly staring into the fire. 'And don't worry about the mess. I can get this place shipshape again in no time.'

Levi shook his head. 'Oh no, you won't. I said before you left that it were time you did what you wanted to do. You've looked after us lot fer long enough. Yer a young woman now an' need a life outside these four walls. To be honest, I 'alf expected yer to stay in London wi' Susan.'

Annie shook her head. 'No, it was nice to go for a visit but I wouldn't want to live there.'

'Why's that?'

She shrugged. 'Just all too much hustle an' bustle fer my likin'. There's traffic comin' at yer from every direction. People everywhere yer look, an' they 'ave some right pea-souper fogs there.'

'What would yer like to do then? I thought yer might give it some thought while yer were away.'

Annie sighed. 'I was thinkin' of tryin' to get an office job or somethin' along those lines, but I wouldn't dream o' leavin' you in the lurch till the missus has perked up again.'

Harry appeared at that moment, and he too seemed pleased to see her.

'He's been givin' me a hand round at the yard,' Levi told her. 'I'm afraid it's all gone to pot a bit since Sid died.'

'In what way?'

'Well, fer a start off we 'ad another break-in an' the thieves made off wi' a load o' the metal I'd collected, an' I ain't been able to sort the rags or do the books either. I've been keepin' me eye on Peggy. She ain't 'erself yet see?'

'I could help there at least,' Annie offered. 'I'm quite good wi' figures. Do you 'ave the ledgers 'ere?'

'I do as it happens.' Crossing to the dresser, Levi took a large ledger from the cupboard underneath it and opened it on the table.

Annie wiped her hands on her apron and studied it for a moment before frowning with dismay.

'Oh dear, at a glance I'd say you have a lot o' people 'ere that owe you money.'

He nodded in agreement. 'I know but I ain't had time to contact 'em.'

'Then after dinner I'll sit down and make a list of them and write out some bills. I'll also pop round to the yard tomorrow and see what's to be done there.'

'Would yer, hinny?' Levi looked relieved; everything had started to get on top of him and with his rounds and Maggie to see to he'd had time for little else. 'I'd be very grateful if yer could, but only on one condition. If you're goin' to help out for a while, you'll 'ave to let me pay yer a wage. It won't be a fortune, mind, but at least you'll 'ave sommat to call yer own.'

Annie would quite happily have done it for nothing but knowing that Levi was a proud man she agreed.

By the time she set off to see Peggy the next morning, Annie had a mound of bills ready to be posted, so she went to the post office first to buy some stamps and post them. With that done she headed for the yard, which looked in a very sorry state. There were piles of unsorted metal and rags everywhere she looked. She sighed as she headed for the door of Peggy's little cottage and tapped on it. When Peggy opened it, she looked pale and had lost a lot of weight, but she still raised a smile when she saw Annie.

'Hello, pet.' She opened the door wider and Annie stepped past her into the room, which, despite everything, was neat and tidy. Ellie, who had a cold so was off school, was reading her story book in front of the fire.

Annie licked her lips, suddenly unsure of what she should say but Peggy clearly understood how she was feeling because she patted her arm and gave her a gentle smile. 'They told you about my Sid then?'

Annie nodded, tears stinging the back of her eyes. 'Yes . . . and I'm so sorry. I've popped round to try an' get the yard a bit sorted for the mister.'

Peggy sighed as she ran a hand distractedly through her hair. She had been doing lots of little jobs about the yard for Levi for some time now. 'Yes . . . o' course. I'm afraid I've let 'im down recently.'

'Of course you haven't. You've had a lot to deal wi' an' it's no wonder you ain't had time to worry about the yard. How are the lads takin' it?'

'Best as could be expected.' Peggy looked so sad that it almost broke Annie's heart. Forcing a smile, she said, 'You can get a nice hot drink inside yer before yer make a start.'

By mid-afternoon, the yard was looking a lot tidier. Annie had carried the rags into the large shed ready to be sorted and the metal had also been sorted into piles ready to be sold to the scrap men. After saying goodbye to Peggy, she made her way back to Swan Lane, stopping to buy some groceries from the corner shop on the way. She felt she had achieved something that day, although Levi's way of doing things seemed somewhat haphazard. He needed someone organised and tidy to sort it out, she decided. And who better than her?

She got back to find Maggie sitting in her usual position by the fire. She had changed into one of her lovely day gowns and had dressed her hair, which hopefully was a good sign, but there was no sign of any food having been made, so Annie began to prepare the evening meal.

Charlie was the first to arrive back that afternoon and her heart gave a little flutter at the sight of him. He had got home late the evening before so she hadn't seen him since returning from London, and she couldn't help but notice how handsome he was.

'Hello, Annie.' He took off his coat and smiled at her. 'It's good to see you back. I think Da was a little afraid you might stay in London.'

She blushed prettily and shook her head. She was painfully aware that since coming to live with the family she and Charlie had been brought up almost as brother and sister, but the feelings she harboured for him were far from those a sister should have for her brother. For a while before leaving for London she had dared to hope that her feelings were returned – there had been the odd tender look, an affectionate touch of her hand – but today he seemed distant again.

As he headed for the stairs, Annie paused in rolling the pastry to say, 'Dinner should be ready in about an hour. I've done one of your favourites – rabbit pie.'

'Ah, thanks. But perhaps you could keep mine warm for me. I have to nip out for a while.'

'Oh!' Annie felt a stab of disappointment. She had been hoping to spend a little time with him that evening, but then she supposed there would be other times, so with a sigh she turned her attention back to her pastry.

Chapter Twenty-Nine

April 1913

Barney hammered the last stake into the enormous tent pegs that pinned down the big top, and paused to wipe the sweat from his brow. He looked across at Mercy, who was just emerging from her mother's trailer with a young man. She seemed to grow more lovely with every day that passed but Barney had seen little of her for the past two weeks. A distant cousin of hers had been staying with her family and they had been forced to spend every available minute together, and Barney wasn't at all happy about it.

Bertrand Russell, or Bertie, was a handsome young chap some two years older than Mercy. He too was of circus stock, and Mercy's parents were quite taken with him – too much so for Barney's liking.

For some time now he and Mercy had been close, although they had had to hide their relationship from everyone. They were both painfully aware that Mercy's parents would be furious if they found out, so they had been sneaking out to see each other late at night or in between shows.

Barney was now a strapping, handsome young man. Lean and muscular from the years of hard work, and the girls in the different towns they visited flocked to him like bees around a honey pot. He had had his fair share of dalliances with more than a few of them, but it was Mercy who held his heart, and he felt jealous of anyone who went near her – her cousin included. Not that he could do anything about it.

It was the first time the circus had come to Nuneaton for some months, and he was intending to visit his own family in the next few days. He just hoped that Bertie would be gone by then and he could command a little more of Mercy's time once more. He had decided he might even invite her to visit his parents' home in Swan Lane.

As he stood glowering at Bertie, Noah came over and nodded towards the entrance flap to the big top.

'Yer can help me lay the sawdust in the ring if yer've finished up here. The first show is in an hour and a half so we need to get a shufty on,' he said.

With a last frown towards Mercy, Barney went to do as he was asked. Inside it was all hustle and bustle with circus folk climbing around the roof fixing lights, and the ropes and swings for Mercy's flying trapeze act, and around the ring, fences were being erected to keep the big cats and the horses in when they performed. The atmosphere was charged with excitement, which was only one of the things that Barney loved about the circus life. Outside the trainers were preparing the animals for the show, and the many stalls and sideshows were being erected. The seats for the audience also needed to be set out, so everyone was focused on their tasks, working in perfect harmony like a well-oiled machine. Barney knew that by the time bedtime approached he would ache in every limb, but he was used to it now and wouldn't have had it any other way.

By the time the public began to arrive for the first show, everything was almost ready and Barney could finally relax a little, before he needed to go to the tent where he would be bare-knuckle fighting later that evening. He found Luca, Mercy's father, setting out the last of the seats for the public around the ring.

'Yer up against Jupiter Payne from Leicester this evenin', an' from what I've 'eard o' him he's good, lad, so be prepared,' he warned Barney.

Barney shrugged; he wasn't overly concerned. It was rare that he lost a fight and once the men in the audience started betting on the two contestants it usually raised a fair sum, much to Luca's delight.

When Luca was finished, he hurried away to get into his ring master's uniform, and going to the tent door Barney lit a cigarette and stared out at the crowds. Already the swing boats were full of laughing children who squealed with delight as they soared into the air, and the various stalls seemed to be doing a roaring trade. He wasn't surprised. It was a beautiful, balmy evening, just the sort to draw folks from their homes. The carousel was full too, but then it was a great favourite with adults and children alike. There was also a long queue at the stall selling candy floss and toffee apples.

Finishing his smoke, Barney ground it out with the heel of his boot and made for his trailer to get changed. On the way he saw Mercy, who had changed into her costume for the trapeze act. With her long dark hair flowing down her back like liquid silk, and dressed in a short, sequinned skirt she looked adorable, and his heart ached at the sight of her. She waved when she spotted him and he paused to watch her disappear into the big top. Once she had done her trapeze act, she would change and go to manage one of the fairground stalls for the rest of the evening. Most of the circus people performed more than one role.

'Don't get yearnin' fer what can never be yours, lad!'

Startled, Barney turned to find himself face to face with the fortune teller, Gypsy Rose Lee. He hadn't been aware that anyone was watching him, and he flushed.

'I was just being friendly,' he said defensively.

She tutted as she leant towards him. 'Don't forget who yer talkin' to, lad.' She scowled as she tapped the side of her nose. 'I knows everythin', an' you an' Mercy were never destined to be together.'

'Everythin' all right there? You two are lookin' very serious!'

They turned in unison to find the bearded lady staring at them. She was always a popular sideshow for the circus-goers and Barney felt sorry for her. She was probably the ugliest woman he had ever seen but she never seemed to mind the public laughing at her.

'We're fine.' The gypsy smiled at her and with a last glance at Barney she went off to get her crystal ball and tarot cards ready for her audience later that evening.

Half an hour later Barney was clad in the shorts he would wear for his fight and on his way to the tent, he checked out how the circus was going. Madame Fifi was putting her five white stallions through their paces in the ring and the children in the audience were watching enthralled. With a smile he moved on to find Matty, an old man who had been with the circus for most of his life, taking bets from gentlemen for the fight ahead.

'It's Jupiter Payne against our own reignin' champion Iron Barney,' he shouted. 'Come an' place yer bets, gentlemen!'

'How's it goin', Matty?' Barney flexed his fingers and stared into the tent. Some men had already taken their seats.

'Good, lad. Yer odds-on favourite to win at the minute, so don't get letting us down now!'

At that moment a huge man strolled around the side of the tent. 'Is this where the fight's takin' place?'

'Aye it is, sir. Will yer be placin' a bet now?' Matty hopefully held his hand out.

The man shook his head. 'Ner, matie. I'm Jupiter Payne.'

Barney gulped. He was a giant of a man with his nose plastered across his face. It had obviously been broken many times. But it wasn't that that Barney found unnerving, nor the fact that he had hands like hams. It was his eyes; they looked like those of a snake, and for no reason he could explain, he shivered. Perhaps this wasn't going to be such an easy fight after all. But only time would tell, so he moved on to do some warm-up exercises behind the tent.

Once the circus performance was over the crowds streamed out of the big top, and soon they were swarming into the hall of mirrors and around the many other fairground attractions. Men started to enter the tent for the fight and it wasn't long before all the seats had been taken and there was standing room only.

Luca appeared ready to do the introductions and he too frowned when he clapped eyes on Jupiter Payne, who was dancing from foot to foot at the side of the ring, throwing punches into the air.

'I reckon you've got your work cut out tonight, boyo,' he muttered.

Barney gave a brave shrug. 'I'll be all right, boss. Yer know what they say – the bigger they are the harder they fall.'

'Hmm, well let's hope yer right; there's a lot o' money ridin' on this fight.'

They entered the tent, and a roar went up from the crowd as Luca, with the grace of a cat, swung himself up through the ropes and into the ring. When the crowd had quietened he took up the megaphone and announced, 'Tonight, gentlemen, we will be watching the fight between Jupiter Payne from Leicester and our own Iron Barney.'

With a flourish the two opponents swung themselves theatrically into opposite corners of the ring where they stood weighing each other up warily.

'Remember, gentlemen, I want a clean fight. No hitting below the belt now. So let the fight begin!'

Another roar went up as Luca left the ring and the two men began to circle each other, their fists held up in front of them. Jupiter Payne looked to be at least twice as heavy as Barney, but Barney was light on his feet and easily dodged the blows aimed at him. They danced from side to side like clumsy ballerinas until suddenly, quite without warning, Barney lashed out and caught Jupiter a resounding crack on the nose. Blood started to spurt from it, and he narrowed his eyes in fury, but never for a minute did he show signs of backing off. By the time the referee called time for the end of the first round, Jupiter's nose was still bleeding and one of Barney's eyes had a dark bruise forming around it, but neither of them were showing any signs of tiring.

The second round went much the same as the first, with both men taking some vicious punches but they continued to hold their own. By the time the bell rang, the crowd were on their feet roaring as the pugilists made for their corners.

During the third round Barney took a heavy punch to the stomach that knocked him to the floor, but he was up and fighting again within seconds. By this time the sound of the audience was deafening. In round four it was Barney who meted out the punishment with a blow to the side of Jupiter's head that had him floored, but like Barney he bounced back to his feet and the fight continued. By now, Barney was beginning to realise that he was up against a formidable opponent and Luca was beginning to look a little concerned as he screamed encouragement at Barney from the side of the ring. But Barney was oblivious to everything apart from the man he was facing as he valiantly battled on.

It was during round eight, when both men were beginning to show signs of tiring, that Barney caught sight of Mercy entering the tent with her cousin at her side. For just a split second he was distracted and that was all it took. Jupiter leapt forward and delivered a crushing blow to the side of Barney's head that made him see stars as the ground rushed up to meet him, and then there was blackness.

From far away Barney could hear the referee counting, ten, nine, eight, seven . . . And then there was nothing.

'Come on now, lad.'

There was a voice. Was it talking to him? Barney struggled to open his eyes but the light hurt and only one of them would open, so he stopped trying.

'I think he's starting to come round.'

Barney recognised the voice. It was Charity, Mercy's mother. But where was he? And why did everything hurt so much? He felt as if he had been trampled on by a shire horse.

'Do you think he's goin' to be all right, Mama?'

He recognised that voice instantly. It was Mercy, and she sounded upset.

'To be sure the chavo will be fine eventually. He just needs time to recover,' Charity replied. 'But it'll be a while afore he's well enough to go into the ring again, I'm thinkin'.'

Barney was touched at the concern he heard in Mercy's voice and with an effort he forced his eyes – or at least his one good eye – to open and Charity swam into focus.

'Wh-what 'appened?'

Charity was bathing his face with a cool, wet cloth, and she smiled. 'You took a hammerin', lad, but rest now.' She gently lifted his head and pressed a cup of cold water to his lips, and Barney was sure nothing had ever tasted as good as it dribbled down his chin onto his bare chest. A worried-looking Mercy was standing beside her mother. 'Is there anythin' I can be gettin' you, Barney?' she asked softly.

He tried to shake his head but it hurt too much and he gasped.

'Be off wi' you now, girl,' her mother scolded. 'An' leave him to my tender mercies. He'll be all right, I'm tellin' you.' And to Barney's dismay Mercy did just that.

'I-I was goin' to see me family tomorrow,' he muttered through split lips.

Charity chuckled as she laid his head back down. 'I don't think you'll be goin' anywhere for a few days.' She gently smoothed the damp hair from his forehead. 'But the good thing is there are no bones broken so after a rest you'll be good as new. Now lie still, I 'ave things to do, but I'll be back shortly.' And with that she lifted the tin bowl of bloody water and quietly left the trailer.

Chapter Thirty

In London, Eve was feeling no happier than Barney. The child she was carrying was now impossible to hide and over the last month she had barely left the plush flat. It wasn't so bad during the daytime when Milly was there to keep her company, but the nights seemed to stretch on and on when Susan was out entertaining her clients, which was most evenings. She and Milly had become close friends during the time she had stayed there. Eve had begged Milly not to tell Davey about her condition and had also told her what she planned to do after the birth. The girl was no fool, and although Susan never spoke of her trade, Milly was very aware of how she earned her living.

'Are you quite sure that's what you want to do?' she had asked Eve when she told her. 'It might be easier said than done to give the baby up once you've seen it.'

'Oh yes, an' how am I supposed to keep it?' Eve had asked with tears in her eyes. Strangely enough, ever since she had felt the child move inside her, her feelings towards it had started to change. After all, she had reasoned, the baby was the innocent in all this and hadn't asked to be born. And although the child had been forced upon her it would still have her blood flowing through its veins. 'I can't even keep meself wi'out a job an' somewhere to live, so how am I supposed to keep a baby?'

Milly had chewed on her lip as she thought of her friend's dilemma. 'Does Annie know about the baby?' she had asked eventually.

Eve nodded. 'An' about what yer plannin' to do for a livin' after it's born?'

Shamefaced Eve had hung her head. 'No, she don't know about that. She don't know what Susan does either. Susan told 'er she works in a hotel.'

The conversation had ended abruptly there when Susan had returned from a shopping spree, and they hadn't spoken of it since.

On this balmy April day Eve was ironing one of Susan's elaborate gowns, which was no easy task, when Susan returned looking faintly dishevelled. She hadn't come home the night before, but Eve was used to that, so she hadn't been overly concerned.

'Are you all right?' Eve asked as Susan sat down heavily on the nearest chair. It was then that Eve noticed a bruise forming over one of her eyes and she gasped in horror. 'Miss Susanne, what's 'appened to you?'

'Oh . . . it's nothing!' Susan tried to wave her away. 'Just one of my clients got . . . shall we say, a little over-enthusiastic.'

'Why, the lousy swine!' Eve had never been one to mince her words. 'He oughter be locked up fer doin' this to you. I'll go an' make yer a nice cup o' hot, sweet tea. They reckon it's good fer shock.' She raced away to the kitchen just as Milly arrived back with a basket full of shopping.

'Some lousy bugger's been knockin' Susan about,' Eve whispered as she filled the kettle. 'She's goin' to 'ave a right shiner on 'er when the bruise over 'er eye comes out.'

Milly shrugged as she placed the basket on the table. 'Well, it won't be the first time,' she stated matter-of-factly. 'It's normal in 'er job. Some o' the punters like it rough.'

'I bet Theo will sort 'im out!'

Milly snorted with derision. 'Theo will probably get paid a bit extra to keep 'is trap shut more like. You do realise that he's Susan's pimp, don't yer?'

Eve's mouth dropped open. '*What*? . . . But I thought he were 'er man friend. She wants to marry 'im, she told me so.'

'Huh! So do all the other women who 'e pimps out. That's 'ow he gets 'em in his clutches. He makes 'em all believe they're special an' that he'll marry 'em one day. But he'll drop 'em all like a ton o' bricks when their looks start to fade an' replace 'em wi' younger models. You just see if 'e don't!'

'Oh, poor Susan. Doesn't she know?'

'There's none so blind as them as don't wanna see,' Milly said flatly as she began to unpack the shopping. 'And she's blind when it comes to 'im. He's got her exactly where he wants 'er. But you go help 'er get undressed. I'll make the tea an' bring it through.'

Eve found Susan sitting where she had left her, her face the colour of putty. 'Come on,' she said cheerfully. 'Let's get you outta them clothes an' into your dressin' robe, then you can 'ave a nice 'ot drink an' rest fer awhile.' She helped Susan into the bedroom and as she helped her remove her gown, she blinked to stop the tears that threatened to fall. There were vivid purple and black bruises up Susan's arms and all across her back, and it was obvious that she'd taken a severe beating.

'Whoever did this to you is worse than an animal,' Eve ground out as she helped Susan into her robe. 'You ain't gonna be able to work for days now till these are all gone.'

'Aw well, I suppose it will be nice to have a little time off.' Susan stroked the girl's cheek. She had grown fond of Eve in the time they'd spent together and already she was feeling guilty for the life she was about to lead her into. Although she was carrying a child, she was such an innocent in many ways.

Milly appeared with her tea then and after she had drunk it, Eve tucked her into bed and left her to rest while she went back to her pile of ironing.

Theo arrived shortly after, being his usual charming self, but for the first time, Eve found herself disliking him.

'Miss Susanne is in bed. She took a beatin' last night,' she informed him shortly.

He strode past her and into Susan's room, closing the door firmly behind him.

'Our Davey were askin' after you last night,' Milly said innocently as she and Eve sat at the kitchen table having a well-earned cup of tea a little later. 'He wonders why yer don't go down into the foyer or come round ours to see him anymore. I suppose you've guessed that he's got a soft spot fer you.'

'An' why do yer think I've stopped?' Eve retorted more sharply than she had meant to. 'Do yer think he'd still be interested when he found out I've got another man's baby growin' in me belly?' If truth be told she had begun to think fondly of him too, but she knew it was hopeless. Her future was set, and although she was nervous about the direction it was going in, she was powerless to do anything about it.

Milly sighed as she carried her cup to the sink. As far as she was concerned what was going on was a downright shame. Eve clearly wasn't sure about the future Susan had mapped out for her, but as Eve had said, what other option did she have?

Suddenly an idea came to her. 'What about if I asked me Ma how she'd feel about lookin' after you an' your baby when it comes? Wi' our lot, a couple more wouldn't make that much difference an' the extra money she got fer lookin' after it while you were at work would certainly come in 'andy. That way you wouldn't 'ave to give the baby up if yer didn't want to.'

Eve chewed on her lip as she thought about it. The idea had taken her completely by surprise. She liked Milly's mother and had no doubt that the baby would be very well cared for. And as Eve had said, it meant she might be able to keep it if she felt that way inclined after it was born.

But then common sense kicked in. 'How would we explain the baby away to Davey? An' worse still, what would 'e think o' me workin' wi' Susan? He still wouldn't want to know me when he found out what I was doin' fer a livin',' Eve pointed out forlornly.

'So get yerself a different job. You don't 'ave to go on the game,' Milly replied.

The idea was tempting, but after a few seconds thought, Eve shook her head. 'I appreciate you carin', but it still couldn't work. Your mam 'as her hands full wi' your lot wi'out me putttin' on 'er. But thanks fer offerin'.'

Milly shrugged. 'I suppose yer right,' she said sadly. 'But I can't 'elp thinkin' yer better than that. Not that I'm knockin' Susan,' she added hastily. 'She's a lovely person. Trouble is, that Theo plays 'er like a fiddle an' she falls for his lies hook, line an' sinker. I just wish she'd wake up an' see 'im for what he really is.'

'Yer know what they say, "love is blind an' makes fools of all of us".' Eve blinked back tears as she tenderly stroked her stomach, then heaving herself out of the chair, she went to make a start on their dinner.

Theo emerged from Susan's bedroom shortly after with a face like thunder, and without a word to either Eve or Milly he stormed from the apartment banging the door resoundingly behind him.

Milly nodded towards the bedroom door and suggested, 'Do you think you ought to go in an' see how she is?'

Eve nodded somewhat reluctantly and went to tap on the door but there was no reply, although she could hear Susan crying. She tapped again, a little louder this time, and when there was still no response, she inched the door open and stepped inside.

'Are you all right, Miss Susanne?' Tentatively she moved towards the bed and Susan turned to look at her, clutching a large white handkerchief.

'Yes . . . yes I'm fine . . . it's just . . .' Her voice broke off and she began to sob even louder as Eve sat down on the bed beside her and took her clammy hand in hers.

She waited patiently for the sobs to subside before asking gently. 'Mr Theo didn't 'urt you, did 'e?'

'Oh no . . .' Susan sniffed loudly. 'It's just that I told him I thought this might be a good time for me to retire from my, er . . . escorting, and for us to get married.'

'I see. An' was he not keen on the idea?'

'Oh, I don't think it's because he doesn't want to,' Susan said defensively. 'It's just that he said he wasn't in a good enough financial position to do that just yet.'

'An' don't he always say that?'

Susan snatched her hand away. 'If you're insinuating that he has no intention of ever marrying me you're wrong,' she snapped.

Eve wondered if she was trying to convince her or herself.

'And now if you don't mind, I'd like to rest.'

Sadly, Eve rose and left the room. Like Milly had said, there were none so blind as those who didn't want to see and from where she was standing, Susan was one of them.

Chapter Thirty-One

Late one evening in April, Annie and Levi sat together looking through the business's ledgers. 'I can't believe what a good job you've made o' these, pet,' he praised. 'They were in a rare old state when you first started workin' on 'em, an' now they're all bang up to date. A lot o' the money that was owin' 'as been paid an' all thanks to you. Well done. An' you've made a difference round at the yard too. I've never seen it so well organised.'

'I'm glad you're pleased,' Annie answered. 'But I think there's still room for improvement.'

Levi cocked his eyebrow. 'Oh aye, in what way?'

'For a start off, now that you're collectin' clothes from the better areas o' town I think it's a shame to sell 'em on to the rag stall. You could ask a lot more for 'em if we sold 'em ourselves.'

Levi frowned as he considered her idea. 'But how could we do that?'

'Quite easily.' Annie had clearly given this a lot of thought. 'There's more than enough room in the rag-sortin' shed to fit a few clothes rails. Peggy has already said that she'd be 'appy to wash an' iron the good stuff an' sell it on fer you.'

'You mean like a sort of second-hand shop?'

She nodded enthusiastically. 'Yes. She only earns a pittance up at the work'ouse an' it ain't always easy fer 'er to find someone to look after Ellie now Sid is gone. If you were to cover the wages she earned there, I reckon you could still make a really good profit.'

He thought about it for a moment. Already it was apparent that despite her tender years Annie had a very good business head on her shoulders. He nodded. 'I dare say it's worth givin' it a go. What else did yer 'ave in mind?'

'Now that Sid's not 'ere the scrap man that comes once a month to collect what you've taken tends to take the lot, but if it were sorted into piles o' the different metals you'd fetch far more. He's only givin' you the basic pay for metal an' steel, but copper an' lead are worth a lot more. I wouldn't mind doin' that.'

'But don't you think you're already doin' more than yer fair share?' Levi worried that the family was putting too much on the girl. As well as running the house, she was also helping him, and he was concerned that it was too much responsibility for her young shoulders. Harry had started an apprenticeship with a butcher in the town and had turned into a right little Romeo, always off out with some pretty young lass or another. When he wasn't working, Charlie seemed to spend most of the time over in Coventry with his circle of friends. He had finished college now and was working in an accountant's office. Barney was still off with the circus somewhere, clearly with no intention of coming back and joining the business, and Maggie was neither use nor ornament but just sat about the house all day expecting to be waited on.

'Are you sure it wouldn't be too much for you?' His eyes were troubled as he stared at Annie.

She smiled. 'Don't forget you pay me a wage now,' she pointed out. It was the first time in her life that she'd had any money of her own and although it was only a modest wage, she was saving every penny she could.

'I'll tell yer what, we'll give yer suggestions a try if you'll let me up yer wages a bit,' he said eventually. 'An' o' course I'd be more than 'appy to pay Peggy fer whatever she does. Is that a deal?'

'Deal,' she agreed and they shook hands on it.

The next morning when Annie arrived at the yard and told Peggy that Levi was happy to try out her idea, they began to sort through the clothes Levi had collected over the last week. In no time at all they had sorted out a pile that would have graced any lady's back, and Peggy bustled away to wash the clothes that needed it and to press the rest. They had agreed they would only sell the best and the rest would go to the rag stall as before.

That evening after arriving back at the yard, Levi looked about the rag shed in amazement. All the rags had been moved to the very back and Annie had hung a clean white sheet in front of them and scrubbed the front of the shed until it was spotless.

'I wonder if you could make me some shelves and put up some hanging rails on that wall over there for me?' she asked Levi. 'Then anyone who wants to try anything on can do so in 'ere. Peggy's got an' old mirror that she's bringin' across so as they can see what they look like in the clothes before they buy 'em.'

'Seems to me you've thought of everythin',' Levi said approvingly as he went off in search of some wood for the shelves. By the time he and Annie left almost two hours later he had fitted two broad shelves and a lengthy clothes rail ready for the garments when Peggy had finished preparing them.

'I thought I'd make a sign tonight advertisin' the clothes to put at the bottom o' the alley,' Annie told him as they clip-clopped towards Swan Lane.

Levi smiled indulgently. Both Annie and Peggy seemed quite excited about the new venture and he'd even seen Peggy smile – really smile – for the first time since she had lost Sid, so he hoped they'd be successful.

Back at the house Levi went to stable Dobbin while Annie went into the kitchen. She had cooked and prepared a large cottage pie for their dinner that morning and it would only need heating up. She found Maggie sitting primly in her favourite chair in a very becoming gown she had ordered from London the week before. Levi had baulked at the price but was reluctant to deny her anything while her mental state was so fragile. She had piled her hair high onto her head and looked more as if she should be going to some very grand event rather than sitting at home all day. She rarely ventured anywhere now apart from to go to St Mary's each Sunday for the morning service.

Levi had just come in when the door opened and Barney walked in. Maggie was on her feet in an instant, clearly thrilled to see him, until she saw the state of his face. Peggy had mentioned to Annie earlier that the circus was back in town, so she wasn't wholly surprised to see him.

'Oh, my *poor* darling! Whatever have you done to your face?' Maggie gasped, throwing her arms around him.

Barney grinned self-consciously. 'It's nothin' really.' He glanced across at his father. 'Let's just say I got it in a fight. I didn't win this time, but the other chap looks worse than me,' he ended hastily. His eyes found Annie then and he smiled at her.

The questions began next. 'How long are you here for? Can you stay for dinner? Will you—'

'*Whoa!*' Barney held his hand up to stop the flow of questions. 'One at a time eh, Ma? Yer makin' me feel dizzy.' It had been three days since the fight and if he were honest, he still didn't feel right, although he was a lot better than he had been. His face still throbbed and he had an idea he might have broken a rib as it hurt to breathe. Charity hadn't been at all happy about him going out and about so soon, but he had wanted to visit his family.

'In answer to yer first question, we should be here fer about a month or so. An' yes, I'd like to stay fer dinner if it ain't no trouble.' He gently put her from him and looked over at Annie. 'But I won't stay if it's gonna put you out.'

Annie gave him a friendly smile. 'It won't put me out at all, the pie is almost big enough to feed the street.'

His parents demanded his attention then as they asked all about what he'd been doing in the time since they'd last seen him, and Annie was pleased to see Maggie so animated for a change. Both

Charlie and Harry arrived home soon after and so it was almost like a family reunion when they all sat down to eat together, and the atmosphere was light. For dessert, Annie had cooked an enormous jam roly-poly, which just happened to be one of Barney's favourites. She served it with a large jug of thick, creamy custard and after two helpings, Barney leant back in his chair and groaned.

'I don't think I'll be able to eat another thing fer at least two days. That were lovely!'

Annie flushed with pleasure at the compliment as she started to clear the table. Charlie stood to help her; he'd made no secret of the fact that he wasn't as pleased to see his brother as the rest of the family was.

'It's good, isn't it?' he hissed to Annie as they washed up. 'He clears off wi'out a word o' warnin', leavin' you an' Da to do all the work, an' me an' Harry to tip some of us wages up, yet when he bothers to come back to see us, from the way me ma carries on, you'd think he were a returnin' conquerin' hero!'

Elbow-deep in hot soapy water, Annie chuckled. 'I dare say she'd be just the same if you or Harry were to go,' she tried to placate him.

'Even so, I'm glad I'm going out tonight if he's going to be here,' Charlie answered resentfully.

Annie felt a little stab of disappointment. He'd been a great help with teaching her how to balance the ledgers, and she'd been hoping that she could go over the last week's figures with him that evening, and tell him about their plans for their little clothes shed.

'I half expected a visit when I heard the circus were in town,' Charlie went on. 'Me an' a couple o' me friends thought we might go down there this Saturday. Why don't you come with us?'

Annie blushed. Had Charlie asked her to go with him on her own she would have jumped at the chance, but she wasn't so keen on going with young men she had never met before.

'I'll see how busy I am,' she said, not wanting to hurt his feelings, and he shrugged.

When the washing up was done and everything had been put away, Annie made a large pot of tea and carried it through to Maggie and Levi, who were still chatting to Barney. Harry had gone out to meet his latest girlfriend and once again Charlie had caught the train into Coventry.

'Da tells me you've been a great 'elp to 'im wi' the business,' Barney told her with a smile that would have charmed the birds off the trees.

'Oh, I ain't done that much,' she answered modestly, and after pouring them all a cup of tea she excused herself and went up to her room to make the poster advertising the clothes for sale, and to get an early night. It had been a very long day.

When she arrived at the yard the next morning, Annie found Peggy had already hung some of the garments on the rail in the clothes shed.

'While I was washin' an' ironin' some o' the things I noticed a few had slight damage on 'em so I got to thinkin'.' Peggy puffed her chest out with pride. 'There were so much material in some o' these gowns that I unpicked 'em an' made 'em into lengths o' material. Look . . .' She crossed to one of the shelves and lifted down some lengths for Annie to look at.

Annie was impressed. 'What a brilliant idea, Peggy.' She beamed at her. 'Some of these would make a wonderful dress for a child or a skirt for an adult, perhaps.'

'That's what I thought. Have yer put the sign out at the end o' the alley?'

'I have, but I shall also add material for sale this evening. I'd better go and sort some o' the metal into piles if you think you can manage 'ere.'

'O' course I can.' Peggy smoothed the material of her skirt and patted her hair, for all the world as if she was going to serve royalty, and settled down to wait for her first customer.

As the morning dragged on, she began to think no one was ever going to come, but at last she heard footsteps in the ginnel and a harassed woman with a young child clutching her skirt appeared. She had a basket full of food shopping and Peggy greeted her jovially.

''Ello, luvvie, if yer lookin' fer a bargain yer've come to the right place. What was it you were lookin' for exactly?'

'Well . . .' The woman eyed the clothes rail warily. 'It said on yer sign outside that yer were sellin' second-hand, good quality clothes at a fair price an' I'm lookin' fer a gown fer me sister's weddin' in a couple o' weeks' time. I were goin' to 'ave a go at makin' somethin' but I ain't that good wi' a needle if truth be told.'

'Then I reckon we might 'ave just the thing 'ere.' Peggy lifted down a very pretty day gown in a soft shade of lemon trimmed with white lace. 'What do yer think o' this one? The colour would set yer hair off a treat. The only trouble is yer might outshine the bride. Would yer like to try it on?'

The woman stroked the gown reverently. It was made of a fine cotton and sprigged all over with tiny sprays of lilacs.

'I'm not so sure I could afford this,' she said honestly.

'Why don't yer just try it on afore yer make yer mind up?' Peggy said persuasively.

The young woman took the dress behind the sheets to undress, and Peggy helped her into the gown. When it was fastened, she turned to face the mirror and gasped with pleasure.

'Oh, it's just beautiful! I feel like a toff in this, but 'ow much is it?'

'Hmm, how about five shillin's? Sommat like that would cost you quite a few pounds if you were to 'ave it made an' it is fer a special occasion. I'll bet there'll be no one else at the weddin' wearin' a dress o' that quality.'

The young woman chewed her lip as she turned this way and that. Even five shillings was a lot of money to her, but eventually she smiled. 'Make it four an' a tanner an' you've got yerself a deal!'

'Eeh, yer drive a hard bargain. I'm practically givin' it away at that price, but all right then. Just be sure to tell all yer friends about us. We've got stock comin' in daily. Oh, an' I've got some lovely lengths o' material, an' all. You could happen make a dress fer the little 'un out o' one o' these, an' then there'd be a pair o' bobby-dazzlers at the weddin''.'

Eventually the young woman left with her gown and a length of blue satin to make her little daughter a gown, and Peggy was thrilled. She had made her first sale.

Annie, meantime, had been busily sorting the metal, when Peggy carried a well-earned cup of tea over to her, giggling when she saw the state of her. Annie's hair had come loose from its pins and her face was smudged with dirt, but she was smiling.

'Crikey, lass, yer look like you've been pulled through a hedge back'ards,' she laughed.

Taking the tea from her, Annie shrugged. 'No pain, no gain. An' look at the difference 'ere already. The mister could be sittin' on a little gold mine if he were a bit more organised.'

Peggy's face became solemn for a moment as she commented, 'I notice yer allus call Levi "the mister". Why is that? He's surely more of a dad to you after all this time?'

Annie nodded. 'He is an' I think the world of 'im. But I don't reckon the missus would be happy if I were to call 'im Dad. She's never encouraged that sort of a closeness. To her I'm just a maid an' I reckon I allus will be. You've allus been more of a mam to me than she 'as.'

Peggy clamped her lips together as she gave Annie a little hug. Annie was telling the truth and it was a crying shame, but she didn't feel it was her place to comment, and after all, Annie seemed happy enough, so she turned and bustled away to get on with what she had been doing.

Chapter Thirty-Two

June 1913

The heat in London was unbearable and Eve stood by the open window of Susan's apartment fanning herself with a newspaper. She felt like a beached whale and waddled rather than walked, and she had forgotten what her feet looked like. It had been many weeks since she had ventured out of the house during the day for fear of seeing Davey downstairs. She wouldn't be able to bear the shame of him seeing her like this and just wanted the whole thing to be over now.

The day before, she had received a letter from Annie and as she read it, she had never felt lonelier in her whole life. Annie was the best real friend she had ever had and she still missed her every day, although she was close to Milly now too. Added to this was the uncertainty of not knowing what was to become of her unborn child. If it was adopted, then she would be free to do what she wanted with the rest of her life, but the temptation to keep it was a constant ache. But what would become of her if she did?

Eve sighed as she stared out at the fast-moving traffic rattling along on the road below. Recently the baby had kept her awake at night with its kicking and it had brought home to her more sharply than ever that this was a real little person who she was about to abandon – just as her own mother had once abandoned her. That knowledge had scarred Eve for life and she wondered if it would do the same for her child?

Turning, she made her way into the kitchen where Milly was preparing some cold slices of meat and a salad for lunch. It was too hot for anything warm.

'How you feelin'?' Milly asked with a smile.

'Oh, yer know . . . fat.' Eve absent-mindedly stroked her swelling stomach.

'Look, yer can tell me to mind me own business if yer like,' Milly said tentatively, watching her closely. 'But are yer quite sure you're doin' the right thing givin' this baby up? Yer don't seem so keen on the idea now as yer did when yer first arrived. I could still talk to me Mam about fostering it for you, you know.'

'I'm not sure,' Eve confessed as she sank down onto one of the chairs that surrounded the kitchen table. 'And thanks fer the offer but I don't think that would work. I'd always feel that I had to be a part of its life an' that wouldn't be fair to it. Trouble is, I ain't got no way o' keepin' it – or meself if it comes to that, so I don't really 'ave much choice but to let it go, do I?'

'But what about Annie? Wouldn't she know someone who could 'elp yer out back at 'ome?'

'I 'ad thought o' that,' Eve admitted. 'But the trouble is, were I to go back there, Mr Taylor-Lloyd might twig that the baby were 'is, an' then there'd be trouble big time.'

'Rubbish,' Milly snorted. 'All you 'ave to say is that it weren't 'is. He's got no way o' provin' it, an' I ain't so sure he'd want to anyway. Why don't yer just think about it at least, cos from what you've said you don't seem too keen on the life Miss Susannne 'as got lined up fer you neither.'

Eve flushed and suppressed a shudder. She had never been that keen on the idea, although being an escort to lonely gentlemen had sounded quite glamorous. She had thought it meant she would be wined and dined by them, but having lived with Susan she now knew that it involved much more than that, and after being violated by Mr Taylor-Lloyd she didn't know how she was going to stand it. A solitary tear slid down her cheek. Everything seemed so awful at present and more than anything she wished she could just see Annie. Struggling up out of the chair she told Milly, 'I'm gonna go an' write to Annie an' see if she ain't too busy to come an' visit us fer a few days.'

Milly nodded. 'Good idea, a visit from yer chum might perk you up a bit.'

She watched with concern as Eve waddled away, her shoulders drooping.

In Nuneaton, Barney's mood was no better than Eve's. He was standing in the shade of the big top watching Mercy and her cousin's progress over the field. They were probably going to have a dip in the stream and jealousy seethed through him. He had expected the chap to be long gone by now but there he still was, larger than life and twice as handsome. And to make matters worse the rest of his family had arrived that day, and Luca was having a party after the performance to celebrate; he could see Charity busily preparing for it as she set up the tables between the trailers.

'Barney!' Luca's sharp voice sliced through his thoughts and Barney twisted towards him, gasping as the sudden movement made his chest throb. His broken rib still wasn't properly healed, although the worst of his cuts and bruises were almost gone now. 'Get round an' exercise the horses, would yer? An' make sure they've got food an' water. They're first in the ring this evenin'.'

'Right y'are, boss.' Barney loped away. Seeing to the horses, or any of the animals, was usually one of his favourite jobs, but today he couldn't seem to focus on anything. Earlier on he had managed to snatch a few moments alone with Mercy, who was as miserable about Bertie's presence as he was.

'I've got a horrible feeling Dad is trying to marry us off,' she had confided. 'And I don't know how I could bear it. It's *you* I love, Barney, but the chances of Dad ever allowing us to marry are zero.'

'If he tries to do that we'll run away,' he had responded. 'No one should be forced to marry someone they don't love. Think about it, we could go somewhere no one knows us an' start a new life together.'

'But how would we live?' she asked tremulously.

He shrugged. 'I'll get us a room an' find a job. We'd manage. Will yer consider it?'

She was prevented from answering when Bertie suddenly appeared and glared at him as he placed his arm about Mercy's shoulders. 'Come on, sweet'eart. Yer dad is lookin' fer us.'

Suddenly Barney had snapped and swinging his fist back he landed a thump on Bertie's chin that almost floored him.

'You get yer 'ands off 'er else I'll *kill* yer,' he roared.

Luckily for Bertie, Noah and Luca appeared to pull him away.

'What's to do 'ere then?' Luca was furious. 'We'll 'ave less o' that talk, Barney, else you'll be getting' yer marchin' orders. Do yer hear me?'

A crowd had assembled by then, and Charity hurried over to rush Mercy away. Bertie rose to his feet and leered at Barney over his shoulder as Luca led him away.

Noah caught Barney's arm as he made to go after them. 'Give it up, man. You've got to get over this silly obsession you 'ave wi' Mercy. You ain't one of us an' Mercy will marry who me dad chooses fer 'er so get used to the idea.' Then he had marched away, leaving Barney to clench his fists as the crowd around them slowly dispersed.

The day seemed to drag by interminably slowly, until finally at about six o'clock the visitors began to arrive and file into the big top. Mercy was to be the second act on after the performing horses and when she appeared from her trailer in her skimpy, glittering costume, his heart began to thud. She really was an incredibly beautiful girl.

For one brief second their eyes locked. It had been hard enough before Bertie had arrived, as Noah had always known that Barney had feelings for his sister and had guarded her jealously, but now things were even more difficult. And then, as if thoughts of him had conjured him up, Bertie appeared behind her and the moment was lost as he possessively took Mercy's arm and walked with her to the big top. With a low growl Barney clenched his hands into fists and turned away.

At last the show was over and the crowd poured from the big top intent on enjoying themselves at the fair. Barney was working on the swing boats that evening, even though he wasn't fully recovered from the fight, and more than one pretty girl eyed him flirtatiously as he pulled on the heavy rope that sent the boats sailing into the air, but he wasn't interested.

Once the crowd thinned, a few of the circus folk lit bonfires, while Charity and the other women placed dishes of food on the tables they had set out earlier, and the party began. The circus band played tunes on their fiddles and the younger ones began to dance, the girls' gaily coloured skirts swirling about them in a rainbow of colours.

Barney sat at the edge of the dancing, his eyes jealously following Mercy who was trapped within the circle of her cousin's arm; it took all Barney's willpower not to go and punch Bertie on the nose and snatch her away from him.

Barrels of beer had been rolled out and as the men drank their fill, the night grew louder with laughter and high spirits. It was pitch-dark, everyone's faces rosy in the glow from the fires, when Luca finally hopped lightly onto a chair and loudly called for everyone's attention. Bertie's parents were standing at the side of him with broad smiles on their faces as a hush fell on the crowd so all that could be heard was the popping of the logs on the fires and the sounds of the night creatures in the surrounding hedgerows.

'I've gathered you all here tonight to make an announcement,' Luca told them with a fond smile at Mercy, who had gone to join him with her head bowed. 'As of this fine evenin', my beautiful daughter Mercy will be betrothed to her cousin Bertrand Russell!

The comin' together o' these two young people will join two o' the best circuses in the whole land. So raise yer glasses, please, an' drink a toast to Mercy an' Bertie. May God bless 'em wi' many children an' many happy years together.'

As a cheer went up from the crowd, Barney felt his legs go weak as he watched Bertie swing Mercy towards him and kiss her soundly on the lips. Mercy looked pale and dazed. Their worst fears had been realised and Barney had to blink hard to stop the tears that were burning at the back of his eyes from falling. Quiet as a mouse he slid into the shadows. The further away he walked the quieter it became as the sounds of the party faded into the distance. Eventually, he threw himself down on the grass beside a hedgerow and beat the ground with his fists as he allowed the tears to flow.

'*Damn Luca and the stupid circus traditions,*' he cursed brokenly. He had loved Mercy from the very first day he had set eyes on her. It had taken her a time to realise that she felt the same about him, and now he was heartbroken. After a time, he pulled himself together, and swiping the tears from his eyes, he thrust his hands deep into his pockets and set off back to the camp. Most people had gone by that time and the fires had burned low, so after doing a final check on the circus animals, as he did each night, he retired to his own small trailer – although he was so distraught he doubted he would sleep.

As he approached it, sounds reached him from the edge of the field. He paused to listen and his heart skipped a beat. It was Mercy and she sounded as if she was in distress.

Without even stopping to think he made his way towards the noise, and he had almost reached her when he heard her threaten, 'Get your hands off me now or so 'elp me, Bertie Russell, I'll kill yer!'

The sound of Bertie's drunken laughter floated on the air. 'Now come on, schweet'eart. We're betrothed now sho why wait fer the weddin' night, eh?'

Fury raged through Barney's veins as he hastened his steps. Mercy was crying and as he drew closer, he saw that her blouse was torn and Bertie was pawing at her naked breasts as she tried to fight him off. And that was when it happened. Barney tried to reach them faster, but his broken ribs prevented it and he saw Bertie launch himself at Mercy as she drew a knife from the belt of her skirt and it sank into his chest. Bertie gave a strangled howl and dropped to the floor.

For a moment, Mercy just stood there sobbing and shaking, but then catching sight of Barney, she flew to him and threw her arms about him. 'Barney. I-I think I've killed 'im!'

He gently put her from him and bent to feel Bertie's pulse. But there was nothing and his eyes were staring sightlessly at the moonlit sky. Barney looked about to make sure they were alone before dragging the knife from Bertie's chest and shoving it into his belt.

'Right, now *listen* to me,' he said sternly as he gently shook Mercy. She was on the verge of hysteria. 'You're to go back to your trailer and say nothing about this to anyone. Do you hear me?'

She nodded. 'Y-yes.'

'Good girl. Go on now.' He turned her about and gave her a little push in the back, and she set off unsteadily over the field. When Barney was sure she was gone, he made his way to his own trailer where he threw the bloodstained knife as far under his bed as it would go before throwing his bloodied shirt after it. There was nothing anyone could do for Bertie now.

He rose early the next day after a restless night and was surprised to find Mercy hovering outside his trailer. There was no one else in sight and he could see how terrified she was.

'I-I'm so sorry, Barney,' she murmured, glancing around to ensure no one else was about. 'But you do understand, don't you? I was only tryin' to defend meself. He were tryin' to . . . to . . .'

'Aye, I understand. The dirty bastard deserved all he got. But you must promise me that you'll say not a word about what 'appened to anyone. It'll be only a matter o' time till someone finds 'is body an' then this place will be teemin' wi' police, but remember, you know nothin! Okay?'

'Okay.'

Her words trailed off as the bearded lady emerged from her trailer, yawning and stretching with her small dog at her feet.

Mercy shot away, and Barney stared after her, desperately trying to think of a way they could be together. Perhaps they should run away? He dismissed that idea almost immediately; it would look too suspicious, so they would have to bide their time.

With a throaty growl he strode away to begin his chores – he didn't feel like any breakfast that day.

Almost an hour later, as the circus folk went about their business, a scream rent the air and they all paused to look towards it, while those who had been having a lie-in appeared at the doors of their trailers.

'What the 'ell is goin' on?' Luca shouted, as he too appeared, bare-chested.

'I don't know but the sound came from over there towards the 'edge,' Barney informed him innocently.

They both raced around there only to stop abruptly when they saw Gypsy Rose Lee bending over a body on the ground.

'Were it you who screamed, Rose?' Luca asked.

Looking up, she nodded, her face ashen. 'I were takin' me dog out an' I come across this young chap 'ere.'

'Is 'e hurt?'

'It's worse than that.' The woman had recovered from the initial shock, and as she rolled the body over onto its back, they gasped as they saw that it was Bertie. His eyes were staring sightlessly up into the early morning sky and his clothes were soaked in blood.

Chapter Thirty-Three

Soon after the body had been found the field was swarming with police and the shocked circus folk stood about, waiting to be questioned.

'Do you know anyone who might have had cause to do this?' an officer asked Luca.

He shook his head. 'Not really. We just announced his engagement to me daughter last night although . . .' He paused to stroke his chin. 'There were a bit of a ruckus, come to think of it. Him an' Barney, a chap that travels wi' us, 'ad a bit of a fight yesterday.'

'I see, and could you tell me where I might find this Barney?'

Luca nodded towards Barney, who remained calm as the policeman approached him.

Mercy, meanwhile, stood with her mother's arm about her shoulders. Dry-eyed but clearly shaken.

As the police methodically questioned everyone, an ambulance arrived and Bertie's body was taken away.

Barney, accompanied by two policemen, went back to his trailer, where they started to question him.

'Could you tell us what your scuffle with Mr Russell was about, sir?'

Barney nodded. 'Mercy were bein' made to marry someone she didn't want an' I didn't agree wi' it.'

'Because?'

'Because me an' Mercy are in love an' *I* want to marry 'er,' he admitted sullenly.

'I see.' The policemen exchanged glances. Here was a motive for murder if ever they'd heard one. 'And was it you who killed Mr Russell?'

'No, it weren't,' Barney said bluntly.

Until the cause of death had been established by the police doctor there was no point in questioning him further, so the officers rose. 'It appears that Mr Russell had been dead for some hours so we'll be asking whether anyone heard anything. Please don't leave the camp. We will need to question you further when we know more details.'

Grim-faced, Barney nodded, and once the door had closed behind them, he put his head in his hands.

It was much later that day before Barney managed to catch Mercy alone for a few minutes. She was sitting in her trailer staring into space, and as much as he had disliked Bertie intensely, he hated to see her so upset. From the trailer next door he could hear Bertie's mother wailing and the deep rumble of Bertie's father's voice as he tried to soothe her.

'I, er ... I'm sorry about what's happened,' she said softly. 'What's done is done and can't be undone, but if I were to tell the truth ...' She paused to flick her long dark hair across her shoulder. 'I can't pretend to be heartbroken – I'd be a hypocrite if I did. But what I can say is ... I didn't mean to kill 'im. I took me knife out just to make him step away from me, but he lunged forward an' ...'

Barney was unsure what to say to this, but then Noah suddenly appeared.

'You didn't 'ave anythin' to do wi' this did yer, Barney?' he said, staring at him accusingly.

'*What?* No, I didn't,' Barney snapped. 'Why would you even *think* that?'

'Cos of your feelin's fer me sister, an' after yer fracas wi' him yesterday ... But ...' He held his hand up to stop Barney from saying any more. 'I also know that in the time I've known yer I've never found yer to be a liar, so we'll say no more.' He turned and strode away. It was his turn next to be questioned, but like everyone else they had already spoken to there was little he could add to help them.

'You'd best go now. It won't look good if you're seen here talking to me,' said Mercy.

Realising she was probably right, he too left and went back to his trailer. There were officers everywhere scouring the area for a likely weapon but as yet they had found nothing. Barney made a mental note to get rid of the knife the first chance he got. It wouldn't do for it to be found in his trailer.

Two days passed before Barney got a chance to speak to Mercy alone again. The story of the murder had made headlines and had been splashed across the front of all the newspapers – although as yet the victim had not been named – and an unusual number of people were visiting the scene of the crime.

He caught her as she was coming out of the big top following her trapeze performance and drew her to the side out of sight.

'How are Bertie's mam and dad?' He knew what a ridiculous question this was the second the words had left his lips.

'Obviously they're devastated.' Mercy looked tired as she fiddled with the beads on her outfit. 'They're takin' 'is body to be buried in Suffolk where the family come from. Me an' me mam an' dad will be goin' wi' 'em to attend the funeral as a mark o' respect.'

He could understand that. After all, be it very briefly, Bertie and Mercy had been engaged to be married, although Barney noticed she wasn't wearing the diamond ring he had given her.

'How long will you be gone for?

'Not more than three or four days, I shouldn't think. Dad is leavin' Noah in charge.'

'I see. Well . . . I hope it all goes well. Thankfully from what I've heard the police are still no closer to workin' out what happened.'

When she looked away, he added hastily, 'It has to stay that way, Mercy. Don't weaken now.'

'Of course I won't. But now if yer don't mind I 'ave to go an' get changed. I'm on the hook-a-duck stall in a minute.'

He watched her walk away before hurrying on to get the horses into their sparkling plumed headdresses ready for their performance.

Barney visited his parents again the following Sunday afternoon and found his mother in an agitated state.

'I want you to leave that circus and come home *right* now!' she told him. 'I never liked you living like that. And what has happened to that young man just goes to prove how dangerous that way of life is. It could have been *you* that was killed.' She shuddered at the thought, and Annie hurried off to fetch her a glass of water. Maggie had been a bag of nerves ever since she had read about the murder in the newspaper.

'But it wasn't me, Ma, an' don't worry, I know 'ow to look after meself.' He gently stroked her hand as she started to cry.

Barney looked towards his father who smiled at him sadly. 'Don't worry, son. It's just been a bit of a shock fer 'er. But tell me, 'ow much longer will yer be stayin'?'

'About another two weeks, I reckon. If the police are finished wi' their enquiries then we'll be movin' on to Nottingham. But 'ow are things wi' you? How is the business doin'?'

'Very well indeed, thanks to that young lady there.' Levi smiled at Annie. 'She's got a right little 'ead fer business on 'er that one 'as.' He told him about the second-hand clothes business she and Peggy had set up. 'Word is spreadin' an' I can 'ardly keep up wi' the demand. The clothes are sellin' like 'ot cakes.'

Barney glanced at Annie admiringly. So, she had brains as well as beauty! She seemed to get prettier every time he saw her. She wasn't as pretty as Mercy, of course, but then no girl measured up to her in his eyes. Still, he was surprised some young chap hadn't already snapped Annie up.

'You should come an' see the show afore we go,' Barney told her. 'I can get you a ring-side seat for nowt.'

Annie shook her head. 'Thanks, but I've got a lot on at the minute. Perhaps the next time you come.'

Barney spent a little longer with his parents, hoping to see his brothers, but as usual, Charlie was out with his friends and Harry was out with his latest young lady.

Shortly after he left, Annie asked Levi, 'Would you mind if I took a few days off next week? I was thinking it was time I went to visit Susan and Eve. She sounded a little low in her last letter.'

She had confided in Levi about Eve's whereabouts and the reason she had left Swan Lane, although she had been careful not to let Maggie know. She didn't want anything getting back to Mrs Taylor-Lloyd.

'Well, I can 'ardly refuse after 'ow 'ard you've been workin', can I?' he replied with a smile. 'Peggy seems to 'ave the clothes shed workin' like clockwork now. I barely 'ave time to get the day's takin's off the cart afore she's sortin' through 'em.'

It was actually turning out to be a very profitable enterprise. Even after paying Annie and Peggy he was still making a profit, and the arrangement had worked well for Peggy since she didn't have to worry about getting anyone to look after Ellie when she went to work now.

'Lovely. I thought I'd go on Monday mornin' an' come back on Friday.'

He nodded his agreement and Annie started to feel excited – she couldn't wait to see Eve again. She had saved some of the clothes that she and Maggie had sorted through, which were far superior to any she had ever owned before – apart from the things Susan had given her – and now that she had altered them to fit her, she could hardly wait to wear them.

That evening, she stayed late helping Peggy sort the clothes, and it was already dark by the time she left for home.

'Eeh, I ain't too 'appy about yer walkin' back alone at this time o' night,' Peggy fretted.

Annie smiled as she shrugged her shawl about her shoulders. 'I'm a big girl now. Ta-ra.'

She was walking across Abbey Green when she suddenly sensed someone behind her and turning she saw Reggie Taylor-Lloyd rushing towards her. Her heart did a little flip. She didn't trust Reggie as far as she could throw him, but even so she tried to be civil.

'Evenin', Reggie.'

As he drew abreast of her she could smell the alcohol on his breath. He had clearly had far too much to drink so she quickened her steps. There was no one on the green and she suddenly felt nervous as he pulled her arm and brought her to a standstill.

'Sho, alone at last eh, me pretty?' he slurred and before she knew what was happening, he tugged her towards him and his slobbery lips tried to find hers.

'Get off, Reggie, you're drunk,' she said heatedly, desperately trying to push him away.

'A li'l drink never hurt anyone.' He laughed, keeping a tight grip on her. 'You should try it sometime. It might loosen yer up a li'l. Come on, how about a li'l kissh, eh? I've been wanting to do this for a long time!'

'Get *off* me!' she stormed, struggling against him. But her anger was turning to fear. He was so much stronger than her and she knew she had no chance against him. Without warning he suddenly lifted one leg and snaked it round behind her knees and she fell heavily onto the damp grass, knocking the air from her lungs.

Tears started in her eyes as Reggie heaved himself on top of her and started to lift her skirt. She opened her mouth to scream but she was too winded to manage more than a terrified croak.

Suddenly a figure loomed out of the darkness and Reggie was lifted from her before being flung to the ground.

'You *dirty* swine!' It was Monty standing over his brother with clenched fists. He aimed a kick at Reggie's chest causing his brother to whimper and curl into a ball. Then, he turned to Annie. 'Are you all right, love?'

Annie was badly shaken, but she managed to nod as he helped her up. 'Y-yes, he just came up behind me and . . .' Stifling a sob, she straightened her skirt and wrapping her shawl tightly around herself, she took deep gulps of air.

'It's all right. You're safe now.' Monty gently took her hand and she clung to it. 'It's lucky I came along when I did. Levi told me you were staying late to help Peggy, so I thought I'd come and walk you back.'

Leaving Reggie lying on the ground, they set off for home.

'Don't tell your parents what he did,' she pleaded when they turned into Swan Lane. 'They'll only say I encouraged him or something. They've got no time for us as it is.'

He sighed. 'Very well, if that's what you want but you can be sure I shall be walking you home in future.'

At the entrance to the drive, she gently kissed his cheek, and for the first time she noticed how handsome he'd grown. He was kind and generous too, and she was grateful to have him as a friend.

'Go on, get yourself inside,' he urged, watching until she was safely through the front door.

Now more than ever, Annie couldn't wait for her trip to London. It would be nice to put some distance between herself and Reggie. She tried not to think of what might have happened if Monty hadn't come along and she thanked God that he had, otherwise she knew she might have ended up in the same predicament as Eve.

Chapter Thirty-Four

'*A*nnie!' Eve gave a cry of delight when she opened the door on Monday afternoon to find her friend looking very smart in a two-piece travelling costume in a lovely shade of blue. 'Blimey, yer look the bee's knees. Why didn't yer write an' tell me yer were comin'?' Taking Annie's elbow, she hauled her into the apartment.

Annie was shocked at the size of her. It was now mid-June with only weeks to go until the baby was due and Eve looked enormous.

'I wanted to surprise you,' Annie told her friend as she took the pin from her bonnet and laid it on the table. 'How are you? You look ready to burst.'

'I feel ready to burst an' all.' Eve rubbed her swollen belly. 'I can't wait fer it to be over. This heat is fair killin' me.'

'I can imagine it is. But not long to go now, eh?'

To her shock, Eve burst into tears and dropped heavily onto a chair. 'No, it ain't, an' between you an' me I'm all confused. It seemed so easy in the beginnin' to say I'd let the baby go when it were born, but since I've felt it kickin' inside me . . .'

'So . . . you're havin' second thoughts?'

'I suppose I am, not that it'll make any difference,' Eve said miserably. 'Susan offered me a way out when I come here, but if I were to turn it down now where could I go, wi' a baby in tow an' all!'

'Surely you could find some sort of job and a room where someone could look after the baby while you work? Especially here in London where no one knows you. You could pretend you were a widow, and nobody would ever know the baby was illegitimate,' Annie suggested. 'And I thought you told me Susan had a job lined up for you?'

Eve bowed her head. She had never admitted to Annie what Susan had in mind for her but now she knew she would have to confide. 'She does but, er... Well, the thing is, now it's growin' closer I'm not so sure I could do it.'

'Do what?' Annie was completely confused now. 'Susan works in a hotel, doesn't she? Isn't that what she wants you to do?'

'Yes, it is . . .' Eve took a deep breath. 'But she never actually told yer what she *does* in the hotel, did she? See, she's a . . . um, she entertains gentlemen, if yer can call 'em that.'

Annie stared at her blankly for a moment, then as she realised what Eve was saying she looked shocked. 'You mean she's a . . . a . . .'

Eve nodded. 'Yes, call it what yer will – whore, prostitute, lady o' the night. It's all the same thing. She's a high class one, admittedly, but men pay 'er to 'ave sex wi' 'em.'

'But what about Theo? He adores her!'

'Huh! Susan likes to try an' convince 'erself 'e does, but in actual fact he's 'er pimp, the one that finds the customers for 'er. He's got a string o' girls workin' for 'im an' he takes most o' the money they earn. That's what Susan 'ad in mind fer me, but first I 'ad to get rid o' the baby.'

Annie was horrified. She had put Susan on a pedestal only to find that she wasn't the person she had thought she was. 'If this is true, we have to get yer away from 'ere afore the baby is born,' she said in a croaky voice.

'Easier said than done,' Eve said sadly.

Suddenly, Annie had a thought. 'I 'ave an idea o' someone that might be able to 'elp yer.'

'An' who would that be?'

'Peggy.'

'Peggy!' Susan frowned. 'An' 'ow could she 'elp me?'

'Her second oldest is due to get married next month so there would be room for you there when he's gone, and I was thinking you could help her with the clothes shed we've started up once the baby 'as come.'

Eve shook her head. 'What? Yer mean come back to Nuneaton. Not on yer nelly! What about Mr Taylor-Lloyd?'

'He need never know the baby is his,' Annie said firmly. 'And even if 'e guessed do you really think he'd want it to become common knowledge? Course 'e wouldn't. His reputation would be in tatters.'

'I suppose there is that,' Eve said doubtfully. 'But what if Peggy ain't keen on the idea?'

'We'll never know if we don't ask 'er, will we?' The more Annie thought about it, the better the idea seemed. 'I 'ad planned to stay on till Friday but I reckon I'll just stay a couple o' nights an' go an' put the idea to 'er. But what about Davey? I got the feelin' you two were growin' close at one time.'

Eve sighed. 'We were, an' 'e's a lovely chap, but I ain't seen 'im fer months. I didn't want 'im to see me like this, so ever since I started showin' I've kept well out of his way. I only venture out for a bit o' fresh air occasionally after I'm sure Davey's gone home of an evenin'.' She stroked the mound of her stomach. 'I suppose I were too ashamed to face 'im. He wouldn't want me anyway, if he were to find out I were carryin' someone else's baby, would 'e?'

'That all depends. I'm sure he'd accept it if he knew the baby 'ad been forced on yer.'

Eve shook her head. 'No, I couldn't stand it if 'e were to look down on me. It's better if 'e never finds out.'

'In that case let me go back an' 'ave a word wi' Peggy. I can't think of any other option, can you?'

Eve shook her head just as Milly appeared with a basket full of food from the market. She smiled when she saw Annie. 'Aw, this is a nice surprise. Miss Susanne'll be pleased to see you an' all.' Then noting the glum expressions on the two young women's faces, she asked, 'What's wrong? You've both got faces on you like wet weekends!'

Eve explained that she had told Annie what Susan did for a living and her plans for her after the baby was born.

Milly sighed. 'I wondered 'ow long it'd be afore you found out. The thing is, though, Miss Susanne ain't a bad person. She's got a good heart an' I reckon she were just tryin' to 'elp Eve out of a bad situation. The problem is she can't see no further than the end of her nose when it comes to Theo. She thinks the sun rises an' sets wi' 'im, an' she can't see that he's just usin' 'er. Or per'aps she just doesn't want to? They do say that love is blind, don't they?'

'I was just telling Eve that I might know someone back at 'ome who might be able to help her out an' give her a place to stay,' Annie told her.

Milly frowned. 'And how do you think Susanne would feel about that?'

Annie shrugged indignantly. 'I don't know and I don't much care. I can't believe she's even thinking of lettin' Eve go into that sort o' thing after what she's been through.'

The sound of the door opening stopped the conversation from going any further, as Susan breezed in.

'Why, Annie, we didn't expect you.' She came forward with her hands outstretched and it was all Annie could do to allow her to touch her. What Eve had just told her had shocked her to the roots and she needed some time to get used to it.

'How is everyone at home? Is this just a social visit or is something wrong with Maggie or one of the family?'

'They're all fine,' Annie assured her. 'I just wanted to come an' see how you an' Eve were. I shall only be stayin' for a couple o' days, though, if that's all right?'

'Of course. You're welcome here anytime and you can stay as long as you like.'

Annie wondered if Susan was hoping she would join her and Theo in the future as well, but hell would freeze over before she'd lower herself to doing that.

'Right, I'll just go and get changed into something a little cooler,' Susan said, tugging at her high-necked day gown. 'And then you can tell me all about what's going on back at home.'

'You won't get tellin' 'er that I've told yer what she does fer a livin' will yer?' Eve pleaded, once Susan had left the room.

Milly looked over at Annie with a worried expression. She could see how shocked the other girl was and couldn't help feeling sorry for Susan.

'It's easy to judge,' she said sensibly. 'But I don't think Miss Susanne ever set out to be what she is. It were Theo that manipulated her into it, so don't judge her too harshly.'

Annie heard the wisdom of what she was saying and nodded. 'Don't worry, Eve, I won't say a word.'

'Anyway, why don't yer tell us all about what you've been up to since yer last visited,' Milly suggested, and so the girls spent the next ten minutes chatting of other things.

The next two days passed pleasantly, and Annie set off for home early on Wednesday morning. Eve was only weeks away from giving birth and Annie was keen to speak to Peggy and explain the situation to her – although if Peggy wasn't ready to offer her a place to stay, she didn't know how she could help her, poor thing. It had become increasingly clear that Eve was regretting her decision to part with her baby, for, as she had told Annie, this little soul would be the only family she had ever known. Like herself, Eve hadn't had the best start in life and things hadn't improved greatly for her when the Taylor-Lloyds had taken her in. And that was why, when the train drew into the station in Nuneaton, Annie set off purposefully to speak to Peggy.

On reaching the ginnel that led to the courtyard, Annie was surprised to see that the clothes shed was locked up with not a sign of Peggy. Normally at that time of the day she would be serving customers or arranging the clothes rails. Frowning, Annie crossed to the cottage and opened the door. The sight that met her eyes made her gasp with dismay. The curtains were drawn and despite the heat outside there was a fire roaring up the chimney, making the room stiflingly hot. Peggy was bending over Ellie, who was lying on the sofa, and when she glanced up, Annie saw that Peggy had been crying.

'Phew, it's enough to roast you in here. What's wrong?' Annie went over and looked down at Ellie, who was covered in an evil-looking rash.

'She broke out in this rash the day you left fer London an' she's gone steadily down' ill ever since,' Peggy told her in a choky voice. 'So I sent fer the doctor an' he told me it's measles. She can't even stand the light now, poor little soul.'

Ellie's eyes were rolling and she didn't seem to be aware of anything going on around her. Sweat was rolling down her forehead and, taking control, Annie told Peggy, 'Go and open that door and let some air in.'

'But the doctor told me to keep 'er warm an' try an' get some water down 'er,' Peggy objected.

'There's a difference between keepin' her warm an' cookin' 'er,' Annie replied, taking her bonnet off. 'Now go an' do as I ask, then fetch me a bowl o' cool water. We'll bathe 'er an' try an' get 'er temperature down.'

Peggy meekly did as she was told. She was totally exhausted and only too happy to have the help.

'Right, now go upstairs an' get a couple of hours sleep,' Annie ordered when the bowl was at the side of her.

Peggy shook her head. 'No, I ain't leavin' 'er.'

'Oh, so when you collapse because you're worn out who'll look after her then? Now go an' do as yer told. You ain't no use to 'er in this state, are you? I'll watch 'er an' if there's any change, I'll come an' fetch yer straight away.'

Peggy reluctantly did as she was told and Annie turned her attention to little Ellie. Levi wasn't expecting her home until Friday so she had all the time in the world to take some of the burden off Peggy's shoulders, and that was exactly what she intended to do. Eve's predicament would have to wait for now.

Chapter Thirty-Five

Levi arrived back at the yard late that afternoon. He was aware that Ellie was ill and had been worried about her. When he walked into the kitchen, he was surprised to see Annie and his face broke into a smile.

'I didn't expect to see yer back so soon, pet.'

'Oh, I decided to come back early,' she told him. It didn't seem the right time to tell him why just yet. 'It's just as well I did. Poor Peggy looks dead on her feet, so I sent her up to 'ave a lie-down.'

He nodded his approval as he stared down at Ellie, who was still feverishly hot. 'And 'ow is the little 'un?'

Annie could hear the concern in his voice. She knew how much he thought of the child, and had it been left up to him she would still be living in Swan Lane.

'Not good,' she admitted as she wrung the cloth out in the cool water again. 'I wonder if we shouldn't get the doctor to come an' 'ave another look at 'er? I think she'd be better in 'ospital.'

'I've already suggested that, but the doctor reckons it would do more 'arm than good to try an' move 'er at the minute. I think he's worried about spreadin' it round the 'ospital an' all. Come to think of it, it might not be such a good idea you bein' so close to 'er. What if you catch it?'

'I'll take me chances.' Annie started to mop Ellie's brow again.

Levi wrung his cap between his hands. 'Is there owt I can do?' he asked.

She shook her head. 'No, you go an' unload the cart. Now I'm back I can open the clothes shed again in the mornin'.'

'Oh, don't get worryin' about that. That's the least o' me worries at the minute. I'm more concerned about Ellie, an' Peggy if it comes to that. She adores this little girl an' I don't know 'ow she'd cope if she were to lose 'er now. Look what losin' our Penny did to Maggie. She's never got over it.'

'Grief is a funny thing an' it takes different people different ways,' Annie agreed.

'You've got a very wise 'ead on yer shoulder's, hinny,' Levi said with a sad smile.

At that moment Peggy appeared from the door leading to the stairs. 'Eeh, why didn't yer wake me?' she scolded gently. 'I must 'ave been asleep fer hours!'

'Yes, you were, an' you obviously needed it. But come an' take over now while I make the mister a cup o' tea, eh? I dare say one wouldn't go amiss wi' you either, an' while I'm at it I'm goin' to make you a sandwich. I bet you ain't been eatin' properly.'

Peggy opened her mouth to tell her she wasn't hungry, but Annie held her hand up to stop her before she could speak.

Once she'd made the sandwich, she stood over Peggy until every crumb was gone and the cup was empty. Swiping her mouth with the back of her hand, Peggy admitted, 'I 'ave to say I do feel a bit better now.' Her eyes fastened on Ellie. 'I just wish this little 'un's fever would break.'

'It will,' Annie said as she carried the dirty pots to the sink and washed them up. 'Now, what were yer cookin' fer the evenin' meal? I dare say the lads will want sommat when they come in.'

Peggy looked guilty. 'To tell the truth I ain't been able to get out to do any shoppin' so they've been going to the café fer their dinner fer the last couple o' days.'

'Right, let's make a list of what you need an' I'll go an' get some shoppin' in for yer. Then when I get back, I'll cook you all sommat. I'll be sleepin' 'ere tonight an' all, so as we can take it in turns sittin' up wi' Ellie.'

*

Two days later, Ellie started to cool down and finally opened her eyes. Annie had been sitting with her and when Peggy came down the stairs to take her turn and saw the little girl awake, she cried with relief.

'Oh, thank God.' She made the sign of the cross on her chest and burst into tears. 'I really thought we were gonna lose 'er fer a while back there.'

'I think we're over the worst now,' Annie told her gently, stifling a yawn.

Soon Ellie had improved to the point where she could eat small titbits that Peggy cooked to tempt her, but she was still very weak so Annie stayed on to help care for her and to reopen the clothes shed.

As word had spread of the decent clothes available at fair prices, they had become increasingly busy and the business was thriving, much to Levi's delight. He had widened his rounds now, calling into neighbouring villages and even as far as the nearby town of Atherstone.

One day as he was unloading the cart after a busy day, he told Annie, 'I can't linger tonight, hinny. Maggie ain't too well an' the house is a bit of a tip.'

Peggy looked round sharply. 'I think it's time you were goin' home now, pet. I don't know what I would 'ave done wi'out you over the last few days, but yer needed at home by the sounds of it.'

'Are you sure?'

Peggy nodded. 'Very sure. Go an' get your bag packed. You can go home wi' Levi.'

As Annie packed her bag, she chewed on her lip. With Ellie being so poorly and one thing and another, she still hadn't broached the subject of Eve coming to stay and now she had missed her chance. For the time being at least, she consoled herself. There was always tomorrow.

When she and Levi entered the house in Swan Lane, Annie glanced around and stifled a sigh of dismay. Every surface was covered in dirty pots and pans and it appeared that nothing had been done since she had left for her trip to London. Maggie was sitting in her usual position in the chair by the empty hearth, her back ramrod straight, her clothes immaculate with not a hair out of place. She didn't even acknowledge them when they entered and Annie saw the worry in Levi's eyes.

'She's started to talk to Penny again,' he whispered.

Annie didn't answer. She could have told him that Maggie had never stopped talking to the dead child, although she had only done it when she was locked away in their bedroom where she thought no one could hear her. But it was a sign that she was becoming worse again if she was openly doing it in front of Levi and her sons.

'I, er . . . I'm sorry about the mess, hinny. It seems everythin' goes to pot if you 'ave a few days off.'

'Oh, don't worry about that,' Annie said airily as she placed her bag down on the floor. 'I'll have it all shipshape in no time. But first, what do you fancy for your dinner? I'm sure I'll be able to rustle somethin' up.'

She hurried away to check on the pantry. 'Not much left in there, I'm afraid, but there is a big tin of ham, some eggs and a few potatoes I can boil, so I'll go and pick some salad from the garden an' get us some tomatoes from the green'ouse an' do us a salad. How does that sound? I can go an' get some shoppin' in the mornin'.'

Charlie came in as she was peeling the potatoes at the sink, and Annie smiled. Her heart no longer did a little flip at the sight of him. She had finally realised that he wasn't interested in her in a romantic way, unlike Monty, who she was becoming very fond of.

He returned her smile. 'Don't worry about doin' me anythin'. I'll be eatin' out with me friends this evenin' an' I think Harry said he'd be havin' dinner at his lady friend's house.'

Annie nodded. They rarely saw him anymore. As soon as he got in from work, he was always off out with his friends, but she supposed he was entitled to go where he pleased.

'Monty were askin' after you yesterday. He wanted to know when you'd be back.' He winked. 'I reckon he's still got a right soft spot for you,' he teased. 'The only downside to that bein' if you took up wi' him you'd have Mrs Taylor-Lloyd as a mother-in-law.'

And Reggie as a brother-in-law, Annie thought, and shuddered. She was still trying to get over what he had tried to do to her.

'I have no intention of takin' up with anyone,' Annie responded shortly, throwing another potato into the pan, and turning her back on him.

It was in the early hours of the morning, as Annie lay awake in her little attic room, that she heard a commotion down in the yard. Quickly lighting a candle, she threw a shawl over her nightgown and crept along the landing, almost colliding with Levi.

'Did you hear it too?' she whispered.

He nodded, and they hurried down the stairs and into the kitchen where they stood for a few moments listening. All was silent now save for the hooting of an owl in the old oak tree outside Annie's bedroom window.

'I'd better 'ave a look around an' just check everythin' is all right.' Levi snapped his braces over his shoulder, and as he opened the door a figure fell into the room.

'Oh, good grief!' Annie's hand flew to her mouth as they looked down at Charlie, who had taken such a beating his face was almost unrecognisable.

'Help me get 'im into that chair an' fetch a bowl o' water to clean 'is face, would yer?' Levi ordered as he hauled his son across the floor.

Annie rushed off to do as she was asked.

'Sh-should I run an' fetch the doctor?' Annie asked fearfully as Levi tenderly wiped the blood from his son's face. He was still out cold but it was soon obvious that the injuries weren't as bad as they looked, although he was going to have two lovely black eyes the next day.

'Not just yet, pet. Let's see if we can bring 'im round first. I reckon most o' the blood 'as come from his nose, but there's no doubt he's taken a right old pastin'. His jacket's missin' an' all!'

Annie bustled away and returned with a glass of water and as Levi tilted his son's head and dribbled the water into his open mouth, Charlie started to choke and come round.

'It's all right, I've got yer, lad,' Levi soothed as Charlie started to lash out.

He blinked up at his father and started to calm down.

After a few minutes Levi asked, 'Who did this to yer?'

Charlie turned his head away, gripping his chest as he tried to sit up straighter. 'I don't know.'

'But yer must 'ave seen whoever it were?'

Charlie winced with pain as he shook his head. His nose had started to bleed again and the front of his shirt was more red than white.

'I didn't. They came at me from be'ind as I were makin' me way across Abbey Green.'

'Then I reckon we should be informin' the police,' his father told him gravely.

Charlie shook his head. '*No!* I don't want no police involved. Do yer 'ear me? Let it go. It was probably just some drunks on the way home from the pub.'

Levi blinked in surprise. 'But what if it were the same person that killed that chap be'ind the circus? They ain't caught 'em yet. If we don't report it, they could strike again!'

'I don't care. I'm tellin' yer, this is the end of it, all right? I'll be fine in a couple o' days.'

Levi wasn't happy but he shrugged. 'Very well, if that's 'ow yer feel.'

All the colour had drained from Annie's face as she watched from the other side of the room. What if Levi was right? Barney had told them about the stabbing and they had read about it in the newspaper. What if it was the same person who had killed Bertie at the fair? If it was then one thing was for sure, none of them would be safe until the killer had been caught.

Chapter Thirty-Six

It was late in June and the circus would be packing up the next day ready to move on. Barney would not be sorry to go. The police were still trying to find the killer and were regular visitors to the camp, but so far their investigations had come up with nothing.

Since Bertie had been killed, he had seen little of Mercy. She was struggling to cope with what had happened, and he'd had little chance to speak to her alone, even had she wanted to, because Noah was watching over her whenever she ventured out of her trailer. Her brother had made it clear that he still suspected Barney, and although he had strenuously denied it, the atmosphere between them was strained to say the least.

Poor Mercy was a bag of nerves, jumping at her own shadow; under the circumstances, though, it was entirely understandable. And now the final circus performance was under way and once the audience had gone, the hard work of preparing to move on would begin.

Barney was standing at the entrance to the big top watching the antics of the clowns in between performances when someone tapped him on the shoulder. Turning he found himself face to face with the police officer heading up the investigation into Bertie's murder.

'It's Barney Lilburn, isn't it?'

Barney nodded and frowned. 'Aye, it is? What can I do fer you?'

The officer beckoned to one of the policemen standing behind him. 'We want to check everyone's trailers again before you move on tomorrow. We're still trying to find the murder weapon. Would you please accompany my officer to yours and allow him to search it?'

Barney's heart sank. He'd forgotten all about the knife he'd thrown under his bed. Luckily, they'd missed it the last time they searched, but his luck might be about to run out. 'What if I do mind?' They had already questioned him twice and he had an idea it was because he had told them of his fondness for Mercy.

The officer produced something from his pocket and flashed it at him. 'This is a warrant enabling us to search every trailer on the field. But perhaps you have something to hide?'

Barney shrugged and led the officer to his trailer, noting that many of the other trailers were being searched too.

He stood back and watched helplessly as the police officers systematically emptied cupboards and drawers until the place looked as if a hurricane had ripped through it. And then one of the officers lifted the bed and he knew he was in trouble.

'So, what's this, sir?' The officer scowled as he held up the bloodstained knife. 'Can you explain it?'

When Barney shook his head, the man blew his whistle and seconds later more officers appeared.

The one holding the knife nodded towards Barney and before he knew it, he was in handcuffs and the policeman was reading him his rights. 'I'm arresting you for the suspected murder of Mr Bertrand Russell. You have no need to say anything but anything you do say may be used in a court of law as evidence against you . . .'

His voice droned on, but Barney barely heard him. Better this than they suspect Mercy, so he held his head high as he was led away.

Mercy was outside her trailer, and when she saw what was happening, she gave a cry of anguish. '*Barney . . . no!*'

He gave her a warning glance as her mother drew her into her arms and then he was in the back of a police cart and ready to face what was ahead.

'Is there a problem 'ere?' Luca asked shortly, hurrying towards the policemen.

'We've just found this knife covered in blood and hidden in this man's trailer, sir. We've arrested him for the suspected murder of Mr Russell and we're taking him to the station for questioning.'

Luca looked dumbfounded as he watched Barney being carted away, but then pulling himself together, he snapped, 'All right everyone! The show's over, so get back to what you were doin'.'

The crowd dispersed and while Charity sat with Mercy, Luca and the men went about their business.

It was the early hours of the morning when two policemen came back to tell Luca, 'We need to question your daughter, sir. We have reason to believe that she and Barney Lilburn were romantically involved. Did you know anything about this?'

'*What?*' Luca looked stunned. 'But that can't be true. Bertie and Mercy had only just announced their engagement that evenin', an' both me an' her mother were happy about it.'

Mercy's teeth were chattering with fear as she listened in to the conversation. Unable to sleep she was sitting on the steps of her mother's trailer so she was able to hear everything. She had been expecting the police to come for her ever since Barney had been taken away. Surely he would have told them it was she who had killed Bertie?

Spotting Mercy, Luca snapped, 'Is there any truth in what they're saying, Mercy?'

'Y-yes, Dadda.'

Grim-faced, Luca stared back at her. 'Why didn't I know about this? I always knew he had a soft spot for you but he should have known that nothin' could ever come of it. We marry our own in this business.'

'Th-that's why we didn't tell you,' she answered in a small voice.

'But none o' this makes any sense,' he muttered as he shoved his fingers through his thick thatch of hair, making it stand to attention. 'Me an' yer mammy were made up about the engagement.'

Mercy hung her head. 'I'm sorry,' she muttered. 'But I never wanted to marry Bertie.'

The police had heard enough and turning to Mercy, they told her, 'We'd like you to come to the station with us now, miss.'

Mercy nodded and allowed them to lead her away.

'Don't say a word till I've got yer a lawyer sorted,' Luca shouted after her, but Mercy didn't answer. She was almost relieved they had come for her in one way. Anything was better than sitting back and letting Barney take the blame. It was time to tell the truth.

That night neither Luca nor Charity slept a wink, and Luca hurried to answer a rap on his door early the next morning. A police officer he hadn't seen before was standing on his step and without waiting for an invite he stepped inside.

'Where is me daughter?' Luca glanced over his shoulder.

'I'm afraid your daughter has been charged with the murder of Mr Russell, sir.' The officer's face was grim as Luca stared at him in disbelief. 'She'll be kept in custody until the case goes to court.'

Luca was as pale as a ghost and there were dark circles beneath his eyes.

'Mercy? But she wouldn't hurt a fly!'

'Unfortunately, it seems she did. She claims she defended herself when he tried to rape her. She's to appear in court sometime next week so until then we request that you all stay put.'

Luca stared across at the loaded wagons. 'But you arrested Barney. You said the knife had been found in his trailer?'

The officer nodded. 'Apparently Mr Lilburn heard a ruckus and when he went to investigate, he found Mr Russell assaulting your daughter. She claims that before he could help her, she pulled out a knife and the victim was stabbed as he lunged at her.'

'Why did you find the knife in *his* trailer then?'

'It seems that Mr Lilburn was trying to protect her and was prepared to take the blame for the stabbing himself.'

Luca sat down heavily. He felt as if he was caught in the grip of a nightmare, and there was nothing he could do about it.

'May I have your assurance that you'll remain here until after the court case, sir?'

'Y-yes. Mercy's mother an meself will have a few days holiday. There's no sense in us settin' everythin' back up again. But will it be all right if the rest of 'em move on if they wish to? We're booked to be in Nottingham tomorrer.'

'I should think that would be in order, sir.' He tipped his cap and left.

Luca now had the unenviable task of telling Charity about the latest developments. She was going to be devastated.

Most of the circus folk were keen to move on. The majority of their money was earned through the summer months and they couldn't afford to miss out.

'I'll put Noah in charge till I can join you all,' Luca told them, and within an hour they started to leave.

During that time Charity had been crying continuously and despite his own despair, Luca's heart ached for her. She adored their daughter.

'I can always stay in 'ere wi' you if that's what yer want?' he offered.

She shook her head, the tears pouring down her pallid cheeks. 'N-no, you go. I'll be fine,' she told him in a choky voice. It was the closest they had been for many long years.

Later that day Barney appeared, and if it were possible, he looked even worse than Mercy's parents.

Luca glared at him. 'They let you go then?'

'Aye, they did, more's the pity.' Barney glared back at him. 'If only Mercy hadn't told 'em what *really* happened I could have done the time for her.'

They stood facing each other and it was Luca who finally spoke when he said, 'Why wasn't I told you two were havin' a love affair?'

'What would 'ave been the point?' Barney said accusingly. 'You made it more than clear that Mercy didn't 'ave a say in who she married. If she hadn't been forced into that position, none o' this would ever 'ave happened!'

Luca's shoulders sagged. 'What do you intend to do now?'

'I'm goin' to stay wi' me folks till I know what's goin' to happen to Mercy, then I'll join the rest o' the crew, unless I'm sacked, that is?'

'You must love 'er very much if you were prepared to do time fer her?'

Barney nodded. 'I'd die fer her if need be. An' furthermore yer may as well know, when she comes 'ome, whenever that might be, I'll be waitin' for 'er!'

'Of course you ain't sacked. Right now we need to stand together,' Luca said brokenly. Times were changing and perhaps he had been too rigid in his ideals, on more than one occasion.

And so an hour later Barney went back to his family for a rest with no idea how long it might be until he saw Mercy again.

Chapter Thirty-Seven

It was the first week in July and Annie knew that if she was going to help Eve she must speak to Peggy now. The baby could come anytime, and now that Ellie was so much better, Annie looked for a chance to broach the subject.

'I was wondering,' she said cautiously one sunny morning as they were preparing to open the clothes shed, 'how you might feel about Eve coming to stay with you till she could afford somewhere of her own? Do you remember her? She used to be a maid for Mrs Taylor-Lloyd next door to us in Swan Lane.'

'Aye, I remember her.' Peggy paused in the act of hanging a gown on the rail. 'She disappeared off all of a sudden if I remember right?'

'Yes . . . she did.' Annie took a deep breath before telling Peggy the whole sorry story.

When she'd finished, Peggy shook her head and sighed. 'The poor girl. No wonder she cleared off the way she did. And you say she's had a change of heart and wants to keep the baby now?'

Annie nodded.

'Hmm. I'm not surprised now you've told me what Susan had lined up for her. Eeh, I dread to think what Maggie would say if she knew how her sister were earnin' a livin'. But what about if she were to bump into Mr Taylor-Lloyd? Wouldn't he guess the baby were 'is?'

'If that happened, which I think is highly unlikely, she'd just deny it. But if anything, I reckon he'd strongly deny it an' all in case word got back to his missus. Can you imagine the ruckus it would cause! Mrs Taylor-Lloyd is an even worse snob than . . .'

When her voice trailed away, Peggy grinned. 'Than Maggie, were you goin' to say? Well, I can only agree wi' that.' She thought for a moment before going on, 'Our Wilf gets wed this Saturday, as yer know, so I will 'ave a spare room then. Him an' Ruth are goin' to stay wi' her parents till they've saved enough to get somewhere. So 'ow about you go an' see the poor lass an' tell 'er she can come any time after that. I can manage on me own 'ere fer a couple o' days. Only till she gets back on her feet an' finds somewhere of her own to live, mind!'

'Oh, Peggy, you are kind.' Annie threw her arms about her and gave her a big sloppy kiss on her cheek.

Peggy blushed. 'Get off wi' yer. Actually, it'll be quite nice to 'ave another little 'un about the place. Wi' Ellie gettin' a bit older now an' goin' out wi' her friends I miss havin' someone to talk to of an evenin', especially since my . . .' She gulped.

Annie's heart went out to her. She knew how much Peggy still missed Sid and hoped the baby might take her mind off her loss a little. Already in her mind she was planning her trip to London. If she went on Friday, she could bring Eve back with her on Monday. She just hoped she didn't have the baby before then or things would get complicated.

She told Levi about her plans that evening and just as Peggy had been, he was disgusted with Mr Taylor-Lloyd.

'The poor lass.' He shook his head. 'And our Susan a lady o' the night, eh? Crikey, I 'ope our Maggie never finds out. She'd 'ave a dicky fit!'

The clothes were now in such high demand that Annie and Peggy could hardly keep up, so the rest of the week Annie was so busy that she barely had time to think of Eve until Friday when she set off bright and early to catch the train. She could hardly wait to tell Eve the good news and hoped she hadn't changed her mind.

The journey was uneventful and shortly after dinner the hansom cab pulled up in front of Susan's smart flat in Russell Square.

Davey was in the foyer and he smiled when he saw her. 'Come to stay with Miss Susanne and Eve, have you?' When she nodded, he sighed. 'I think I've upset Eve. I haven't seen 'er for months now.'

'Oh, I'm sure you ain't.' Annie would have liked to explain why Eve was keeping out of his way but felt it wasn't her place. 'Anyway, I'd best get on. This bag is gettin' 'eavier by the minute.'

'I'll carry it for you,' he offered, but she shook her head and hurried along the corridor. 'Bye fer now, Davey.'

He watched her go with a forlorn expression and she couldn't help but feel sorry for him. She knew Eve liked him as much as he liked her, but her pride had got in the way, and there was not a thing Annie could do about it.

Both Milly and Eve were in when she got to the flat and Annie's eyes stretched wide when Eve answered the door. She was so big that she looked as if she was about to burst.

'Crikey, you're huge!' Annie smiled as Eve gave her a welcoming hug.

'I'd almost given up on yer,' Eve said with a catch in her voice. 'I thought per'aps Peggy had said no to yer idea?'

'Quite the opposite,' Annie assured her. 'It's just that we've 'ad a lot goin' on back 'ome, an' this is the first chance I've 'ad to come an' get you. Ellie was ill, then Barney's young lady was arrested for murder at the circus in the Pingle fields, an' it's been splashed all over the papers an' . . . Oh, but never mind about all that fer now. I'm 'ere wi' good news. Peggy's son gets married tomorrer, so there's an empty room fer you there if you still want it.'

'*Really?*' Relief flashed across her face.

'It looks like I got 'ere in the nick o' time,' Annie teased.

'I know; this 'ot weather is bloody killin' me. But what am I goin' to tell Susan? She's been so good to me.'

'I'm sure she'll understand. We'll tell 'er together tonight, eh? Now 'ow about a cold drink? I'm parched.'

Once Milly had fetched her a glass of lemonade, Eve and Annie chatted about what they'd been up to since they last saw each other while Milly tackled a pile of ironing.

Half an hour later, the door opened and Susan breezed in with Theo behind her.

'Ah, my dear. How nice it is to see you.' Susan smiled a welcome.

Theo advanced on Annie and gallantly kissed her hand with a smile that would have charmed the birds from the trees. 'I hope you are here for a while?'

'No, just for a couple of nights unfortunately,' Annie replied, quickly withdrawing her hand. Knowing what she did about the man, he made her skin crawl.

'That's a shame but I'm sure we'll persuade you to come and join us eventually.' With a little bow he followed Susan into the lounge, leaving the three young women in the kitchen.

'Don't get saying anything about why I'm here in front of Theo,' Annie whispered to Eve. 'We'll wait until he's gone before we tell Susan that you're leaving. I wouldn't trust that man as far as I could throw 'im, an' he ain't goin' to be 'appy when he knows you've 'ad a change of 'eart.'

'I 'ope he don't take it out on Susan,' Eve fretted.

Milly shook her head. 'Don't get worryin' about that. Miss Susanne is still very much in demand wi' the gentlemen an' he ain't goin' to risk losin' her an' all. But I don't know 'ow our Davey is goin' to take the news,' she ended sadly. 'There ain't a day goes by when he don't ask after you when I get in from work.'

Eve shrugged. 'I'm sorry about that. If things 'ad been different . . . But they ain't, are they? Do you really think he'd still think so much o' me if he knew about this?' She patted her bulging stomach and sniffed back a tear. 'Anyway, I reckon when I go back to Nuneaton, I'm gonna go with the widow story. I'll say

I met me husband soon as I moved to London an' was widowed soon after. That way, no one need know that this one 'ere is a bastard. It'll save any embarrassment for Peggy, won't it?'

'I suppose it would,' Annie agreed. 'Although I don't think Peggy would worry too much about that anyway. But let's take one step at a time. We need to tell Susan you're leavin' first an' hope she ain't too angry about it.'

A little later that evening they got the opportunity to do just that when Susan joined them in her pretty lounge.

Annie and Eve exchanged a glance and licking her lips, Eve began tentatively, 'Susan . . . I, er . . . 'ave somethin' I'd like to tell yer.'

Susan had just poured some sherry into a cut-glass goblet and settling her silken skirts around her, she smiled. 'You're going to tell me that you're leaving, aren't you?'

Both Annie and Eve gasped.

'B-but 'ow did you know?' Eve asked.

'I noticed that on Davey's day off you go shopping and it's always baby clothes that you come back with. Why would you buy them if you had no intention of keeping the child?'

Eve guiltily bowed her head and Susan squeezed her hand. 'Do you have somewhere to go?'

Eve nodded. 'Yes, Peggy 'as agreed I can stay wi' 'er till I can find a job an' somewhere of me own to live. I-I'm so sorry I've let yer down.'

Susan sighed. 'Don't be. I don't blame you. All I ever wanted was a man to love me and a baby of my own. I still hope that Theo will turn out to be that man one day – till then . . . Well, we do what we have to do, don't we? So, if there is a way you can keep this child and manage, do it with my blessing.'

'B-but what will Theo say? Will you be in trouble?'

'You just leave Theo to me,' Susan said quietly. 'To be honest, I've been thinking for a while that you aren't cut out for the sort of job I do. I don't think you would have been happy.' She turned her attention to Annie. 'And you, young lady. What do you intend to do with your life?'

Annie frowned. 'What do yer mean?'

'I mean that ever since my sister took you from the workhouse you have done nothing but look after the family and be at her beck and call. But what you should realise is that you're a very beautiful young woman with a good head on your shoulders. You could be anything you want to be. And I know how much you think of Levi, but it's time you started to think of yourself now.'

'I'm quite 'appy as I am,' Annie said defensively. But deep down she knew that wasn't entirely true. Susan was right, though. She did think a lot of the mister. After all, he was the closest thing to a father she had ever known and she often wondered if her birth father would have been anything like him. She had given up her dreams of being reunited with her real family many years ago, but recently the underlying yearning to find out who they were had risen to the surface again, niggling away at her – not that she had the foggiest idea of how to ever go about it. And then there was Monty. Ever since that horrible night when he'd rescued her, she'd felt a little more drawn to him. Perhaps it was time she made a point of spending a little more time with him?

She smiled at Susan. 'Don't you go worryin' about me. I've got me 'ead screwed on, an' yes, I have got ambitions, but I don't want to talk about 'em just yet till I've discussed an idea I've 'ad wi' the mister.'

'Good, I'd hate to see you waste your life when you have so much going for you.' Susan patted her hand. 'And now if you'll both excuse me, I'm going for a lie-down. I have an appointment with a very influential gentleman late tonight.'

After she'd gone, Annie and Eve lapsed into a thoughtful silence as they each considered what the future would bring. For Annie, it seemed rich with possibilities, and she suddenly couldn't wait to get on with it. Eve, on the other hand, was full of dread. Much as she couldn't wait for her baby to be born, their future was uncertain and fraught with difficulty. One thing she did know, though: she would do everything in her power to ensure they never saw the inside of a workhouse.

Chapter Thirty-Eight

Early on Monday morning, Eve packed the rest of her things into her bag and glanced around. 'I can't believe I'm really goin'.'

'Well, you are,' Annie assured her. Susan had stayed out the night before, so they had already said their goodbyes, and all they had to do now was get themselves to the train station. 'I don't understand why yer want to set off so early though. We'll 'ave a good hour's wait at Euston afore the train is due if we leave now.'

'I want to go before Davey starts work,' Eve said sadly.

Annie shook her head. 'I still think you should 'ave been honest wi' him. I think Davey really likes you an' if he knew how the baby 'ad come about he might 'ave still accepted it an' you two could have made a go o' things.'

'As you say – *he might 'ave*. But there's no guarantee, is there? No, it's better like this.'

'Have it your own way.' Annie shrugged and lifted their bags. 'If you're sure, we'll get goin'. I'll hail us a cab outside. There's no way you're gonna be able to walk far like that, an' the last thing I need is fer you to go an' have the baby on the train.'

Eve grinned and winced as the baby kicked her. 'As far as I'm concerned, once we get to Peggy's it'll be the sooner the better. It's torture lumpin' this lot around in this 'ot weather, believe me.'

They left the flat and had just reached the foyer when Davey suddenly appeared and stared at Eve in shock.

'Wh-what are you doin' here so early?' The colour had drained from Eve's face.

287

'Our Milly told me you were leavin' this mornin' an' I wanted to say goodbye. But she never told me about *that*?' He stabbed his finger towards Eve's swollen stomach. 'No wonder you've been avoidin' me!'

'Ah well, now you know why, don't you?' Eve's chin was up, although her eyes were unnaturally bright.

Annie looked helplessly from one to the other, not knowing what to say to try and make the situation any better.

'Aye, I do. Don't let me keep yer.' Davey looked so hurt that Annie couldn't help but feel sorry for him. Though she knew she'd had the best of intentions, perhaps it would have been better if Milly hadn't told him that Eve was leaving.

'We, er . . . we'd best be on our way, Davey. Look after yerself. Ta-ra fer now.' She nudged Eve towards the entrance and out into the road. Luckily there was a cab passing and after flagging it down she and Eve climbed into it. Only then did Eve give way to tears.

Annie put her arm about her. 'Shush, this ain't goin' to help anythin', is it now? What's done is done an' you have to move on.'

'I know,' Eve sniffed, taking the handkerchief Annie handed to her and mopping her wet cheeks. 'I just feel so bad about hurtin' Davey. He's such a nice chap.'

When they reached the station, Annie hustled her onto the platform and found them a bench to sit on while they waited for the train. They had been there for half an hour when Annie noticed Eve was looking uncomfortable. 'Are you all right?'

'Yes . . . I think so . . . I've just got an awful backache. I reckon it's sittin' on this hard bench.'

Eve's cheeks were flushed. But then it was unbearably hot, so Annie hoped it was just down to that. The alternative didn't bear thinking about.

Eventually they boarded the train, but as the morning wore on Eve's backache got worse and Annie started to get seriously concerned. Eve had been walking up and down the corridor outside their carriage for the last hour or so and looked more uncomfortable with every moment that passed.

When the train finally drew into the station, Annie breathed a huge sigh of relief and helped Eve out onto the platform, but they had gone no more than a few steps when Eve suddenly clutched her stomach and doubled over.

'I-I think the baby is comin',' she gasped.

Annie flew into a panic; normally they would have walked the short distance to Peggy's courtyard in Abbey Street, but today Annie didn't dare risk it. 'Right, sit here on this bench and watch the bags while I run outside and see if there's a cab to take us to Peggy's.'

Without waiting for an answer, she was gone like the wind, soon returning with a cab driver who glanced nervously at Eve. He lifted the bags while Annie helped Eve outside where they somehow managed to get her into the cab.

'Hold tight, ladies,' he said, as he clambered up into the driving seat. 'I don't want yer givin' birth in me cab.' He urged the horse forward and Eve groaned and clutched at her stomach.

Thankfully Peggy was outside in the clothes shed when the cab pulled up at the end of the ginnel and when Annie told her what was happening, she hurried back with her to help Eve inside while Annie paid the driver and fetched the bags.

They had just entered the kitchen when Eve felt a warm gush of fluid between her legs. 'Oh no, I reckon I've just wet meself.'

'No, you ain't, pet. Your waters 'ave just broke.' Peggy was completely in control as she turned to Annie. 'Get some newspapers an' towels an' go an' spread 'em across me bed, then run an' tell Old Ma Bates we're goin' to need her. But tell her not to rush. First babies have a habit o' takin' their time. She could be hours yet.'

Annie did as she was told while Peggy helped Eve into a chair. 'Now you sit there while I make yer a nice cup o' tea,' she ordered. 'An' don't get panickin'; we've got everythin' under control, an'

Old Ma Bates has been deliverin' the babies hereabouts fer years. She delivered all mine. Just try an' time how far apart the pains are.'

By the time the tea was mashed, Annie was back, looking anxious. Peggy chuckled. 'Don't look so worried, pet,' she urged, for Annie looked worse than Eve. 'Everythin' is comin' along nicely. Although I have to say I didn't expect to have a new baby under me roof quite this soon.'

Soon after Eve confirmed that the pains were coming approximately every eight minutes and Peggy nodded, unconcerned. 'Aw, you'll be ages yet.' She took a sip of her tea. 'Get that drink down you an' just remember, givin' birth is the most natural thing in the world.'

She finished her tea and went back outside to finish what she had been doing, leaving Annie with strict instructions to fetch her if anything should change and to get as much water on the boil as she could. Throughout the afternoon Annie paced up and down the kitchen like an expectant father. Old Ma Bates had been to check on Eve and had said much the same as Peggy, and told Annie to fetch her when the pains grew closer together.

Late in the afternoon, when Levi drove Dobbin into the yard, Annie went out to greet him and told him what was happening.

He shook his head. 'By! I'd like to strangle that dirty bloody Taylor-Lloyd for what he did to that poor young lass. He should be ashamed o' himself!'

'Huh! Blokes like him think it's their right,' Peggy said. 'But it'll be best fer Eve if he never finds out this baby is his, so try an' keep yer temper.' She ordered Annie to go back to Eve and while she was helping Levi empty the cart, Ma Bates reappeared.

'Right, I reckon it's time we got yer upstairs to have a look how far along you are,' she told Eve, whose face was as pale as a ghost's. Then to Annie, 'Get that hot water on again, lass. I reckon she's comin' close now.'

Annie had already placed a pile of towels at the side of Peggy's bed and she had lined a drawer with a blanket for the baby. Minutes later she carried the first steaming bowl of water upstairs and then all she could do was wait.

Very slowly the light began to fade as the evening wore on, but still there was no sign of the baby coming. Annie had bitten her nails down to the quick by that time and refused to go home with Levi until she knew that both Eve and the baby were all right. She had been taking bowls of hot water upstairs constantly for hours but as yet they hadn't been needed and she was growing concerned.

Eventually she gave Ellie her supper and tucked her into bed. After that, the time seemed to pass even more slowly. Sometimes the sound of Eve groaning floated down the stairs, and each time Annie's heart missed a beat. Poor thing, she was clearly in agony but Annie couldn't do a single thing to help her. It was gone nine o'clock when Peggy came down the stairs looking worried and harassed to fetch a cup of tea for herself and the midwife. Annie bustled over to the sink to boil the kettle and make the tea as Peggy wearily sank down onto one of the hard kitchen chairs.

'How is she?' Annie asked fearfully.

Knowing it would be pointless to lie, Peggy shook her head. Everything had started so well but now she feared things were not progressing as they should. 'Not well,' she admitted. 'If the baby ain't here in the next half an hour I want you to run fer the doctor. Old Ma Bates is concerned that the baby is too big for her to birth it. She's been so brave, bless her, an' she's done everything Ma Bates told her to, but she's exhausted an' I don't know how much longer she can go on.'

'In that case I'm goin' to get the doctor right now,' Annie told her. She couldn't bear to think of her friend suffering. 'I'll just make this tea an' then I'm off. I just hope the doctor ain't out on a call.'

'It might be a good idea,' Peggy admitted and Annie realised things must be very serious indeed.

When Annie hammered on the doctor's door minutes later, she was relieved when his wife answered it and assured her that the doctor was there. Annie hurriedly told him what was wrong and after slipping his coat on and grabbing his bag he accompanied her back to Peggy's cottage.

He went straight upstairs after instructing Annie to boil yet more water, and the waiting began again.

Upstairs the doctor frowned as he looked at the poor soul writhing on the bed. 'And how long has she been like this?' he asked as he rolled his sleeves up and snapped his bag open.

'Two or three hours now,' Ma Bates answered. 'An' she ain't got any further, although she's been pushin' wi' all her might.'

'In that case I think it's time we did something to help this baby along.' Lifting a lethal-looking scalpel from his bag, he approached the bed and made a small cut before saying, 'Now on your next contraction I want you to push with all your might. Can you do that for me?'

'I-I'll try,' Eve whimpered. She was so weak that she could barely speak, and a tear rolled down Peggy's cheek as she squeezed her hand.

Soon after the doctor nodded. 'Right, here it comes, now *push*!'

With one final effort Eve did as she was asked and suddenly the baby's head was out.

'Stop . . . stop now,' the doctor barked suddenly. 'The cord is around the baby's neck. Just pant for me while I try to loosen it!' Again, he bent to her and a few moments later, he said, 'Now, push again. One last time and the baby should be here!'

Eve bent her chin to her chest and strained as best she could and finally, she felt the baby slither out of her.

Tears of relief streaked down her cheeks, until she realised that the baby wasn't crying. Leaning up on one elbow, she saw the doctor pressing hard on its little chest and blowing into its mouth, as Peggy and Ma Bates looked on with frightened eyes.

'What is it?' she cried in panic. 'A boy or a girl? And why isn't it crying?'

Peggy tried to reassure her. 'It's a little boy, pet. But he had a hard time coming and the doctor is just helpin' him a bit.'

The doctor lifted the infant after a time and smacked him hard on the bottom, but still there was only silence. Eventually the doctor laid him down and gently covered him with a blanket.

He turned to Eve. 'I'm so very sorry but your baby was still-born,' he told her gravely. 'I did everything I could but I'm afraid it was too late.'

'B-but he can't be!' She shook her head in disbelief. 'You're lying to me, you must be. I want to see him!'

Blinded by tears, Peggy gently lifted the baby and placed him on his mother's chest.

Staring down at him, Eve felt as if her heart was breaking. 'This is me punishment fer not wantin' him when I found out I were pregnant,' she said in a cracked voice. He was unbearably beautiful with hair the exact same colour as her own, and he looked so peaceful, she was sure that any minute he would open his eyes and look up at her.

'It's no one's fault,' the doctor said wearily. Eve had lost a lot of blood and he was more concerned about her at the moment. There was nothing more he could do for the baby.

Eve clung on to her little son, committing every tiny feature of his face to memory as the doctor delivered the afterbirth and stitched her up.

Annie had come upstairs by that time, and she too was heart-broken at the loss of the baby.

'What do we need to do now?' Eve asked dully.

'We need to send fer the undertaker,' Peggy told her gently. 'That's if yer want him buried properly? If not—'

Eve looked panicked. 'O' course I want him buried properly. But how much will that cost?'

'I shall pay for it,' Annie told her firmly. She knew that Eve didn't have much money. 'And he'll have the best funeral we can for him.'

'Thank you,' Eve said humbly. 'I'll pay yer every last penny when I'm back on me feet.'

When the doctor was satisfied he had done all he could for Eve, Annie paid him and he left, promising to call into the undertaker on his way home. And still Eve clung to her son as if she never intended to let him go.

'Let's give 'er a little time alone wi' him,' Peggy suggested, and she and Annie quietly slipped from the room.

'I'm so sorry,' Eve whispered as her tears dripped onto her baby's face. 'I had such plans fer you an' me. We were goin' to 'ave such good fun.'

Downstairs the mood was no lighter as Annie mashed yet more tea while they waited for the undertaker to arrive. He came almost an hour later, bearing the tiniest coffin they had ever seen. Peggy took him upstairs, and after he'd taken the little body away, Annie and Peggy comforted Eve as best they could.

What had started that morning as the beginning of a whole new adventure for Eve had turned into the worst day of her life.

Chapter Thirty-Nine

August 1913

'I've been thinking,' Levi said to Annie and Maggie one evening as they sat outside enjoying the balmy night air. 'I reckon it's time we 'ad us all a little holiday.'

'What!' Maggie looked shocked. They hadn't had a holiday since shortly before Penny had died and as far as she knew, Annie had never had one at all, apart from her breaks with Susan in London.

'Why not?' He grinned at her. 'All we have to do is shut up shop and go. I doubt Charlie and Harry will want to come so they can look after Dobbin. An' I think we should take Peggy, Ellie an' Eve, an' all – if they want to come.'

'And what sort of holiday did you have in mind?' Maggie questioned.

'I was thinkin' o' the coast somewhere. We could go by train an' book into a hotel fer a few days. I think it'd do us all a power o' good.'

He folded the paper he had been reading. Mercy had been sentenced to twenty years in prison for murder, but he didn't mention that to Maggie. She worried about Barney being with the circus enough as it was without having to read about that, so he would make sure that the paper disappeared. This, he felt, was a case of see all, say nowt!

'But wouldn't that sort of a holiday be rather expensive?' Annie asked. She had been saving every penny she earned and didn't want to spend it frivolously, although she had always longed to see the sea.

'It'd be my treat. You, Peggy an' Eve have certainly earned a break.' Levi leant back in his chair and smiled.

Finally, Maggie nodded. 'I suppose a breath of sea air wouldn't go amiss,' she admitted, thinking back to the happy time they'd had with Penny and the boys at the seaside. It all seemed such a long time ago now.

'Right, so I'll put the idea to Eve an' Peggy tomorrow an' we'll go from there.'

Monty breezed round the corner just then and smiled. 'Evening all. I was wondering if you fancied a stroll, Annie?'

Levi had noticed how much attention Monty had been paying to Annie recently and wondered if anything would come of it. The young man certainly seemed to be smitten with her and to his mind she could do far worse.

'I thought we could go along the canal,' Monty went on hopefully.

Annie nodded. 'All right. I'll just go and get a shawl. The nights are beginning to draw in and it can get nippy.'

As they set off, Annie glanced around anxiously. Reggie had been a bit of a nuisance again lately; waiting for her every time she set foot out of the house, and his unwelcome attentions were beginning to make her a little nervous. It was only when they reached the bottom of Tuttle Hill and branched off towards the canal and along the tow path that she began to relax.

'Is everything all right?' she asked Monty, who seemed unusually quiet.

He frowned. 'Yes . . . but . . . Well, I heard a rather unpleasant rumour today and wondered if you could tell me if it's true or not.'

Annie didn't like the sound of that but she nodded. 'I suppose so, if I can.'

'The thing is, I heard that Eve is living with your family's friend Peggy in the courtyards in Abbey Street. And I also heard that shortly after arriving back here she gave birth to a child. The rumour is that she must have been carrying the child when she ran away and that it was my father's baby. Is there any truth in that?'

Annie swallowed. She'd been dreading this happening and wasn't sure what to say. Would telling the truth achieve anything other than a lot of heartbreak and unpleasantness? So, deciding to stick to the story she and Eve had decided on, she crossed her fingers and told him, 'Eve told me that she met and married the baby's father shortly after arriving in London.'

'Phew!' Monty looked relieved. 'Thank goodness for that. Had it been true and my mother ever found out there would have been ructions. Poor Eve, though. The baby died, didn't it? And what happened to the father?'

'Oh, er, he was killed in an accident shortly after they were wed.' It seemed that one lie was leading to another and Annie hated it. 'If I were you, I'd forget all about it, for Eve's sake. She's had a rough time and I think she just wants to put it all behind her.'

'I can understand that, poor thing,' Monty said sympathetically.

Changing the subject she told him all about the proposed holiday. 'I've never seen the sea,' she admitted, her eyes sparkling.

Monty smiled as he tucked her arm into his. 'Then let's hope you enjoy it. You certainly deserve a break. I only wish I could come too.'

When Levi put the idea to Peggy and Eve the following morning, Eve was less than enthusiastic.

'I could stay 'ere an' keep the clothes shed open,' she pointed out. The last thing she felt like doing was gallivanting about, as she was still grieving for her baby. But Peggy wagged a stern finger at her.

'We've both suffered terrible losses over the last few months, my girl,' she scolded. 'An' I reckon it's a grand idea, just what the doctor ordered. When were you thinkin' of goin'? And is Ellie invited?'

'The week after next all bein' well, and of course Ellie will come with us.' Levi was pleased they'd agreed, albeit Eve was somewhat reluctant.

'Might as well go an' make the best o' the good weather afore we're properly into autumn, eh?' Levi commented. 'Now we just have to decide where to go.'

'Southend?' questioned Maggie when Levi told her where he had in mind to go. She pulled a face as she folded her hands primly in her lap. 'But Mr and Mrs Taylor-Lloyd have just come back from the South of France! Southend is so . . . so working class, don't you think? *Surely*, we could afford to go somewhere a little more upmarket!'

'Not if there's six of us goin' we can't.' Levi's smile faded. 'Annie's never seen the sea, nor 'as little Ellie. An' both Eve an' Peggy 'ave suffered bereavements, so I reckon it would do 'em the world o' good.'

'Annie is quite old enough to pay for her own holiday. You do give her a wage now, don't you? And as for Eve . . . Well . . . wasn't the child she lost illegitimate? Why are we paying for her holiday?'

'Aye, Eve's baby was illegitimate, thanks to that old lecher next door,' Levi snapped. 'If it were up to me, I'd have him horse-whipped an' run out o' town, but I reckon it's a case of the least said the soonest mended in this case.' He hadn't intended to tell her about Mr Taylor-Lloyd but she had annoyed him and it had just slipped out. Still, there was nothing he could do about it now. 'The poor girl needs to get 'er life back on track.' He went on. 'Her an' Annie spent most o' their childhoods in the workhouse an' as for Peggy . . . well, I thought she were your oldest friend. She's been there fer you through thick an' thin, so I thought you'd be happy to give her a break.'

Maggie looked uncomfortable and squirmed in her seat. 'I sup-pose Peggy is my best friend,' she admitted grudgingly. 'But what would she wear to go on holiday? Her clothes are so drab. You men don't think about those sort of things.'

'Happen that's cos she's never 'ad the money fer fancy togs,' Levi answered. 'But that can soon be sorted. We've enough fancy clothes in that shed to rig 'er out – the girls an' all. So what do yer say? Are you up fer it or what? Cos I'll tell you now, I'm goin' whether you decide to come along or not.'

Maggie's back was ramrod straight as she glared at him. 'In that case I shall come,' she agreed. 'And we can only hope that none of them shows us up. I take it we will be staying in a hotel?'

'Of course.'

'Then you'd best get yourself fitted for a new suit too, because your clothes aren't much better than theirs.'

He shook his head in irritation and left the room.

Levi told Annie the next morning that she, Peggy and Eve were to help themselves to anything they liked from the clothes shed.

Peggy was all of a dither when she found out. 'Ooh, I ain't too sure about this,' she told Annie. 'It don't seem right.'

Annie chuckled. She had far more clothes than Peggy because while she was in London Susan had given her some lovely gowns that she no longer wore, but she knew Peggy didn't have much in the way of fancy clothes, apart from the one second-hand gown she had treated herself to for her son's wedding a few weeks before.

'Levi wouldn't tell you to do it if he didn't want you to,' she assured her as she started to rifle through the clothes.

Half an hour later she had selected two very pretty day gowns that she thought would fit Peggy, along with some petticoats that looked almost brand new, and a two-piece costume that would be perfect to travel in.

'Go and try them on, and make sure you let me see you in them,' she urged. 'I can serve the customers if any come.'

'Very well, but I don't feel right about it,' Peggy grumbled as she set off for the cottage with the clothes across her arm.

When she returned wearing the first gown, Annie hardly rec-ognised her. Peggy usually wore drab colours because they were more serviceable, but this gown was a cream linen sprigged with tiny rosebuds. It was tight into the waist and fell gently to the floor showing off her figure to perfection. She was staring at her so hard that Peggy blushed to the roots of her hair.

'It's too young for me, ain't it?' she wailed. 'I bet I look like mutton dressed as lamb.'

'No, you do *not*!' Annie shook her head vehemently. 'It really suits you; in fact you look ten years younger and quite beautiful. An' you'll look better still when I've done yer hair for you.'

'Why, what's up wi' me hair?' Peggy self-consciously patted the unbecoming bun on the back of her head.

'I bet you've got lovely hair when it's loose,' Annie declared. 'So, I want to try a few different styles out on you before we go away. Now go an' try the next gown on, eh?'

Peggy obediently went to do as she was told and returned in a pale-blue gown trimmed with white lace at the collar and cuffs. Again, it was fashioned in the straighter style that ladies favoured now and it was the exact same colour as her eyes.

Annie beamed at her. 'You look amazing,' she assured her. 'And while you've been gone, I've found you a nice blouse an' skirt too.'

'An' just how am I supposed to pay fer all this lot?' Peggy groaned. 'I ain't made o' money, yer know? An' we've still got to sort some clobber out for Eve an' all.'

'Don't you get worryin' about that. Levi said there's no charge fer either o' you. He reckons you've more than earned a few togs.'

A customer appeared just then, and they were both kept busy for the next hour so there was no more talk of the holiday, but Annie was sure Peggy looked a little more cheerful and knew that a break and a bit of clean sea air would do her a power of good. She could hardly wait for them to go.

Chapter Forty

In Nottingham, where the circus was now settled for the next few weeks, Barney watched Charity trudge towards her trailer. Her shoulders were slumped as if she was carrying the weight of the world on them and all the sparkle seemed to have gone out of her. He supposed it was because she was missing her daughter, and he wished there was something he could do to cheer her up. But since Mercy's arrest, Luca and Noah guarded her like watchdogs and it was hard to get a word alone with her. Now, however, neither of them were anywhere in sight, so seizing his opportunity Barney hurried over and relieved her of the empty buckets she was carrying.

'Just fed the horses, have you?' he said cheerfully.

Glancing up at him she nodded.

'Not too much, I hope? You know they don't perform right on full bellies.'

'I think I've been feedin' 'em long enough to know how much to give 'em by now,' she snapped.

'Yes . . . o' course yer do. I didn't mean to offend yer.'

She sighed and turned to look up at him. 'Sorry, Barney, I'm just . . . oh, I don't know . . .'

'Yer missin' yer daughter,' he said gently. 'That's understandable. I am too.'

Tears swam into her eyes. There were dark circles beneath them and he had to stop himself from throwing the buckets down and taking her in his arms.

'Twenty years she got,' she said brokenly. 'It ain't fair. I'll be old afore she gets out. That's if she survives it. Yer know she hates bein' in confined spaces.' The tears spurted down her pale cheeks as she lifted her gaily coloured skirts and plodded towards her trailer.

Barney watched helplessly, knowing there was absolutely nothing he could do to ease her pain, before placing the buckets next to the feed sacks and heading back to his trailer.

Later that evening, as the crowds began to spill into the big top, he saw Charity wearing Mercy's pretty trapeze costume. She had taught Mercy all she knew, and had now taken her daughter's place, and although she was in her late thirties, she was still a fine figure of a woman. Hers was always the first act, and he loved hearing the audience ooh and ahh as she swung effortlessly about the roof of the tent. He wondered what was different about her and suddenly realised it was her hair. Normally she wore it tied back but this evening it hung down her back as sleek and shiny as a raven's wing. He frowned. It looked beautiful, but wearing it like that could be dangerous should it get tangled on one of the swings, so he hurried over to her.

'Charity, you forgot to tie your hair back.'

She shrugged. 'So?'

'So, it could be bloody dangerous,' he told her with a glare. 'Go and get a ribbon for it.'

She glared right back, her fists on her slim hips, her legs apart. 'And since when have you had the right to tell me what to do?'

'I ain't, I'm just thinkin' o' yer safety.'

'Well don't bother. I don't care what happens to me,' she retorted, and with a toss of her head, she turned and left him standing there.

Once the audience had taken their seats, the ringmaster in his smart costume and black top hat announced the beginning of the show. 'And now, Miss Charity on her flying trapeze.'

To squeals of excitement from the children, Charity appeared in the spotlight, her costume glittering in the bright light. She shinned the rope as easily as a monkey to get to the many swings suspended from the roof of the big top and as she swung effortlessly from one to another Barney watched with his heart in his mouth. He had a bad feeling about this performance and couldn't wait for it to be over.

It seemed to go on forever, but at last she was nearing the end when, as one of her hands reached for a swing, her long hair tangled in the rope. A gasp went up from the audience and time seemed to stand still for a moment as Charity desperately tried to save herself, but the swing slipped from her grasp and she plummeted to the ground landing with a sickening thud, her arm bent beneath her at an unnatural angle.

Children were crying and women were screaming as Luca rushed forward to drop down beside his wife, shouting her name. There was no response from Charity and in one swift movement, he swept her into his arms and ran out of the tent as someone else shouted for the audience to stay in their seats before introducing the next act.

Barney was already waiting for Luca at the back of the tent as he emerged with Charity in his arms.

'We need to get her to the hospital,' he shouted, laying her gently on the ground. 'Bring the trap round *now!*'

'Is she breathing?' Barney asked.

Luca bent to listen to her chest and nodded.

Barney let out a sigh of relief. Minutes later the trap was there, driven by one of the clowns, still in his costume with a ridiculous red nose on.

Very gently they lifted her onto the back of the trap and as Luca climbed in beside her Barney tried to join him but he shook his head.

'No, you stay here. There's no point in us all going. Try an' keep everythin' runnin' smoothly.'

The clown whipped the horse into a trot and all Barney could do was watch them go with a sinking feeling in the pit of his stomach.

That evening was the longest Barney could remember. Every minute felt like an hour but at last the show was over and the crowd started to disperse to the fair. It was then that Barney saw the trap coming back, with Luca sitting beside the clown who had now removed his nose and wig. But there was no sign of Charity.

'How is she?' Barney asked before the horse had even come to a standstill.

Luca seemed to have aged ten years as he climbed wearily down and swiped the hair from his forehead.

'They've kept her in but God willin' she's goin' to be all right. Her arm is broken an' she has concussion but as the doctor pointed out it could 'ave been a lot worse. She's been very lucky to survive that fall.'

'Thank God,' Barney whispered. He had noticed that Luca and Charity seemed to be having more to do with each other since Mercy had been imprisoned and hoped there might be a way they could overcome their differences – whatever they were. They clearly still cared about each other, even if they couldn't see it. But there was still work to do so he turned and went to get on with it. The show had to go on.

Early the following afternoon, Barney went to the hospital armed with a large bunch of flowers.

Charity was propped up in bed at the end of a long ward with a cast on her arm and her hair spread about the pillow, her face as white as the sheets.

'Didn't I tell yer yer should have tied yer hair back?' he said as he approached.

She managed a small smile. 'Yer did an' I knew yer were right but I don't care anymore.'

Barney scowled. 'What do yer mean, yer don't care anymore? Do yer think Mercy would like to see yer like this? You've got to come to terms wi' what's happened to her.'

'I-I can't . . .' She began to cry. 'I miss her so much an' I should 'ave seen how much you two cared fer each other. I'll never forget that you were willin' to go to prison for her.'

Barney shrugged. 'That's what love does for yer,' he said softly, then he quietly left the ward.

Outside he lit a cigarette and sagging back against the wall, he took a long drag as he tried to shut out the image of his beautiful Mercy trapped in prison like a little bird in a cage.

Charity returned three days later having been given strict instructions to rest. There wasn't much else she could do with the heavy cast on her arm anyway. The circus women fussed around her like mother hens, making her food and helping her to wash and dress, so it wasn't until around midday the next day that Barney had a chance to speak to her alone again.

She was lying propped up on her bed in the trailer, and when she saw him, she looked away.

'How are you?' The words sounded ridiculous – he could see that she was in a bad way, but he didn't know what else to say.

'I'll live,' she murmured. 'But I have come back to some good news.'

'Oh yes?'

'Luca informed me that the lawyer he employed to defend Mercy has put in for an appeal on her sentence. He believes that it should be reduced to manslaughter rather than murder. She was only defending herself, after all. And she didn't really stab him, he lunged towards her onto the knife.'

Barney smiled, really smiled, for the first time since Mercy had been locked away. 'Then let's just pray the appeal is successful, eh?'

Chapter Forty-One

'Right, are we all ready for the off then?' Levi asked as the last of the luggage was loaded onto the cab – Maggie had taken enough clothes to last for at least a month.

'Yes, I think so,' Maggie began to pin her newest hat onto her head and glanced around for anything she might have forgotten as he urged her towards the door.

They clambered into the cab with Peggy complaining. 'Eeh, there ain't enough room in 'ere fer another pea,' she groaned as she pressed up against Eve with Ellie pressed tightly against her other side. 'I told yer I should've met yer at the station.'

Annie giggled. She couldn't help but be excited at the thought of her first glimpse of the sea. Although she wasn't much looking forward to the journey as they would need to change trains in London, but at least she had packed enough sandwiches and drinks to make sure they didn't go hungry.

Soon they arrived at the station and after their luggage had been placed in the guards' van at the back of the train, they climbed aboard to find their carriage.

'Can I 'ave a bucket an' spade to make sandcastles when we get there?' Ellie asked innocently.

'Course yer can, pet,' Peggy assured her and the girl pressed her nose against the window, excited to watch the world flash past.

Once they had changed trains in London, Annie unpacked the food and they dug in. They still had at least another couple of hours to go before they reached their destination, and Ellie was growing bored.

'Let's have a game of "I spy",' Annie suggested and soon everyone apart from Maggie was joining in. When Ellie eventually grew tired of the game, she thankfully fell into a doze and didn't wake again until they drew into the station at Southend, where the ritual of unloading the luggage began all over again. Soon, though, they were in a cab rattling towards the hotel, and as the sea came into view Ellie clapped her hands with delight.

The hotel was everything they could have wished for and as they entered the luxurious foyer Annie felt as if she was entering a different world. It was perched on the clifftop overlooking the estuary and once Levi had collected their keys and they were shown to their rooms on the first floor, they were delighted to find that each one had a sea view. Levi and Maggie had one room, Eve and Annie were in the next, and Peggy and Ellie were in the one next to them. They were tastefully furnished with large, comfy featherbeds and Peggy confessed this must be what it was like when you died and went to heaven.

It was late afternoon, so after a quick wash and change they all met downstairs to eat in the hotel dining room. Peggy's eyes stretched wide with dismay when she saw the prices on the menu, but Levi waved aside her concerns. 'You're on holiday so have whatever you like,' he told her with a kindly twinkle in his eye. It was lovely to see her looking more like the Peggy he remembered before she had lost Sid.

He ordered a steak that almost covered the plate when it came, while Peggy, Annie, Ellie and Eve all ordered chicken. Maggie ordered seafood and they agreed that everything was cooked to perfection. After the main course Ellie was treated to an ice cream sundae that made her eyes pop when she saw it, and they finished off with coffees for the grown-ups, and lemonade for Ellie. And then the little girl could be put off no longer, and she insisted on going down to the beach.

Maggie declined to go with them, saying she preferred to rest in her room, but everyone else set off in fine high spirits. Within minutes of setting foot on the sand Ellie had kicked her shoes off and was racing around like a spring lamb.

'We'll get you a bucket and spade tomorrow,' Levi promised her as he tussled her hair affectionately. He still missed her living with them but at least he knew she had a wonderful home with Peggy; he just wished that Maggie could have an ounce of her compassion sometimes. They spent a pleasant hour wandering along the beach as Ellie collected shells and paddled in the rock pools, then as the light began to fade, they turned and headed back to the hotel.

When they entered their rooms, they were surprised to discover that their curtains had been drawn and their beds turned back for them.

'Crikey, 'ow the other 'alf live,' Peggy giggled. 'I reckon I could get used to this.' She had never been waited on before. Turning to Levi, her smile left her. 'I dread to think 'ow much all this must be costin'.'

He tutted, but his eyes were smiling. 'Don't you get worrying about that. We're only here for a week so just enjoy it.'

When he entered his own room a few moments later, he was delighted to find Maggie looking happier than she had in years. 'Oh, the indoor bathrooms here are just *wonderful*!' she gushed. Mrs Taylor-Lloyd had had one installed, and she was wildly envious of it. 'I insist that when we get home, we look into getting one for ourselves.'

Levi's heart sank. It sounded like it was going to be a very costly exercise but knowing his wife as he did, he knew she wouldn't stop going on about it until she had one. Still, they were there to enjoy themselves so he said nothing. He didn't want to spoil things.

There followed an almost idyllic week. One day Levi took them on a boat trip and they spent a lot of time on the beach, where Ellie made sandcastle after sandcastle. They walked along the pier and by midweek, they all had a slight tan, for the weather had been perfect, with cloudless blue skies and sunshine. Even Peggy and Eve had got a little colour back in their cheeks and Levi couldn't help but notice how pretty Peggy looked, with her hair hanging loose about her shoulders in her pretty second-hand dresses.

Every morning, they had a hearty breakfast at the hotel and during the day they ate toffee apples, ice creams and candy floss before returning to the hotel for their evening meal. Maggie chose not to go with them for much of the time as she had discovered that Southend had a very nice little shopping centre, so she went there most days instead. She bought herself yet another new bonnet and two very pretty blouses and a skirt, and Levi teased her that at the rate she was buying they'd never be able to get everything home.

Annie ventured into the town herself one day to get small gifts for Monty, Charlie and Harry. For Monty she bought a very smart fountain pen, for Charlie a book of sonnets that he had been after for some time, and for Harry there was a rather nice tie.

'Why don't you treat yourself to something?' Levi asked.

She smiled and shook her head. 'I don't need anything,' she assured him.

He stroked her hair gently. Over the years he had grown to love her and he now looked upon her as a daughter.

But all good things must come to an end and soon it was time for them to return to reality.

'I hope Charlie's taken good care of old Dobbin,' Levi commented as he helped Maggie to pack their cases.

'Of course he will have,' she answered shortly.

They were all quiet on the journey home. Ellie had cried when she waved goodbye to the sea and Levi promised her that he would bring her again. She was fast asleep long before the train reached the station and she didn't even stir as Levi carried her to a waiting cab for the final part of their journey.

On the way to Swan Lane, they dropped Peggy, Eve and Ellie off at the courtyard before carrying on to their own home.

Harry was in on his own, as Charlie was out with friends. Once Levi and Annie had carried the luggage in, he shot off to the stable to check on his beloved horse while Maggie took her hat off and frowned at Harry.

'And what's with the glum face?' she questioned. 'I thought you'd be pleased to see us, but you look as if you've lost a bob and found a tanner.'

He gave a nervous little cough and tugged at the collar of his shirt. 'Actually, Ma, I've got somethin' to tell yer.'

'Go on then, spit it out.' She turned to the mirror and began to remove her coat.

'I, er . . . well, the thing is I'm gettin' married . . .'

'You're *what*?' Maggie turned with a look of horror on her face, hoping she had misheard him.

'But you're so young. What's all the rush and . . .' As something occurred to her the colour drained out of her face. 'You haven't gone and got some tart in the family way, have you?'

'Becca ain't no tart,' he said defensively. 'I've been seein' her fer some time. Well . . . a few months at least.'

'Is this the butcher's daughter you're talking about?'

He nodded miserably, keeping his head bowed.

'You young *fool*!' his mother snapped. 'How could you be so stupid!' But when she thought of it, she realised things could have been worse. At least Rebecca's father owned a reputable, thriving shop.

'Do her parents know?'

He nodded.

'Hmm, and I dare say they're no happier with the news than I am!'

'They ain't so bad now they know I intend to do right by her,' he said sullenly.

'And when is this wedding to be and where do you intend to live?'

'The weddin' will be next month an' we'll be livin' wi' Becca's parents fer a time. I'm already workin' fer her dad, so it makes sense.'

'I see. In that case I suppose we should start to organise the wedding.'

Harry shook his head. 'There's no need. Becca's parents are seein' to everythin'. It's only goin' to be a very small do wi' close family at the registry office.'

Maggie looked horrified. '*The registry office*! Surely you can do better than that? What will people think? You could at least have a church wedding and a decent reception.'

'I don't much care what anyone thinks,' Harry informed her. 'It's how me an' Becca want it. Just simple wi' no fuss.'

Feeling in the way, Annie slipped out of the back door and it wasn't long before Monty appeared through the gap in the hedge.

'I saw the cab bring you back. Did you have a good holiday?' he enquired, thinking how well she looked. But then she always looked good to him.

'Yes, yes we did thanks.' They strolled to the bench under the apple tree and sat down, enjoying the silence for a moment.

'I, er . . . thought I heard some shouting from the kitchen just now. Is everything all right?' he asked eventually.

Annie nodded. 'Yes. Just Maggie and Harry having a little tiff.' She didn't feel it was her place to tell him about the forthcoming wedding, although she had no doubt he would hear about it soon enough. Harry would probably tell him about it himself.

She went on to tell him about the lovely hotel they had stayed in and how much Ellie had loved the beach before standing up again and stretching.

'Right, I think I'll go in and grab an early night. It's back to the grindstone tomorrow.'

311

He rose with her. 'Of course. How about we go to the picture house tomorrow evening? They're showing *Saved from the Titanic* with Dorothy Gibson.'

Everyone had been horrified the year before when the *Titanic* had sunk on her maiden voyage after hitting an iceberg, and many hundreds of people had perished in the icy ocean, and now films were being made about it.

They both enjoyed the silent movies that were becoming so popular, but Annie shook her head, although she would have liked to go – she liked spending time with Monty. 'I won't this time, Monty. I've got so much to do after being away for a week that I need to catch up.'

'I understand, another time.' He smiled but it was hard to hide his disappointment and suddenly he blurted out, 'Look, Annie . . . we've always got on, haven't we? And I was wondering . . . Well, would you consider walking out with me? Properly, I mean, as my girl.'

Annie bit her lip. She'd known for a while that Monty's feelings for her went beyond friendship, but as fond as she was of him, she wasn't sure if she was ready to commit to anyone just yet.

'The thing is,' she began, hoping to spare his feelings. 'I think the world of you – you know I do. But I don't want to walk out or get seriously involved with anyone just yet. And anyway, can you imagine what your mother would say if she found out we were walking out together as girlfriend and boyfriend. She'd have a fit! I've never been more than a glorified maid to her. Even so, I might not have had the best start, but I want to make something of my life.'

'But you could . . . we could do it together, and I don't give a damn what my mother says!' he said desperately.

She shook her head. 'I'm sorry, Monty. I wouldn't hurt your feelings for the world but as I said, I'm not ready. Let's just keep things as they are for now at least, eh?'

She gave his hand a gentle squeeze and hurried away. *What a homecoming.* First there had been Harry's bombshell about getting wed and now this from Monty. She almost wished she was back in Southend again.

And the day wasn't over yet, for just as she was falling asleep later that evening, she heard a bang and a crash in the kitchen and the sound of Levi's bedroom door being flung open as he flew downstairs to see what was going on.

Pulling her dressing robe on, Annie followed him to find him standing over Charlie's inert frame on the kitchen floor.

'Light the lamp,' Levi told her. 'And get me some water and a rag to wipe 'is face. It looks to me like he's had another pastin'.'

'But *why*?' Annie gasped as she saw the blood on Charlie's face. 'This is the second time this 'as happened yet Charlie wouldn't hurt a fly. Why is he bein' picked on?'

Levi said nothing as he dragged a cushion from the chair and lifted his son's head onto it. He had his own thoughts on what might have happened, but they were so terrible that for now he preferred to keep them to himself and pray that he was wrong.

Chapter Forty-Two

Barney was like a cat on hot bricks as he helped to take the swing boats down, keeping one eye open for Luca who had attended court in Warwick for Mercy's appeal that morning. The circus would be moving on to Lincolnshire that evening and everything was hustle and bustle as the men took down the rides and loaded them onto the wagons. He was praying that when Luca did appear he would have Mercy with him. After all, how could she be found guilty when she was only defending herself. Then, from the corner of his eye he saw two figures in the distance striding towards him. One of them had long flowing black hair and his heart started to beat a tattoo in his chest as he stopped to watch them advance.

It was only as they grew closer that he realised the woman wasn't Mercy, it was her mother.

Racing towards them he gasped, 'Where's Mercy? What's happened?'

Charity looked pale and thin, her bright clothes hung off her and without even acknowledging him she carried on to her trailer.

'The judge accepted that she acted in self-defence and it wasn't premeditated,' Luca told him dully. 'But even so, the stabbin' resulted in Bertie losin' 'is life, so he reduced her sentence to five years fer manslaughter.'

'*Five years!*' Barney felt as if he had had all the air sucked out of his body. Five years of never speaking to her, of never seeing her lovely smile; it sounded like a lifetime to him, and yet it was certainly better than the twenty years she was originally sentenced to.

'So is there nuthin' else we can do to get 'er out?'

Luca wearily shook his head. 'Not a bloody thing, boyo. She's done the crime and now she has to pay the penalty, simple as that. An' the worst thing is I blame meself. All the circus lasses are taught 'ow to defend 'emselves from an early age. It were me as taught 'er to use a knife an' encouraged 'er to allus carry one. An' further-more, I'm expectin' trouble from Bertie's family. They ain't gonna be none too pleased to know that her sentence 'as been reduced. Huh! So much fer the two families mergin'. I reckon we're gonna 'ave to keep us eyes peeled from now on cos we could have a war on us hands.'

The war began two weeks later in the middle of the night while the circus folk slept. All was quiet until a sudden shout went up. '*Fire!*'

Bleary-eyed men and women spilled out of their trailers and grabbed buckets of water. The gaily painted horses on the carousel were engulfed in flames but after half an hour of hard work they managed to douse the fire.

'Do yer reckon this were the work o' vandals?' Gypsy Rose Lee asked, swiping the back of her hand across her sooty face.

Luca shook his head. 'It could have been, but it could also have been the work o' the Russells. I reckon we're gonna have to have someone on night watch from now on. If it had been the big top we'd have been in serious trouble. As it is we might be able to sal-vage the carousel but the whole thing will want a total repaint an' we ain't gonna get a chance to do that until the winter.'

Barney volunteered to keep watch for the rest of that night while the others returned to their trailers sick at heart to think that one of their most popular rides would be out of action for some months.

The fire had made the animals fractious, and Barney spent a lot of the night going round the various enclosures trying to reassure them. Thankfully, there were no further incidents so at first light, he slipped away, fell into bed and was asleep in seconds.

315

The next day, during a rare quiet time, he went to see Charity, who had huge dark circles beneath her eyes. Her usually glorious hair looked limp and matted and he found her sitting staring into space. She didn't look as if she had had a proper meal, or a bath for that matter, since her daughter had gone to jail.

'Er . . . is there anything I can get fer you?' he offered as he took the kettle to the tiny stove and lit the gas beneath it. She looked in need of a good strong cup of tea.

'Not unless yer can bring me daughter back to me.' She started to cry. 'Why did the silly young fool 'ave to go an' admit to stabbin' Bertie like that?

'I was more than willin' to do the time fer her!' Barney pointed out sadly.

'I know yer were, but she obviously didn't want you to take the rap fer sommat yer didn't do.'

Barney lifted the teapot and spooned some tea leaves into it. What could he say?

'She had her whole life ahead of her.' Charity sighed. 'Whereas me . . . Well, all I had left were her.'

Barney frowned. He desperately wanted to ask why she and Luca had nothing to do with each other and why they lived in separate trailers, but it wasn't the right time. It was none of his business anyway. He made her a sandwich and a cup of hot sweet tea before going to get on with his daily chores. As Luca had told him when he had joined them, no matter what happened, the show must go on.

Two weeks later, as Barney was enjoying a quiet drink with Betty, the bearded lady, he asked, 'Do yer know why Luca an' Charity don't live together, Betty? I mean I know they're married an' they have Noah an' Mercy, yet I never saw 'em so much as pass the time o' day till all this happened wi' Mercy.'

Betty scowled. 'Let's just say sommat happened a long time ago an' Luca washed 'is hands of 'er.'

'So if that's the case why is Charity still here?'

'Circus folk don't believe in divorce, son,' she stated solemnly. 'An' if yer want my advice yer'll not go delvin'. Some things are best left well alone.'

It was obvious she wasn't going to say anything else on the subject, so Barney shrugged and said no more, but he was still curious.

Chapter Forty-Three

October 1913

'This is gettin' ridiculous,' Peggy said one morning as she tried to make room for yet more clothes on the hanging rails in the shed. 'We ain't got room to swing a cat around in 'ere now that Levi has took to goin' further afield.'

Annie nodded in agreement. She still had an idea in mind to further their venture but as yet she hadn't discussed it with either Peggy or Levi. As well as the clothes, she had now started another line. She had realised that some of the metal Levi collected was still in good condition – far too good to be sold for scrap – so she had created a separate area in the courtyard where people could buy kettles, saucepans, buckets, bowls and anything that was still in usable condition for a knock-down price. Like the clothes, they were selling like hot cakes, so much so that Levi had finally given in to Maggie's demands and was having their smallest bedroom converted into an indoor bathroom. Maggie was in her element and had been boasting about it to everyone she met.

She had opted for a rather large claw-footed bath, a large sink and a flushing indoor toilet. The house was swarming with men fitting pipes that would feed the appliances from an enormous copper in the kitchen, while others were outside digging a cesspit for the toilet to flush into. The whole house was in chaos, but Annie was sure it would be worth it. It would be nice not to have to venture down the garden to use the toilet in the winter.

Her concern for Maggie had deepened since getting back from holiday for, more and more, she was catching her talking to Penny.

Thankfully the new bathroom had given her a diversion and she had seemed slightly better for the last couple of weeks, but Annie wondered how long it would last.

Maggie had now managed to form a circle of friends from the church, although Mrs Taylor-Lloyd wasn't amongst them, and once a week she would hold a coffee morning, at which she insisted Annie serve the drinks in her finest bone china cups and saucers. Annie found the whole thing highly amusing. The ladies would arrive like peacocks, each trying to outdo the other in their dress and the amount of jewellery they wore. The visitors clearly thought Annie was the maid, for Maggie never introduced her as a family member, but she wasn't concerned. She had realised long ago that Maggie would never accept her as a daughter, and it no longer troubled her.

As she got older, she was thinking more about who her birth parents might be. The bitterness at being abandoned as a newborn had long since gone. Now she could only imagine that her mother must have been in dire straits to do what she did, and she felt nothing but pity for her. Had she spent all these years wondering if her baby had survived the workhouse? she would wonder whenever she took out the beautiful, brightly coloured silk shawl she had been found in. She could have no way of knowing but she hoped one day to find out.

'Penny for 'em'.' Peggy's voice brought her thoughts sharply back to the present and she grinned. 'You were off wi' the fairies.'

'I was. I was thinking of Maggie's coffee mornings. I expect there'll be more of them once the indoor bathroom is finished.'

'Huh! There'll be no stoppin' her,' she chuckled, hanging another gown on the rail. 'She'll be plyin' 'em wi' that much tea an' coffee afore they go that they'll 'ave to use it. But how are things back there apart from her ladyship? It's Harry's weddin' next week, ain't it?'

'Yes, and I think Maggie is quite pleased about it now. She's a bit disappointed that it's only going to be a small do, but that was what Harry and Becca wanted.'

'Ah well, let's just hope he ain't makin' a mistake,' Peggy said quietly. 'Young Becca has been spoilt rotten by her parents', bein' their only child, an' I can't imagine her bein' easy to live wi'. And what about you? Ain't there nobody has caught your eye yet? It shouldn't be all work an' no play for a girl your age.' She had had a sneaky feeling that Annie had been sweet on Charlie at one time, but she seemed much closer to Monty now. She was also aware that Reggie Taylor-Lloyd still had his eye on her, but Annie seemed to be handling that and avoided him whenever she could.

'I'm quite all right as I am,' Annie said quietly.

'Oh yes, so you wouldn't still be sweet on young Charlie then?'

'No, me an' Charlie are . . . Well, we just get along,' Annie muttered. 'Although I admit I did 'ave feelin's fer him.'

'Aye, well it's perhaps as well yer over it, yer've been brought up as brother an' sister, an' I can't see Maggie would ever 'ave been happy if it had ever developed into anythin' more than that. You'd do better settin' yer sights a bit further afield, like on young Monty next door. Now there's a good chap. You could do far worse fer yourself an' it's as plain as the nose on yer face that he thinks the world o' you. Allus has!'

Annie sighed. 'Peggy will you *please* stop tryin' to marry me off. I'll get married when an' if I'm ready, I've got plenty of time. Why don't you concentrate on fixin' Eve up instead?'

Peggy shook her head. 'There'd be no point in tryin'. I reckon she's still stuck on that young man she met in London. Davey, weren't it? She still talks about him all the time, an' it's a cryin' shame. The way things have turned out wi' her losin' the baby they could have made a go of it. Trouble is she's too proud to speak to him now. Still reckons she's soiled goods.'

Annie thought of what Peggy had said all day, and late that evening when everyone was in bed, she sat down to write a letter to Susan. They still kept in touch and Susan had been saddened to hear of the baby's death. Perhaps, she thought, Susan might have a little word in Milly's ear, who in turn might have a word in Davey's? It was worth a try.

The weather was turning, the trees were beginning to shed their leaves and there was a distinct nip in the air now. The bathroom was almost completed, and life went on in the same humdrum way, but Annie was beginning to feel restless. There was so much she wanted to do, so she decided it was time to speak to Levi about her ideas.

'I was thinking,' she began cautiously as they sat together that evening after Maggie had retired, 'that it's time we expanded the business a bit.' She handed Levi a cup of cocoa and joined him on the sofa.

'Oh, yes? An' what did you 'ave in mind?'

'Now the second-hand clothes business is doing so well, I thought . . . I thought perhaps if you could afford another horse and cart and employed someone else to double your rounds, we could afford to rent a shop in town where we'd have more room to show the stock to its best advantage. We could buy in a few affordable ready-made clothes too, to give a better selection, and we could start to stock other things, like hats and shoes, and what have you. What do you think?'

Levi stared thoughtfully into the fire. 'But who would run the shop? You and Peggy do it between you at present cos you still keep this place runnin'. It would mean an awful lot o' extra work. An' I'd have to work out if it could be profitable after buyin' another horse an' cart. There'd be another wage to pay an' the rent on the shop an' all.'

'I know all that,' Annie admitted. 'An' I've already done some sums. Look.' She lifted a sheet of paper up on which she had written the estimated prices of what everything would cost. 'Admittedly we'd be makin' no profit fer a few months while you recouped what you'd laid out an' paid all the wages, but this is what we make roughly each week now.' She stabbed her finger at an amount written on the paper. 'An' wi' double the space an' double the merchandise to sell within no time we'd be coinin' it in. What do yer think? Will you at least think about it?'

'Aye, I will, hinny,' he promised and, satisfied that she had planted the seed, Annie sat back to enjoy her drink.

The following day when Levi got back to the courtyards after doing his rounds, he told her, 'I might go down to the cattle market tomorrow an' see what horses they've got for sale. I ain't promisin' anythin', mind.'

A little bubble of excitement stirred in Annie's stomach, but she said no more. It would be better to let Levi do things in his own time. He had enough harassment from Maggie without her adding to his woes.

Sure enough, the next morning Levi set off for the market and Annie went to join Peggy in the yard. She told her of the idea she had put to Levi and after thinking about it for a few minutes, Peggy nodded. 'Yer know, that ain't such a bad idea. We certainly do enough trade 'ere to branch out a bit. But is there enough room in the stable at Swan Lane to house another horse?'

'Oh yes, there are two stalls there.'

As it was market day the town was busy and soon their first customers began to arrive so there was no more time for them to talk.

It was almost lunchtime when Levi reappeared leading a lovely dapple-grey horse by her reins.

'This is Spirit,' he informed Annie and Peggy, looking pleased with himself. 'I got a right bargain with her. One of the farmers at the cattle market is selling all his livestock and his farm to go and live in Wales so I bartered him down.'

'Oh, she's just beautiful.' Annie smiled as she stroked the horse's nose.

'An' she's only nine years old so she's got years o' work in her yet. I just hope her an' old Dobbin take to each other,' Levi said as he too stroked the new addition to the family. 'Anyway, I'd best get her to the house. I've still got time to do me afternoon round but I reckon I'll take Dobbin as usual today till I've tried this little lady out. She won't be doin' much, anyway, till I've found me another cart an' someone to drive it.' He set off with a spring in his step.

Thankfully, as Annie discovered when she got home that evening, Dobbin and Spirit were getting along like a house on fire.

However, Maggie was far from happy about the new addition and wasted no time in making her feelings known. 'What were you thinking, bringing another horse here?' she ranted at Levi. 'Isn't it bad enough that we have to have the other smelly old thing at the back of the house?'

'May I remind you that that *smelly old thing* helped to buy this house you live in and the clothes on your back,' he retaliated. 'Not to mention the fancy new bathroom you insisted on.'

'I-I'm quite aware of that,' Maggie said in a quieter tone. 'But the neighbours aren't going to like it. They'll be complaining of the smell.'

'Me an' Annie keep that stable clean at all times and the smell is minimal,' he pointed out as he washed his hands at the sink. 'But perhaps if it bothers you that much, we should think of selling this place and going back to live in Abbey Street. Nobody cares how many animals you have there, seeing as most of them keep pigs in their yards.'

'Oh no . . . I, er . . . as you say, I'm sure it will be all right. But why didn't you tell me you were thinking of getting another horse, and why do we need one anyway?'

'I didn't talk to you about it because you don't normally want to get involved with my work.' He stared at her levelly and she flushed.

'But if you're askin' now, I can tell you that I intend to start another round. It will mean takin' someone else on and buying another cart but even after the cost of another horse to feed and shoe and another wage to pay, I think we will still be considerably better off. While I'm at it, I'm also considering rentin' a shop in town.'

Now her ears pricked up and he had her full attention. 'A shop!' She seemed quite excited at the thought. 'What sort of a shop?'

'A second-hand one.'

'Oh!' She scowled.

He could hear the disappointment in her voice. 'Is there anything wrong with that?'

'Er . . . it just sounds a little . . .' She struggled to choose the right words. 'What I'm trying to say is . . . won't that attract a certain type of customer?'

'If you mean working-class folk 'as are on a low income, yes it will. That's just the market I'm aiming at.'

She wanted to say more but one look at his face told her that he was in no mood to hear it, so instead she glowered at Annie, who was peeling potatoes for dinner, and sank into her chair where she snatched up a newspaper. A second-hand shop indeed! She dreaded to think what her lady friends would say when word got out. But it hadn't happened yet. Let the workmen finish the bathroom and then she would go into battle with Levi to prevent it if need be.

She had no doubt Annie would have had a hand in this. Her and her bright ideas. She'd be in line for a tongue-lashing too, but for now she would bide her time.

Chapter Forty-Four

Before they knew it, Harry's wedding day dawned and everything in the house was hustle and bustle as they got ready. As expected, Maggie was dressed in a completely new outfit, and much to Levi's disgust she had insisted he had a new suit too.

'I feel as if this damn thing is chokin' me,' he groaned as he tugged at the collar of his shirt.

Maggie chuckled as she adjusted his cravat. 'Oh, just stand still while I get it tied properly. It's nice to see you dressed up for a change. I could almost take you for a gentleman.'

Harry appeared with Charlie, who was to be his best man, looking handsome in their new suits, although Harry seemed subdued. Levi chuckled. 'Crikey, me lad, cheer up. You look like yer goin' to a funeral instead o' yer own weddin'. An' where's Annie? We should be settin' off fer the registry office any time now. It wouldn't do fer the groom to be late to his own weddin', would it?'

The words had barely left his lips when Annie appeared looking a vision in a blue satin gown Levi had collected on his rounds. Peggy had painstakingly washed, ironed and altered it for her until it fitted like a glove, and she looked beautiful.

'Why, hinny, you'll put the bride to shame lookin' like that,' Levi told her fondly.

Annie blushed, trying to ignore Maggie's scowl. It wasn't often she got a chance to dress up. She knew that had it been left up to Maggie she wouldn't even be going to the wedding, but Levi had insisted and she intended to enjoy the day.

At the registry office, they took their places to wait for the bride. When she arrived, wearing a white satin gown and veil and carrying a bouquet of white roses, everyone agreed she made a truly stunning bride.

Monty, however, only had eyes for Annie, who seemed oblivious to the fact.

Peggy, Eve and Ellie were also there, but apart from them there was only the bride's immediate family. The short service was followed by a small reception lunch in a hotel in town and by mid-afternoon it was all over, and the bride and groom accompanied Harry's in-laws back to what was to be his new home.

Returning to Swan Lane, Maggie was quite tearful, and Levi linked her arm through his. 'Come on now, pet,' he soothed. 'They're growin' up an' they're all gonna fly the nest sooner or later. You'll 'ave to get used to it.'

'I know that,' she sniffed as she dabbed at her cheeks with a tiny lace hankie. 'But he's so young, and despite the fact his in-laws own a shop, he could have done so much better for himself had he not got the girl in the family way.'

'Have yer forgotten that you were younger than Harry is when we got wed?' Levi pointed out.

Charlie, who was walking behind them with Monty and Annie, raised an eyebrow and they both grinned.

'I suppose seeing as we've got the rest of the day off, we could go out somewhere?' Annie suggested hopefully to Charlie and Monty. She was worried about Charlie; he spent hardly any time at home, and when he was there, he was subdued and offhand. There was something wrong, she could sense it. Or perhaps it was just that a young lady had caught his fancy. The idea would have been painful at one time but she was getting used to not seeing so much of him now.

She was not surprised, when Charlie shook his head. 'Sorry, but I'm off out to meet friends when I've got changed.'

'You and I could do something, though?' Monty suggested hopefully.

'No, it's all right. I've got plenty to do really, and I suppose I should help Peggy get ready for opening tomorrow,' she replied, failing to see the look of disappointment that crossed Monty's face. The last thing she wanted to do was give him false hope.

Over the next few days Annie was surprised to find that with only four of them living in the house the workload seemed so much lighter – there was far less washing and ironing to do for a start.

'That's two down and one to go,' Annie commented to Maggie the next morning.

'And just what is that supposed to mean?' Maggie snapped as she sipped at her tea from her favourite china cup.

'It doesn't mean anything,' Annie answered calmly. The days when she stood to attention when Maggie addressed her were well and truly over. 'I was just wondering if this house will be too big for just you, me and the mister if Charlie moves out as well.'

'And why would he do that?' Maggie looked worried. 'He hasn't mentioned leaving, has he?'

'No, of course he hasn't.' Annie wished she hadn't said anything. Maggie had been very temperamental since the wedding and was clearly missing her youngest. With Barney off with the circus she only had Charlie now, and she was clearly pinning all her hopes of a successful future for one of her children on him.

It was sad, Annie had to admit. Maggie had lost the daughter she adored to a terrible accident; Barney had run off to join a travelling circus; and now Harry had been forced to marry before he felt ready. It was no wonder Maggie was clinging on to Charlie.

Levi finally found his second cart a few days later. It had belonged to a farmer who had invested in a larger one and Levi considered, after some bartering, that he had got it for a snip. He had given Dobbin quite a bit of time off while he took Spirit on his rounds to train her, and now he just needed another driver who could begin a new round collecting in the nearby villages of Mancetter and Witherley, as well as Atherstone. He could then extend his round to Bedworth.

'Why don't you let me do it?' Annie suggested as they were all having dinner one evening.

Levi looked shocked. 'What? Why, I've never heard of a female rag-an'-bone collector. I reckon you've been readin' too much about these suffragettes demandin' equal rights to men. They're gettin' theirselves into loads o' bother accordin' to the papers. Lots of 'em, includin' their leader, that Emmeline Pankhurst, got their-selves arrested in London not so long ago when they went on the rampage smashin' shop winders!'

'And why shouldn't women be treated the same as men?' Annie said heatedly.

'I agree with Levi on this one,' Maggie butted in. 'A woman's place is in the home, looking after her family.'

'Oh really, in that case, why do I do most of the work around here?' Annie questioned boldly.

Maggie gasped with indignation and her mouth opened and closed before she eventually stuttered, 'You do it because you are the maid here.'

Annie's eyes flashed fire as she stood, hands on hips, glaring at her. 'Yes, I suppose I have been all these years,' she ground out. 'Although when you took me from the workhouse, I was foolish enough to think I was going to be a member of the family.'

'But you *are* a member o' the family, hinny,' Levi said worriedly. He could see this fast developing into a full-scale row.

Annie tossed her head, setting her dark hair flying. 'But I *still* want to do the new round.'

'I thought you were plannin' to run the shop when we find one? I've got me eye on one that's comin' up for rent soon, as it happens.'

Annie shook her head. 'Eve is more than capable of doing that and this is something I *want* to do, for now at least. It will mean that you'll have to take over the running of the house, though, because I'll be working longer hours,' she told Maggie boldly.

Maggie looked horrified. 'But who will serve my friends when I have my coffee mornings?'

'I'm quite sure you're more than capable of serving them yourself.' Annie's chin rose defiantly. 'After all, you must have run your own home and cared for three children before I came to live with you.'

Maggie had no answer to that and merely glared back at her.

'All right . . . all right.' Levi held his two hands up in a gesture of defeat. 'If you're really sure it's what you want, we'll give it a go, but I shall want you to come out wi' me fer a few days first to make sure yer know what to do. An' I suggest you take Dobbin, an' I'll take Spirit cos she's younger an' takes a bit more handlin' than the old boy.'

'Fair enough.' Annie nodded and made for the door. If Maggie was going to take over the running of the house again there was no time like the present, so she left her to prepare the dinner.

As agreed, Annie joined Levi on his rounds. She had wrapped up well in layers of her oldest clothes, for the leaves were coming down off the trees like confetti and there was a nip in the air as they moved into autumn.

The collections went well and so, confident that Annie could manage alone, Levi agreed that she could now begin her own round.

One week later, Annie got Dobbin harnessed to the cart and set off for Atherstone with a smile on her face. It was time to prove herself. There was a large sack dangling from the back of the cart with a shovel to clean up any mess Dobbin made along the way, and Annie soon discovered that keen gardeners were more than happy to buy it for their rose bushes. Rather than visit Atherstone on the first day, she decided to try her luck in the slightly closer village of Mancetter. The maids who answered the doors to her were shocked to see a girl doing the job, but Annie soon won them round with her pretty smile and at the end of her first day, when she turned old Dobbin for home, she was feeling quite proud of herself.

'Eeh, you've done grand fer yer first effort,' Peggy said with a grin as she helped her unload in the courtyard. 'An' what a selection o' things you've got.' There was even a tin bath on the cart.

Annie beamed. 'I know it's got a hole in it but it can be sold for scrap.'

'Too right,' Levi said approvingly. He had half expected her to turn for home early with not much to show for her first day in the cold, but he should have known better. When Annie made her mind up to do something she usually did it, and he was proud of her.

Three days later, Annie horrified Maggie when she came downstairs dressed in an old pair of Harry's breeches, tied at the waist with string and an old coat of Levi's, that was at least four or five sizes too big for her.

'*Good grief!*' Maggie's eyes were almost popping out of her head. '*Please* don't tell me you're going out onto the streets dressed like that! Whatever will people think?'

Annie chuckled as she tucked her long hair into a cap, yet another thing she had found that Levi didn't wear anymore. 'I don't much care what anyone thinks. And these trousers will be so much more practical for hopping up and down off the cart. Skirts tend to be far too cumbersome. And as for the coat . . . well, the weather is turning cold and this will be so much warmer than anything I have.'

Maggie sniffed disapprovingly. Over the last few days since Annie had started the new round, she had been forced to take over most of the running of the household again and she wasn't at all happy. She much preferred to be waited on and was beginning to realise just how much work Annie had done for all those years, not that she was ready to admit it.

'All I can say is you look a fright!' Maggie pursed her lips, but it had been a long time since she could hurt Annie's feelings, so after snatching a hasty cup of tea Annie went to fetch Dobbin from his stable.

Back in the kitchen Maggie was fuming. As far as she was concerned it was quite unacceptable for a young lady to leave the house looking as Annie did and she intended to have words with Levi at the first opportunity.

The opportunity came that evening as she and Levi sat having a cup of cocoa.

'Did you happen to see how Annie was dressed today?'

'I did indeed,' he chuckled.

Maggie frowned. 'But *surely* you're not condoning her walking the streets looking like that? It's bad enough that she's doing a rag-and-bone round, but this is just too much! What will people think of her – or us – for letting her go out like that? And another thing, now that she's your employee and no longer has a big part in running the house, isn't it time we told her to move out? She could afford a room somewhere now she has a regular wage, and with her gone, I could get another maid into her room.'

Levi stared at her for a moment, his face set. 'Do you mean to tell me that after fetchin' her from the workhouse as a child, all these years on you still don't consider her a member of our family?' His eyes were glittering dangerously. 'And as for how she's dressed . . . well, as she said it makes more sense to wear trousers. I'm surprised she 'asn't broken her neck before now havin' to get on and off the cart in heavy skirts.'

Maggie opened her mouth to protest but he held his hand up to stay her words. 'Enough said,' he growled ominously. 'And Annie stays. Is that clear? You might have no feelin's for her, but I look on her as my daughter, so we'll hear no more about her leaving until she's good and ready to, do you hear me? Finally, you can forget about gettin' another maid. There's only the four of us here

now and if Annie could keep the house going when the whole family was here then I'm sure you can manage it now. What's the point
of me doubling the rounds if you're just goin' to carry on spending
frivolously? A maid indeed! I sometimes think you've forgotten
your roots, Maggie Lilburn.' He slammed his cup down onto the
small table at the side of the chair and stamped off to bed, leaving
Maggie fuming silently.

Chapter Forty-Five

November 1913

'So what do you think, hinny?' Levi asked as Annie peeped into the back room of the shop on Bridge Street in the town centre. It had just become available and he was keen to hear Annie's opinion.

'Bein' so close to the market there will be a lot of footfall going past,' she commented. 'And there's a good yard out the back where we can store some of the metalware. It has a small kitchen where we can make tea an' a toilet in the yard. Then there's the rooms upstairs. I suppose we could rent 'em out and the rent could go towards the rent on the shop. I think it's just perfect!'

Levi beamed with satisfaction. He had thought so too but Annie's comments confirmed it. 'It looks like we have us a shop in that case. I'll go and pay the first month's rent right away.'

His words fell on deaf ears, for Annie was already planning how the place should be set out.

'You could perhaps make a little fitting room over here in case anyone wants to try any of the clothes on,' she suggested, pointing to the far corner. 'An' we can use all these shelves for metalware over this side of the shop. It could do with a coat of paint though, just to brighten the place up. Funnily enough, I picked a couple of old mannequins up yesterday from a seamstress who's just retired. Peggy could put 'em in the window with some of the nicer gowns displayed on them to attract customers in.'

'In that case, you go and get the paint and I'll go and get the deal done,' Levi told her with a broad smile.

Peggy was almost as excited as they were when they told her the news later that day. They had already decided that she and Eve would run the shop between them.

Peggy had suggested that Maggie could perhaps help out in the shop but Levi had laughed at the idea. 'Can you *really* see Lady Maggie servin' in a shop, let alone a second-hand one? Why, she would die a thousand deaths if Mrs Taylor-Lloyd or one her posh friends saw her in there!'

Chuckling, they had all been forced to agree with him. Sadly, he had acknowledged some time ago that since moving into Swan Lane Maggie had become a snob. He hardly recognised her from the woman he'd married, but it didn't stop him loving her and he hoped that in time she would soften again.

Now, while Levi went to seal the deal for the shop with the landlord, Annie went to buy paint and brushes. Later that day they took Peggy and Eve to see the place and they were almost as excited about the new venture as Levi and Annie were.

'What are yer goin' to call it?' Peggy queried.

Levi looked surprised. He hadn't thought that far ahead and didn't have a clue.

'Why don't yer name it "Annie's Bargains"?' Peggy suggested. 'The shop were her idea, after all.'

Annie flushed while Levi beamed. 'I reckon that's an excellent idea. I'll have to see about gettin' a signwriter on to it straight away.' And while the others continued to make plans for the shop, he shot off to do just that.

Annie and Levi were late getting home that evening and Maggie wasn't in the best of moods. 'Don't blame me if your dinners are ruined,' she said tartly. 'I've been keeping them warm in the oven, but they're probably shrivelled up by now.'

Even her bad mood couldn't put a dampener on Annie and Levi's spirits, though, and laughing Levi caught Maggie around the waist and danced her around the kitchen. 'Sorry about that, pet.

But never mind. Turn the oven off and I'll take you to have a look at the new shop and we'll go for a meal somewhere to celebrate.'

'What, with you two dressed like that?' Maggie was horrified. 'Why, I doubt any decent restaurant would let us in with you looking like a pair of vagabonds.'

'All right, we'll go and get changed first,' he offered.

She pushed him away and shook her head. 'No, not tonight. I haven't had time to get ready,' she said peevishly. She didn't like the sound of this second-hand shop and had told him so in no uncertain terms.

'Suit yerself.' Levi looked disappointed but he didn't argue – he knew it would be useless when Maggie had a bee in her bonnet.

'So when shall we start to get the shop ready?' Annie asked as they were eating their meal. It was very dry as Maggie had predicted, but they didn't dare to comment.

'Hmm, I've been thinkin' about that an' about the only day we 'ave really is a Sunday.'

'I was thinking we might rope Monty and Charlie in to help with the painting?' Annie suggested.

He nodded. 'Well, yer know what they say, "Many hands make light work". The more we can rope in the merrier,' he said cheerily, his happy mood restored. He didn't tell Maggie what they had decided to call the place just yet, though. He had an awful feeling it wasn't going to go down too well.

That Sunday, Levi, Annie, Peggy, Eve, Charlie and Monty entered the shop armed with paint and brushes, and by the end of the day the place looked clean and fresh. While the women painted, Levi and the men erected a small fitting room in one corner with a curtain around it to shield the customer. When they'd finished they were pleased with their efforts.

'I'll come round tomorrow and give the kitchen and the toilet out the back a good clean if you can manage the yard,' Eve offered to Peggy as they locked up, and tired but happy they headed for their homes.

It had been decided that during the week, Levi would transport all the clothes and items ready to go into the shop after his rounds so that they could hopefully open the doors to the public the following Monday.

Peggy was there on Tuesday hanging the clothes on rails and filling the shelves when the sign-fitters arrived to hang the new sign above the shop door. When it was done, she went outside to admire it. *Annie's Bargains* stood out in large gold letters over a dark blue background and Peggy thought it was beautiful, although she shuddered to think what Maggie would make of it.

Levi took Annie, along with Charlie and Monty, to see it that evening when they'd finished their rounds, and she felt a little rush of pride to think that she had contributed to the start of the new business. Maggie had pleaded a headache and didn't want to go but Charlie and Monty were very impressed. And now Annie could hardly wait for the opening.

As planned the doors were opened to the public the following Monday but the first day didn't go as they had hoped. Many shoppers stopped to peer through the window but few ventured inside and Eve was a little disheartened.

'Now look 'ere,' Peggy scolded. 'Rome weren't built in a day! It'll only take a few to come in an' get a bargain an' the word will spread; you just mark my words. It took a few days for word to spread about the clothes business in the yard as well. I shall start sendin' everyone round to the shop now an' that'll give me more time to concentrate on sortin' an' gettin' everythin' ready to go on the rails.'

Sure enough, throughout the rest of the week things gradually improved, although after paying the rent they were still nowhere near taking enough to make a profit, and Annie started to panic.

'What if it doesn't take off?' she said to Peggy worriedly. 'It was all my idea and I'd hate to think I was costing Levi money.'

'Oh, ye of little faith,' Peggy snorted with a shake of her head. 'Patience is a virtue. It'll happen.'

On the next market day, which attracted a lot more shoppers and farmers' wives into the town, things did improve and shortly after lunchtime that day Maggie decided to finally pay a visit.

'Hello, Maggie,' Eve greeted her when she entered the shop.

'Who put *that* there?' Maggie demanded through gritted teeth, stabbing a finger towards the sign.

'Oh, the sign you mean. It's nice, isn't it?' Eve was flustered and didn't quite know what to say. 'Er . . . I believe Levi chose it cos openin' the shop were Annie's idea,' she ventured timidly.

Maggie scowled. 'I can't believe he'd do that. Why didn't he call it Penny's after our late daughter?'

'I don't know, missus, you'd 'ave to ask him,' Eve answered meekly.

'Oh, don't you worry, I *will*!' Maggie glanced around the shop and wrinkled her nose. 'Is every single thing in here second-hand?'

'At the minute yes, but I believe the mister an' Annie 'ave plans to start stockin' some affordable ranges o' new clothes. The whole point o' this shop is to be affordable fer people who are on a budget.'

'Yes, I can see that,' Maggie said scathingly and turning on her heel, she stomped away.

That evening, when Levi and Annie called in after dropping their loads off at the yard, Eve warned them, 'Be prepared. I reckon yer in fer a roastin' when you get home. The missus called in earlier an' she weren't best pleased when she saw the sign. She didn't seem too impressed wi' the inside o' the shop either, to be honest.'

Levi pursed his lips; he'd been expecting this. 'In that case we'd best get 'ome an' face the music, hinny,' he told Annie. 'But you just leave 'er to me. I'm ready for 'er!'

The second they entered the room they noticed the frosty atmosphere.

'So, what's your explanation for the sign above the shop door?' Maggie spat, glaring at Levi.

He moved to the sink to wash his hands and when he'd finished, he turned to face her. 'The shop was Annie's idea so it seemed fair to give her credit for it. The lass has worked her socks off fer all of us ever since the day you took 'er from the workhouse, so I think it's time we showed her some appreciation.'

'Why couldn't you have called the shop after our Penny?'

He leant towards her. 'Penny is gone, God bless 'er little soul, an' Annie is alive.' And when Maggie opened her mouth to argue he snapped, 'I don't wanna 'ear another word from you if you ain't got nuthin' good to say! You ain't the woman I married anymore. She stood by me an' worked side by side wi' me, but now all yer do is complain an' take, take, take.'

Maggie reeled back in shock as Annie sidled past with her cheeks burning and headed for her room.

'Furthermore, an' I may as well tell yer now,' Levi went on. 'I'm fully intendin' to make Annie a partner in the business. I've already spoken to me solicitor about it. The girl deserves it an' nowt you say will make me change me mind. An' now I'm off to the pub. I feel in need of a few jugs of ale.'

He slammed out of the room leaving Maggie to sink into her chair as shock coursed through her. Levi had never been a big drinker or frequented the pubs as most working-class men did. Nor had he ever been quite so harsh with her before. It made her think, and she looked back at her behaviour and wondered if she was the cause of the change in her husband. Deep down she knew she had been demanding and a little unfair. Slowly she made her way to bed, where she lay awake for a long time, Levi's words racing through her mind. In all the years they had been married, she had always been able to count on her husband, secure in his love. But she wondered now whether she had pushed him away once too often. The thought made her heart ache, and there and then she promised that she would make more of an effort with Levi and Annie.

Levi slept in Barney's old room that night and was shocked the next morning when he and Annie came down to the kitchen to find the fire lit and the kettle bubbling on the stove.

'I thought I'd make sure you had a hot drink and some food inside you before you go out in the cold,' Maggie said meekly, putting two bowls of porridge on the table.

Levi blinked, wondering if this was really his wife. 'Er . . . that's very kind o' you,' he said in a small voice, glancing towards Annie, who looked just as shocked as he was.

After finishing their breakfast, they set out into the bitter morning.

'That were a turn up fer the books, eh?' Levi commented as they strapped the horses to the carts. 'Let's hope it's the start o' better times to come. Now you be careful today. There's been a frost an' the roads will be slippery. Don't get stayin' out all day if yer get too cold.'

Annie set off with a smile on her face. She had no idea what Levi had said to Maggie the night before but whatever it was she was certainly in a kinder mood this morning and Annie, too, hoped it would be the start of happier times to come.

Chapter Forty-Six

It was the week before Christmas when Annie woke up to an eerie grey light. Slipping out of bed she crossed to the window to find it was iced over with a lacy pattern. Breathing on the glass she scrubbed at it with the sleeve of her nightdress and stared out at a white world. It looked as if everything had been painted with silver and although it looked beautiful, she knew there would be no going to work today, especially as the snow was still falling. Shivering, she pulled her robe on and went down to the kitchen where she found Levi and Maggie sitting at the table drinking tea.

'Looks like we've got ourselves a day off,' Levi told her. 'The roads will be treacherous, and I can't risk Dobbin or Spirit breaking a leg.'

'Never mind, I can always go and help in the shop.' Annie poured herself a cup of tea and joined them, just as Charlie came through the door from the hall. They had all been in bed when he came in the night before and Maggie squawked with dismay when she saw that he was once again boasting a black eye and a split lip.

'*Oh no!*' She was up in a flash leading him to a chair. 'What's happened now? This is the third time in a matter of months.'

He shrugged her arm off and frowned. 'It were just some kids larkin' about outside the train station,' he muttered.

'I'd hardly call this *larking* about,' she snapped indignantly. 'We should report them to the police. Did you recognise any of them?'

'Just leave it will you, Ma.' He was scowling now and Maggie backed away from him. There was something not right about this, she could feel it, but it was obvious Charlie wasn't going to tell them what had really happened.

'Well, at least let me clean you up a bit?' she offered, but again he held his hand up to keep her at bay.

'I told you I'm all right, didn't I?' And with that he turned and went back to his room, leaving his mother to bite her lip.

'Let him be, pet,' Levi urged. 'He clearly don't want to talk about it.'

At that moment the back door opened, and they got their second surprise of the day when Barney appeared with a rucksack slung across his shoulder.

'Barney!' Maggie squealed with delight as she flew across to him. 'Oh, this is a lovely surprise. We weren't expecting you.'

He dropped his rucksack onto the floor, gave his mother a hug, and crossed the room to hold his hands out to the flames flickering up the chimney.

'I decided to come 'ome fer Christmas if that's all right wi' you,' he told Maggie.

Her smile broadened. 'Of course it is.' She was delighted as always to see him. 'You should have let us know. I'll need to get your room aired for you.'

'I didn't decide till last night,' he admitted as his eyes lit on Annie. She seemed to get prettier every time he saw her. 'We're overwintering in Nottingham this year and I thought seein' as there's nowt much to do that I'd come back and spend the holiday wi' family.'

'I'm very glad you have,' Maggie assured him. 'We're having the Christmas tree delivered today so you can help decorate it tomorrow like you used to do when you were little.'

'We'll see.' Barney grinned as she slipped away to make some fresh tea. It would be the first Christmas he'd spent without Mercy since he had joined the circus, and he hadn't been able to face staying at the circus without her, although he wouldn't tell his mother that.

'So how did you get here?' Levi asked.

'I managed to get the mail train through to Coventry and hitched and walked from there,' Barney answered.

Levi told him about Harry's wedding and the new shop, and the next hour passed in the blink of an eye. At one point Annie slipped away to get dressed and came down wearing a warm woollen skirt with a shawl about her shoulders. Maggie nodded her approval. It was nice to see her dressed as a girl for a change – Annie seemed to spend half her life in men's breeches now.

'I'm going to the shop to help,' she told them. 'I might as well, seein' as the roads ain't fit to take Dobbin out.'

'I'll come with yer,' Barney said, rising from his seat. 'I'm curious to see it.'

They set off side by side, slipping and sliding along the icy pavements. Eve had just opened the shop when they got there and Barney was impressed.

'Who'd 'ave thought me dad, a humble rag-an'-bone man, would ever end up wi' his own shop an' a posh house in Swan Lane, eh?'

'It's doin' really well,' Eve told him proudly. She'd always had a bit of a soft spot for Barney when she was younger, but he had never even noticed her.

'Is there anythin' I can do to 'elp while I'm here?'

Eve nodded. 'Actually, there is . . . the rooms upstairs need clearing out but we ain't had time to tackle 'em yet, what wi' bein' so busy in 'ere. If you wouldn't mind carryin' some o' the heavier stuff down that would be a great 'elp. If you just dump it in the yard, Levi can clear it when he has time. I think he's thinkin' o' lettin' them rooms out when we can get 'em respectable.'

Barney made his way up the narrow staircase to the two small rooms above. As Eve had said they were full of rubbish but Barney wasn't afraid of hard work and by lunchtime he had all but cleared them.

'Crikey, they look so much bigger,' Annie told him approvingly when she went to check how he was getting on. 'And they're actually not in bad shape. I reckon a quick lick o' paint an' they'd be liveable. Whoever moved in could use this room as a small sittin' room an' the other one as a bedroom. They can always use the kitchen downstairs at the back o' the shop, so they should be quite comfortable.'

Barney, who was well used to living in the close confines of a trailer, chuckled. To him they seemed enormous. 'Get the paint an' I'll get 'em done. I might as well make meself useful while I'm 'ere,' he offered.

Levi visited the shop later that afternoon. He had spent the day working at the yard and when he saw what Barney had done, he was very pleased. He'd recently started to collect unwanted furniture on his rounds, and he stroked his chin thoughtfully. 'I reckon I've got enough decent stuff round at the yard to furnish this place,' he told them. 'But I won't be able to bring it round till the roads improve. It'd be too heavy to carry.'

'I'm sure I could sort out a couple o' pairs o' curtains from down in the shop,' Eve told him.

'There we are then, sorted. We could have this place ready to rent for early in the new year, but let's just enjoy Christmas first, eh?'

They nodded in agreement, feeling pleased with everything they'd achieved that day.

'How is Monty doing?' Barney asked Annie when they made their way back to Swan Lane later that day.

'Oh, he's fine. I've been so busy I haven't seen too much of him lately.'

Barney raised an eyebrow and glanced at her out of the corner of his eye. 'Really? I thought you two might be walking out together by now. Monty's never made a secret of the fact that he's fond of you.'

'I'm fond of him too,' Annie admitted.

'I see. So, do yer think anythin' will come of it?' When Annie flushed, he frowned. 'You've not still got a soft spot for our Charlie, 'ave yer?'

Annie was shocked. 'No, but how did you know I ever had?'

He looked worried. 'It was as plain as the nose on yer face, but I'm glad yer over it now. I, er . . . just don't think anythin' would ever 'ave come of it,' he said as tactfully as he could.

'And why is that? Is it because you think the missus wouldn't approve?'

'Oh no, no, it's nothin' like that,' he hastened to assure her. 'It's just that . . . Well, to be honest, I don't think our Charlie is the settlin' down sort. Me dad were tellin' me he's taken a few good hidin's lately,' he went on.

She nodded. 'Yes, he has. You don't think he's mixed up in anythin' shady, do yer? What I mean is, he spends an awful lot of 'is time in Coventry so he could be mixin' wi' anybody.'

'If you mean, do I think he's doin' anythin' illegal, no I don't. Charlie ain't the sort.'

'I just 'ope yer right,' she answered worriedly as she flicked some falling snow from the end of her nose. She was sure it must be turning red and she had lost all feeling in her hands and feet. 'But I ain't so sure. Peggy has hinted that she's 'eard some rumours goin' round about him.'

'Oh aye, what sort o' rumours?'

She shook head. 'I don't know, she wouldn't say. Yer know what Peggy's like. She ain't one to gossip.'

They had reached the house by that time and rushed inside, glad to be out of the cold, so the conversation was over.

The family spent a pleasant evening decorating the tree. Even Charlie stayed in to help because of snow on the tracks that had prevented the trains from running, so Annie was in a pleasant mood when she retired to bed that evening.

Her happy mood increased tenfold when Annie went round to Peggy's to help get some more clothes ready for the shop the next morning. Eve had gone ahead to open the shop and Annie and Peggy were chatting when there was a knock on the kitchen door – they had chosen to work in there that morning rather than in the shed because of the freezing temperatures. Peggy was in the process of repairing a seam on a gown and she spat out the pins she'd had clamped between her lips. 'Get that would yer, Annie. I've no idea who it could be.'

Annie quickly crossed the room to do as she was asked and gasped with joy when she saw who was standing there. '*Davey!* Why . . . what a lovely surprise. What brings you to this neck of the woods? Come in, come in!'

She took his arm and almost hauled him over the doorstep, closing the door quickly behind him. Turning to Peggy, she said, 'Peggy, this is Davey Froggett. His sister Milly works for Susan in London.'

'Then yer very welcome, lad.' Peggy smiled at him. 'But if it's Eve yer after she's round at the shop.' She had heard Eve wistfully mention Davey so many times that she felt she almost knew him.

He dragged his hat off, looking embarrassed, and smiled shyly. 'It *was* her as I was after, actually. I would have come sooner but some o' the trains ain't been runnin' properly fer a few days.'

'Not to worry, yer 'ere now an' I'm sure Eve will be thrilled to see yer. Now come an' get warm by the fire while I make you a nice hot drink. Then Annie can walk yer round to the shop an' take over from Eve so you two can 'ave a little time together.'

He sat down looking awkward. 'How is Eve?'

'Oh, yer know, ploddin' along,' Peggy told him. 'But I think she'll be surprised to see you.'

He licked his lips before admitting, 'Milly told me a few days ago that Eve lost her baby, so I wondered if . . .' His voice trailed away.

Warming to the young man, Peggy patted his hand. 'You were wonderin' if there might still be a chance fer you?'

'I, er . . . suppose I was.'

'All I can say is that's somethin' you'd 'ave to ask Eve, but if I'm right I think she's still very fond o' yer. An' yer do know, I hope, that that baby were forced on 'er? Eve is no little floozy who's loose wi' her favours.'

He nodded again and took a mug of tea from Annie.

'So will you be all right on yer own here if I take him round to the shop?' Annie asked once he'd drained the mug.

Peggy nodded. 'Right as ninepence. Go on, get away wi' yer. Eve is goin' to be tickled pink.'

Annie practically bounced along Abbey Street as she pictured how thrilled Eve was going to be when she saw Davey.

Outside the shop they paused to look through the window to where Eve was serving a customer.

Annie peeped at Davey and saw that his eyes were fastened on Eve, so she opened the door, setting the little bell above it tinkling. Eve turned to look towards them and when she saw Davey the colour drained from her face and her hand flew to her mouth.

She blinked as if she could barely believe what she was seeing before choking, 'D-Davey . . . what are you doing here?'

He smiled, his eyes locked on hers as he stepped forward to take her hands. Annie suddenly felt in the way, so she walked past them to serve the customer who was still standing by the counter.

'Why don't you two go into the kitchen?' she suggested tactfully.

She watched with a smug expression as Eve led Davey away. If the looks on their faces were anything to go by, she had a feeling this was going to be a very happy Christmas for them, and she couldn't be more pleased about it.

It was almost an hour later before they emerged with Eve blushing prettily as she told Annie shyly, 'Davey has asked me to marry him . . . and I've said yes.'

'Oh, that's just *wonderful* news!' Annie did a little jig of excitement. 'But I hope that doesn't mean you'll be going back to London, Eve?'

Eve shook her head. 'No, we talked about it and Davey said he'd be happy to come here to live. That way I can carry on working in the shop, for the time being at least. It will mean we have to find him a job though and somewhere for us to live.'

'Well, we can solve half of that problem straight away,' Annie pointed out. 'There are the rooms upstairs, which would be more than big enough for the two of you.'

Eve's face lit up even more, if that were possible. She felt as if she was caught up in a wonderful dream and just prayed that she wouldn't wake up from it.

'And when is the happy day to be?' Annie asked.

Eve and Davey smiled at each other. 'Just as soon as we can get a registry office booked. We only want a little do. But I will 'ave to go back to London after Christmas to get all me stuff an' tell me ma what's 'appening,' Davey told her joyously.

'I'm sure Peggy would let you stay wi' us till then,' Eve told him. It was going to be the happiest Christmas she'd ever had and hopefully the start of many more.

'Look, you two get off to tell Peggy the good news,' Annie encouraged. 'I can handle things 'ere till closin' time an' lock up. Go on, now.'

Only too happy to oblige, Eve skipped away to fetch her coat and the young couple left, starry-eyed and hand in hand.

Chapter Forty-Seven

Things continued to get better when Susan turned up on the doorstep of Swan Lane two days before Christmas Eve. Theo had had to go abroad on business, she told them, although Annie didn't believe a word of it, and suspected that Susan didn't either. Nevertheless, she was happy to see her. Peggy, Eve, Davey and Ellie would be joining them for Christmas dinner. Flo had tried to wangle an invite for her crew as well, but Maggie had skilfully got out of it, much to Flo's disgust, saying that with Barney being home and her visitors she wouldn't have room to seat them all.

The only one of her family who would be missing was Harry, who would be spending his first Christmas away from home with his new wife and his in-laws.

It was on Christmas Eve when Annie was preparing to go to her room that Levi stayed her and handed her an envelope.

'What is it?' she asked with a smile.

'It's a document drawn up by my solicitor to say that from the first of January next year you are a partner in my business.'

Annie gasped. 'But what does that mean? And why me when you 'ave sons?'

'If it weren't for you and your hard work and ideas, I wouldn't be earning a fraction of what I do now,' he told her honestly. 'And as for my sons . . . I think that rather speaks fer itself, don't it? Barney has his own life wi' the circus, Harry is an apprentice to 'is father-in-law, an' Charlie ain't interested in the business. From that date, twenty-five per cent of all profits will be paid into a bank account I've set up in your name, so hopefully in time you'll 'ave a nice little nest egg to fall back on. Call it yer birthday present! I've also been thinkin' about young Davey an' I wondered 'ow you'd feel about 'im takin' over your round? You've done a grand job of it but now yer introducin' new clothes into the shop an' custom is growin' it really needs two o' you in there. Plus, I'll need someone there to do all the orderin' etc. What do yer think?'

'I think it's an excellent idea,' Annie told him in a wobbly voice. 'And thank you.'

He gave her a fatherly hug and she skipped away upstairs where she stood clutching the document to her chest as she stared out of the window at the snowy night.

The following day passed in a blur of laughter and good spirits. The only two who seemed slightly subdued were Susan and Charlie, but the rest of them didn't let it spoil the day. Gifts were exchanged, and Maggie and Susan went to the morning service at St Mary's while Peggy and Annie cooked the dinner.

The meal was a success: the pork and the goose were cooked to perfection, as were the roast potatoes and the vegetables to go with them. Following the main course was a selection of desserts. There was a flaming Christmas pudding that Annie had had sitting in brandy for months, a cream-topped trifle and hot mince pies, and by the time everyone had eaten their fill they all declared they couldn't have managed another mouthful.

After dinner the men settled down with glasses of port and the newspapers while the women and Ellie had a game of Ludo.

'I don't like the way this Balkan war is goin',' Levi told Barney.

His son nodded in agreement. 'I 'ave a 'orrible feelin' it could affect us.'

'So do I,' agreed Charlie, who also read the newspapers religiously.

Maggie, who had been eavesdropping, clapped her hands and told them sternly, 'That's quite enough of that sort of talk, thank you very much. It's Christmas Day and I won't have you discussing such things.'

'All right, boss.' Levi winked at his sons, unwilling to spoil the happy atmosphere.

Later that evening, as Annie stood watching them all, she realised that over the years, despite the ups and downs, these people had somehow become her family. Admittedly she still longed to learn of her true parentage and hopefully one day she would, but for now she felt lucky to be where she was.

The following evening, after everyone except Annie and Charlie had retired to bed, she made them a mug of cocoa. She felt at ease in his company now that she had got over her childhood crush and grinned as she asked him, 'Did you ever realise that I had a soft spot for you when I was younger? At one time I actually thought you felt the same about me.'

He looked embarrassed and gently took her hand. 'O' course I knew yer cared. An' I *do* still care fer you. Yer the best little sister any bloke could ask for.'

She shook her head. 'No, you've misunderstood me. It's . . . well . . . the truth is I thought I was in love wi' you. But now I realise that you perhaps have a young lady in Coventry?'

His hand went rigid in hers and he tugged it away as if it had been burned, a look of horror crossing his face.

He shook his head. 'You've took me a bit by surprise. I mean I never realised . . .' He groaned as he ran his hand distractedly through his thick mop of hair, making it stand on end. 'The thing is, I don't 'ave a young lady.'

'Oh . . . then I was mistaken.' This wasn't going at all as she had hoped but she didn't want to make him feel bad.

Looking contrite he took her hand again and lowered his head. 'The thing is . . .' He gulped as he tried to find the right words. She deserved to know the truth. 'The thing is . . . I'm not like other chaps. You see, I . . . well, I *do* have a special friend in Coventry, that's why I'm always over there.'

Annie blinked, confused. 'But you just said—'

'I said I haven't got a girl. My special friend is a man. Do you understand what I'm sayin'?'

When she still looked confused, he sighed. 'Did you never wonder why I got beaten up? Why the blokes at school never had time for me? I . . . the truth of it is, I love a man. *Now* do you understand me?'

Shock registered on her face as she stared at him open-mouthed. 'You mean you're a . . .'

'I'm a homosexual, or whatever yer want to call me. I've known it since I was a small boy. When all the other lads were having crushes on girls, I were more interested in them. Hence the good hidin's. God knows, I never wanted to be, and I fought against it fer a long time, but we can't 'elp how we're made, can we? I'm so sorry; I love yer dearly as a sister, but that's all you could ever be to me. You need to find a normal chap, someone who'll love yer as yer deserve to be loved.'

Annie was shocked.

'D-do the mister an' missus know?' she asked in a wobbly voice.

He shook his head. 'I've kept it from them up to now, though I dare say they'll find out eventually. But hopefully I'll have moved away by then. My, er . . . friend and I are thinking of going to live abroad. France, perhaps, where no one knows us . . . I'm so sorry, Annie.'

'It's all right.' She swiped the back of her hand across her wet cheeks, feeling desperately sorry for him. 'As you said, we can't help how we're made, and I hope you and your friend will be very happy. Meanwhile your secret will be safe with me.'

'Actually, there are rumours floatin' around, so I don't think it will be a secret fer much longer,' he said sadly. 'I think Peggy 'as a good idea fer a start off.'

Annie remembered the many times Peggy had tried to tactfully steer her away from Charlie towards Monty, and now it made sense, as if the pieces of a jigsaw were slipping into place.

'Does Monty know?' she asked.

He nodded. 'Yes, Monty's known since shortly before we left school,' he admitted.

'I see. So, when are you thinkin' of leaving?'

He shrugged. 'There's no definite date yet but I 'ope it will be soon. Me friend is slightly older than me and a barrister. He's applied for a job in France and if he's lucky enough to get it then we'll be off.'

She rose slowly. It seemed there was no more to be said. 'I'll wish yer goodnight then, Charlie.'

'Goodnight, Annie . . . And, Annie, just remember, Monty adores you and he's a good bloke.'

'I know he is, there's none better,' she said quietly, and turning about she made her way up to her room where she paced the floor as she tried to put her thoughts into some sort of order. How could she not have guessed? Now that he had confessed, she saw all the signs had been there, but she had never seen them. Perhaps she hadn't wanted to. Poor Charlie.

Eventually she crossed to her drawers and took out the shawl that was all she had of the mother who had once abandoned her. Going to the window, she stood gently stroking the silky material as she gazed out at the white world beyond. A feeling of peace crept through her. She was now eighteen years old. She had survived being abandoned at birth and the strict regime of living in the workhouse, then being taken into a household where she had been treated as little more than a maid by the lady of the house – although Levi and the rest of the family had more than made up for that. She had also survived Reggie's unwelcome advances. There were dark clouds on the horizon and people were saying the country was on the verge of war, but she didn't want to think of that right now. The next part of her life was before her. Very soon now she would have part shares in Levi's business and somehow, she would find a way to trace her birth family.

After a time, she changed into her nightclothes and slipped between the cold sheets staring at the dancing shadows on the ceiling. She would make this business work, she vowed to herself, and one day she would own her own businesses and shops – lots of shops, in fact! And then there was Monty. She smiled into the darkness. All her life she had longed for a family and a home of her very own. Perhaps if she opened her heart to him the fondness she felt for him would turn to love? Eve and Davey were about to find their happy ending, so maybe it was time she did too. On this thought she slept. The future looked bright and she could hardly wait for the next chapter to begin.

Acknowledgements

As always, I shall have to start by thanking my long-suffering husband, who supplies me with endless cups of tea and who encouraged me to write my very first book. Not forgetting the rest of my amazing family who are used to me disappearing off to scribble down ideas at the drop of a hat. And of course, to all my loyal readers who keep me writing with their wonderful reviews!

To all of my wonderful team at Bonnier Books. What can I say? There are too many of you in the Rosie Team to mention you all by name but you know who you are and you all go that extra mile to make sure each of my books is as good as it can be. I'm so lucky to work with such a talented and supportive, caring team. And then there's my very talented agent Sheila Crowley, who has been right behind me since I joined her some years ago. To Gillian Holmes, my brilliant copy-editor and to my proofreader, Jane Howard. Thank you so much. I couldn't do this without each and every one of you!

Rosie GOODWIN

Want to keep up to date with the latest from Rosie Goodwin?

With exclusive content from the author herself, book updates, competitions and more, the Rosie Goodwin newsletter is the place to be if you can't get enough of Britain's best-loved saga author.

To sign up, you can scan the QR code or type the link below into your browser

https://geni.us/RosieGoodwin

Hi everyone,

Here we are again with another brand-new book on the shelves. This is the *The Rag Princess*, the first of my Rags to Riches trilogy in which we meet Annie.

Abandoned on the steps of the workhouse as a young child, Annie has always yearned to discover her true parentage and have a family of her own. When she is eventually taken from the workhouse by the Lilburn family, she hopes that her dreams are about to come true, but sadly she soon discovers that this isn't going to be the case as Maggie Lilburn treats her as no more than an unpaid skivvy. Even so, Annie quickly bonds with Levi, Maggie's husband, the local rag-and-bone man, and he treats her as a daughter. She also forms strong bonds with their three children. There are lots of trials ahead for Annie but she is a strong character and overcomes everything that is thrown at her. As she grows older, she joins Levi on his rag-and-bone cart and proves herself to be a very shrewd young business woman.

Book two in the trilogy, *One Woman's War*, will be released in spring next year and in this one we will follow Annie through World War I, when she becomes a nurse who goes to work in the field hospitals in France.

The third of the trilogy, *The Winter Bride*, will be released in autumn 2026.

I really came to know Annie through this journey and hope you will all love reading about her as much as I enjoyed writing about her.

·MEMORY LANE·

It's been a wonderful year so far for me, beginning with the success of the last of my Flower Girls collection, *Our Sweet Violet*. She went straight into the *Sunday Times* top ten after three days of sales and stayed there for some weeks, so many thanks to all of you who bought the book.

And then of course I was shocked to hear I had been shortlisted for the page turner category at The British Book Awards. It was the first time a saga had ever got through to the shortlist in thirty-five years, so although I didn't win, I felt very honoured, and what a night it was! It was an occasion I shall never forget. I can truly say now that I trod the red carpet and me and some of my wonderful team at Bonnier had a brilliant evening. I met so many famous authors and celebs. I was a little in awe.

Anyway, it's time I got back to work now. I'm very much enjoying keeping in touch with you all via my newsletter, where I keep you all informed about what I'm up to, and I love receiving your messages. Do keep them coming, and happy reading!

Take care.

Love,
Rosie xx

One Woman's War

Set during the First World War, Annie's story continues after *The Rag Princess* in *One Woman's War*, the second book in the Rags to Riches trilogy.

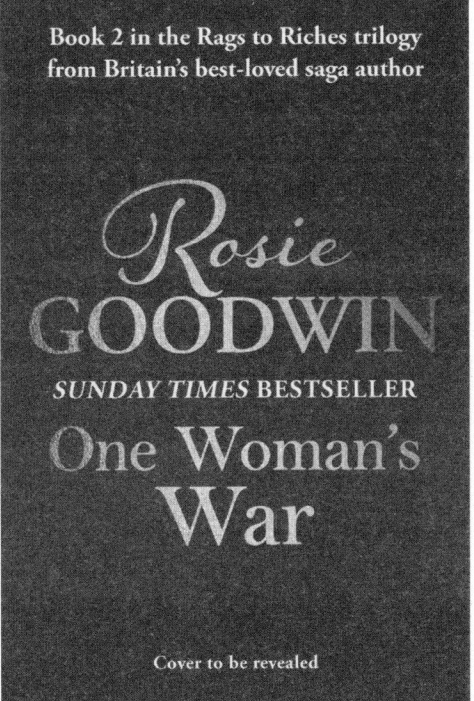

Book 2 in the Rags to Riches trilogy from Britain's best-loved saga author

Rosie GOODWIN

SUNDAY TIMES BESTSELLER

One Woman's War

Cover to be revealed

Coming Spring 2026

The Rags to Riches trilogy

Get to know Annie over the
course of three books in
a brand-new series from
Rosie Goodwin

Coming soon

The Flower Girls

Meet Lily, Daisy
and Violet in this
collection by Britain's
best-loved saga author,
Rosie Goodwin

Available now

The Lost Girl

Can Esme lay the ghosts to rest to save
herself and find the life she deserves?

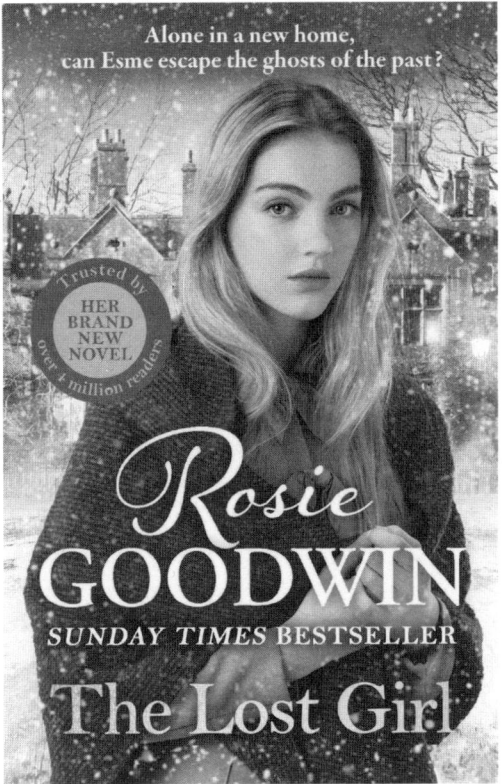

Available now

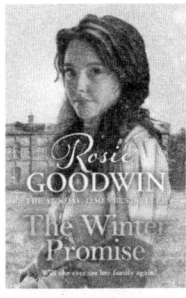

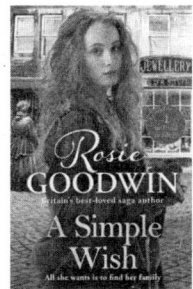

The Days of the Week Collection

Have you read Rosie's collection of novels inspired by the 'Days of the week' Victorian rhyme?

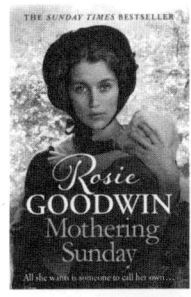
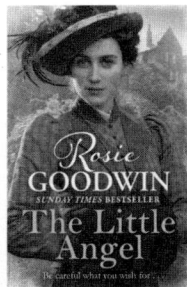

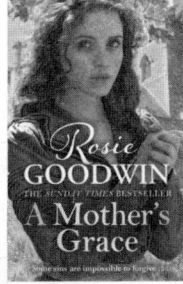

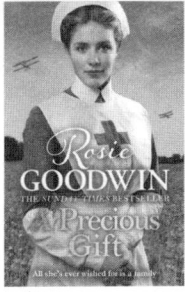
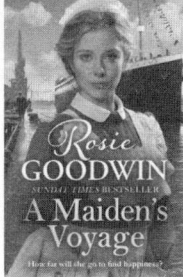
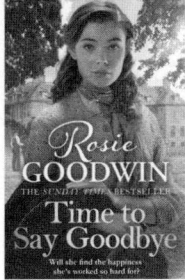

Available now

·MEMORY LANE·

Introducing the place for story lovers – a welcoming home for all readers who love heartwarming tales of wartime, family and romance. Join us to discuss your favourite stories with other readers, plus get book recommendations, book giveaways and behind-the-scenes writing moments from your favourite authors.

·MEMORY LANE·

www.MemoryLane.Club

f www.facebook.com/groups/memorylanebookgroup